For Otis, with all my love

Thank you . . .

To Darley Anderson for spotting the potential in my first few chapters and encouraging me to write on. Without his wisdom, this book wouldn't exist. Also, to his wonderful team, particularly Emma White, Madeleine Buston and Zoe King.

To Suzanne Baboneau and Julie Wright at Simon & Schuster for agreeing to publish *Bridesmaids* in the first place and then, with Libby Vernon, editing the book so brilliantly.

To my friends and former colleagues at the *Liverpool Daily Post* and *Liverpool Echo*, for providing at least a smidgen of inspiration for this book's (completely fictional) newspaper and its journalists.

To my parents, Jean and Phil Wolstenholme, for their love and support – and for being the best unpaid publicists any author could wish for.

To Nina and Peter, Will and Gemma, Gregg and Hannah and all the other friends whose weddings have, over the years, provided ample material with which to write *Bridesmaids* and probably at least ten sequels.

Finally, special thanks to Jon Brown for the best wedding I ever attended (my own) and for the love, encouragement and extra childcare duties which fell to him while I was writing this book.

Chapter 1

The Forest of Bowland, Lancashire,
Saturday, 24 February

My best friend is due to get married in fifty-two minutes and the hotel suite looks like day three on the main field at Glastonbury.

The room is strewn with random items of wedding paraphernalia – and I include the bride herself in that category. Grace is still in her dressing-gown, with only half of her make-up done. I, meanwhile, have spent the last ten minutes frantically trying to revive the flowers in her hair after she trapped them in the car door coming back from the hairdresser.

I give her curls another generous whirl of spray and throw the empty can onto the four-poster bed.

'You're sure it's all secure now, Evie?' she asks, hurriedly applying her mascara in a huge antique mirror. I've used enough hairspray to keep Trevor Sorbie in a comfortable retirement, so am reasonably confident.

'Definitely,' I say.

'It doesn't look unnatural though, does it?' she goes on, picking up a tub of bronzing balls.

I tentatively touch her curls. They feel like they're made of fibre-glass.

'Course not,' I lie, strategically re-positioning bits of foliage over some of the thirty-odd hairgrips. 'Your flowers are perfect. Your hair's perfect. Everything's perfect.'

She looks at me, entirely unconvinced.

We're in the bridal suite at the Inn at Whitewell, in the Forest of Bowland, a piece of countryside so beautiful it inspired Tolkien's Shire in *The Lord of the Rings*, and so tranquil that the Queen herself has said she'd like to retire here. Which is fair enough because she's probably in the 0.001 per cent of the population who could afford to.

In any case, we haven't even looked at the scenery; there just hasn't been time. And the gorgeous suite with its sweeping window and antique chic is completely wasted on us at the moment.

'Great! Excellent. Good! Thanks,' Grace says breathlessly. 'Right. What now?'

Why she's asking me, I don't know. Because nobody could be less qualified to advise on an occasion like this.

First of all, I'm just not used to this wedding malarkey. The last one I went to was in the mid-Eighties, when my mum's Cousin Carol married the gangly love of her life, Brian. Within three years he'd run off with a seventeen-stone painter and decorator. Carol was devastated, despite the undeniably professional job her rival had done on their hall, stairs and landing.

For those nuptials I wore a puffball skirt and wouldn't let go of the pageboy's hand all day. If I'd known then that that was going to amount to one of my life's most meaningful relationships, I'd have tried to remember his name.

Which brings me to the second reason why Grace would be better off asking the grandfather clock in the corner for advice: I doubt very much that I'll ever be getting married myself.

Before you get the wrong impression, I should explain an important point. It's not that I don't *want* to get married – I'd love to. I just don't think I ever will.

Because the fact is – the very *worrying* fact is – that I have now reached the grand old age of twenty-seven and can honestly say that I have never been in love. I've never even come close to being in love. By which I mean I've never actually managed to stay with someone for longer than three months. In short, I am to commitment what Pamela Anderson is to AA bras. A very poor fit.

The funny thing is, I encounter plenty of people who think this ought to be a cause for celebration. They assume that my inability to be tied down makes me young, free and thoroughly liberated.

But that isn't how I feel. Like everyone else, I read *The Female Eunuch* in sixth form and didn't shave my armpits for three weeks, but I just *know* emancipation isn't meant to be like this.

A typical case is Gareth, with whom I split up last week. Gareth was – *is* – lovely. Nice smile. Good heart. Decent job. Lovely. And, as usual, it all started well, with pleasant evenings over a bottle of Chianti in Penny Lane wine bar – near where I live in Liverpool – and lazy Sunday afternoons at the cinema.

But we'd barely been together four weeks – he was suggesting a three-night caravanning holiday with his mum and dad in North Wales – when I knew that it was just too late.

3

I had ceased to think about the cute little dimple in his chin and couldn't stop thinking about the dirt under his toenails. And the fact that the most intellectual thing on his bookshelf was a copy of *Auto-Trader*. And – oh well, I won't go on.

Suffice to say, I'm aware that nothing he did or said was all that terrible and, certainly, it doesn't compare with what some women have to put up with. Yet, while I kept telling myself there were worse things a man could do than think that George Eliot was that bloke from *Minder*, I knew deep down he wasn't for me.

Which is fine. Except they never seem to be for me.

Anyway, after a gap of twenty-two years, I've now got three weddings lined up in one year and I'm a bridesmaid at every one of them. Although if today's dramatics are anything to go by, I'm not sure my nerves are up to it.

'Shoes!' Grace declares as she stomps around the bedroom, flinging items out of the way.

I look at the clock: thirty-one minutes to go. Grace is now pacing around like a teenager waiting for the results of a pregnancy test. She picks up her lip-brush and hesitates.

'Maybe I should get my dress on now,' she says. 'No, wait, I need my stockings. Oh, hang on, should I touch up my hair with the tongs first? What do you think?'

What do I know?

'Er, stockings?' I offer.

'You're right. Yes. Stockings. Christ, where are they?'

Chapter 2

I would like to say it's just the wedding that has prompted today's pandemonium, but this scene is a microcosm of Grace's life over the last five years. During that time, her stress levels have been not just through the ceiling, they've been through three floors, a well-insulated loft and a roof as well.

The onset of this hysteria coincided with her return to full-time work after her daughter Polly was born four years ago. It graduated to a terminal case when baby number two, Scarlett (which is the colour of Grace's face at the moment), came along last November.

The contents of Grace's bag are chucked onto the floor one by one before she eventually locates her stockings.

'I really must be careful with these,' she says.

Sitting on the edge of the bed, she tears open the packet, removes one, and puts her toe into the foot of it with all the delicacy of a bricklayer pulling on a pair of Doc Martens. Predictably, her foot goes straight through the end of it with a rip that makes my hair stand on end.

'Oh fff . . .' she begins, but as four-year-old Polly walks in from the bathroom, she just about stops herself from saying something she'd regret. 'God! God! God!' she goes on. 'They were my only pair. And they cost eighteen quid!'

'What?' I am incredulous. 'For eighteen quid they shouldn't just be toe-proof, they should be able to withstand a nuclear explosion.'

Twenty-six minutes left. I may be a novice but I know enough to be aware that we should have made more progress than this. The whole place is starting to take on the air of an episode of *ER*.

'Look,' I say. 'What can I do to help?'

'Er, Polly's hair,' Grace shouts, sprinting into the bathroom in search of her necklace.

'Come on, Pol,' I say brightly. But the prospect of smearing Molton Brown moisturiser into the carpet seems more appealing to Polly.

'Come on, sweetheart,' I repeat, trying to sound firm and friendly, as opposed to desperate. 'We really need to do your hair. *Really*.'

There is barely a flicker of recognition as she starts on the naran ji handwash.

'Right, who wants to look like a model?' I ask, searching for something – anything – that might persuade her to oblige.

'Me!' she exclaims, jumping up. 'I want to be a model when I grow up!'

I can barely believe my luck. Last week she wanted to be a marine biologist.

I tie Polly's soft blonde curls into two bunches, add a variety of sparkly clips, and look at the clock. Twenty-three minutes to go. My own dress is still hanging on the back of the door and all I've managed to do with my make-up is cover up the spot on my chin with some Clearasil.

Deciding that my best tactic is to do a rush job on myself so I can then get the bride into her dress, I go into the bathroom and, perching on the edge of the luxurious roll-top bath, I start to apply my make-up with all the precision of a three-year-old in an Expressionist painting competition.

When it is done, I grab my dress from the back of the door and pull it painstakingly over my head, taking care not to leave any deodorant snowdrifts down the side. Then I look in the mirror and survey the results.

Not bad. Not exactly J-Lo, but not bad.

The dress flatters my figure and that's always a bonus when nature has bestowed on you a classically English build. It's not that I'm fat. In fact, taken overall, my weight is near enough average. It's just that the top half of my body (flat chest) and the bottom half (big bum) somehow look like they should belong to two different people.

My shoulder-length hair is mousy by nature but has been borderline blonde for several years, courtesy of an early *Sun-In* addiction which has graduated these days to full-blown highlights.

Today, it has been painstakingly curled – sorry, *tousled* – into a 'natural' look that took precisely two and a quarter hours and enough high-definition hair products to bouffant a scarecrow. And despite the haphazard application of my make-up, as well as the lingering annoyance of that zit, I'm starting to feel like I've scrubbed up pretty well today.

I'm just about to leave the room to attend to Grace, when I spot my bag at the side of the sink and realise I've forgotten something. Something crucial. Something that will finish off the look like nothing else. My 'chicken fillet' boob enhancers.

More dramatic than a Wonderbra and – at £49.99 – significantly cheaper than surgery, I've been dying for a suitable occasion to try these out. I shove them down the front of my dress and wiggle them into position, before I turn to look at the results.

I can't help but smile.

I still wouldn't make much of a *Nuts* cover girl, but it's an improvement on what nature has bestowed on me. (Or not bestowed, should I say.) I'm just about to show my new assets off to Grace when I hear a yell coming from the adjacent room.

The bride is having a showdown.

Chapter 3

'The chocolate favours have WHAT?' shrieks Grace, gripping the hotel phone furiously.

'Melted?' she asks, her face growing redder. 'How can they have melted?' She puts a hand on her forehead.

'Okay, how bad are they? I mean, are they still heart-shaped?' There's a pause.

'Arrrghhh!' She slams down the phone. Ouch.

'So they're not still heart-shaped?' I ask tentatively.

'Apparently they now look like something you'd find in a litter tray,' she says, forlorn. 'I haven't got a bloody clue where my tiara is. Has anyone seen my tiara? Oh God, now I've lost that too.'

'No, you haven't,' I say, trying to induce some calm. 'It's bound to be around here somewhere.' Although we will need a satellite navigation system to begin to know where.

'Mummy,' Polly announces, 'I've got no knickers on.'

Grace slumps onto the bed. 'This is *great*,' she says. 'I'm getting married in about fifteen minutes. I've got a hole in my stockings, I can't find my tiara, I've just found a fake-tan streak on my knee, and now it seems I'm incapable of getting my daughter out of the room with any underwear on. Not only am I now at risk of being carted off by social services but I am also, officially, the worst bride in the world.'

I sit on the bed and put my arm around her. 'Cheer up, Grace. You just need to put things in perspective. It's only the biggest day of your life,' I joke.

She wails. Look, I'm trying.

'I'm meant to be walking down the aisle looking as elegant as Audrey Hepburn,' she says. 'At the moment, I feel about as elegant as . . . as . . . *Peggy Mitchell*.'

I burst out laughing. 'Don't be so ridiculous,' I say. 'You're at least three inches taller than Barbara Windsor.'

I see the faintest trace of a smile.

'Look, what is the point in panicking?' I continue. 'It's not like Patrick won't wait for you. So what if you're a bit late? And besides that, whatever you may think, you look *gorgeous*.'

'Do I?' She sounds sceptical.

'Well, you will do soon,' I say, looking at her dressing-gown. 'Come on, it's time to step things up a gear.'

And then I go into bridesmaid-overdrive, assaulting Grace with her toupe tape, nail polish, bronzing balls, lip gloss, bronzing balls (again), then, finally, the dress, which it takes both of us – plus Polly – to squeeze her into.

Just when I think we're all done, with time to spare, it becomes clear that the drama is not over yet.

'Oh bugger!' Grace shouts suddenly. 'I left my earrings downstairs with my mum. Evie, I'm so sorry but you're going to have to go and find her.'

I look at the clock again. I feel exhausted.

By the time I've located Grace's mum, secured the earrings and am heading for the stairs, I note that there are about four and a half minutes to go. But as I start dashing up the stairs, something – or should I say *someone* – stops me in my tracks.

He is quite simply one of the most stunning-looking men I've ever seen. 'Ruggedly handsome' is the phrase that springs to mind – as in, gorgeous but not so perfect he's dull or pretty. He's got smooth and tanned skin, chiselled features and eyes the colour of warm treacle. His nose is slightly crooked but it hardly matters. He's got a body so tight he'd make Action Man look like he'd let himself go.

My pace slows as I walk up the stairs, and my heart-rate quickens as I realise he's looking right at me. Brazenly, I find myself holding his gaze as we step closer to each other. Then, as our paths are about to cross, the most incredible thing happens.

He looks at my breasts.

It's only for a split second, but there is no doubt that it happens. In fact, it's so blatant I'd almost describe it as *a gawp*. His eyes widen conspicuously and I even detect a faint intake of breath. As he drags his eyes away and continues on his way downstairs, I can't help shaking my head in disbelief.

Part of me is appalled at how deeply Neanderthal this otherwise god-like creature turned out to be – and I remind myself of my personal vow never to judge a person on their looks. The other part of me is quietly pleased at the apparent effectiveness of my recent John Lewis purchase.

It is therefore with a slight spring in my step that I open the door to the bridal suite.

'Ta da!' I say. 'One set of earrings.'

Grace turns around to look and gasps – before collapsing into hysterical giggles.

'What?' I ask, bewildered.

'I'm not having you in my wedding photos looking like that,' she cackles, barely able to contain herself.

'Like what?' I ask, pleased that I've done something to make her relax at last. But as I look down, the cause of her mirth becomes horribly apparent.

Chapter 4

My cleavage has been attacked by two rogue jellyfish. At least, that's what it looks like. My chicken fillets, the ones I was so very chuffed about, clearly felt restricted inside my dress – and have ridden up to make a break for freedom.

In fact, they nearly made it: my two 'completely 100 per cent natural-looking' breast enhancers are now poking out of the top of my dress for all the world to see. Or should I say, for him – Action Man – to see. Which feels rather worse than just *the world*.

'I don't believe this,' I say, furiously yanking both fillets from my cleavage. In the absence of a barbecue, I chuck them in the bin.

'Just think of it as God's way of saying you were born flat-chested for a reason,' Grace tells me kindly.

'I'm glad you find it amusing,' I say.

'Sorry.' Grace is clearly trying not to snigger. 'But you must admit it's *quite* amusing.'

I look across the room and see that Charlotte, Grace's other grown-up bridesmaid, is back – having spent most of the morning sorting out flower arrangements – and even she is trying to suppress a smile. Which means it must be bad,

13

because Charlotte is possibly the sweetest person in the known universe.

'Don't worry, Evie,' she comforts me. 'I'm sure nobody noticed. They may have just thought they were part of your dress.'

I resist the temptation to tell Charlotte that the one person who did see it couldn't have noticed more if they'd jumped out and slapped him on both cheeks.

'No, you're right,' I say. 'Thanks, Charlotte.'

I feel a stab of guilt for not having found some time to help her get ready for today. It isn't that Charlotte's not pretty, because she most definitely is. She's got skin that I'd kill for – smooth and clear like a baby's, with gorgeous rosy cheeks – and eyes so big and gentle they could belong to Bambi. I remember thinking when I first met Charlotte – years ago now – that she reminded me of an eighteenth-century milkmaid: gloriously soft and round and wholesome.

But while Charlotte does have natural assets, it's fair to say she doesn't make the most of them. To be horribly blunt, there are contestants at Crufts who will have spent longer on their hair than she has today. And although Charlotte wouldn't be Charlotte without her ample curves, she never dresses to flatter them. Her bridesmaid dress today is so tight, it looks dangerously close to cutting off her circulation.

'It's nearly time,' I say, holding Charlotte's hand and squeezing it.

'Yes,' she replies, looking utterly terrified.

Grace thrusts a bouquet into my hand.

'Right, you two,' she says. 'We can't stand around discussing Evie's cleavage all day. We need to get down that aisle – and quick.'

Chapter 5

It is difficult not to get caught up in the magic of a day like today.

Even someone as prone to cynicism as I am can't help but dwell on all things *uncynical* at such a time. Like how incredible it must be to love someone so much you want to grow old and incontinent with them.

Because it's not just the spray tan that has given Grace the glow she's got today. It's Patrick, the man she's about to marry. And the fact there isn't a doubt in her mind that he's the man for her, for ever.

'What's the matter?' whispers Charlotte as we wait outside the main room for the ceremony to start.

'Nothing,' I say. 'Why?'

'You sighed, that's all,' she replies.

'Did I?' I whisper, a bit surprised.

She smiles. 'Don't worry, Evie,' she says. 'You'll meet someone special one day.'

You're more of an optimist than me, Charlotte.

As I follow Grace down the aisle to 'What a Wonderful World' sung by Louis Armstrong, I spot Gareth among the guests and my thoughts swing back to the last time I saw him, sniffing into his napkin as I told him our relationship was no more.

I attempt a 'no hard feelings' smile but he pointedly turns away to concentrate on his Order of Service. I bite my lip for a second. What's wrong with me exactly? Gareth wasn't that bad. *None* of them were that bad.

I glance over to my left and another of my exes, Joe the TV producer, catches my eye and winks. Okay, maybe *he* was that bad. Smug as ever in his Paul Smith suit and sunbed tan, I can smell the four litres of Aramis he's probably bathed in from the other side of the room.

I haven't seen Peter the musician – the third of my failed relationships – here today, but I know he's somewhere, playing with his tongue ring and rattling the ubiquitous key chain that I'm convinced is welded to him.

Grace and Patrick meet at the front and exchange nervous looks. I suppose even if you have spent the last seven years together, signing up for potentially the next seventy is enough to make anyone's stomach do a few back-flips.

The pair met when they were trainees at the same law firm and, even though that was years ago now, Grace's friends knew as soon as we met him that Patrick was the man for her. There was an immediate connection between them – and two kids and three mortgages later, it's still obvious to anyone who meets them.

The registrar is an eccentric-looking woman in an A-line skirt that probably wasn't very fashionable in 1982 when I suspect she bought it. It looks like the sort of thing Trinny and Susannah would spit on then set fire to. As she introduces the first reading, it suddenly strikes me that there was one person I hadn't spotted as I walked down the aisle.

He of the deep brown eyes and chiselled jaw. *Action Man.*

No, this is good news. This means that one of the most monumentally cringeworthy incidents of my life is something to which I need never give a second thought. Because the only person who witnessed it isn't even a guest at the wedding. I can forget it now. Completely.

I think about the definition in his features and the smooth skin that just got better as I moved closer towards him. And as I remember his smell – a heady combination of sultry aftershave and clean skin – I find myself slumping in my seat. Like hell this is good news.

Action Man, where are you?

Chapter 6

Our friend Valentina is giving the reading. It's only meant to be a one-and-a-half-minute speech, but you'd be forgiven for thinking she was about to collect an Oscar. She glides to the front and, as she steps onto the platform, conspicuously lifts the hem of her crimson chiffon dress to reveal more of her never-ending bronzed legs than were already on show.

Valentina has been part of our circle of friends since she latched onto Charlotte in Freshers' Week at Liverpool University. They made as unlikely a twosome then as they do now. Poor Charlotte was the desperately shy girl who'd hardly been out of Widnes. Valentina was the exotic-looking Amazon who'd been everywhere, done everything, and all in all was about as shy and retiring as the average *Penthouse* centrefold.

Valentina tried her hand at various careers when she left university – personal shopper, *Hollyoaks* extra, upmarket restaurant hostess – before settling on one of the things at which she genuinely does excel. She is now a professional tennis coach and apparently making quite a name for herself. Although I'm told that's at least partly because she wears skirts so short they'd make a gynaecologist blush.

If you asked me my opinion of Valentina, I'd say that, deep down, she's a decent cove. But that's not a universally held opinion, since her idea of a great conversation is other people listening to how she is always being mistaken for Angelina Jolie.

As Valentina puts her notes on the lectern, she looks up to check that the Best Man has been taking notice and, judging by the appreciative look on his face, there is little doubt of that. With a pout and flick of her dark glossy hair, she prepares to address her audience.

'Ladies and gentlemen, before I start my reading, can I just say how *overwhelming* I personally have found it, that two of my closest friends are getting married today,' she gushes.

'When they persuaded me to do a reading I really couldn't have been more pleased to play such a *significant* part in the most momentous day of their lives.'

Grace and Patrick exchange looks. Far from needing any persuasion, Valentina had sulked so much when Grace explained that she wanted to keep the bridesmaids to a minimum that Grace had only agreed to the reading to shut her up.

'The blessing I am about to read is one which has been used in Native American weddings for centuries,' she continues. 'You may be interested to know, however, that the author of it is actually still unknown. It's a beautiful piece of prose and I hope that when you hear it, you'll agree that it is truly fitting for a day like today.'

She composes herself dramatically as the registrar looks at her watch.

'*Now you will feel no rain, for each of you will be the shelter for the other.*'

She pauses for effect.

'*Now you will feel no cold, for each of you will be the warmth for the other . . .*' Et cetera.

After Valentina's performance (and it is a performance) the service seems to pick up speed and in no time at all, Grace and Patrick are walking back down the aisle as man and wife, to the loud applause of their guests. Polly and I are next in the procession, holding hands as she skips along. Charlotte skulks somewhere behind us.

I try to avoid smiling at the guests, given that there seems to be an ex-boyfriend wherever I look. But just as I am attempting to keep my eyes fixed firmly ahead, something draws my attention to the far corner of the room. *He's* standing by a window which overlooks some of the most beautiful scenery in the country. But he makes an unbeatable view all by himself.

My pulse starts racing and I grip Polly's hand tighter. It's Action Man. And he's looking right at me.

Chapter 7

My face flushes as our eyes meet and I turn away in embarrassment, my mind whirling with thoughts of those bloody chicken fillets. I bend down to whisper to Polly.

'You were such a good girl during the ceremony,' I tell her, more to give the impression that I'm preoccupied than anything else.

She looks at me as if to say: 'What *are* you on about?'

I can still feel his eyes burning into me as we almost reach the door. Sod the chicken fillets, Evie, I think, *just look at him.* The applause is ringing in my ears as I turn slowly towards him. He's clapping enthusiastically, and when he sees me look over, he smiles. It's a soft, friendly smile – one that is completely, utterly confident.

Which is the last thing I feel at the moment.

Ridiculously, I look away again, without smiling back, without holding his gaze, without *anything*. My eyes focus on Grace's dress and I feel like kicking myself. The fact that I've just noticed I'd done two of her ivory buttons up wrong is the least of my concerns.

When we reach the drawing room, Grace and Patrick kiss while champagne corks pop and the guests pour through to congratulate the happy couple. I grab a glass of bubbly from a passing waiter and only just stop myself from knocking it back in one as I monitor the door, which he's going to have to come through sooner or later.

Not that I know what I'll do when he does.

The drawing room is soon a riot of people and it's difficult to keep track of who has come through the door as there are so many of them. But as I sense someone by my side, my heart leaps.

Chapter 8

Grace is looking no less stressed than she did *before* the ceremony.

'Evie, listen,' she says, 'I need your help again. Can you get everyone outside? We've got to start doing the photos.'

I look around at the guests tucking into a lavish champagne reception in a cosy drawing room filled with roaring open fires. My task, if I choose to accept it, is to get them all out – even the ones in strappy high-heeled sandals – onto a wind-swept terrace in February.

'You give me all the best jobs, Grace,' I say. 'I think it might take me until next weekend.'

In the absence of knowing where to start, I pick the group of people next to me.

'Er, hi,' I say. 'Er, could I please ask you all to make your way into the garden for the photographs? Thanks. Thanks so much.'

I move on to the next group and say the same.

Five groups later I realise that this ever-so-polite technique is getting me precisely nowhere. I'd get more response talking to the wedding cake. So I decide to start tapping people on the shoulder as well.

'Er, yes, hi, hello,' I say. 'Really sorry to interrupt, but do you think you could make your way into the garden? The photographer's ready.'

Nothing. I cough – my aim being to be polite but authoritative. In other words, to get people to start doing as they're bloody well told.

'The photos are about to be taken,' I say, with a definite firmness now. 'Could you make your way into the garden . . . *please?*'

This is starting to get really annoying. I am either invisible or people are more interested in the booze and smoked salmon blinis than standing outside for half an hour being told to say 'chocolate biscuits'.

Hmm. Okay, so I knew it was going to be a challenge. I need to get bossy. Very well – I can do bossy. I resist the temptation to stand on a chair, but decide to give it all I've got anyway.

'LADIES AND GENTLEMEN,' I bellow, aware that all I'm lacking is a bell and a town-crier's outfit. 'PLEASE MAKE YOUR WAY OUT INTO THE GARDEN AS THE PHOTOGRAPHS ARE ABOUT TO BE TAKEN.'

The whole room stops talking and turns to look at me as if I'm a stripper who's been booked as the star turn at a Women's Institute meeting. Obviously, I was rather louder than I thought.

I suddenly realise that I was so close to the poor bloke next to me that I just might have punctured his eardrums. He's visibly cringing, and I hadn't known what that looked like until now. He turns around slowly with the clear intention of discovering the source of this outburst and I realise that I've got nowhere to run.

The second I see his face, my heart sinks. At least nobody could accuse me of not knowing how to make a first impression.

Chapter 9

I decide that there's only one way to redeem this situation – and that's to say something funny. To make Action Man think, Okay, so this woman has twice acted like she's just escaped from the local asylum but, my goodness, isn't she just the wittiest, most amusing individual I've ever met? That would at least go some way to remedying this disaster.

I try to conjure up my best, most side-splitting line, to lighten the atmosphere and ideally make him want to take me home immediately.

'Er, ah! Er, erm . . .' I splutter. 'Sorry about that.'

Move over *Monty Python*.

He smiles. 'Don't worry about it,' he says. 'You've got an impressive set of lungs, that's for sure. Although don't take that the wrong way, will you?'

I relax – slightly – and try again. 'I bet you say that to all the girls,' I reply, attempting to brazen out the fact that I haven't felt more embarrassed since . . . well, since I saw him on the stairs an hour ago, actually.

'Not exactly,' he says, laughing. 'Although I admit not all the girls take your approach.'

My face gets hotter. 'Okay, I admit it,' I confess. 'I'm

embarrassed.' I don't know why I'm telling him this, when he can already see that my cheeks look like they've got third-degree sunburn.

'Don't be,' he says, nodding over to the doors. 'It's done the trick.'

The guests are pouring onto the terrace.

'Thank God for that,' I sigh.

'Is this what being a bridesmaid involves these days?' he adds. 'I didn't think you had to do anything other than stand around looking pretty.'

'Looking pretty is really my main duty for the day,' I agree. 'That and deafening the guests.'

'Well,' he says, 'may I say you do both exceptionally well.'

I try to stop myself grinning. 'Thank you,' I say instead. 'I'm Evie. Very pleased to meet you.'

I offer my hand to shake and he reaches out and holds it firmly. But before he gets the chance to introduce himself, we are interrupted.

'Evie, you naughty thing! I hope you're not trying to steal my date!'

Valentina is pretending that she's joking, but she now has hold of Action Man's arm in the sort of grip that could get her a job as a parole officer.

'I was just introducing myself to your friend,' he says, turning back to me. 'I'm Jack. Lovely to meet you. And hear you.'

Before I can think of anything to say, Valentina beats me to it.

'Jack, there's someone you've just got to meet,' she says, pulling on his arm and giving him little choice in the matter.

So off they go. Action Man and the Amazon.

Bloody, bloody, bloody hell.

Chapter 10

What a disaster. In fact, the worst outcome I could have dreamed of. I'd have preferred to discover that Action Man – sorry, Jack – was a trainee monk having just taken a strict vow of celibacy. Or that he was gay. Yes, gay would have been nice. I could have lived with gay.

Instead, aside from the most obvious issue, i.e. that he's here on a date with someone else, the fact that that someone else is Valentina is catastrophic. Because, put simply, being a boyfriend of Valentina's is not exactly a good character reference. I haven't met a man she's been out with yet who doesn't fit every one of the following criteria.

Must be obsessed with looks – both his own and hers – to a deeply unhealthy degree.

Must hang on her every word.

Must remember to make a flattering comment involving her resemblance to some starlet or other as often as possible.

Finally, and most crucially: Must be as intellectual as the average episode of *Teletubbies*.

Action Man, Jack, Whatever Your Name Is: you can be as ruggedly handsome as you like, but unfortunately that's now about the only positive thing I can say about you.

I look over to the bar and realise to my horror that Joe, Gareth and Peter are huddled together talking, apparently having formed an Ex-Boyfriends' Club. Oh deep joy. I can only imagine what the conversation must be. They're probably comparing voodoo dolls.

'You haven't seen Grace, have you?' asks Charlotte, her soft voice snapping me out of my trance. 'The photographer is waiting for her.'

'I'll go and look for her,' I say, glad of a distraction.

I finally find Grace in the marquee where the wedding breakfast is being prepared.

'Why can't everything run smoothly?' she frets. 'I should be the world authority on wedding etiquette by now, I've read so many bridal magazines, but things are still going wrong.'

My friend is holding a champagne glass in one hand and rocking Scarlett with the other.

'What now?' I ask.

'There has been a mix-up with the table plans,' she says, blowing a stray bit of hair from her face. 'When I faxed them over to the hotel last week, the machine apparently chopped off the edge of the top table, including where Patrick's mum and dad were meant to be sitting. Now they've not set up a table big enough to accommodate them and they can't change it without dismantling the whole thing.'

'Didn't they wonder where the groom's mother and father were?'

'I think they assumed they were dead,' she says.

Neither of us can help laughing.

'Well, why don't Charlotte and I just step down from the top table?' I suggest. 'The staff can easily slot us both onto other tables. That way, Polly can still be up there with you, and there will be enough room for Patrick's mum and dad.'

'Don't you mind?' she asks, looking relieved.

'Of course not,' I tell her. 'Rather that than spark a diplomatic incident with your new in-laws.'

She grabs me and kisses me on the cheek.

'You're a star, Evie,' she says. 'Remind me to ask you to be a bridesmaid at all my future weddings!'

Only after the photos have been taken do I get to have a look at the amended table plan and realise exactly what I've let myself in for.

They've put me next to Jack and Valentina.

Chapter 11

'How is it that there are ninety guests here today and I manage to be put next to Valentina and her trophy boyfriend?' I ask. 'Did I torture kittens in a past life or something?'

Charlotte tries to stop herself from smiling. 'She's not that bad,' she says. 'I think she might be insecure.'

We both look over in Valentina's direction.

'Kelly Brook?' she's saying loudly to one of the ushers. 'Oh, that's funny, because most people tell me I look like Angelina Jolie . . .'

'I *know* she's not that bad,' I say, 'but insecure? She couldn't be more secure if she were padlocked and guarded by MI5.'

Charlotte giggles.

'Anyway, let's see who's on your table. Oh, lucky you!' I say, nudging her.

Charlotte has been put next to Jim, Grace's favourite cousin. He's a trainee cameraman with the BBC, who has been roped into doing the wedding video today. Although he's a year or two younger than us, he is one of the nicest people you could ever hope to meet. Secretly, I have always thought he would make a perfect partner for Charlotte.

'Jim's lovely, you know,' I tell her, not very subtly.

Charlotte blushes and looks away. She does this all the time – often for little apparent reason – and I know that she despairs of this trait, as with one rush of blood to the head, her entire thoughts are laid out for the world to see. In this case, if I know Charlotte, I can see very plainly that she's got a crush.

'What's up?' I say softly. 'You have been introduced to Jim, haven't you?'

'Er, yes,' she replies. 'I've met him once or twice before.'

'Don't you think he's nice?' I add.

'Hmm,' she says, her cheeks now the colour of a particularly full-bodied Valpolicella.

'You could do worse, you know,' I tell her.

'I don't know what you mean,' she says, fiddling with the strings on her satin bag.

'Charlotte, you don't have to hide these things from me,' I say, holding her hand. But she still looks like a teenager during a parental chat about contraceptive methods.

'I'll drop a few hints if you like,' I offer when she doesn't reply.

'No!' she says immediately. 'Please, Evie, *no*.'

'Okay, okay,' I say, deciding it's time to back off. For now. I know only too well that if Charlotte gets herself too worked up, she'll go out of her way to avoid ever speaking to Jim again. The poor girl definitely needs my intervention somewhere along the way, I don't doubt that. Charlotte has only ever had one boyfriend – Gordon, a damp-proofing specialist – who was uniquely lacking in a single interesting feature. His one talent was that he could tell you everything you never wanted to know about the differences between dry and wet

31

rot, which, believe me, are many and varied. That was years ago, however, and Charlotte is more than overdue another romantic liaison.

Before we sit down to eat, I go to powder my nose and triple check for stray boob enhancers, cabbage in my front teeth, and that I haven't accidentally tucked my skirt into my knickers. Then I take a deep breath and head back to the marquee to locate table five. Jack is already there by himself. I contemplate making a diversion so I'm not left talking to him alone, but he sees me and raises his eyebrows casually in recognition.

Oh no – help me, someone. I'm stuck with Valentina's eye candy already.

Chapter 12

'It's the bridesmaid with the big voice,' says Jack cheerfully as I approach our table.

I should be relieved that he's chosen that, and not the earlier incident, to remind me of, but I still can't help sounding slightly irritated.

'Am I not going to be allowed to forget that?' I ask.

'I won't mention it again, I promise,' he grins. 'So, how do you know the bride?'

I've chit-chatted with enough of Valentina's beaux over the years to know that the next couple of hours are likely to be as excruciating as a dodgy Brazilian wax. But I tell myself to be polite. I don't suppose it's his fault if he's as bright as a 5-watt pygmy bulb.

'We went to Liverpool University together,' I say, before realising he appears to be waiting for me to elaborate. 'We shared a house in the last two years.'

'But you're not from Liverpool originally?' he asks, studying my accent.

'Not far away,' I say. 'About forty-five minutes north.'

'It's a great city,' he says. 'I love it.'

'So you don't live there yourself?' I ask, annoyed with myself for wanting to know.

'I've just moved there,' he says. 'With work.'

Under other circumstances, I'd pursue this as a line of conversation, but the last thing I want is for him to think I'm interested.

'I didn't know Valentina had a new boyfriend,' I say instead, wondering immediately why I'm bringing this up.

'We've only actually been out together once before,' Jack tells me. 'I'm a member of her tennis club.'

I look up to see Valentina flouncing towards us as if she's at Paris Fashion Week, before sitting down and putting her hand conspicuously on Jack's knee. Our conversation comes to an abrupt halt.

'I'm really not sure about this dress,' she muses, inching the hem up. 'Jack, what do you think? I can't decide whether it shows off too much leg.'

She crosses her legs slowly – to show exactly how much leg there is. Jack's eyes are drawn to them momentarily, before he looks away. If I didn't know better, I'd think I could detect a slight sense of embarrassment.

The other guests on our table start to arrive, beginning with two of Grace's aunts. Auntie Sylvia and Auntie Anne are both lovely, tiny women who are dressed today as visions of dusty pink and powder blue, respectively. They both have huge hats, candyfloss perms and meticulously co-ordinated outfits that look like the sort of thing you'd find in a catalogue distributed with the *Mail on Sunday*.

Their husbands, Uncle Giles and Uncle Tom, have spruced themselves up just as much as their wives, although without quite the same panache. Uncle Tom has made a daring attempt at a comb-over, with just a handful of straggly hairs clinging to his scalp for dear life. I'm finding it difficult to tear my eyes away from it.

'Ay up, love,' says a voice I recognise immediately.

I leap up and hug Georgia, another of my old university friends, who is here with her new fiancé, Pete.

Georgia is by far and away the wealthiest individual I know, but to the untrained ear you'd never guess it – the accent is more Daphne Moon than Princess Di.

Georgia's dad grew up in near-poverty in Blackburn and is a self-made man whose company is now the largest manufacturer of plastic bags in Europe. It is perhaps because of his background that Georgia and her family are the most down-to-earth millionaires you could ever hope to meet. She'd be the first to admit she loves to spend, but she's also exceptionally generous and sometimes gives the impression of not being entirely comfortable with her wealth.

'So, how's your practice-run as a bridesmaid been, Evie?' she asks.

'Good,' I tell her. 'I might even have worked out what I'm meant to be doing by the time it's your wedding.'

When we left university, Georgia was one of the few who didn't remain in Liverpool and, although we stayed in touch, the rest of us didn't see nearly as much of her as we would have liked. That's all changed in the last couple of months since the preparations for *her* wedding really got underway. We have had to meet up for so many dress fittings I'm starting to imagine what it must feel like to be a shop dummy.

'I love your outfit, by the way,' I tell her.

Georgia always looks fantastic. Today she is wearing a cream suit which I'd guess is YSL – her favourite – and a simple but beautiful diamond necklace.

'Oh, cheers, love,' she says. 'It was from Top Shop.'

I smile. If that suit is from Top Shop then I'm a world champion Sumo wrestler. But I'm not going to be the one to 'out' her.

When our first course arrives, Jack turns and asks if I could pass the pepper. But as I reach over for it, Valentina interrupts.

'Don't worry, Evie, I've got one here,' she says, touching Jack's arm as she hands it to him. 'You know,' she says, lowering her voice and closing in on him, 'I've read somewhere that pepper is supposed to be an aphrodisiac.'

I don't know why, but I suddenly feel a bit ill.

Chapter 13

'Tell me, Pete,' says Valentina to Georgia's fiancé. 'Are you interested in tennis at all?'

'I'm what you'd call an armchair fan,' Pete responds, flashing a grin at his future wife. Georgia splutters into her drink.

'What he means is that the last time he played he was so unfit he nearly ended up in Casualty,' she says.

'Thanks for your support, love, it's touching,' he jokes. 'You'll be telling people I'm a crap shag next.'

'I'd be delighted to give you a lesson,' says Valentina, handing over one of her trademark red business cards. 'I've done some fabulous work on Jack's forehand, as I'm sure he'll tell you. Not that Jack's forehand wasn't above averagely skilled in the first place,' she adds, flashing a suggestive smile.

We're onto the dessert course when it registers that Jack and I have barely exchanged a single word since we sat down. No tragedy as far as I'm concerned – obviously – although I am starting to question Valentina's sanity these days.

He has turned to me on several occasions, only to be hauled back as if she's got him on a set of reins. So far, she's asked him to check whether her lipstick is smudged no less than four times, and I suspect she'd prefer to fake her own sudden death rather than let him enter into conversation with anyone other than herself.

The sole exception to that is Pete, with whom Jack has been allowed to share a brief discussion about their passion for rugby. It ended abruptly, however, when Pete suggested he join him in an executive box next weekend. The invitation was for a single spare place only.

The only significant drawback to all this for me is that I am stuck with Uncle Giles to my right. I should stress that I have nothing at all against Uncle Giles, who is, to all intents and purposes, a lovely man. But if I hear another word about his collection of nineteenth-century shotguns I may have to ask if I can borrow one to put myself out of my misery.

'Shotguns have been my thing since I was a teenager, you see,' he tells me.

'You'd get an ASBO for that these days,' I joke, but he just frowns and moves on to the enduring qualities of British craftsmanship.

I take the opportunity of this interlude to have a peek at what Charlotte is up to on table 14, and am pleased to see that she and Jim are deep in conversation. At least, Jim is. Charlotte is shredding her napkin nervously and is now surrounded by so many bits it looks as if she's just come in from a blizzard. Still, it's a start. And I must say, he looks promisingly interested.

Chapter 14

Grace's dad looks so relieved to sit down after his speech you'd think he'd just addressed Wembley Stadium. It was the shortest, quietest speech in the history of wedding speeches, but we all laughed at his one joke anyway and clapped furiously at the end.

Next up is Patrick, who is used to public speaking and looks significantly more comfortable than his new father-in-law did. He straightens his jacket – the tails he desperately didn't want to wear today – and runs a hand through his thick blond hair. Grace looks up at him proudly.

'May I say on behalf of both myself and . . . *my wife*,' he begins, grinning at Grace's new title, 'how delighted we are that so many of you have made it here today. Grace and I have been together for the last seven years, and I can honestly say that every day I think to myself how lucky she is to have met me . . .'

The room collapses into laughter at what turns out to be the first of many of Patrick's acceptably lame quips.

Only when he is nearing the end of his speech do I sense someone looking at me. I glance around at Jack and our eyes meet for the third time that day. Even as it's happening, I know it's a ridiculous thing to do. His date is sitting right next to him and I've already decided I'm not interested. Definitely not interested.

But I can't help myself studying his undeniably beautiful face as the hint of a smile, a smile I'd almost call flirtatious, appears on his lips. The room erupts into rapturous applause as Patrick finishes and Jack and I snap out of . . . *whatever the hell it is we're in.*

As the clapping dies down, Valentina has a momentary lapse in concentration and Jack seems to seize the opportunity.

'Have you been a bridesmaid before?' he asks me.

'Never. Have you?'

'I'm afraid not,' he smiles. 'I was a pageboy once, but velvet culottes and a dickie bow aren't a good look when you're fifteen. I didn't enjoy it much.'

I find myself laughing. 'Well,' I say, 'it *is* the rule at weddings that everyone else involved in the ceremony has to look rubbish so that they don't upstage the bride.'

He raises his eyebrows. 'So what went wrong with you?'

Before I can even contemplate an answer to this, Valentina grabs him by the hand and whisks him up from the table.

'You still haven't met the bride and groom properly,' she says firmly.

It's amazing how she can sound like a cerebrally-challenged Bunny Girl one minute and a Victorian schoolmistress the next. Jack has little choice but to go with her, although I'm certain I detect a slight frown as he does so.

'So, Evie,' says Uncle Giles, interrupting my thoughts. 'You were asking about barrels earlier.'

Was I?

I spend the next ten minutes trying to get away from Uncle Giles and when I eventually do, I head straight for the ladies, where I know I'm safe. Grace is already in there and we go into adjacent cubicles.

'Jack's a bit of all right, isn't he?' she shouts over.

I hesitate. What's the right way to approach this question, I wonder. Jack's definitely a bit of all right, but there is one major problem with him.

'He's very much Valentina's type,' I say dismissively.

Grace pauses. 'What, you mean stupid?' she asks. 'I don't think he is, actually. Val says he got a First at Oxford and is now the chief executive of some charity or other.'

I unravel some loo roll silently. Okay, so he's been to a posh university and has a good job. That just means he falls into the 'no commonsense' category.

'Evie?' Grace says.

'Yeah?' I reply.

'Oh, you'd just gone quiet, that's all.'

We come out of our cubicles simultaneously and she looks at me, narrowing her eyes accusingly.

'What?' I ask.

'You fancy him,' she says.

I take on the indignant air of someone wrongly accused of farting in a lift. 'I do *not!*' I say, and march over to the sink to wash my hands.

'Look, don't worry, your secret's safe with me. Just don't tell Valentina, for God's sake. She's had enough of a mouth on her because I didn't make her a bridesmaid. You getting off with her date would send her over the edge.'

'Grace, I have absolutely no intention of *getting off* with

41

anyone,' I say, slightly exasperated. 'Unless it's escaped your notice, you managed to invite three of my ex-boyfriends to this wedding, so it would hardly be appropriate even if it were true.'

'I'm not apologising for that,' she says. 'Only one of them was an ex when we drew up the invitation list. You've managed to get through two others since then.'

'Well, look, Mrs Smug Newly Wed,' I say. 'Just because you've found a gorgeous, intelligent bloke you fancy enough to spend the rest of your life with doesn't mean it happens quite so easily for all of us.'

'So none of the men you've ever been out with have been good-looking or intelligent then?'

I frown. She knows she's got a point.

'Look,' she says. 'Maybe you just need to alter your expectations a bit. The initial romance wears off in any relationship.'

'Faster in mine than most though,' I say, feeling thoroughly depressed now.

She smiles and raises her eyebrows. 'Anyway, if you did fancy Jack . . .' she says.

'I don't!' I interrupt.

'Well, I'm just saying *if* you did . . . I wouldn't worry about Valentina too much. You know how many men she gets through, and he's apparently just split up with his long-term girlfriend – which I'm guessing means the Valentina thing is his way of getting over it. She's a consolation shag, I bet you.'

I pause for a second, determined not to give too much away. Grace's words get me wondering though.

'So,' I say idly as we head back, 'you do think they're shagging then?'

Chapter 15

Nice Cousin Jim is taking a break from filming guests and is standing at the bar alone. Which is very frustrating as I'd rather hoped by now that he'd be huddled in a corner whispering some of Byron's juicier poetry into Charlotte's ear.

'Hi, Jim. Er, where's Charlotte?' I ask. I'm being as subtle as I can be, given my aim is for him to have proposed by next week.

'I'm not sure,' he says. 'I haven't seen her since dinner. Can I get you a drink?'

'I'm fine. She's lovely, Charlotte, isn't she?' I muse, sipping my wine casually.

'Yes,' he says. 'Yes, she is lovely.'

'I honestly don't think I've ever known anyone so kind, or generous, or intelligent, or just generally all-round fantastic,' I add, hoping I'm not laying it on a bit thick.

'She's a really nice girl, no doubt about that,' he says.

'*Isn't* she?' I agree. This is showing tremendous potential.

'Oh, there she is now,' he says, pointing to the other side of the marquee, where Charlotte is deep in conversation with Grace's mother.

I don't believe this. By some miracle the table planners

put her next to a man she fancies – a man who describes her as 'lovely' – and at the first opportunity, she goes off to talk to Grace's mother. Oh Charlotte, what am I going to do with you?

'Is everything all right?' asks Jim.

'Er, yes – why?'

'You were shaking your head, that's all.'

'Oh, was I?' I say. 'Sorry. Er, I was just thinking about the latest council tax rises. Tsk, terrible, aren't they? Anyway, would you excuse me?'

I am crossing the marquee with Charlotte firmly in my sights, when I spot Jack on the other side of the room. He is chatting with Georgia's fiancé Pete and, just as I am wondering what they might be talking about, he looks up and catches my eye. Then he raises his hand and . . . *waves*.

As I contemplate how to react, I realise that I've stopped walking and am rooted to the spot. I am genuinely torn about what to do here. To wave back would be a clear declaration of interest, and that's the last thing I want. But not to do so looks just plain rude.

'Evie, *there* you are,' says a familiar voice from behind me.

I freeze. And as I turn around slowly I realise that the decision has been made for me. It's Gareth. And it's the first time we've spoken since our break-up.

'Listen,' he says. 'We must talk.'

Oh, God. Must we?

'Don't look so worried,' he says.

'I'm not,' I tell him. Actually, I very much am. I've been avoiding Gareth all day now, because I instinctively know he'll want to have a discussion about 'our relationship', a prospect I find about as appealing as a medieval torture session.

44

'I really think we need to have a discussion about our relationship,' he says.

'Do you?' I ask, with a sinking feeling in my gut. 'I'm not sure now's a good time, Gareth.'

'It's as good a time as any,' he says firmly. 'And I really do think it's important. The thing is, Evie, I've just got to know something.'

'Oh?' I say, scanning the room for an escape route.

'The reason you split up with me. Was it,' he looks around to see if anyone is listening, 'was it *the underwear?*'

A group of guests a couple of tables away start laughing and, even though I know they can't hear us, I shift uncomfortably. Just the thought of the underwear – his hideous Valentine present purchased from the Classified Section of a publication called *Hot and Horny* – would elicit a hysterical response anywhere. I never did try it on but couldn't help thinking that, even with the two big holes in the chest as ventilation, all that rubber had the potential to induce one hell of a rash.

'I can't pretend I wouldn't have preferred La Perla, Gareth. But no,' I add hastily, not wanting to appear cold-hearted, 'it really wasn't that.'

But it's too late. His puppy-dog eyes are looking at me as if I'm a vivisectionist. I feel a stab of guilt.

'Then what, Evie?' he wails. 'For God's sake, what was it?'

Then Gareth sniffs. I say sniffs, but it would be better described as a grunt. A grunt so long and loud it sounds like a cappuccino machine about to spontaneously combust. This can only mean one thing: we're heading for emotional melt-down.

'Don't cry,' I plead, grabbing his hand. I mean it too. And

not just because Grace's Uncle Bob and Auntie Marion are looking over.

Gareth produces a threadbare piece of tissue from his pocket and gives his nose the most almighty blow I've ever witnessed. A blow so forceful his eyes look in danger of popping out. Then he scrunches up the tissue and, instead of putting it back in his pocket, chucks it idly on the table next to us.

I try to concentrate on what he's saying, but suddenly find it very difficult to focus on anything other than the content of his tissue, which looks alarmingly like something from *Ghostbusters*.

'I'm not going to cry,' he says with a brave, wobbly smile. 'I'm not going to cry.'

Then he pauses for a second. '*Ohhh! Evieee!*' he blubs.

I pull my eyes away from the tissue, suddenly torn between despising myself and being desperate to get out of there. There is only one thing for it. I turn to Gareth, grab his arm and look intensely into his eyes.

'Gareth,' I say, gripping his elbow. 'We *do* need to talk about this. You're absolutely right.'

Gareth couldn't look more surprised if I'd suggested we elope to Finland and adopt twelve reindeer.

'Oh,' he says. 'You agree then? That we ought to talk?'

'Absolutely. But the thing is, I can't. Not just now anyway. I've got to go and help Grace's mum . . .' I scan the room for inspiration '. . . with the napkins.'

He looks at me as if I'm insane.

'What do you need to do with the napkins?' he asks. 'Everyone's finished eating.'

'They're a fire hazard,' I say authoritatively. 'You can't just go leaving that amount of paper around the place, it's against EU regulations. One stray cigarette and this place will be like the *Towering Inferno*. With no Steve McQueen on hand to rescue us.'

He scrunches up his face. 'I've never heard anything like that before,' he says. 'Besides, weren't they linen?'

'Even worse,' I gasp. 'I'm sorry, Gareth, I'm going to have to go. We'll catch up soon. *Promise*.'

Chapter 16

Charlotte spent the first eighteen years of her life in a dormer bungalow in Widnes, which is Cheshire, but not the wealthy part where none of the women's breasts are real.

She had two loving parents who stayed together for the sake of the children for so long they almost forgot they couldn't stand the sight of each other. These days, she works for the Inland Revenue doing ... well, I must admit I've never quite worked out what she does exactly. Whenever she tells anybody about it, you can see people's eyes glazing over, the way my Great Aunt Hilda's do when the nursing home has given her too many pills.

The point is, Charlotte's background isn't very exciting. But that hardly explains why she's as *desperately* shy as she is and why she has a love-life which isn't so much bad as non-existent.

'So, how come you went off chatting to Grace's mum?' I ask her casually, after I've finally prised her away from an in-depth conversation about why gypsy grass has gone out of fashion in the floristry world.

'Why not?' she asks.

'Well,' I say, wondering how to put this, 'I just thought

you and Jim looked like you were having a nice chat, that's all.'

She looks slightly confused. 'Well, we were. But then I had a nice chat with Mrs Edwards too.'

'Okay, what about?' I ask, feeling that this has got to be challenged.

She frowns. 'Sudoku, mainly.'

I pause. 'Sudoku?'

She shrugs. 'Yes. Well, why not?'

'Do you like Sudoku?' I ask.

'Well, no.'

'Have you ever even played it?'

'Um, no.'

'Do you have any interest in it whatsoever?'

'No, but I don't mind talking about it.'

'Charlotte,' I say, 'unless you're going to tell me that Mrs Edwards has a black belt in Sudoku, I can't see how that can possibly be more interesting than talking to Jim.'

She blushes as she realises what I'm getting at. I immediately feel guilty.

'Listen,' I tell her softly, rubbing her arm, 'all I want to say is: Jim thinks you're lovely.'

I can tell I've sparked her interest.

'It's true, I promise.'

'We just sat next to each other, that's all,' she says.

'And so – what was he saying?'

'Okay, okay,' she says, taking a deep breath. 'Well, we were talking a lot about music.'

'And?' I prompt.

'Well, he loves Macy Gray and plays the guitar in his spare time.'

49

'Just like you!' I exclaim.

'I can't play the guitar.'

'No, but you love Macy Gray.'

'*David* Gray,' she corrects me.

'Don't split hairs,' I tell her. 'Honestly, you were made for each other. Come on, come back over and have a chat with him.'

We are suddenly distracted by some male voices coming from beyond the pillar next to us. It's not that they are being particularly loud – it's hardly quiet in here anyway – but the content of their discussion is something we can't help over-hearing.

'It's a shame I'm not a single man any more,' one of them is saying. 'Some of the women here you wouldn't kick out of bed. The one who did the reading was bloody *spectacular*.'

I roll my eyes. The only thing more annoying than Valentina trying to attract so much attention is the fact that she usually succeeds.

'That bridesmaid was a bit of all right, too – the one with the dirty-blonde hair,' says the other – and I realise they're talking about me. 'A bit flat-chested but definitely fit.'

Talk about a backhanded compliment. I tut and am about to go back to my favourite topic of conversation when another voice chips in.

'What about the other one though – the fat bird?' says a voice.

My eyes widen. I know immediately who they're talking about.

'Who, Shrek's ugly sister?'

They fall about laughing and I listen, dumbstruck, as

Charlotte's face crumples. I try to think of something to do to stop her hearing what I fear may be coming next.

'I wonder how many pies you have to eat, to fill a dress that size?' someone else sniggers.

'Enough to bankrupt the whole of Wigan if she ever gave up!'

Cue another round of drunken laughter.

Charlotte's cheeks are blazing. She's trying to look brave but her lip is quivering and I can tell she is dying inside. Oh God, I'm going to have to stop this.

'How much would you have to be paid to shag her?' someone says, and it's at this point I realise that I really can't let this go on.

'Right, that's it,' I declare, not knowing exactly what I'm going to say to them, but certain that I've got to do something.

'Evie, please don't,' Charlotte implores me.

'Why not?'

'Because you'll just make it worse,' she says. 'Please don't make me any more embarrassed than I am.'

'*You've* got nothing to be embarrassed about,' I tell her.

'Please, Evie,' she repeats. 'Just leave it.'

I briefly consider not doing anything, but when I hear what comes next, I swiftly change my mind.

'It'd have to be a hell of a lot of cash,' comes the reply. 'It would be like getting stuck under a giant airbag.'

'Evie,' says Charlotte, her eyes welling up. 'Please don't say anything. I beg of you.'

Her words ring in my ears as I step beyond the pillar and come face to face with the three men, still not having a clue what to do. I'm looking directly at them, but they're completely oblivious, caught up in the humour they assume is harmless, but is actually anything but. I know I can't betray Charlotte, but I've got to shut them up. Quickly.

What I do next is something spontaneous. You could call it instinct. You could call it a moment of madness. Either way, it has the benefit of me being absolutely sure that it will work, on a certain level at least.

I throw my drink over them.

I say throw, but the technique I opt for might be better described as a 'spray' – the sort of thing Formula One racing drivers employ after a particularly triumphant victory. The difference is, these men don't enjoy it. You can tell by the amount they splutter and swear and by the fury and bewilderment with which they start picking bits of lemon out of their hair. I can honestly say that after about six glasses of wine and champagne, together with a massive injection of adrenaline, I genuinely don't know who's more surprised about the whole episode, them or me.

'Er, sorry,' I manage to get out. 'I slipped.'

I spin around as fast as I can and grab Charlotte's elbow to make a sharp exit. As we start to make our way through the crowd, I soon realise that the crowd has in fact become *an audience*. Grace's Uncle Giles is looking at me as if I'm utterly psychotic. Auntie Marion has her hand over her mouth in horror. Little Polly's eyes are almost popping out. But the worst is yet to come.

'Did you do that on purpose?' whispers Valentina gleefully, clearly as amused as everyone else is amazed.

'Of course not, don't be silly,' I grunt, glancing at Jack by her side.

I wonder if what I've just said would convince anyone.

The look on his face would tend to indicate not.

Chapter 17

Common sense tells me I really ought to stop drinking after that little display, but the glass of champagne Grace has just poured for me is about the only thing I've got to take solace in at the moment. Besides, sobering up is never a good tactic at a wedding. Not when everyone else is doing the direct opposite with such conviction.

'So you think Charlotte's okay now?' asks Grace, when I've brought her up to date.

'Who knows?' I say. 'I dragged her to the ladies straight after it happened, but she didn't really want to talk about it, no matter how much I tried. She just kept saying she was fine. Obviously, I could tell she wasn't, but you know what Charlotte's like when she closes up: I don't think even the SAS could get any information out of her when she's made her mind up not to talk.'

I pick up a handful of peanuts from the bowl in front of us and as I start to eat them, become aware that Grace is suddenly distracted. I look up and see why: her new husband's lips are attached to her cheek.

'Hello, wife,' says Patrick, looking suitably loved-up – and a little bit squiffy.

'Husband. How the hell are you?' she asks, smiling.

'All the better for being a married man,' he tells her, kissing her on the lips.

'Oh, for God's sake,' I complain. 'I know you're newlyweds, but you're putting me off my peanuts.'

'We're married now, so if we want to snog in public we can,' Patrick replies. 'It's all official.'

'You're not meant to *snog* in public when you're married,' I tell him. 'You're meant to *argue* in public – didn't anyone tell you?'

Patrick sits down to join us.

'So how do you feel?' I want to know. 'Different?'

'What do you mean?' he asks.

'I mean,' I say, 'now you're a married man, do you feel different from yesterday – when you were young, free and single?'

'I was still thirty-four yesterday,' he says. 'But in answer to your question, I'm not sure exactly. I don't think so – not yet, anyway. Although ask me tomorrow – I might thoroughly regret the whole thing.'

Grace digs him in the ribs.

'Do *you* feel different?' he asks Grace, obviously not certain about what he wants the answer to be.

'Yeah,' she says. 'Good different.'

He leans over to kiss her again. They look totally and utterly in love.

When Grace had a schoolgirl crush it was on the dashing-but-dangerous Han Solo, not the nice-but-not-as-interesting Luke Skywalker. So in some ways it wasn't a surprise that she ended up with Patrick and not with any of the men she'd been out with before. Her previous 'serious' boyfriends – one in sixth form and one at university – both lasted for over two years, but it was obvious that neither was 'the one'.

It's not that they weren't nice. They were probably *too* nice. Patrick has an edge about him and, in all honesty, that was far more of an attraction.

What that meant in practice was that – well, put it this way, he had played the field. Patrick had dated so many women before he met Grace that he made George Clooney look like the Pope.

Which is and always has been heartening for someone like me. Because if Patrick, former confirmed bachelor and committed Lothario, can fall in love, have two children, stay faithful for seven years and even get married, then there must be hope for someone as hopeless as me.

'Doesn't look like this wedding's going to be consummated tonight,' Grace tells me later, looking over at Patrick as he sways slightly while talking to some guests.

'But it's your first night as man and wife,' I argue. 'It's *got* to be a toe-curler. Those are the rules.'

'I've never seen him so drunk,' she says, shaking her head. 'I don't think even my new Agent Provocateur undies are going to be sufficient tonight.'

'I thought those things came with a certificate guaranteeing a shag,' I say, but as Patrick's swaying becomes more pronounced, I believe she could be right. The only thing that's going to spark him into action tonight is a defibrillator.

'Mummy, will you come and dance with me?' asks Polly, tugging at Grace's skirt.

'When the disco starts, I promise I will,' she says. 'I've still got to say hello to some people.'

'It's starting now, Mummy,' she insists.

'Have you asked Daddy?' Grace wants to know.

'Yes, but he's too drunk,' says Polly.

Grace isn't really in a position to argue.

'You know she's right,' I tell her, nodding towards the dance floor.

'What, about Patrick being drunk?' says Grace. 'Oh yes, I think we've established that.'

'No, I mean about the disco starting,' I correct her. 'Aren't you supposed to be up there for a first dance?'

Putting her champagne down, Grace grabs Patrick by the hand. I follow them to the edge of the dance floor, as the other guests gather around and the music for their first dance starts.

'Evie, will *you* dance with me?' Polly pleads, tugging at my skirt now.

'I can't, sweetheart,' I tell her. 'It's your mummy and daddy's first dance. Nobody else is allowed to join in.'

'Why not?'

'That's just the way it is,' I reply, realising that this isn't a very philosophically constructed argument.

'That's stupid,' she says sulkily. 'Muuummm!' she shouts. 'I want to dance too!'

The guests next to her start chuckling. It's a good job she's cute.

Patrick pulls Grace towards him dramatically and swings her down so her back is arched *à la* Scarlett O'Hara. It's only the fact that he nearly drops her that betrays his state of intoxication. In some ways it adds to the display, although I suspect from Grace's expression that she's concerned he's going to break her neck.

The guests are certainly lapping it up, and the clapping

and cheering get louder as Patrick swings Grace across the dance floor, obviously reckoning he'd give Fred Astaire a run for his money.

I look down and suddenly realise I've lost Polly. I'm not overly concerned as she's been running around all day, but I am surprised that she's given up on finding a dance partner so easily.

However, as I look back at the dance floor, I soon spot her little figure.

She's found someone to dance with.

Chapter 18

Jack has lifted four-year-old Polly up by the waist so that her shoes are three feet off the ground, and he has her arm held out in a waltz position.

He's gently spinning her around, but containing their movements to a small corner of the dance floor, obviously to make sure they don't upstage the bride and groom. But to be honest, that's a bit difficult. Because the eyes of virtually every woman in the place are glued on him.

They're mesmerised by the ripple of Jack's biceps as he keeps tight hold of Polly, on the wide, smiling eyes and the sensuous curve of his buttocks, now tantalisingly defined after his jacket has been discarded.

At least, I imagine that's what they're mesmerised by.

'*Look* at that bum!' gasps some woman next to me. I can only assume she isn't referring to the one belonging to the hefty middle-aged waiter laying out the buffet.

'Come and join us!' shouts Grace, beckoning Jack and Polly into the centre of the dance floor with them.

Polly looks as if all her Christmases and birthdays have come at once, as Jack twirls her around and around in the centre of the dance floor while she giggles uproariously, loving the attention. When the song finishes and Jack puts Polly down, I make a decision. I'm going to go and talk to him.

I know he's with Valentina. I know I've made a complete idiot of myself today. I know I've got three ex-boyfriends hovering about. But it doesn't matter. I have got to talk to him, if only for one reason: to prove to myself that my instinct was right. That the very fact of him being here with Valentina makes him as dim-witted and shallow as everyone else she's ever gone out with. Regardless of whether he's an Oxford-educated chief executive. Of a charity.

I take a deep breath and start walking towards him. But suddenly, there is a tap on my shoulder and I spin around.

'Evie, we've got to talk.'

Oh, no.

'There's still so much we need to say to each other.'

No, no, no, no, no. This is getting ridiculous.

'Somehow, we've kept missing each other all day,' Gareth tells me, with an expression so pained he looks constipated. 'I don't know how. But anyway, I've caught you now. So we can talk properly.'

'Gareth,' I say, 'I know we need to talk. I know.'

'So, how about it then?' he asks.

'Now just really isn't a good time.'

'I'm starting to get the impression that you're avoiding me, Evie,' he says, narrowing his eyes.

'Me?' I am a picture of innocence. 'Honestly, I'm not. It's just that . . . I need to go and choose some music.'

He screws up his face. 'But they've hired a disco,' he objects.

'Oh no, the disco man's not hired,' I say. 'He came free with the hotel. They threw him in with the chicken drumsticks.

59

The problem is, he'll only play Neil Diamond tracks unless you tell him otherwise. I mean, I love "Cracklin' Rosie" as much as the next person, but sometimes you just need a bit of Britney. So I've got to go. Sorry.'

'Wait,' he says, and grabs my hand. 'I wanted to give you something.'

'What?' I ask, a familiar feeling of dread washing over me.

'It's a symbol of our relationship, Evie,' he says, looking worryingly profound.

'Er, right.' I am torn between trying to imagine what he's talking about and really not wanting to know at all.

'A symbol of everything that went wrong,' he continues. 'A symbol that shows how much I'm prepared to change.'

It's at that very moment that it dawns on me exactly what he's about to give me, and it sends a shiver down my spine. He's got an engagement ring, I just know it! He has that demented glint in his eye.

'Oh Gareth, no,' I gulp, as he reaches into his inside pocket. 'I mean, I'm just not ready. I'll *never* be ready.'

He grips my arm and looks deep into my eyes. 'I know, Evie,' he says softly. 'That's exactly what I'm trying to tell you. I know you weren't ready.'

'What do you mean?' I ask.

As he pulls something out of his inside pocket and starts to unwrap it, it soon becomes clear that it isn't an engagement ring.

In fact, it's the only thing I'd rather see less than an engagement ring.

It's *the underwear*.

The underwear he bought me from *Hot and Horny* magazine. The black rubber underwear with two holes in the chest. The underwear that should have *Perve Magnet* written across the front.

The blood drains from my face as he whips it out of his pocket like a matador.

'I mean this,' he says. '*This* is where I went wrong. No matter what you said before, I just know it, and this is proof to you that I'm willing to change.'

Chapter 19

It's 12.05 a.m. and I'm self-righteously sober. Actually, that's not strictly accurate. I'm nothing like sober. But compared with a number of the other guests I am a bastion of ladylike virtue and sobriety. Which is a miracle, really, when you consider the earlier shenanigans with Gareth.

As we'd stood there in the middle of the marquee, he brandishing *Hot and Horny's* finest as everybody else bopped around to 'Sweet Caroline', I can honestly say that I have never been more acutely aware of my surroundings.

There was really only one thing for it.

I snatched *the underwear* from Gareth's hand, turned around and ran out of the marquee as fast as my legs could carry me – until, that is, I crashed straight into Auntie Sylvia and Auntie Anne.

They took one look at what I was holding and appeared to come close to simultaneously passing out. The offending item is now stuffed into a sanitary-towel bin in the ladies cloakroom, which is hopefully where it will stay until someone wearing protective clothing comes to take it away to be incinerated, along with everything else in there. Which I can't help thinking feels like a fitting end for its existence.

Anyway, I have been laying low for the last couple of hours. Which means that, not only have I managed to give Gareth the slip, but it's also allowed me to quietly witness a number of alcohol-induced highlights elsewhere in the party.

Valentina has been the star of the show. In fact, courtesy of her newfound friends Moët & Chandon, she has provided more entertainment in the last hour or so than a travelling circus. As I sit at a table at the side of the dance floor, perfectly happy to have some solitude, I watch in amusement as she high-kicks her way around Uncle Bob.

'Can I join you?' someone says behind me.

I turn around and my pulse quickens. It's Jack. With whom, by now, I'd completely given up on ever engaging in conversation.

'Yes. Sure. Absolutely. Why not?' I gabble, sounding about as cool as the average school nerd.

As he pulls up a chair, our eyes are drawn back to the dance floor, where Valentina has now moved onto the Can-Can.

'I think you may have stolen the show before with your dancing,' I say.

'Oh, I think we can safely say it was Polly who stole the show,' he smiles. I'm not so sure. 'Anyway, I believe you're a reporter at the *Daily Echo*?'

I take a sip of my drink and nod, and then look to see what his reaction is. Some people, believe it or not, don't like journalists.

'The reason I ask is that I've been in the *Daily Echo* myself a couple of times,' he goes on.

'You're not a convicted criminal, are you?' I ask.

'No, no,' he laughs. 'At least, they've not caught me yet.'

'So why have we featured you?'

'I work for a charity called Future for Africa,' he explains. 'We create sustainable projects in the third world – helping farmers to help themselves – as well as running some refugee camps. Your paper did a fantastic feature about us just over a year ago. It was a double-page spread. We were really struggling at the time and I can't tell you how much it helped. We just couldn't have bought the publicity.'

I don't know why, but this surprises me. The closest Valentina's ever been to going out with someone with a social conscience before is when she tried to seduce a trainee vicar she met in second year at university.

And as the two of us start talking, by the intimate glow of a single tea light and with the disco feeling like it's miles away, I discover a lot that surprises me about Jack.

His background, for a start. Despite his now high-flying job and hard-to-place accent, he went to a comprehensive where the average GCSE grade would only get you a job asking, 'Would you like fries with that?' a hundred times a day.

He was the first person in his family to go to university, and that university happened to be Oxford, where he got a First in History. He travelled all over the world in a gap year, before finally landing a job with the charity at which he has now risen to the rank of chief executive.

These days, he loves kids but loves African kids the most and says he wants to adopt at some point in his life. He is a lapsed vegetarian (the smell of bacon after a night out saw the end of it) who reads about two books a week – everything from Dickens to Lee Child.

The only thing he watches on TV is old episodes of *Frasier*, and instead he listens to so much radio that he's embarrassed to say he knows exactly what is happening in *The Archers* in any given week. He is obsessed with sport, and he loves spicy food (especially Thai), expensive red wine and tortilla chips.

Oh yes, and he's recovering from a broken heart.

Chapter 20

The details about Jack's break-up are relatively thin. It happened recently. They'd been together a while. There's no chance of them getting back together.

I sit and nod, taking it all in, looking as if I empathise thoroughly, as if I know *exactly* what he's going through. But, obviously, nothing could be further from the truth. I haven't got the foggiest what he's going through, since the closest I've ever been to having a 'serious' relationship is with the woman who has highlighted my hair for the last five years.

The fact is, this is a subject to which I have virtually nothing to contribute. At least, not without admitting to my appalling track record in the romance stakes – and I'm not about to do that in a hurry.

Why not? Well, I just don't want him to know that I'm about as good at relationships as I am at intergalactic travel.

Anyway, I shouldn't give the impression that the conversation has only been about him. Far from it. I have found myself telling him about everything – from the dad I can't remember, to my pursuit of a great journalistic career, and the fact that I'd only had time to shave one leg before we walked down the aisle. (I don't know why I let that one slip. I regretted it immediately.)

'What's it like, being at a wedding where you hardly know anyone?' I ask him.

'I've enjoyed it. You soon get to know people. There's you, for a start,' he says, and I can't help noticing that my heart is pounding faster again. 'And Pete and I have become friends for life tonight. I've never met anyone before who's quite as obsessed about rugby as I am.'

'Do you play yourself?' I ask.

'Yeah, I do. I know being wrestled to the ground by fifteen blokes every Saturday isn't everyone's idea of fun, but I love it.'

I can't work out whether it is prompted by this image, or by the fact that I have finally drunk too much champagne, but I do feel very hot all of a sudden.

'You two – together again! Humph. I'm shtarting to think I should be getting jealous!'

You might have thought Valentina would have sobered up now, after all that dancing. Not on the evidence before us.

'I think I've got a bit dirty shomehow,' she says, flopping onto Jack's knee.

'Have you had a good dance?' I ask politely.

She lifts up her skirt to demonstrate that the back of one leg and the front of the other is covered in a black streak of grime.

'Yesh, but I have abpholutely no idea how this could posh-hhibly have happened. Have you, Evie?' she asks me.

Jack, who is trying to ensure she doesn't fall off his knee and injure herself, looks over to me.

'I think it's because you did the splits, Valentina,' I say.

'The splits? Did I really? Ha! I amaze myshelf shometimes.'

Jack and I catch each other's gaze.

'And everyone else,' I say, smiling.

She grabs Jack's glass, obviously realising it's been, oooh, minutes since she last had something to drink, and almost slides onto the floor in the process. He manages to stop her, but not easily. The veins in his neck are bulging as he lifts her up into his arms.

'I think I'd better get Valentina back to the B and B,' he pants.

'Yeah. Of course,' I say.

'Jack, I . . . think . . . I think . . . we should go and have a good old dancsh,' says Valentina, her head wobbling from side to side. He pulls her in tighter to make sure he's not going to drop her.

'It was lovely meeting you,' he tells me.

'You too,' I reply.

'Enjoy the rest of the evening,' he adds.

'Oh, I think I'm going to go now anyway,' I shrug.

'Right,' he says.

'Yep,' I say.

'Bye.'

'Bye.'

And off he goes. With Valentina in his arms.

Which feels horribly, horribly wrong.

When Jack has left, I scan the room to see if Charlotte is still around and realise that she must have gone to bed, like most of the other guests seem to be doing. The disco man is packing up now and I see no particular reason to hang around, especially as Gareth is still loitering somewhere like a particularly determined Klingon.

As I lean over to pick up my bag, I spot something on the chair next to me. It's a phone. A phone that can only be Jack's.

Chapter 21

Sunday, 25 February

I manage to get down for breakfast just before they stop serving. I find Patrick and Grace, polishing off huge plates of smoked salmon and free-range scrambled eggs.

'So did he perform all right?' I ask, as Grace and I meet at the juice table. 'Or have you had more romantic experiences sitting on the tumble dryer?'

'The latter, I'm afraid,' she says, pouring herself a large glass of orange. 'He couldn't even stand up, never mind get it up. Still, we have got two weeks in the Maldives to look forward to, so there's plenty of time for him to make it up to me.'

'Assuming his hangover wears off any time soon,' I grin. The bags under Patrick's eyes currently look like they could be carrying a week's worth of shopping.

'Anyway, how did you get on after we left?' she asks.

'Fine,' I say. 'What do you mean?'

She narrows her eyes. 'You know what I mean,' she says. 'I *mean* Jack. Did you make any progress?'

I look at her as if she couldn't have suggested anything

more ludicrous – as if she'd asked me about my budding relationship with Ken Dodd.

'I don't know where you've got this idea from that I fancy Jack,' I say. 'I mean, he's very nice and all that . . .'

'Not thick – like I told you,' she interrupts.

'No, not thick,' I agree.

'Exceptionally good-looking,' she goes on.

I nod.

'He's certainly what some people might call attractive,' I say, determined to remain non-committal.

'Including you?' She raises her eyebrows.

'Look, for God's sake, he's going out with Valentina,' I say. 'Why on earth are you trying to set me up with him?'

She shrugs her shoulders. 'I don't know, I suppose I reckon you'd be good together,' she says. Then she shakes her head. 'No, you're quite right, I don't know what I'm talking about.'

I pour myself some pear juice.

'So you *don't* think we'd be good together?' I mumble.

She laughs and puts her arm around me.

'Anyway,' I say, 'if you must know, I may not have seen the back of Jack this weekend anyway.'

'Oh?' She looks interested.

'He left his mobile phone here last night, and I've got the dubious pleasure of dropping it off at the Crown and Garter where he and Valentina are staying.'

Grace stifles a giggle. 'Good luck,' she says.

An hour later, I find myself in the reception of the Crown & Garter, face to face with a hotelier who looks about 132 years old.

'So, you think they may have already checked out?' I ask, Jack's mobile phone in my hand.

'Oooh, I'm not sure,' he says, doddering over to a large, leather-bound diary. 'My wife Edith tends to look after these things, you see. But she had her varicose veins done on Friday and is out of action for a few days. So it's just me. And I'm afraid I'm probably not as on top of things as she is.'

His shaking fingers turn the pages onto February of last year.

'I don't think we've got anybody by the name you're after,' he says. 'Are you sure you've got the right hotel?'

I help him turn the page.

'I think it's *this* February you need to look at,' I say gently, turning it to the right page. I scan its columns silently myself.

'Look, there they are,' I say, seeing Valentina's name. 'Room 16. So do you have a record of whether they've checked out?'

He frowns. 'I know I'm meant to,' he says, starting to look around the desk. 'But I think that's in another book. My wife Edith is better at this sort of thing than me. Only, she had her varicose veins done on Friday.'

'Right,' I say. 'Well, perhaps somebody could go and knock on their door. You know, to see if they're still there?'

'That's a wonderful idea,' he says, shutting the book. 'That would solve the problem!'

I smile. 'Great,' I say.

'A very good idea,' he reiterates.

'So, will you ask someone to go up there?' I ask.

He thinks for a second. 'Oh, well I would do, but I'm by myself, you see,' he says. 'My wife Edith has had her varicose veins done.'

'Okay – well, maybe you could go?' I suggest.

'Oh no, I couldn't do that,' he says. 'I need to man the desk in case there's a rush on. You see, Edith has—'

'Had her varicose veins done, I know,' I say.

71

I look around at the empty reception. The chances of there being a rush on in the next five minutes are so slim they're anorexic. But I haven't the heart to argue with him.

'Right,' I say instead. 'What do you suggest then?'

'Only one thing for it,' he concludes. 'You'll have to go up and see them yourself.'

Chapter 22

The noises coming from Room 16 are really not what I want to hear. They consist of long, guttural snores that are audible from the other end of the corridor and bear an uncanny resemblance to a heavy-duty pneumatic drill. They can only mean one thing: Jack *must* be in there with Valentina.

I take a deep breath and wonder what the hell I am going to do. Coming face to face with a couple who've obviously just spent the night shagging like two randy racehorses – what else explains the fact that they're still sleeping it off at 11 a.m.? – is not an attractive prospect.

And even less so, given who the couple in question are.

I bend down to study the bottom of the door and see if there is a gap big enough for me to just slide the phone under and run. But you wouldn't fit a credit card under it. There is no way around this. I'm going to have to knock and get it over with.

Closing my eyes, I give a number of short, sharp thuds before standing back, my heart jumping with the sort of anxiety only dentists usually have the ability to provoke.

But nobody comes to the door – and the snoring continues at a volume that would rival a volcanic eruption. Taking another deep breath, I try again, this time hammering with more conviction, before standing back and waiting.

But after another minute of vainly hoping that the snoring will stop and someone will come to the door, I realise a more direct approach is in order.

'Valentina! Jack!' I shout, pounding on the door with my fist.

The snores come to an abrupt halt and are replaced by a series of grunts. Someone is stirring.

'Jack!' I say through the door, feeling like a complete idiot but at least wanting to warn him what to expect when we come face to face. 'Er, I've got your phone here. I've just come to drop it off.'

The ensuing commotion inside Room 16 involves so many crashes, bangs and other bizarre noises that anyone could be forgiven for thinking it was occupied by a hippopotamus with Attention Deficit Hyperactivity Disorder.

As the door swings open, I steel myself to get this over with as quickly as possible.

'Jack—' I begin.

But it isn't Jack who's opened the door at all.

'*What?* Oooh. What time is it?'

Valentina looks as if she has spent the night in the darker recesses of hell. If I didn't know any better, I'd say her hair had been backcombed by a chimpanzee. Her eye make-up is smeared down both of her cheeks and would make Marilyn Manson appear a fan of the natural look by comparison. But worse than that is her skin. It's not even grey. It's *off grey*.

'Valentina,' I say. 'I wonder if you could give this to Jack for me? He left it at the Inn at Whitewell last night.'

'*What?*' she says. 'Oooh. Come in.'

'Oh God, no – no, really,' I say, unwilling to come face to face with a post-coital Jack rolling around Valentina's bed. 'Can't you just give it to him for me?'

But as she grabs me by the arm and hoists me into the room, I have very little choice in the matter. Inside is a scene of utter devastation. There are so many clothes, shoes and bags draped over the furniture that it looks as if a bomb has gone off in Dolce & Gabbana.

The bedclothes are tangled up in a ball at the bottom of the bed, the bedside lamp has fallen over, and a G-string so tiny you could mistake it for dental floss is hanging on the bathroom door.

As for Jack, he's nowhere to be seen.

Chapter 23

'Ohhh,' groans Valentina, throwing herself down on the edge of the bed. 'Something doesn't feel right. I mean, I'm never at my best in the morning, but something *really* doesn't feel right today.'

'Are you okay?' I ask, genuinely never having seen such dramatic effects of a hangover before.

'It's my mouth,' she whimpers. 'There's something wrong with my mouth. Oh my God, it's . . . it's . . . *furry*. And it tastes like . . . like I've been licking a pavement. Ohhh no, it's not just my mouth, it's my head as well. My head is *throbbing*.'

'Well, you won't be the only one who feels as if their lives has been pickled this morning,' I point out.

Valentina tries to prise her right eye open, but it's cemented together with a gruesome combination of sleep and four layers of mascara.

'Are you suggesting I'm hungover?' she says indignantly.

I pause for a second.

'Valentina,' I begin, 'you single-handedly drank more than the average rugby team yesterday, you look like you've spent the night sleeping rough, and it's taken me precisely eight and a half minutes of banging on the door to wake you up. Call me Miss Marple, but, yes, I think you've got a hangover.'

'I never get hangovers,' she says dismissively as she unsuccessfully attempts to stand up unaided. 'Oh! Maybe I've developed some sort of illness that has caused my tongue to swell up and make me go half-blind. Maybe Jack gave it to me! He *has* just come back from one of his places in deepest Africa and could have brought anything with him. Now, where's the bathroom?'

I help her up as she tries to make her way into the corner of the room. But Valentina takes a tumble and bangs her leg on a chair.

'Argghhh!' she screams.

'Oh dear,' I say.

'Argghhh!' she screams again.

'Oh, come on, it can't have hurt that much.' I am starting to run out of patience.

'It's not the fact that it hurts that bothers me,' she says, screwing up her face. 'It's that I'm going to have a huge bruise on my leg now, which means I'll have to wear trousers. And I *hate* trousers.'

'Well, I'm sure you can live with them for a few days if it means covering up such a horrendous disfigurement as . . . as a one-inch bruise,' I say.

'Evie,' Valentina tells me, 'I haven't got the sort of legs that should be covered up.'

'Yeah, yeah,' I answer. 'The very idea is like putting polystyrene tiles on the ceiling of the Sistine Chapel, I suppose?'

When we get into the bathroom, she sits on the loo, unable to stand up in front of the mirror.

'Pass me my make-up bag, will you?' she croaks.

77

'Who do you think I am, your bloody chambermaid?' I sigh, but I pass it to her anyway.

Valentina starts rifling through her bag, throwing various items of cosmetic creams, powders and formulas onto the floor as she does so. I pick up one of them – an Estée Lauder cellulite serum – and idly examine the label.

'I haven't got cellulite, just for the record,' Valentina tells me. 'I'm taking precautions for later life.'

After surrounding herself in anti-wrinkle formulas, bronzing mitts, facial scrubs and God knows how many more cosmetic concoctions, she finally locates a bottle of Optrex and is about to start squirting it into her eyes.

'Don't you think you'd be better trying to get all that crap off your face first?' I suggest.

'What crap?' she asks.

'Your make-up,' I tell her.

Valentina stops what she's doing immediately.

'What?' she says, starting to hyperventilate. 'What did you say?'

'Calm down,' I tell her, not sure why she's getting so excited.

'I left my make-up on last night? Is that what you're saying? Surely not. No, I wouldn't. I couldn't. No way. *Never.*'

She leaps up, hysterical.

'*Oh my God!*' she squeals. '*WHAT will it have done to my pores?!*'

Valentina scrabbles to the sink and for the first time today is greeted by her own reflection. She gasps for air, speechless.

'No . . . no . . . no . . .' is all she can say. 'This isn't happening. Dear Lord God, tell me this isn't happening.'

'Don't be ridiculous,' I say, as I sit her down onto the loo again and pass her a wipe so she can start to take her make-up off.

She drags it across a cheek, her expression utterly dejected.

'It's not that bad,' I say, wondering why I'm indulging her.

'Do you really think so?' she asks pathetically.

I sigh. 'Well, you're no Brigitte Bardot this morning, that's for sure,' I can't help saying.

'Ohhh!'

'But look,' I continue, desperate to shut her up. 'A nice shower will sort you out, I'm sure.' Privately, I think she needs significantly more than ten minutes of ablution under a Gainsborough shower.

'What's that?' Valentina says suddenly, peering at the back of her leg.

'Ah,' I say. 'You did the splits last night. I think that muck is from the dance floor.'

'Not that,' she whimpers, and peels something away from the sole of her foot. On closer inspection it turns out to be a cigarette butt.

She puts her head in her hands and starts to sob.

'This,' she says, 'is the worst goddamn day of my whole goddamn life.'

Chapter 24

Valentina has showered, dressed, and spent forty minutes applying concealer underneath her eyes. She looks much better than she did an hour ago, i.e. less like a zombie, but she's still not in what you'd call a good mood.

'If this old fool doesn't get me checked out sharpish,' she hisses to me down at the reception, 'I'm going to become very annoyed.'

'Beautiful morning, isn't it?' smiles the elderly hotelier.

'Hmm,' she says, lifting up her Jackie O sunglasses briefly to flash him a look.

'Have you managed to do any walking during your stay?' he asks cheerily.

I stifle a giggle. Valentina is wearing a pair of £350 Gina shoes with Gucci jeans, and is carrying a top-of-the-range Louis Vuitton travel system. She couldn't look less like a walker if she had no legs.

'No,' she says, without even the hint of a smile.

'That's a pity,' he says. 'The views in the Trough of Bowland are magnificent.'

'Perhaps next time,' I tell him, thinking someone's got to fill the gap in conversation.

Now she shoots me a look.

'Is my bill nearly ready?' she asks tersely. 'I really do have to get going.'

'Oh, sorry, dear,' he says. 'Listen to me wittering on while you're waiting. Things will be much better when my wife Edith is back on her feet. She's just had her varicose veins done. Anyway, your bill's just coming now.'

'As a matter of interest,' Valentina says, 'the man I arrived with yesterday, Mr Williamson – *Jack* Williamson – has he checked out from his room yet?'

The hotelier thinks for a second. 'The man you were with yesterday . . . yes, strapping fellow with dark hair, I know him. Oh, he checked out a long time ago. He was up bright and early, in fact.'

'Was he now?' says Valentina, obviously even less happy now.

'So do you want to take his mobile?' I ask when we get outside. 'I mean, I presume you're going to see him again soon?'

'I doubt it,' she says furiously. 'If he's checked out this morning he's left without even saying goodbye to me. Never mind without *sleeping* with me. And I don't know how you work, Evie, but that's the sort of behaviour I just don't tolerate on a second date.'

'Right,' I say, feeling a surge of optimism. 'I'll have to think of another way of getting it to him. Have you got his address? I'll take it round there myself.'

She thinks for a second, then snatches the phone from me.

'Now you mention it,' she says, 'I am going to have to go round to see him anyway. I need to arrange his next tennis session. So *I'll* take the phone.'

'Oh,' I say, hating myself for feeling so disappointed and for not being able to think of a good reason to wrestle it back off her.

Valentina opens the boot of her car and starts piling her luggage into it.

'So . . . do you think you'll forgive him?' I ask, unable to stop myself. 'You know, for leaving without saying goodbye?'

She gets into her car, pulls down the visor to look in the mirror.

'I may do,' she says. 'It depends on what happens when I go and see him. Which I'm going to do right now. Now, how do I look? Passable?'

'Well, yes,' I say reluctantly. 'Definitely passable – but not your best. I mean, you said that yourself.'

I'd feel a bitch saying this to anyone else, but this is Valentina we're talking about – and I don't think a ram-raider driving a tank could dent her ego.

'Well,' she sighs, 'given that most people would kill to look like my idea of passable, I think that's probably good enough. Anyway, even Penelope Cruz gets bags under her eyes sometimes. Catch you later!'

And off she goes, with Jack's phone on her passenger seat.

Chapter 25

Red Cat Farm, Wirral, Friday, 9 March

'So, when was it that your pig first started to speak French?' I ask, my notebook and pen poised.

'Ooh, it were a while ago,' says the farmer, who looks as if it's been a while since he washed. 'We 'ad a farmhand from over there, see. We tried to tell 'im to speak proper, but he insisted on talking foreign. Well, Lizzie 'ere just seemed to pick it up.'

'Right,' I say, nodding in an attempt to hide the fact that I think this story is the biggest load of swill I've heard all year. 'I don't suppose there's a chance he – sorry, *she* – could let us hear a few words?'

He sucks his teeth. 'She don't just do it on demand, love,' he says.

I feel like saying that, given that a photographer and I have come all the way over here to interview the bugger, surely a little '*Oui*' isn't too much to ask.

'Well,' I say instead, 'do you think we could do anything to help persuade her?'

'A bit of cash might not go amiss,' he says.

Great. So the pig will only speak French if I pay him. She's obviously more skilled than I realised.

'Sorry, but we don't pay,' I say. 'We're a local paper – we don't have the budget.' Which isn't strictly true, but I can't believe we'd pay anything for this story, short of the pig launching into a perfect version of Serge Gainsbourg's *'Je t'aime . . . moi non plus'*.

This really isn't my week, and quite frankly, this story is just about the last straw. I've been a reporter with the *Daily Echo* now for almost eight months, and was starting to feel pretty optimistic about the way my career was progressing. Okay, so at first I was writing little more than two-paragraph 'nibs' – that's news in briefs (which is nothing to do with underwear) – about school fetes and car boot sales. None of which, in case you haven't guessed, was threatening the shortlist for any major journalistic prizes.

But, gradually, the news desk started to trust me a bit more, and the two-para nibs became single columns, then the single columns became page leads, and somehow, I started to find my name on the front page every so often, covering everything from court cases to human interest stories.

This week, however, it all went wrong. Horribly wrong. Because this week was when our News Editor Christine – who described me as being 'overflowing with enthusiasm and potential' in my first company appraisal – went on maternity leave.

Her replacement is the terminally sleazy Simon, who can't see my potential because he's too busy looking at my arse. He has bombarded me with school fete nibs and picture stories for what he smirkingly refers to as his 'soft news slots'. In fact, the stories have been so ridiculous, you'd have to be soft in the head to call them news.

Hence the reason for my being here in a farm 'over the water' at the far end of Wirral – and barely even on the *Daily Echo*'s patch – praying that Lizzie the Gloucester Old Spot will ask someone for a croissant. *New York Times* here I come!

Okay, so it's not just this. It's the fact that I have spent the last five days attempting to find out what happened when Valentina went round to Jack's house – and failing miserably. Grace is away on honeymoon, so she's out of the game as far as gossip is concerned. I've attempted to grill Charlotte about it but, bizarrely, Valentina doesn't appear to have told her anything. And I'm certainly not going to ask Valentina herself about it.

So why am I so desperate to know?

God knows.

I've spent the last five days asking myself that, in between hammering out pieces about bilingual pigs and dogs with eating disorders.

'What a pile o' shite this is,' whispers Mickey, the photographer. Mickey isn't known for his excessive amounts of patience, but in this case he's undoubtedly right.

'Listen,' I tell him. 'We both know this animal can't speak French, any more than I can speak Mandarin. But the thing is, Simon wants a story about it and I can't go home completely empty-handed. Shall we just try to get the photo done with and then go?'

'She bloody well can speak French,' protests the farmer, obviously having overheard me. 'But she won't do it if she's under stress. And you coming in 'ere telling her she's not capable won't be helping.'

We eventually manage to persuade him to pose for a

photo with Lizzie in exchange for a few glossy copies of it to hang on his wall. Mickey, still muttering under his breath, takes it in record time.

'I remember when this used to be a paper of record,' he complains to me.

'Don't blame me,' I reply. 'I'm as chuffed to be here as you are.'

'So,' says the farmer, 'when will it be in?'

'I'm not sure yet,' I say. 'It's one of those stories that we call "hold-able". If the city centre is razed to the ground, I'm afraid it doesn't go in until the next available slot.'

Which will be never, if I've got anything to do with it.

'Only I've got the nationals interested too,' he says, 'so you'd better get in there quick.'

'Thanks for the tip,' I say, trying not to smirk. 'Come on, Mickey, let's go.'

Chapter 26

Alderley Edge, Cheshire, Saturday, 17 March

Another Saturday, another dress fitting. But this time, it's for the wedding of Georgia and Pete. And this time, the budget is so big it should be listed on the Stock Market.

'How much is this wedding costing exactly, Georgia?' asks Valentina idly as she examines a rail of dresses which, tellingly, don't even have price tags.

'About two hundred grand at the last count,' says Georgia, immediately looking like she wished she hadn't let it slip. 'I mean, not that it matters what it's costing. We could be getting married in Chorley Register Office, for all I care.'

'Thank God it's already booked,' mutters Valentina.

The reality is that Georgia's big day couldn't be *less* like a session at Chorley Register Office. In fact, the ceremony is happening in the Isles of Scilly and is on course to be so lavish, it will make the average royal wedding look like something out of *Coronation Street*.

Georgia is having six bridesmaids and we're all here today for fitting number two, in a boutique so upmarket that even the dummies in the window have attitude. Actually, that's not strictly true. We're all *supposed* to be here, but Grace, typically, is late following a domestic crisis caused by Polly having fed the rabbit some leftover chicken jalfrezi.

Georgia's two younger cousins are also here and today is the first time we have met them. Beth and Gina are both in their early twenties and are so pretty you could mistake them for younger sisters of Catherine Zeta Jones. Valentina could barely hide her disappointment when they arrived.

Then, of course, there is Charlotte, who looks about as cheerful at the prospect of being a bridesmaid again as the average Death Row prisoner.

'You okay?' I ask, as she sits down next to me on a velvet stool.

She nods and attempts a smile.

'It's not really your sort of thing this, is it?' I whisper.

'Not really,' she says. 'I've put on at least half a stone since Grace's wedding. I've not weighed myself, but I know I have. Only my Evans cords would fit me this morning.'

I put down the bridal magazine I've been flicking through and place a supportive arm around her. Then, the curtain is pulled back and Georgia emerges in her wedding dress, smiling from ear to ear.

'What do you think, girls?' she asks, twirling around as her gorgeous silk skirt skims the floor. She does look amazing and even Valentina joins in our cacophony of approval.

'Well, I've got to admit it,' I tell her. 'You scrub up well.'

'Do you think so?' she says, grinning excitedly.

'Absolutely. I think you should have gone for more frills though judging by some of these,' I joke, nodding at my wedding magazine. 'Some of the dresses in here look like those little dolls my grandma used to put over her toilet roll.'

'Are you excited, Georgia?' asks Charlotte softly.

'Hysterical might be a better word,' Georgia replies. 'I don't know what I'll do once it's all over though. It's taken a year and a half to organise this wedding. I've forgotten how to talk about anything other than bloody tiaras and calla lilies. My conversational skills are destroyed.'

'Apparently,' says Valentina, fixing an enormous, elaborate tiara onto her head, 'some couples, once they're married, struggle to find anything in common because all they've talked about beforehand are things to do with the wedding.'

I roll my eyes.

'It's a *well-known fact*,' she says indignantly. 'It's fully recognised by the psychology profession. I read it somewhere – *Glamour* magazine, I think. Now, what do you reckon?' She turns away from the mirror to show us her tiara.

'Lose the tan and you'd look like the White Witch,' I tell her.

She narrows her eyes.

'Just joking,' I say.

But something has been bothering me about the way Valentina's behaving today, something I've been trying to put my finger on since we got here – and have only just done so. It's been a full twenty minutes and she hasn't mentioned Jack yet.

Chapter 27

Charlotte has the look of someone five seconds away from their first-ever bungee jump. In fact, all she's been asked to do is go behind the curtain with the dressmaker to try on her dress.

'Why don't you go next, Evie,' she says, her eyes imploring me to take the pressure off.

'Yeah, okay, no problem,' I say.

Our dresses are called 'Peony Dream' and are strapless, calf-length and as obscenely expensive as everything else to do with this wedding. As I pull mine on, the fit is, mercifully, near enough perfect – which means that unless I develop a craving for pasties and Big Macs between now and the wedding, I won't have to have another fitting.

'There,' I say, pulling back the curtain to the same round of applause that Georgia, Beth and Gina have all had.

'You don't think that's a bit saggy at the bust, do you, Evie?' Valentina asks in an innocent tone. 'Not everyone can get away with that sort of cut.'

'It fits perfectly,' Georgia jumps in diplomatically. 'Evie, you look fabulous.'

When I've changed back into my jeans I sit myself down next to Charlotte.

'You know Jim's going to be at the wedding, don't you?' I whisper. 'Georgia liked Grace's wedding video so much she's asked him to do hers.'

'I believe so,' she says.

'So, are you going to talk to him this time?' I say, nudging her gently. 'Or just spend the entire afternoon talking about teabags or something equally fascinating with Auntie Ethel?'

She giggles.

'Oh, do you like Jim, Charlotte?' Valentina is like a heat-seeking missile when it comes to gossip. 'Why didn't anyone tell me? I hate being the last to know these things.'

Charlotte blushes. 'So Evie thinks,' she says.

Valentina ponders for a second.

'He'd look a lot better with a couple of inches off that hair, you know,' she tells Charlotte. 'You might want to ask him to consider it if you end up going out with him.'

'I didn't even say I liked him,' she protests, going redder still.

'I think we need a plan of action to get you two together,' Valentina decides.

I groan.

'Georgia, why don't you put them next to each other on the seating plan?' she continues, apparently oblivious to how uncomfortable she's making Charlotte feel.

'Er, do you want me to, Charlotte?' Georgia asks hesitantly.

'No,' she says. Then: 'Well, yes, okay. I mean, if you like. It makes no difference to me.'

Valentina gasps as she picks up a floor-length Vera Wang number and holds it against her body to admire herself in the mirror. I use the distraction to lean over to Charlotte again, this time whispering so quietly I'm certain nobody can hear.

'Sorry about that.'

'It's okay,' she says.

'But the thing is,' I continue, 'I only mentioned it because I think he might fancy you.'

She frowns.

'He virtually said so at Grace's wedding,' I add.

Okay, so I might have slightly embellished the conversation, but it's all for a good reason.

'Fancies me?' she asks.

'Well, he said you were lovely,' I whisper. 'And the way he said it, it definitely amounted to the same thing.'

'So, Georgia,' Valentina says loudly, cutting short my conversation again. 'The guests at your wedding – are many in your sort of social circle?'

Georgia smirks. 'I obviously socialise with them,' she says. 'If that's what you mean.'

'Yes, of course,' says Valentina, pausing. 'I suppose what I mean is do they have a similar sort of, well, standing?'

'Standing?' echoes Georgia.

'*Financial* standing,' says Valentina, begrudging the fact that she's had to spell it out.

'Ah,' says Georgia. 'You mean are there any filthy rich, eligible men? Loads, love, loads. I promise.'

Valentina grimaces. 'Oh Georgia,' she says. 'I can't believe you think I'd be so crude as to only be interested in someone for their money.'

I can't let this conversation go without exploring what's behind it.

'Are you single again then, Valentina?' I ask, trying to look like I'm only vaguely interested.

She pouts. 'At the moment, yes,' she says. 'I decided I

ought to be concentrating more on making some "me time". Plus, Jack was very nice and everything, but not really my type.'

'When did this happen?' I ask.

'Oh, I let him know the day after Grace's wedding,' she says.

'Right,' I say nonchalantly.

'You're more than free to go after him, Evie,' says Valentina smugly. 'I mean, he was very upset when we split up, obviously, but you never know – he might be after a meaningless fling with someone to get over it. And I know you're good at that sort of thing.'

Chapter 28

Valentina doesn't bother closing the curtain to get changed.

She just unzips her dress and lets it drop to the floor so she is completely naked except for a pair of satin high heels and a thong so small it looks like you'd need a microscope and a pair of tweezers to get it on.

Okay, so her body is perfect in every way – high breasts, neverending legs, and a backside so pert an airbrush couldn't improve it. But I think everyone would feel more comfortable if she behaved a little less like someone who'd just checked into a Swedish nudist colony.

Turning her head to admire herself from behind in the full-length mirror, she runs a hand slowly across one of her buttocks.

'I hope I've not put any weight on since last time,' she says. 'I haven't been going to the gym as much as usual lately.'

'It must be terrible to have to live with all that cellulite,' I tell her. 'There are support groups for people afflicted as badly as you, you know.'

She tuts and turns around to let the assistant help her get her dress on. As I continue flicking through a magazine, Charlotte nudges me.

'Do you like Jack?' she breathes.

I think about this for a second, then find myself smiling.

'It goes against all my principles, given that he's been out with Valentina,' I say. 'But, yes, I think I do.'

'What are you going to do about it?' she asks.

'Good question,' I reply, the implications of what I've heard only just dawning on me.

'Valentina's the only link between us,' I continue. 'Perversely, now they've split up, I can't think of any obvious opportunities to see him again. Short of becoming a stalker, that is, and I don't think I'm capable.'

'Thankfully,' she giggles.

But the smile is soon wiped off Charlotte's face. Because there is only one more person left to try on their dress, and that's her. As she heads behind the curtain, she pulls it back right to the end, checking that there are no gaps anyone could see through. The assistant goes in to try and help her, but is sent away – and for a good ten minutes, there is nothing but silence coming from behind the curtain.

Finally, I creep over and try to murmur to Charlotte without attracting too much attention from anyone else.

'Are you okay in there?' I ask.

'Wait! Don't come in!' she says, slightly hysterically.

'Okay, okay,' I say. 'I wasn't going to. I was just wondering how you were getting on. You've been an awfully long time.'

Suddenly, the boutique door flings open and it's Grace, looking slightly dishevelled and out of breath as usual.

'How's the rabbit?' I ask.

'Rooney? Well, the vet says he's going to have a sore bum tomorrow,' she says. 'But we've managed to avoid major surgery. How's things?'

'Fine,' I say, walking over so I can talk to her privately. 'We're just waiting for Charlotte to come out, but I think she's determined to stay behind that curtain until the wedding is over.'

Grace flashes me a knowing look. Just as I'm about to go and check again if Charlotte is okay, we hear a scream. Oblivious to the fact that someone is still in there – it has been nearly quarter of an hour now – the assistant has whipped back the curtain. And I've never seen such a terrible look on anyone's face in my life.

Chapter 29

'I'm sorry,' she's saying to Georgia, her lip trembling. 'I really am sorry.'

At first I can't work out what Charlotte is trying to apologise for. But then, as I follow her eyes downwards, all becomes clear. She was right about the extra half-stone. Charlotte's dress is now so tight that if she even attempts to breathe she's going to do herself a serious injury.

'Charlotte,' says Grace, trying to fill the excruciating silence. 'You look really, er, nice.'

She's immediately embarrassed by her own insincerity. And just as I'm trying to think of something appropriate to say myself, I notice that there are tears spilling down our friend's face.

'Charlotte, why are you crying?' I say tenderly. 'It's okay, honestly. You've got nothing to be upset about.'

She tries to open her mouth, but nothing is coming out. I put my arm around her as the others rush over to her too.

'Come and sit down here,' says Georgia, beckoning her towards a velvet footstool.

The tears are streaming down Charlotte's cheeks now as she walks across the room, guided by Georgia. I try to think of something profound to say, something meaningful enough to make her obvious pain go away.

'Do you want a cup of tea?' I ask, realising it's not quite what I was looking for.

She shakes her head silently. As she goes to sit down on the footstool, the room takes on a strange quietness. All six of us are watching her, her eyes red and swollen, her face almost bereft of expression.

It is perhaps because of the intensity of the moment that we can hear the tear before her backside even hits the seat. Or maybe it's just because the resulting hole is so big. Either way, the sound of Charlotte's dress ripping as she sits down on a footstool is heart-stopping.

And it's not just me who thinks so either. Grace and Georgia have their hands over their mouths. Valentina and Beth are both wide-eyed to the point of looking like cartoon characters. Gina's jaw seems to be only several inches away from the floor. And the dressmaker, quite simply, looks as if she's about to faint.

Almost robotically, Charlotte stands up again to look at the evidence in the mirror. It's spectacular – a foot-long rip running like a gaping wound right down the middle of the bodice. It's not even on the seams, but the bodice itself – and the sheer impossibility of fixing it is making everyone's head spin.

'Let me see,' squeals the dressmaker, and she grabs Charlotte by the arm to turn her around. But just when we thought things couldn't get any worse, as Charlotte's waist twists, there is another loud rip. Now the tear is a foot and a half long.

'Argghhh!' says the dressmaker.

'Oh God,' says Georgia.

'Fucking hell,' I add.

Chapter 30

There is something about being British that makes us ascribe to a simple cup of tea the sort of healing properties you wouldn't even demand from a Harley Street psychiatrist.

It doesn't seem to matter what disaster befalls us, whatever death or destruction throws itself in our path, the reaction is always the same: 'I'll put the kettle on then, shall I?'

'Would anyone like another?' says one of the assistants, popping her head around the door.

'Can you make sure it's Assam this time,' says Valentina, handing back her cup.

The thing is though, it somehow works. At least, it has on Charlotte. Although, admittedly, it might not just be the PG Tips that have done it. Charlotte has spent the last half-hour revealing some of her innermost thoughts to myself, Georgia, five other bridesmaids, and a dressmaker who clearly thinks that if she's going to have to fix that dress, she at least wants to hear all about what was behind its undoing.

The thoughts Charlotte has revealed are ones that she's never, ever told us about before, which is unbelievable really, given that our relationship has lasted longer than the average marriage.

With hindsight, they are thoughts that I probably should-n't have been surprised about. But the fact is, I *was* surprised. I couldn't have been more surprised if she'd confessed to having a secret career as Alan Titchmarsh's private lap dancer.

It turns out that lovely, soft-spoken Charlotte – Charlotte who, ironically, never sees anything but good in people – can see nothing but *bad* in herself. And behind the shyness that I'd always assumed was just in her nature lies a self-esteem so low it defies gravity. Charlotte, it appears, *doesn't* like her milkmaid curves and gorgeous rosy cheeks. In fact, she despises them.

'I know I've never really said anything, but I have always felt like this,' she says as she sips her tea, her hands still shak-ing slightly. 'I was teased at school for the way I look, and although people don't say anything to my face any more, I know what everyone thinks about me.'

'Charlotte,' I say, shaking my head, 'what people think of you is that you are a fantastic, *lovely* person who—'

'Well, that's all fine,' she interrupts. 'But don't pretend that even you, even my best friends in the whole world, don't look at me sometimes and think: What a blinking mess she is.'

'Actually, Charlotte, I don't thin—' I begin again.

'I'm not having a go at any of you,' she interrupts. 'I mean, how could I? I *am* a mess. I'm overweight, I don't know how to dress properly and I've never put on lipstick in my life. I wouldn't even know how.'

'We always just thought you were just . . . comfortable . . . with the way you look,' says Grace.

'No, Grace, I'm not,' she says. 'I hate myself.'

'It does have an effect on your confidence when you feel that you don't look your best,' sighs Valentina. 'I don't want to leave the house sometimes when my eyebrows are overdue.'

Everyone ignores her.

'The point is,' Charlotte continues, 'I know happiness isn't necessarily about being slim and gorgeous, but I have enough experience of being fat and plain to know it's not about that either. I'd love to look as nice as any of you.'

I am about to repeat my reassurances when it strikes me that, actually, she may be right. At least partly. If looking better would make our friend more confident, then why on earth wouldn't we help her do that?

'Listen, Charlotte,' I say, 'I love you just the way you are and so does everyone else here. But if you really feel this strongly about it, we'll help you.'

'What do you mean?' she asks.

'I mean we'll give you a makeover.'

She looks sceptical.

'Seriously,' I continue, 'we'll help you to get fit, we'll help you to do your hair and your make-up, we'll help you pick your clothes – and anything else you want help with, for that matter!'

'Charlotte,' gasps Valentina, 'I'll introduce you to the director at *Andrew Herbert* if you like! He'll have you looking like Jennifer Aniston in no time. Oh, this is so exciting!'

'I'm sure it can't be that easy,' she says.

'Nonsense,' says Grace. 'You've got a lovely face, but everyone looks better with some make-up.'

'I actually think the biggest problem is my weight,' she says.

'Right then, you can sign up to WeightWatchers,' I suggest. 'In fact, we could all go to give you some moral support. You'll love it, Valentina.'

'Couldn't you just start throwing up instead?' says Valentina, pulling a face. 'It did wonders for Princess Di.'

I tut.

'Do you really think this sort of thing would help?' asks Charlotte.

'Yes!' we all say in unison, and she starts giggling.

'Oh God, but what about this dress?' she says. 'I'm so sorry, Georgia, I really am.'

'What are you on about?' Georgia says firmly. 'It's challenges like this that dressmakers thrive on – isn't that right, Anouska?'

'Sure, no problem,' replies the dressmaker begrudgingly. 'We'll get another one ready in time. No problem. Yeah.'

Charlotte suddenly has a sparkle in her eye and, later, when I catch her by herself I can't resist seizing the moment.

'You've just got to promise me one thing,' I tell her. 'If we succeed in pulling off this makeover, you've got to start putting in some effort with Jim.'

This time she laughs out loud.

'Fine!' she says in mock exasperation. 'Whatever you say, Evie. Whatever you say!'

Chapter 31

Liverpool city centre, Saturday, 24 March

I only know one person who would even consider getting married in a cowboy hat and feather boa, and that is my mother.

'I think it's quite fun, don't you?' she asks, posing in front of the full-length mirror.

'You look like J.R. Ewing in drag,' I tell her.

She pulls a face. 'How did you ever get to be so conventional?'

'All kids have got to rebel against their parents,' I say. 'Being conventional was the only option open in my case.'

She ruffles my hair, something she's done for as long as I can remember and will probably still be doing when I'm collecting my pension. It used to drive me insane, but now it's just one of a long list of my mother's unique characteristics and, given that it's one of the less eccentric ones and that it doesn't attract too much attention from upstanding members of the public, I've decided I can live with it.

'Have you thought about something a bit more *demure*,' I ask, thinking back to what the magazines in the bridal shop said. But the second I've said it, I wonder why I bothered.

She doesn't do demure, my mum. Demented maybe, but not demure.

'You mean boring,' she says, continuing to look along the rail. 'Oh, this could be nice.' She picks up a traditional-looking floor-length dress. My hopes rise momentarily.

'I wonder if they'd do it in gingham?' she muses.

My mum is getting married later this year to Bob, whom she has been dating for six years. To say they're made for each other is an understatement. Because while I'd previously considered my mother to be a one-off, she and Bob couldn't be more suited if they came as a matching pair.

He is a bearded philosophy lecturer who is permanently clad in Jesus sandals so unfashionable only the Almighty Himself could carry them off. She is a yoga teacher with a fondness for clothes that come in such an alarming array of colours I'm sure some people must risk having a fit if they look at her for too long.

Both of them have a permanently chilled-out expression on their face that always makes people think they've been smoking dubious substances. While I can't testify to what they got up to in the seventies, I strongly suspect that in both cases they were just born like that.

I'll never think of Bob as a father, but I'm glad he and my mother are getting married. She deserves to be happy and he'd do anything for her – so long, of course, as it doesn't involve anything that might challenge his vast list of ethical views on everything from the pollution of Formby beach to the treatment of moon bears in China. Not that my mum would ever challenge those – her own list is long enough to fill the *Yellow Pages*.

But as I've grown up, I've come to realise that, despite her feeding me more lentils as a child than can be good for anyone's digestive system – I was twelve before I had my first Wagon Wheel – and the fact that her idea of a family break was six nights camping at Greenham Common, Mum is undoubtedly one of the good guys in life.

My dad, on the other hand, whom she met on an Indian ashram in 1972, disappeared when I was two. I sometimes think I can remember him, but then wonder whether what's in my head are just ideas about him that have been pieced together from old photos and snippets of information I've picked up over the years.

I wouldn't say my mum exactly shies away from talking about him, but the subject rarely comes up and I certainly don't push her on the issue. It can't be easy, having the father of your child simply leave the house one day and never turn up again. He had apparently popped out to buy some LSD, which tells you all you need to know about him. Other people go out to buy a pint of milk and don't come back. My father couldn't even run away respectably.

'Do you know,' she says, frowning at the rail, 'I don't think I'm going to go for a wedding dress at all. I'd just look silly in any of these. They're not me.'

'You haven't even tried any on yet,' I say, getting worried now. 'Oh God, you're not thinking about wearing your usual gear, are you? I'm telling you, Mum, if you wear one of your purple mohair jumpers and painted clogs, I'm boycotting this wedding.'

'Don't be horrible,' she says, but she's smirking.

'You need something *special*,' I insist.

'It'll be special no matter what I wear,' she says. 'Who cares what I've got on, really? Besides, I've left it very late now. They probably couldn't even get one ready for me in time.'

'I'm sure they could,' I say. 'Go on, just go and try a few on. For me. Please.'

She pulls a face like a sulky teenager whose iPod and mobile phone have been confiscated and grabs a handful of dresses from the rail before wandering off behind a curtain. The shop assistant looks at me in the same sympathetic way I've seen people look at Grace when Polly is playing up.

My mum tries on five dresses and by the time she has decided to abandon the sixth one I start to think she may be right. They're all lovely on the rail, but somehow they don't look right on her. They all look weird. By which I mean normal. And, quite frankly, normal isn't her style.

'Shall we just have a little break?' she says hopefully. 'Oh, go on, Evie. *Please?*'

Chapter 32

For proximity's sake, we settle on one of the cafés in the Met Quarter, although given that you can't move for trendy executives, footballers' wives and designer junkies in here, I'll admit that we look a little out of place.

I go for my usual cappuccino while Mum orders a herbal tea that looks and smells as if someone has washed their socks in it. She opens her newspaper, the *Guardian*, which she buys every day even though she has complained about it 'going too right-wing' for the last fifteen years. She also buys the *Daily Echo* religiously, though I suspect from the fact that she asked recently whether we'd given much coverage to a newly-released book of Afghan poetry that she doesn't actually read it all that often.

I pull a copy of one of Grace's old wedding magazines from my bag and turn to the inside back page, where there's a list of things we should have done so far. The reception is booked, so that's one tick at least. Sort of, anyway. The wedding party is being held in a field near Mum's house, and Wendy, her friend who runs a health-food shop, is doing the catering. It will be a sumptuous feast of nettle soup and mung bean falafels. I can't wait.

'I suppose I'd be wasting my time asking whether you've ordered the flowers yet?' I say.

'You don't need to do that yet,' she says. 'There are three months left.'

'Two and a half,' I correct her. 'And, anyway, according to this you do. Mind you, this says you're meant to have sent out cards telling people to expect an invitation soon. What's the point in that? Why don't you just invite people?'

'Capitalism,' she says knowingly. 'They want you to buy two sets of cards. Anyway, we don't need cards. I thought I'd just mention it to people when I bump into them.'

My heart sinks, and not for the first time today.

'Mum,' I say, trying to stay calm, 'you can't do that. I know you don't want things to be too formal, but I've been to better organised sixth-form parties.'

'You worry too much,' she says. 'It'll be fine. If you want to send out cards, then do. But I'm not bothered and Bob certainly won't be either.'

I can see that being a bridesmaid at this wedding is going to involve significantly more than it did for Grace's wedding – although it isn't as though I haven't got plenty of people to share the burden with.

As well as myself, my mother has asked nine other people to be bridesmaids, including Grace (who could probably do without the hassle), Georgia (who was looking forward to some wedding-free time), Charlotte (who is traumatised enough with the preparations for Georgia's wedding) and Valentina (who's thrilled – she has a star part again).

'I take it you haven't invited anyone else to be a bridesmaid recently?' I ask.

'No, I haven't actually,' she says. 'Although I don't know

why you're so bothered about it. It'll be nice. The more the merrier.'

'I'm bothered about it because, while I'm not saying you ought to be a slave to convention . . .'

'Heaven forbid,' she interrupts.

'. . . getting married, in case you hadn't noticed, is a *ceremony* – which by its very definition follows certain conventions.'

She frowns.

'All I'm saying is, you've got to follow at least *some* of the rules,' I say.

'What rules am I breaking?' she asks.

'You're only meant to ask a *select few people* to be your bridesmaids,' I huff. 'My friends would have been happy as guests. I mean, you didn't even go to Grace's wedding.'

'Only because Bob and I were in Egypt.'

'Ah, yes, your Egyptian holiday . . .'

Mum pulls a face as if to request I don't express my opinion on this again.

'We enjoyed it, I've told you,' she says.

What's wrong with Egypt as a holiday destination? you may ask. The pyramids, a Nile cruise, Tutankhamun's tomb. Marvellous.

Well, yes, except my mum's Egyptian holiday featured none of those and would be enough to give your average Thomas Cook customer heart failure. Her trip was organised by an environmental group and involved my mum, Bob, and a number of other like-minded lunatics waking at 5 a.m. every day to spend six hours picking up tampons and other unsavoury bits of pollution from the banks of the Nile. I worry for her sometimes.

'Anyway,' she continues, 'all your friends were really pleased when I asked them to be my bridesmaids. Especially Valentina. Lovely girl.'

'You won't be saying that when she tries to upstage you on your own wedding day,' I mutter.

I excuse myself to go to the loo, and when I come back I see something that alarms me slightly. My mum has my mobile phone in her hand. The reason I feel so uncomfortable with this sight is because technology and my mother are not happy bedmates. This is a woman who thought blogging was something to do with deforestation.

'I tried to answer this for you,' she says. 'I thought it was ringing but I think it turned out to be one of those text thingies.'

'Let me see,' I say, taking the phone from her and narrowing my eyes. I just know this was the newsdesk trying to get hold of me for a big story. I can feel it.

'What did you press?' I ask.

'Nothing!' she protests.

'Well, don't worry about it then,' I say, still slightly uneasy, but slipping my phone into the pocket of my denim jacket anyway.

She pauses for a second. 'Okay, I might have pressed something,' she says guiltily.

I raise an accusatory eyebrow.

'I didn't mean to, I was just trying to answer it for you.'

'Okay,' I say. 'Was there a message there?'

'Yes,' she says.

'Do you remember what it said?'

'Er, something about a wedding from someone called John. No, sorry, Jack. That's right, Jack. It was definitely Jack.'

Chapter 33

I almost spit out my coffee.

It is now weeks since Grace's wedding and I haven't heard nor seen anything of Jack. Which is exactly what I'd expected, given that he and Valentina are no longer an item – although I'd be persuaded of the existence of Father Christmas before I'd believe she dumped him.

But one thing's for sure: I haven't stopped thinking about him. Which has been a bit annoying, really. I'd be sitting down to bash out a story, when all of a sudden he'd pop into my head, just like that. With his deep brown eyes and his broad shoulders and his smooth skin and . . . well, when you've got a deadline in twenty minutes, I promise you there's nothing more offputting.

Anyway, even more annoying than that is something which has also been invading my thoughts, and it's this: Jack and Valentina no longer dating is a problem in itself. As I told Charlotte, Valentina was the only link between him and myself.

The result of this is that since I discovered the news of their break-up, I seem to have spent a disproportionate amount of time musing about all manner of scenarios in which I might 'bump' into him again.

Could I, for example, offer to do a special feature for the paper on his charity? I dismissed that as too unethical: I can't just go writing special reports on organisations because I happen to keep waking up in a guilty sweat after dreaming about their chief executive. Besides that, it's too obvious.

So, could I take up tennis and join Valentina's club? I dismissed this as impractical: I'd never be able to act with her hovering about all the time showing more flesh than the average swimwear model. Besides that, it's too obvious.

Could I hang about in the coffee shop near the charity's offices? I dismissed this as far too similar to the behaviour of some of my ex-boyfriends. Besides that, it's too obvious.

So, after spending an annoyingly large amount of time focusing on cunning ideas about how I might get to see Jack again, I'm still doing exactly that. Focusing. In fact, I've been focusing so much I'm starting to develop a headache. Now this: a text message from the man himself. Except my mother has gone and zapped the bloody thing.

'Can you please try to remember what it said, exactly?' I ask, trying not to sound too exasperated.

'Oh, I don't know,' she says. 'Something about a wedding – that was it. I tried to get the words to move down, you know, the way they do on a word processor, but they all just disappeared. Stupid thing, if you ask me. Maybe there's a fault on it.'

'The only fault is with your common sense,' I sigh. 'Just think, will you, Mum? This was someone I met at Grace's wedding. Does that help?'

'Not really,' she says vaguely. 'It said something about Georgia and Pete's wedding.'

Georgia and Pete's wedding. Why would Jack be texting me about their wedding?

'Is he one of your new boyfriends?' she asks.

'No,' I say grumpily.

'You really ought to relax more, you know,' she says. 'You seem to get terribly stressed out sometimes, Evie. Why don't you start coming to reiki with me?'

I scan through my phone book to find the entry for Georgia. When she picks up, the background noise is so loud it sounds like she's speaking from the inside cylinder of a vacuum cleaner.

'How you doing?' she asks brightly. 'I hope you're sticking to your beauty regime – I don't want any zits on my wedding photos.'

'I'm exfoliating so much my cheeks are raw,' I tell her. 'Anyway, where are you? I can barely hear you.'

'Flying out for one last check at the venue,' she shouts. 'It's the helicopter you can hear.'

Georgia is getting married in an exclusive hideaway of a hotel on one of the most secluded Isles of Scilly, just off the coast of Cornwall. Which I'm sure will be gorgeous, but apparently isn't exactly the most practical place to get to and from when you're organising a wedding.

'I'll be quick, then,' I say. 'Can you think of a reason why the guy who Valentina brought to Grace's wedding would be sending me a text message about your wedding?'

But she's drowned out again by the sound of the propellers.

'Are you there, Georgia?' I shout, and am conscious that the woman on the table next to us must be delighted at me bellowing away while she's trying to have a peaceful cup of coffee. 'Georgia, I can't hear you!'

'I've got you now,' she shouts back. 'I feel like I'm in *Apocalypse Now*. What did you say?'

'I just said, can you think of a reason why the guy who Valentina brought to Grace's wedding would be texting me about your wedding?'

'You mean Jack Williamson?' she says.

'The very same.'

There's a pause. 'None at all,' she says.

Great. My mother's got it wrong.

'I mean, I've no idea why he'd be texting *you* about it,' she adds. 'He *is* coming to the wedding though.'

Chapter 34

My head spins as I try to think of a possible reason why Jack would be going to Georgia's wedding now that he and Valentina are no longer an item.

'How is he going to your wedding?' I ask Georgia. 'I mean, you hardly even know him.'

'He and Pete have been going to the rugby together almost every weekend since Grace's wedding,' she tells me. 'Oh, hang on, you're breaking up . . .'

Her voice disappears again. I put my phone down with shaky fingers.

'Have you sorted it out?' asks my mother.

'Not yet,' I say, and start keying in a text message.

Have u got a number 4 Jack? Have Forward Planning meeting at work 2moro and have 2 do story about charities.

I press Send and fire it off to Georgia's fiancé Pete. Then I take a sip of my coffee, which has now been standing for so long it's almost chilled.

It seems to be forever before he responds with the mobile number. I scroll further down. *P.S. Forward planning? Family planning, more like!*

Cheeky sod. I resist the temptation to tell him that I

wasn't the one who texted first, but I suspect that might not look as cool as I'm hoping to appear. Now I've got this phone number, I feel like Indiana Jones after he's found the lost Ark. It's exactly what I wanted, but I'm buggered if I know what I'm going to do with it now.

I start composing a text.

Had technical problem. Can u pls re-send yr message?

Oh, no. Far too practical. Aloof, even. I'm missing a trick there, surely.

Can u resend yr text? It's so good I want to read it twice!

God, no. That couldn't be any cornier if it had bunions.

Can't read yr text . . . and am dying to. Can I have another?

None of them feel right, but I've got to pick one. I reluctantly go for option one, although regret it the second it goes. Text was invented for flirting but the one I've just sent is about as likely to set his pulses racing as a party political broadcast.

'Well, shall we hit the road?' says my mum, folding away her paper and leaving it on the table. 'I don't know about you, but I've had enough of weddingy things for one day.'

If I was a better bridesmaid – and daughter, for that matter – I would protest and insist that she continues in the search for the perfect dress. But I've got other things on my mind now.

'Okay,' I say, jumping up from my seat. 'I'll get these.'

I'm standing at the counter waiting for my change when my phone vibrates. I take it out of the top pocket of my denim jacket and see immediately that it's from him. I open the message.

Just wondered if you would be on duty on the 8th, looking pretty and deafening guests?

116

I immediately become conscious that I am smiling and that the woman standing next to me laden with designer bags is looking at me as if I've just escaped from somewhere. I turn my back and start tapping into the keypad.

Thought u promised not to mention that again. I go to send it then stop. His message was definitely flirty, so I need to step things up a little. I add the words: *I'll forgive u – just this once.*

Not slutty, but slightly cheeky, I think. I tuck my phone back into my pocket, unable to stop smiling, and pay up before heading back to collect my mum. My pocket vibrates again.

Good. Would not want to be in yr bad books. See u at the wedding (looking forward to it).

Excellent. Even flirtier. Right – how to respond?

I decide to do a draft first. Just to make sure that what I write is absolutely right. But for some reason I'm stuck for ideas about how to reply. I start bashing out fantasy texts – ones that I have no intention of sending, but they might just help me work out what I'm really going to write.

Me too. PS. Will u carry ME to bed instead this time?

I chuckle to myself and start to scrub it off. There is no way I'm going to go that far. Amusing thought though. Just then, I am interrupted by a familiar voice.

'Evie! I'm starting to think you might be following me!'

Chapter 35

It's Gareth. *Again.* I say *again* because I have now bumped into him three times since Grace's wedding, which is a situation I couldn't feel less comfortable with if I was wearing a pair of size four drainpipes.

'Hello, Gareth,' I say despondently.

'Hi! Mrs Hart,' he adds, grinning and extending a hand out to my mum. 'I've heard so much about you.'

'Oh, it's Ms actually,' she says, smiling and shaking his hand.

There is an awkward silence.

'This is Gareth, Mum,' I say reluctantly. 'He works at the university with Bob. He does their admin.'

'There's a lot more to it than just admin,' he corrects me.

'Oh, sorry,' I say. 'I didn't mean . . . well, sorry.'

There's another awkward silence.

'So, how *are* you, Evie?' he says, grinning again. 'You're looking really great.'

I'm struggling to say, 'You too,' because, sadly, nothing could be further from the truth. Gareth has developed an angry-looking rash on his forehead and hasn't shaved for so long that he's starting to look like Tom Hanks in the last half-hour of *Castaway*.

'Er, thanks, Gareth,' I say.

'Congratulations on your impending nuptials, Mizz Hart,' he says to my mum.

'Oh, well, thank you. Will you be coming to the wedding?' she asks innocently. I try not to groan audibly.

'If I'm invited,' he beams.

Oh God. I know what's coming next.

'Oh well, consider yourself invited,' Mum says brightly.

Were it not for the fact that she makes her living from teaching yoga, I would kick her very hard in the shin right now. As if sensing my thoughts, she announces that she needs to pop to the health-food shop.

'I've run out of ginkgo biloba. Won't be long,' she adds, leaving Gareth clearly wondering which language she's speaking.

'Evie, we never got to have a proper chat about our relationship,' he says, his forehead starting to crumple.

I've got nowhere to run.

'I know,' I tell him. 'But I'm just not sure there's anything left to say.'

'Well, the thing is,' he says, 'I've been putting a lot of thought into all this and, well, you've always said you've got a commitment problem. I want to help you with it.'

The thought is as appealing as treating a mouth ulcer with a packet of salt and vinegar crisps. I try to remain unfazed.

'Gareth, listen,' I say. 'There's nothing you can do to help. It's just the way I am. I'm not ready to make a commitment to anyone yet.'

'But you're *nearly thirty*,' he says.

'*Not for another three years!*' I shriek.

The puppy-dog eyes come back and are now so mournful I'm convinced he's been taking lessons from a basset-hound.

'I'd just hate to see someone like you left on the shelf, that's all,' he tells me.

I'm tempted to enquire whether he really thinks a comment like that will help his cause but I decide, in the light of the fact that his lip is starting to quiver, not to say anything.

'I know I hurt you, Gareth,' I say softly.

'You did hurt me, Evie, you really did,' he says.

'And I'm sorry,' I continue. 'I am really, really sorry. I'm an idiot. You're a lovely man. You'll find someone who deserves you some day, you will.'

'But I really feel that you and I made a connection,' he says.

I'm not sure I can make this any clearer.

'I'm sorry, Gareth,' I continue. 'I really am. Sorry for hurting you, sorry for not being able to make a commitment to you. I'm just really, really sorry.'

He's about to say something else, but as I see my mum walking back towards us, I decide to make my move.

'Look, here's my mum,' I say. 'I've really got to get her back – it's starting to rain.'

'You've got a brolly,' he tells me.

'Oh, er – yes, I know. But she's got *a disorder*,' I say, leaning in to whisper to him.

'A disorder?' he asks, frowning. 'What kind of disorder?'

'She goes just *bonkers* whenever she comes into contact with rainwater,' I tell him. 'It's called, er, *Gremlins Syndrome*.'

He scrunches up his face. 'What, you mean like in the film?' he asks.

'Exactly,' I tell him. 'It's not a pretty sight. I'd hate for you to get stuck in the middle of something like that.'

He's about to question me further when my mum appears by our side.

'Right, all done,' she says brightly, holding up her shopping bag.

Gareth takes a cautious step backwards.

'Sorry we couldn't talk for longer,' I shout, dragging my mother away.

'Bye, Evie,' he shouts back with a worried look on his face. 'See you at the wedding.'

Bugger, bugger, bugger.

'Mum, do you know what you've just done?'

'What?'

'He was someone I used to go out with,' I tell her. 'He's the last person I want at your wedding.'

She doesn't look overly concerned with this news. 'I thought he seemed nice,' she says.

'You think *everybody* seems nice,' I point out.

She frowns. 'You're the one who used to go out with him.'

The thought makes my stomach churn. 'I know,' I say grimly.

'Anyway, just because you've split up with someone doesn't mean you can't still be friends,' she says.

'I know.' Although I've managed to comprehensively disprove the theory so far.

I suddenly realise that this diversion has meant I haven't responded to Jack's text yet, and the thought brightens my spirits immediately. I take my phone out of my pocket to reread my message, but as I look at the screen, my stomach lurches. It says Message Sent.

Oh bollocks. I've sent the draft. He's going to think I'm such a tart I make Abi Titmuss look like a Sunday School teacher. I'm going to have to send him another one immediately, explaining myself. But how the hell do I explain that?

Panicking, I start composing another text. *Sorry – just a joke. I'm not a nymphomaniac, honest!* and press Send immediately.

A couple of minutes later, another arrives. It's from him. One line.

I'll try not to be too disappointed.

Chapter 36

Grace and Patrick's house, Mossley Hill, Liverpool,
Friday, 30 March

Grace has broken out into a sweat again. Not the soft, glowing sort on the average deodorant advert model. More the red-faced, hair-stuck-to-your-forehead sort.

'I wish I was back in the Maldives,' she groans, bending down to look under the bed for her shoes. 'I could cope with the pace of life there.'

'Is there anything I can do to help?' I ask, looking at my watch and thinking that the entire hen night will have graduated to tequila shots and male strippers by the time we finally arrive.

'Er, yeah,' she says, throwing on her top. 'I'm sure there is. Let me think . . . I know, go and ask Polly if she's seen my shoes. The ones with diamonds on them.'

Polly is downstairs watching *Sponge Bob Square Pants* and is so transfixed that I bet it would take nothing less than an alien invasion of the living room to snap her out of it.

'Hey, Pol. How's it going?' I ask.

'Good,' she says, barely blinking.

'Have you seen your mum's shoes?' I ask. 'The ones with the diamonds on them?'

'No,' she says. I can hardly see her lips move.

'You're sure?'

'Hmm, yes,' she says.

'Right,' I say, wondering what to do next.

'Evie,' she says, as I'm heading out of the room. 'Why have they got diamonds on them?'

Now that's more like it.

Why is one of Polly's words *du jour*, along with *What? Where?* and anything else that marks the start of a question. Lately, from the minute she wakes up in the morning to the minute she goes to bed, Grace, Patrick and anyone else she comes into contact with is bombarded with questions, questions and more questions. The FBI could take lessons from her.

Tonight, we've covered topics as varied as religion: *Why does God make people and then make them die?* Try answering that one when you're trying to put your eyeliner on; physics: *What is there in the sky after the clouds?*; maths: *How many numbers are there?*; military history: *When did wars start?*; cinema: *Why was Simba – the Lion King – born?*; sex education: *Why was I born?* and a whole wealth of miscellany including: *Who would win a fight between Superman and King Kong?* and *Why does Mrs Harris* (her teacher) *have a moustache even though she's a lady?*

It's proof, according to Grace's mum, that she has 'an inquisitive mind'.

'I think they're there just to decorate them, just to make them look pretty,' I say.

'Why do they need to look pretty?' she asks.

I can see this has the potential to be a long philosophical

discussion, and with the taxi booked for 7.30 p.m. I'm not sure we've got time.

When I get upstairs to check on Grace's progress, she is flinging random items of junk out from the bottom of her wardrobe. There's old coat-hangers, plastic bags full of tights, a box full of half-used moisturisers and crusty make-up, and about six or so pairs of shoes, one of which actually has cobwebs on them. Piled up, it is the sort of collection you'd see in the scruffy corner of a car-boot sale.

'Shit,' she says suddenly. 'Can you look at my curling tongs?'

The tongs have started to burn a hole in the dressing-table and are emitting the sort of aroma you'd expect from a rusty barbecue. I prop them up next to a bottle of tanning lotion as Patrick shouts from downstairs.

'Is Scarlett's bum meant to look like this?'

Grace takes a deep breath and runs downstairs, followed by me. I'm not sure what light I can shed on the issue, but at least it's getting us closer to the door.

'Hmm,' Grace says as she bends down to examine the evidence. 'She's got nappy rash. Just let her dry out for five minutes then put a load of Sudocrem on.'

'Right,' says Patrick.

'You're obviously not as familiar as I am with the complete works of Miriam Stoppard or you'd have known that,' she adds.

She's clearly joking but I can't help noticing that Patrick flashes her a look – a look that's almost dirty. It's the sort of expression Valentina throws shop assistants if they suggest she's anything over a size eight. And it's not one I've ever seen Patrick give before, particularly not to Grace.

'Are you sure we've got some Sudocrem?' he shouts through to Grace in the kitchen.

'Yes,' she shouts back, having finally found her shoes.

'You're sure?' he asks.

'Positive,' she replies.

'Because there's none in here.'

'There is.'

'There's *not*, I promise you,' he tells her firmly.

'I promise you there is,' she says. 'I bought some last week.'

'Well, you can't have put it in here,' he says.

'I did.'

'You *can't* have,' he says. 'Because it's not here.' His face is now so thunderous he looks less like a corporate lawyer and more like a military dictator.

I know it's only a low-key domestic, but I'm standing here, stunned into silence, because it's so unlike Patrick and Grace. They just don't row. Not usually, anyway. But *something's* going on here, that's for sure, because there is enough resentment coming from Patrick alone to keep a Relate counsellor going until Christmas.

Grace walks into the living room, moves him to one side and starts rifling through the nappy box, before producing a tub of Sudocrem.

'Oh,' he says. 'I hadn't realised that was the stuff you were talking about.'

'The fact that it's got *Sudocrem* in big letters on the side of the tub wasn't a giveaway?' she enquires. Again, it's a light-hearted jest, the kind both of them usually make all the time.

But Patrick doesn't see it that way. He mutters something under his breath as she heads out of the room but Grace, diplomatically, decides not to ask for a repetition. As it happens, she doesn't need to.

'Mummy,' says Polly, 'what's a pain in the arse?'

Chapter 37

'Is everything okay between you and Patrick?' I ask when we eventually make it into a taxi.

'Oh God, yes,' she says dismissively as she attempts to finish tonging her hair while we belt it along the Dock Road. It's only half-done at the moment, which means while one side of her hair is so straight it could have been ironed, the other side looks like it has been transplanted from Leo Sayer. 'He's just being a bit of a grumpy old man at the moment, that's all. It's nothing. Oh, bugger.'

Grace's BlackBerry is ringing so she thrusts the curling tongs towards me like some sort of relay baton, to root around in her bag for it. She studies the number which has come up and lets out a long sigh.

'It's Adele,' she says dejectedly. Her boss.

'Well, don't answer it,' I tell her.

She hesitates, biting her lip so much you'd think she was battling with the sort of moral dilemma nations go to war over.

'I've got to,' she says eventually.

'Don't!' I say. 'You're on a hen night. You're meant to be wolf-whistling at barmen and getting so drunk you can't remember your husband's name. This is not the time to be speaking to your boss.'

She bites her lip again and looks out of the window. I know exactly what she's going to do.

'Hi, Adele,' she says cheerfully, as she answers the phone. 'Oh, right. Oh, sorry. Well, I did stay late every night this week and . . .' She pauses to listen '. . . but you see, I thought I *did* get that report to you . . .' another pause '. . . oh well, if it wasn't right . . . Yes. Okay, yes. I understand. I'll see what I can do.'

She puts the phone down and lets out another huge sigh.

'What?' I say.

'I'm going to have to go back,' she says.

'Why?' I shriek. 'Grace, it's eight o'clock on a Friday night. What can you possibly need to do that can't wait?'

'Oh, it's just a report she'd asked for – I won't bore you with the details. But she needs me to do something else for it tonight.'

Grace is about to lean forward to re-direct the taxi driver, and I know I've got to act. Thankfully, I'm faster than she is.

I lean over and grab her BlackBerry.

'What are you doing?' she asks.

I open the taxi window and hold my arm – and the BlackBerry – out as the wind from the Mersey whistles past it.

'Evie, what are you doing!' she screams. 'Do you know how much they cost?'

'Yes,' I lie. I have about as much knowledge and interest in these executive toys as I do in mechanical engineering.

'Look, I don't care,' I add. 'Promise me you're not going back.'

'Evie, *come on!*' she says. 'Give it to me! That's company property!'

'Promise me,' I tell her sternly.

'I can't – I'll be sacked,' she says, almost whimpering now.

'Do you really think that being sacked is a likely prospect?' I ask. 'I mean, how many other employees do they have who would even *consider* leaving a hen night to go and start writing a report?'

She shrugs.

'Come on now,' I say. 'Promise me?'

'So what the hell do I say to Adele?' she asks.

'Here,' I say, pulling the phone back in. 'I'll compose a text message for you. Honestly, leave this to me.'

She rolls her eyes and starts shaking her head, but at least she's starting to see the funny side of it.

Dear Adele, I write. 'Let's keep it vague at this point, I think,' I tell Grace. *Family emergency,* my text continues. *Will explain all on Monday. So sorry but I can't help with the report. Grace.* There, perfect.'

'So what do I tell her on Monday?' she asks.

I shrug.

'You've got two days to come up with that,' I tell her. 'Do you expect me to do everything around here or what?'

Chapter 38

When Georgia chose Simply Heathcotes as the venue at which to kick off her hen night, I have to say I was a little sceptical.

It is one of Liverpool's best restaurants, housed in a stunning glass and granite building in the heart of the city centre. And while I'm not saying the off-duty city types, sophisticated couples and out-of-towners don't look like they know how to enjoy themselves, I just know that if I'd come out for a nice dinner, I wouldn't be entirely chuffed to find myself put next to a hen party.

But as Grace and I make our way past the tables and to a private dining room on the first floor, it's plain that we'll be discreetly tucked away – and won't lower the tone elsewhere. Which is a good job really. Because as we walk in, Georgia is unwrapping a gift from one of her fellow 'hens' – a ten-inch bright blue vibrator that on first glance looks more like Darth Vader's light sabre.

'We thought you'd never get here!' she shouts, attempting to keep the L-plate pinned on the front of her dress out of her soup.

Tonight may be Georgia's night, but there is one other hen

our eyes are immediately drawn to. Charlotte. Okay, so I got a sneak preview earlier after spending the day with her on a mammoth shopping trip, followed by a session at the hairdresser. But with the look now complete – courtesy of a famous Valentina makeover – she is nothing less than stunning.

'Bloody hell!' I say. 'Charlotte, what happened to you?'

'*Fabulous*, isn't she?' says Valentina, admiring her handiwork.

'You look *unbelievable*,' I add. 'Really, you do.'

Charlotte blushes. 'Thank you,' she says, smiling.

As well as her gorgeous new haircut and Valentina's make-up, Charlotte is wearing an ultra-feminine raspberry-coloured jacket, which shows off a cleavage to die for. As I told her when I helped her pick it out, no one is a better judge, since I'm about as voluptuous as the average greyhound.

'She looks amazing,' says Grace, as we slip into the two seats saved for us at the other end of the table. 'How's her diet going?'

I glance back over to Charlotte and see that she's chosen a salad. While she's too far away for me to be certain, I'd bet anything she's told them to hold the dressing.

'It's early days,' I say, 'but she did really well in week one at WeightWatchers.'

If the truth be told, Charlotte didn't just do really well, she positively put me to shame. She lost six pounds and was rewarded with a round of applause from the other slimmers and a free packet of low sugar liquorice chews. I, on the other hand, lost 0.2 pounds and was rewarded with a sceptical look from the leader when I told her I couldn't understand it because I'd stuck to the plan religiously. I decided not to mention the curry takeaway I'd had in front of my *Lost* DVD on Thursday.

'Six pounds in seven days,' I continue. 'And she's showing no sign of giving up. The way she's going she'll be calculating the *Points* value of oxygen before long.' I beam at them all. Then I turn to Grace.

'Anyway, listen,' I whisper in her ear. 'I haven't had a chance to tell you what happened.'

'What?' she says.

'Guess who texted me?'

'Who?' she asks, buttering some bread.

I raise my eyebrows and grin.

'*Who?* Come on, we'll be here all night at this rate!'

I check that nobody else is listening then lean closer to her. 'Jack,' I say, trying not to grin too inanely.

'Oh *really?*' She is raising her own eyebrows now. 'Would this be the same Jack who you're definitely, definitely, one hundred per cent not interested in?'

'There's no need to be like that,' I tell her.

'Go on then, what did he say?' she asks.

I pause for a second, then dig out my mobile to show Grace the texts, realising I'm behaving like a giggly sixth-former.

'You've saved them?' she asks, amused.

'Couldn't resist,' I shrug.

And, do you know, I can barely believe it myself.

Chapter 39

By the time we've got through dessert – and a hefty amount of wine – the conversation around the table has started to resemble an episode of *Trisha*. The subject of debate is probably inevitable under the circumstances: the pros and cons of being married.

On the cons side is Leona, one of Georgia's former neighbours, a woman who is expensive-looking in every way and so skinny she must have been on Atkins since birth.

'All you need to know about married life,' she says in between healthy mouthfuls of Chablis, 'is that you argue more and shag less.'

Everyone laughs, but tonight we're all coming down on the side of Georgia, the blushing bride.

'Oh, for goodness' sake,' she says, laughing. 'Grace, back me up here – marriage is fantastic, isn't it? Go on, tell her – I know I can count on you.'

Grace puts down her knife and fork. For some reason she looks lost for words.

'Grace?' I prompt, thinking I might just have to prod her with her fork to snap her out of it.

'Oh, sorry,' she says. 'It's great. It's lovely. Yes, it *really* is. Lovely.'

'So, does it bring you closer together?' asks Georgia.

'Er, well, it's difficult to say,' replies Grace evasively.

I frown. I can't help thinking we'd all hoped for a little more enthusiasm here.

'What I mean is, Patrick and I have always been close,' Grace continues. 'Besides, it's different when you've got kids. Nothing brings you together like they do. I mean, try dealing with a screaming baby at two a.m. when you've both got work the next morning. That's a bonding experience if ever there is one.'

Georgia smiles, apparently happy with this interpretation.

'So you're glad you did it?' she asks.

Grace hesitates again. 'Absolutely,' she says, a little too firmly. 'Yes, absolutely. I mean, it was a bloody good party at the very least, wasn't it?'

When the meal is finished we head to Mathew Street which, with its packed bars and clubs, is a far more conventional setting for a hen party. Despite the temperature being only a few degrees above freezing, most of the women are wearing the sort of attire you might expect for the climate of, say, Fiji. The men, meanwhile, are just wearing appreciative looks.

'I hope you don't mind, Evie,' says Georgia. 'Everyone offered to carry some of my hen-party presents in their handbags so I didn't have to cart everything round myself. I think you ended up with the fluffy handcuffs in your bag while you were in the loo.'

'I thought it felt heavier,' I say, 'especially since I have been saddled with Grace's curling tongs too somehow. Still, the handcuffs may come in handy. If that Leona woman keeps going on about how awful marriage is, we could always attach *her* to some railings somewhere.'

Georgia laughs as we arrive at the door to a retro club which was one of our staple nights out when we were students. As the door shuts behind us, we are bombarded with the opening bars of 'Native New Yorker' and Valentina wastes no time in refamiliarising herself with the dance floor.

Hands on her waist, lips pouting, she flings her coat on a chair *à la Saturday Night Fever* and strides her way into the centre of the dance floor, hips swinging like a professional showgirl. Or possibly ladyboy.

'What do you reckon?' I say to Grace and Charlotte. 'Shall we join her? Or do you want to sit this one out at first?'

Personally, I'm dying to hit the dance floor. But the get-out clause at the end is for Charlotte's benefit, as I know she usually finds dancing as appealing as doing the can-can naked down Church Street.

But I'm about to be surprised.

'I'll come with you, Evie,' she says, and I raise my eyebrows in disbelief. 'Why not?' she adds, smiling nervously.

Charlotte might dance in a quiet, understated way – but she dances all right. And, three or four tracks in, she actually looks like she's enjoying herself.

'Charlotte,' shouts Grace over the music. 'I know I said this before but you really do look amazing, you know.'

'Thank you, Grace,' she replies. 'I know I've still got a long way to go.'

'Have you?' I wonder out loud. 'You look like a different person already.'

'I still need to lose a lot of weight,' she says, 'but I'm absolutely determined I'm going to do it.'

'Well, good for you,' says Grace.

'I mean, I'd love to look like you,' adds Charlotte.

'Me?' Grace looks genuinely surprised by this.

'Absolutely you,' she says. 'You're attractive, you've got a beautiful family. I'd kill to be in your shoes.'

A look of realisation suddenly washes over Grace's face.

'I *am* lucky, aren't I?' she says, smiling.

After a good half-hour of dancing to the sort of tracks that were last in the charts before I was on solids, Grace looks ready for a breather.

'Do you fancy another drink?' she mouths, competing against the Jackson Five.

I nod, and she and I make our way to the bar as Charlotte, unbelievably, stays with the others.

'White wine?' asks Grace.

'Please,' I say. 'Although I think we're the only ones in here not drinking alcopops, you know.'

She grimaces. 'If I wanted the sort of e-numbers that are in those, I could have stayed at home and eaten one of Polly's strawberry mousses,' she says. 'Ooh, before I forget, you have still got my curling tongs, haven't you?'

'Yes,' I tell her. 'I've got your curling tongs, I've got Georgia's furry handcuffs, and in fact I've got enough of other people's junk in this bag to hold a Bring and Buy sale. Now, am I getting these drinks or are you?'

Just as she's about to produce a twenty-pound note, we can feel someone's presence behind us.

'Let me get these,' says a vaguely familiar voice.

I turn around and can barely believe my eyes.

'Jack!' I gasp, with such enthusiasm that I sound like a swooning Jane Austen character on crack.

I'm going to have to learn some subtlety, I really am.

Chapter 40

Jack isn't as good-looking as I'd remembered. He's better.

'How are you, Evie and Grace?' he asks, smiling.

'I'm fine,' says Grace. 'And you? I've not seen you since the wedding. Listen, thank you so much for the present – it was beautiful.'

Jack spurned the wedding list and bought Grace and Patrick an Indonesian wall-hanging. Not only is it supremely tasteful and completely unique, but it also has the added benefit of being a great excuse to replace the Whitley Bay landscape that Patrick's mother gave them four Christmases ago.

'I'm glad you liked it,' he says. 'I was torn between that and a rather impressive set of garden gnomes.'

'You made the right choice,' she laughs.

'I thought you might say that,' he says. 'And how are you, Evie? It's nice to see you instead of just texting. It's not really the same as a proper conversation, somehow, is it?'

'I'm great, actually,' I reply, trying to think of something good to say, something that will spark a brilliant conversation and make me sound fabulously intelligent. 'Er, I didn't expect to see you here,' I add.

Genius at work, Evie. How about *Do you come here often?* next time.

'It's not one of my usual haunts,' he replies. 'But someone at work is leaving today so I decided to come out for just a pint. Although that was six hours ago, I must admit.'

'Naughty you,' I say. Oh God, what have I been drinking?

'Listen, Evie, I'll be back soon,' says Grace, obviously excusing herself for my benefit. 'I've just got to go and speak to Charlotte.'

She grabs her bag and heads back to the dance floor.

So, here I am, alone with the man himself.

Jack smiles again. 'So, you've heard I somehow made it onto the guest-list to Georgia and Pete's wedding?' he says.

'I *have* heard,' I nod. 'Which presumably means that you're the reason Pete has been spending so much time at the rugby lately instead of getting ready for his big day.'

'Ah,' he says. 'Guilty as charged. I hope Georgia will forgive me.'

'Oh, I'm sure she will.' I am finally managing something halfway akin to a conversation. 'Anyway, don't let it go to your head. I think half of the country has been invited to this wedding. It's going to be more like a football crowd.'

Jack laughs and gazes into my eyes. Just looking at him makes the blood rush to my face. I take a sip of my wine, feeling strangely nervous and excited.

'How many people are going?' he asks.

'A good couple of hundred, I think,' I say. 'Although there are only a few of us out tonight. A handful of us went for a meal and . . . now this. A blast from the past.'

'Well,' he says. 'It's a lovely surprise seeing you.'

'Really?' I am starting to feel a little more relaxed now, a little cooler about the whole situation.

'Yes, really,' he says. 'I mean, I had a good time at Grace and Patrick's wedding. If you'd let me, I think I probably could have talked all night.'

I laugh quietly, feeling confident enough now to say something a little bit flirtatious.

'Well,' I say with a smile, 'I think I probably *would* have let you.'

Jack holds my gaze and my blood starts racing again. The chemistry between us is unmistakable. Nothing is said, but our expressions speak volumes. He knows it and I know it. And I'm absolutely loving it.

'Ay luv, have you gorra pen?' asks a woman next to me, leaning on the bar.

'Mmm,' I reply, making sure I don't take my eyes off him. I'm not about to break this gaze in a hurry.

I reach into my bag to search for the pen I know is in here somewhere. Determined my eyes won't leave Jack's, I root around in it with one hand.

'I pulled the most gorgeous bloke you've seen in your life about twenty minutes ago . . . only my mobile's broken and I can't find anything to write his number down with,' grumbles the woman, but I can't engage in conversation with her. Not now. I just can't do anything other than look at Jack.

I dare to smile – the hint of a smile – and he returns the favour with heart-stopping effect.

Distractedly, I pull Grace's curling tongs out of my bag and put them on the bar to make some room in my bag. As soon as my hand goes back in there, I locate the pen and pass it to the woman.

'Thanks,' she says. Then she just sniggers and leaves. And with a very strange look on her face too.

I think nothing of it as I turn back to Jack. Until I realise he has a very strange look on his face too.

Feeling a little miffed that the spell between us has somehow been broken, I pick up Grace's curling tongs to put them back in my bag. When they are approximately one foot in front of Jack's face I realise something.

I'm not holding a set of curling tongs after all.

I'm holding Georgia's ten-inch vibrator.

Chapter 41

The vibrator was blue in the restaurant. Under the disco lights, it is fluorescent. In fact, it's so fluorescent, you could land a plane with it. I know panicking is the worst possible tactic I could employ in such a situation. But quite frankly, I can't think of anything else to do.

My eyes wide, I grip the vibrator and stuff it firmly back into my bag, hoping against all hope that Jack hasn't realised what it is. But the sheer conviction with which I plunge it back in there manages to set something off. And the vibrator starts *vibrating*.

Panicking madly now, I stuff my hand back into the bag and desperately try to find the OFF button without having to get the vibrator out in public again. But as I frantically feel my way around the thing, my hands sweating and my heart pounding, I realise to my horror that there are at least four different buttons to choose from.

Instinct takes over and I start to press every one of them – my thinking being that *one* of them must shut the damn thing down.

But they don't. Instead, the vibrator launches into an elaborate thrusting movement, the sort you'd expect to see on the production line of an automotive plant.

My bag begins to take on a life of its own, jutting in and out as if it's inhabited by a manic small animal being given a series of electric shocks. I feverishly start pressing the other buttons, the sound of Barry White's 'My First, My Last, My Everything' providing the backdrop to this horrific display. But whatever I press just makes the thrusting get faster and the vibrations get harder . . . and harder . . . and harder.

Conscious of being less than a foot away from the man of my dreams while I wrestle with a ten-inch electronic dildo, my mind starts racing with possible tactics. I am on the verge of throwing the bag over the bar and shouting, 'Bomb!' when finally, mercifully . . . it stops.

Sweating, shaking, I look up at Jack.

'Everything okay?' he asks.

I gulp. 'Er, yes,' I reply, straightening my back and putting my bag on the floor, as if what just happened was the most normal thing in the world.

'Everything okay with *you*?' I ask, realising immediately what a ridiculous question this is. *He's* not the one who's just had a fight with Ann Summers's finest and lost.

'Yes, everything's cool,' he says.

'Er, Jack, *ahem*,' I say. 'Obviously, that wasn't mine.'

'What wasn't?' he says.

'That . . . that . . . *item*,' I whisper.

'You mean the vibrator?' he says.

'It was Georgia's!' I jump in. 'She thought she'd given me the handcuffs, you see, and—'

'*Handcuffs*?' he repeats.

Oh God.

'Fluffy ones,' I offer, by way of an explanation.

Just as I'm about to lose the will to live, I realise something.

143

Jack is smiling. In fact, if I'm not mistaken, he looks thoroughly amused by the whole episode. I can't decide whether this is a good or bad thing.

'I suppose you think that was funny?' I ask.

'*Fawlty Towers* eat your heart out,' he says, and again gives me that wide, heart-stopping smile.

I laugh, feeling slightly relieved now, which is at least an improvement on just mortally embarrassed. I look over to the dance floor, where Valentina now has her arms draped around the neck of a Ricky Martin lookalike and is grinding her hips like a champion flamenco dancer. Charlotte has somehow ended up with a bloke who looks as if his usual Friday nights are spent rehearsing for a future appearance on *University Challenge*. I start to wonder where Grace could be when I see her battling her way through the crowds to reach us.

'Evie,' she says breathlessly when she gets to us. 'I'm going to have to leave.'

I look up at Jack with a sinking feeling. For God's sake, Grace, I can't go yet, I think. But as my mind races with excuses to stay here with Jack, I suddenly realise her face looks drained of colour.

'What's the matter?' I ask.

'It's Polly,' she replies, clearly distraught. 'She's in hospital. She's had an accident.'

Chapter 42

As Grace and I run down the street, our feet sodden with slimy street water and rain belting down onto our faces, I realise she is relying on me to know where we're going. We reach the main road, with headlights streaming past us and squealing groups of girls hurrying into the doorways of night-clubs to avoid getting wet.

At first glance, Grace and I might look like them, but we're not running to get out of the rain. We need a taxi and fast. So why won't any of them stop?

With each set of headlights I see coming towards us, I hurl myself into the road with my thumb out, but they all just swerve around me and beep. Who wants to pick up two women who look like we do? They probably think we're drunk. The fact is, we're both as close to sober now as we've ever been.

'Come on, this way,' I say, grabbing Grace's hand. We run for what seems like hours, but is probably only a few minutes, until we reach a taxi rank. But there is a queue of about forty people. I race to the front and grab the coat of a guy who is getting into a black cab.

'Hey, what the fuck—'

'Please,' I beg. 'There's been an accident. My friend's little girl has been taken to hospital. We need this cab – *please*.'

He looks me up and down, then looks Grace up and down and clearly realises we're not just two charlatans trying to jump the cab queue.

'Come on, Becky, get out,' he says to his girlfriend inside.

'What?' says the woman, uncrossing her long, fake-tanned legs. She's wearing a short, designer dress and, despite the rain, her hair and make-up are still perfectly intact. 'I've waited twenty minutes for this taxi. I'm not getting out now.'

'Get out,' he repeats.

'No,' she says. And then, when he leans into the car and grabs her by the arm, 'Ow! You sod! Get your bloody hands off me!' But she's got the message and reluctantly climbs out.

'Thanks,' I say to both of them and we jump into the back.

'Alder Hey Hospital, please,' I tell the cabbie. 'Accident and Emergency.'

The driver throws me a knowing look; there's only one reason you'd be going to Alder Hey A&E at this time of night and it's not a happy one. He swings the cab around and slams his foot down on the accelerator.

I sit on the fold-down seat opposite Grace and grasp her hands. She still looks stunned.

'So what do you know?' I ask.

She shakes her head, an expression of desperation and bewilderment on her face.

'Not a lot,' she says. 'I mean, I'd been texting Patrick all night. First of all to try and make up with him after our spat. But he just wasn't responding. And I was getting so pissed off with him and . . . well, then I thought perhaps he'd just fallen asleep in front of the telly.'

She takes a deep breath.

'Go on,' I say.

'So, I told myself just to forget it and have a nice time. So I did. I went to dance with Charlotte and two blokes,' she starts sniffing, 'but when I went to the loo I looked at my phone. There were five missed calls.'

'And has he left a voice message?' I ask.

She nods. 'Just the same as the text – very brief. He just says that Polly's had an accident and they're on their way to Alder Hey.'

'Well,' I say, 'she might just have twisted her arm or something.'

Grace looks out of the window as we trundle along and her lip starts quivering.

'But she might not have,' she says.

I squeeze her hand.

'The thing is,' she continues, 'Patrick is usually Mr Pragmatic when things happen. I panic, he keeps his cool. That's the way it is. But he didn't sound very cool, not this time.'

Even though the most rational part of me is saying that this is probably nothing – a broken arm, a bumped head, maybe – there's also a big part of me saying, actually, it might be more than nothing.

I've worked at the *Daily Echo* for less than a year now, but in that time I've covered all manner of horrific stories involving kids. You just assume that that sort of thing happens to other people. Not your best friend's daughter. Not Polly.

Despite the taxi driver's impressive pace, the journey seems to be taking forever.

'Oh Evie,' says Grace, tears welling up now, 'I can't stop thinking about all the questions Polly asked me today – you know how she does. I was trying to get my hair washed when she kept asking me about why dogs have tails – or something. Do you know what I said?'

I shake my head.

'I said: "They just do, Polly". What sort of a mother says "They just do"? Why couldn't I have taken the time to answer her?'

She bursts into tears, sobbing uncontrollably and struggling to get her breath. I jump over and sit next to her, putting my arm around her as tight as I can.

'Grace, don't be silly,' I say to her as the taxi pulls up at the hospital. 'You're a wonderful mother. And everything will be fine. I know it.'

I'm just praying I'm right.

Chapter 43

'I hope she's okay,' says the cabbie, as I hang back to pay him and Grace rushes into the reception. 'Your mate's little girl, I mean.'

'So do I,' I say, handing him a twenty-pound note.

'Oh, I don't want paying, love,' he says.

'But it's a Friday night,' I point out.

'Just go and be with your pal,' he says, pushing my twenty back.

I haven't got time to argue.

'My daughter's just been brought in, in an ambulance,' Grace is saying to the receptionist. 'Her name is Polly Cunningham.' She sounds weirdly calm.

'Just one moment, please,' says the receptionist, as she starts bringing something up on her computer.

'Right,' she says, 'if you'd just like to go through those double doors on the right then follow the corridor along to the desk, they'll be able to help you there.'

We run down the corridor, but before we reach where we're going, I can see Patrick walking towards us, with Scarlett in his arms.

'Patrick!' shouts Grace, and launches into a run.

'I've just come out to try to phone you,' he says when they meet. 'She's *fine*. Just a few cuts and bruises, they think, but absolutely fine.'

The look on Grace's face tells me she doesn't know whether to kiss him or hit him.

Polly, it turns out, fell down the stairs. When I say she fell, it sounds more like the sort of stunt for which Hollywood film stars would need a specially trained double. She'd gone into Grace and Patrick's room – something she's taken to doing recently when she wakes in the middle of the night – and when she'd seen that neither of them was there, had thought it a good idea to go looking for them downstairs.

Which would have been fine, except she tried to do it in the dark and in her new, slightly too long Barbie nightgown. By the time she reached the bottom stair, she was actually unconscious. Patrick, obviously, phoned for a paramedic and, although she had come round by the time they arrived, they decided to take her into hospital to check her over. In the event, she didn't break a single bone, which apparently makes her some sort of medical miracle.

'I bet you had a shock,' I say to Patrick.

'You better believe it,' he says, shaking his head.

'At least Scarlett slept through the whole thing,' he adds, nodding over at the baby in her portable car seat.

The baby is a vision of peace and contentment, fast asleep with only her little dummy moving as she sucks it.

'I'm sorry we rowed,' Grace says softly.

'Me too.' And Patrick leans over to kiss her on the forehead.

I sense my presence is no longer wanted.

'Anyone fancy a coffee?' I ask. 'I'm sure there'll be a machine in here somewhere.'

I do a complete tour of the hospital – twice – before I manage to locate a coffee machine. In the event, it runs out of coffee after I've only bought two of them and leaves me with a chicken soup I suspect went in there in powdered form in 1972.

When I get back, Polly is still having a final, precautionary X-ray and, to my disbelief, Patrick and Grace appear to be having another domestic.

'Well, I'm sorry, but I think one of us needs to get Scarlett home,' Patrick is saying. 'She's going to want to be fed if she wakes up.'

'I'm sure the hospital will let us borrow a little bit of formula milk to keep her going,' says Grace.

'You can't ask them to do that,' he replies.

'Why not?' she asks.

'Well, because it's a hospital. They can't just go giving handouts to visitors.'

'I'm not a visitor,' says Grace. 'I'm the parent of a patient that's just been admitted.'

'It doesn't matter,' he says. 'Scarlett isn't the patient, Polly is.'

'Look, I'll pay them for it if need be,' she says impatiently. 'I'm sure they're used to this sort of thing.'

'Don't be so ridiculous,' he says.

'I'm not being ridiculous,' she says.

'*Look, you two!*' I leap in, and they both turn to look at me. 'I've brought you some coffee.'

I hand them over, glad at least that I've managed to shut them up.

'Sorry if they look like the contents of a washing-up bowl,' I say.

'I don't mind,' says Grace. 'I'll drink anything that's warm and wet at the moment.'

'Hmm,' says Patrick, sipping his and pulling a face. 'Well, it's definitely wet.'

'Listen, I'm going to get going,' I say. 'You don't need me hanging around.'

'Oh, Evie, thanks so much for coming with me,' says Grace. 'You're a real friend.'

'No problem,' I reply. 'If you ever hear of any four hundred-metre races in which the runners have to wear high heels, sign me up.'

'Sorry as well that you had to leave Jack behind,' says Grace. 'You looked like you were enjoying yourself there.'

'Oh, don't worry about it,' I say, trying to look on the bright side. 'I'm just glad Polly's okay. Anyway, there's always Georgia's wedding. That's not long now.'

'No,' says Grace. 'Not long. See you, Evie.'

'See you,' adds Patrick.

Why do I suspect I'm just leaving them behind to start on Round Two?

Chapter 44

Daily Echo *newsroom*, Wednesday, 4 April

Now here's a journalistic dilemma: how do you make a page 23-nib about plans to extend the opening hours of an NHS walk-in centre interesting?

I sit and study the press release, the newsroom alive with activity around me. Jules, to my right, is bashing out the splash – a breaking story about a terrorism plot, centred around a Liverpool chippy, which police uncovered only this morning. Laura, opposite, is on the phone to the emergency services, getting a quote for her page 1 anchor piece about a four-car pile-up on the M56. Even Larry, the twenty-two-year-old work experience guy, is finishing off the caption for the front-page picture.

'It's with you!' shouts Jules, dashing over to the newsdesk, as Simon, the News Editor, opens up his story – ready to give it a quick-fire once-over before it is pinged to the sub-editors.

I look at my press release again and sigh. I can't remember when Simon last asked me to write something for that day's edition – something to get my adrenaline pumping. In fact, I can't remember when Simon last asked me to write something that would prompt anything other than a sudden onset of narcolepsy.

'It's with you!' shouts Simon, as the Chief Sub picks up the story, ready to lay it on page 1 and slam a headline onto it.

I am still searching for some inspiration, but can't help thinking I'd be more inspired watching a job-lot of Dulux dry.

'Right, Evie Hart,' Simon shouts to me after he's sent the last story through. 'Get over here.'

My heart leaps. Maybe I had him all wrong. Maybe he's about to give me a breaking story for the next edition. Maybe I'm about to have my name on page 1 today, after all. I dash over to the newsdesk, my notepad and pen poised in anticipation.

'Right, Hart,' he says, managing to look down my top and as if he's about to kill me at the same time. 'I wonder if you could explain something to me.'

I hesitate. 'Yes?' I say.

'How you were scooped.'

'Sorry?' I ask, every story I've written in the last two weeks racing around my mind. 'I mean, which story?'

'Our four-legged friend,' says Simon.

'Sorry, Simon,' I repeat. 'I don't follow you.'

'*The pig!*' he snaps, with an expression that tells me I'm about as likely to be handed a hot exclusive today as I am the title of Miss World. '*The pig that spoke Italian.*'

'It was French, actually,' I say, but I can sense as soon as I've said it that he considers this about as relevant as its favourite colour.

'I don't give a fucking toss if it was Swahili,' he screams, slamming a paper down in front of me. 'It's in the *Daily Star*.'

I gulp as I come face to face with the picture of Lizzie the

Gloucester Old Spot and her owner. I don't know which one of them looks more smug.

'I thought you said that piece was holdable?' he says.

'I thought it was,' I splutter.

'Didn't you ask whether he was speaking to the nationals?'

I cast my mind back to my conversation with the farmer and consider for a second whether there is any point in trying to lie here. Morally, I have no qualms whatsoever about trying to pull a fast one over Simon, who I am starting to think has all the charm of a sewer rat. It's just that lying isn't exactly my forte. In fact, I'm about as convincing a liar as I am an Olympic javelin contender.

'He did mention that,' I admit eventually, hating myself for being so sheepish. 'But, I've got to confess, I didn't believe him. I never thought the nationals would be interested, short of the pig reciting every verse of the *Marseillaise*.'

Simon shakes his head and I feel like I'm standing in front of the Headmaster for the fourth time this week.

'Listen, girly,' he says, glancing down my top again. 'You've got a lot to learn about recognising a story. And let me tell you this, in case I've not made myself clear: a talking pig is a good story in anyone's book. Particularly since it's got a better grasp of languages than half the GCSE students in this country. Now, get out of my sight.'

When I get back to my desk my eyes bore into my computer screen and I quickly become a seething mass of resentment, imagining all the things I *could* have said to Simon . . . but didn't.

Okay, so I messed up. Catastrophically, according to the News Editor. But *Daily Star* or not, this is a story about a talking pig. It's not going to bring down governments or halt the spread of global warming. Besides, I wrote the thing weeks ago. I might have said it was holdable, but I didn't mean until Christmas 2009.

Picking up my press release, I make a vow to myself. I am going to get a page 1 exclusive for this paper if it's the last bloody thing I do.

Chapter 45

It's quite difficult to drown your sorrows when the person you're with will only drink Diet Coke because there are too many *WeightWatchers* points in anything else.

'Oh, come on, Charlotte,' I say. 'Just have a little glass of Pinot Grigio with me, why don't you? I'm sure I read somewhere that you burn off more calories lifting a glass of wine to consume it than it actually contains.'

'That's celery,' she says. 'And no, I can't, Evie. Not now I've already come so far. I'm determined.'

'Sorry,' I say immediately. 'Don't listen to me – you stay on the straight and narrow.'

'Valentina will be joining us in a minute,' Charlotte tells me. 'She's been on a date. She'll have a glass of wine, I'm sure. It apparently didn't go according to plan.'

Within five minutes, Valentina has appeared at our side and is flinging herself onto the chair next to us.

'I need a glass of water,' she says, putting her hand on her forehead dramatically.

'Not you as well,' I say.

'No, you're right,' she says. 'I might have already had a fair bit tonight, but I'm afraid I'm in shock. Can I have a Chardonnay, please?' she asks a passing waiter.

'So come on, tell us,' I say. 'What happened on your date?'

'You wouldn't believe it,' she says.

'Try us,' I reply.

'Okay, well . . . Zak is the guy I met on Georgia's hen night. And he seemed *perfect*. Six foot four inches of Latin gorgeousness. Runs his own business – as a property developer, he said. Anyway, he phoned last week to ask me out to dinner and didn't even flinch when I suggested *Le Carriage*.'

I raise an eyebrow.

'Proposing somewhere you need a second mortgage to eat at is a very good first test, Evie,' she tells me. 'So, I arrived twenty-five minutes late—'

I raise the other eyebrow.

'You'd have to be *desperate* to arrive any earlier than that,' she says firmly. 'Anyway, you wouldn't believe this, but he wasn't even there yet.'

'Was he stuck in traffic?' I offer.

'That's the thing,' she says, wide-eyed and incredulous. 'No. He just *rolled* in there, half an hour late with no explanation.'

'That must have been annoying,' says Charlotte.

'An understatement, Charlotte, an understatement,' says Valentina, taking a large gulp of her wine as it arrives. 'Not least because I'd made an effort. I'm talking new heels *and* a facial. I was only telling myself on the way there that if it took longer than ten minutes for him to want to spend the rest of his life with me, I'd be amazed.'

I bite my lip, suppressing a smile.

'Anyway, let me get to the story,' she continues. 'I'm

waiting at the bar when he arrives, and when he gets there, the waiter asks him what he'd like to drink. Do you know what he ordered?'

I shake my head.

'A Bacardi Breezer,' she says. 'A *green* one, if you will. In *Le* goddamn *Carriage*!'

Charlotte and I both snigger.

'They made him up a cocktail instead,' she says. 'But then, we sit down and he looks at the menu. And I realise he's pulling a face.'

'Oh dear,' I say.

'So he says: "I hate all this foreign shit". Can you believe it? "What foreign shit would that be?" I ask him. "Well," he says, "what's this when it's at home: pow-lett?" He was referring to the *poulet*.'

I put my hand up to my mouth, more enthralled by this story than I can possibly have imagined.

'"It's chicken," I told him. "Oh, is that all?" he says. "That'll do then. Does it come with chips?"'

I start to laugh, but Valentina appears not to find any of this remotely amusing.

'Oh look, I won't go on,' she says. 'But let me just tell you, he spent the rest of the night shovelling pieces of chicken into his mouth like a caveman, not even mentioning my outfit, and then, to top it all off, he assumed I was paying! Ha! As if!'

'Gosh,' says Charlotte. 'You wouldn't think someone who was a property developer would behave like that.'

'That's another thing,' says Valentina glumly. 'He wasn't a property developer at all. He was an estate agent. A *trainee* estate agent.'

'So you didn't sleep with him?' I ask.

'Certainly not!' she says. 'I wouldn't dream of sleeping with someone who wanted *me* to pay for a meal.'

Do you know, it's funny, but I feel better already.

Chapter 46

The Isles of Scilly, Saturday, 7 April

When Georgia told us this place was amazing, she wasn't joking. We flew into the main island in the Scillies, St Mary's, yesterday evening with a red sun glistening on the water and it almost looked like we were landing in the Seychelles rather than a part of the UK.

Of course, when you do land, it is immediately apparent that you're not in the Seychelles because there's a chip shop, three pubs and a Spar-type supermarket selling copies of *heat* magazine and packets of Benson & Hedges. But still.

We then travelled by speedboat to a smaller, more rugged island which gives the impression of being virtually unin-habited apart from the hotel. And what a hotel: sumptuous and trendy at the same time, with the added bonus of an utterly breathtaking position on the edge of the Atlantic. This place has got just about everything going for it.

Today, there is not a cloud in the sky and as I stand on the bleached-wood terrace of Georgia's honeymoon suite, there is only a soft breeze whispering against my skin. The steps lead down to a private beach, where the sand is fine and pale and the sea is crystal clear. In fact, the only thing that has disturbed the view all morning is Valentina doing a Pilates routine which involved lots of bending over with her arse in the air.

'This place is gorgeous,' I sigh.

'It's great, isn't it?' says Georgia, who is sitting at the stool of a baby grand piano in her wedding dress, all ready for the ceremony. 'I love it here. It was where we spent our family holidays as a kid.'

'Not Butlins, then?' I ask.

'Look, I'd have enjoyed Butlins just as much, I'm sure,' she insists.

'Yeah, yeah, whatever you say,' I tease.

The suite is big and luxurious, but also unfussy in a way that only really expensive places can get away with – with coir carpets, whitewashed furniture and the odd impressionist seascape on the walls. There are still more than forty-five minutes to go before Georgia gets married, but in stark contrast to the scene before Grace's wedding, she seems to have been ready for ages. Predictably, I can't say the same for my best friend.

'Did you see Grace earlier?' asks Georgia quietly.

She has been heroically attempting not to panic about the fact that one of her bridesmaids appears to have gone AWOL.

'Er, briefly,' I say.

'Because she's getting me a bit worried now,' Georgia continues. 'I've been calm all morning and now look at me.' She holds out her hand to demonstrate how much it is shaking.

'She'll be here,' I say, as convincingly as possible. 'Honestly, don't worry.'

Suddenly, the door bursts open.

'Sorry! I know I'm late,' says Grace, wearing that permanently frazzled look she does so well.

'Tracking you down this afternoon has been like trying to trace Osama Bin Laden,' I say.

'I know, sorry,' she says again. 'I've had Adele on the phone complaining about a deal I've just done, I've had my mother on the phone complaining that Scarlett won't eat puréed steak and kidney pudding, and I've had the dry cleaners on the phone complaining that I still haven't picked up the rug I dropped off three months ago.'

'Grace,' I say, 'what you really need is your own personal customer services department.'

'Well, look, you're here now,' says Georgia, throwing the last bridesmaid dress in her direction. 'So just go and get this on and be quick about it.'

'Yep. Right. No problem,' says Grace, catching the dress. She turns, striding towards the dressing room, where she collides with Valentina at the doorway.

'Oh . . . Grace,' says Valentina with barely disguised horror at the vision before her. 'Do you need to borrow . . . a new face?'

Grace frowns. 'Thank you, Valentina, you look gorgeous too,' she says, and barges past her.

'I know,' smiles Valentina. 'I've just been tested for allergies and discovered I have a lettuce intolerance. I gave it up last week and think my skin is glowing already.'

Just then, Charlotte emerges from the dressing room, all dressed and ready.

'Wow! You look great!' I say excitedly, prompting her to blush immediately.

Which is a shame, because if ever she had no reason to blush, it is now.

At its most basic level, Charlotte is wearing a bridesmaid

dress *that fits*. As well as the visible weight loss, her hair and make-up – courtesy of the combined efforts of both myself and Valentina – are a vision of sophisticated glamour so far removed from the old Charlotte, she could be another person.

'I'm so pleased with your look, Charlotte. I've got *such* hidden skills, haven't I?' muses Valentina. 'And I actually think hair and beauty therapy is probably the area in which I excel the most.'

'You said that about fellatio last week,' Georgia points out. 'You told me you could make a man's hair stand on end.'

'Oh yes,' smiles Valentina. 'That too.'

Chapter 47

The ceremony is short and touchingly sweet. Georgia cries, Georgia's mother cries, Valentina pretends to cry and those of us close enough can even see Pete's lip wobbling a bit.

It takes place on an enormous terrace overlooking the bay, with the sun warming our skin and an audience so big I feel as if I know what it's like to play the Royal Albert Hall.

I spend the entire ceremony with my back to the guests, wondering where Jack is sitting and whether it's obvious I'm squeezing my bum in to try to make it look smaller.

Like many of the guests, he wasn't due to arrive on the island until this morning, but I know he's here because Grace saw him having brunch. He had fruit followed by scrambled eggs and toast, apparently. Granary. Two slices, no butter. I think Grace has a future career in the Secret Service, if she ever wants one.

As Georgia and Pete kiss for the first time as man and wife, my spirits lift, knowing that I'm about to come face to face with Jack again. If I actually manage to locate him, that is.

I walk down the aisle behind the happy couple, Valentina

and Beth, and in front of Grace, Charlotte and Gina, trying to seek him out as surreptitiously as I possibly can.

Suddenly, I feel a prod in the back and glance over my shoulder to see what Grace is drawing my attention to. I spot him immediately. Looking over at our procession is the only one of my ex-boyfriends here today. Fortunately, it's one of the few I actually don't mind being here.

Seb and I went out together at university for seven whole weeks, which at the time was a performance I was pretty pleased with – although had I known I'd still be single so many years later, I might not have been so self-congratulating.

Seb eventually suffered the same fate as all my subsequent romantic dalliances, but the whole thing was undoubtedly a more bittersweet affair.

I can't even remember what it was that made us split up, but what I do remember is that there was no sense of relief when it happened. Far from it. In fact, at the time I'm sure I actually regretted it. I even thought about telling him, but by the time I'd got my act together it was too late and he was with someone else.

Anyway, why this blip in an otherwise unshakably predictable pattern should have occurred I've never been able to work out. But the plus side to all this at least is that bumping into him – and it's been at least two years since the last time – isn't anything like the traumatic affair it is with the others.

When he catches me looking at him, Seb smiles and holds up his hand to give me a little wave. I smile back but am prevented from waving both by convention and by the bloody great bouquet I'm carrying; it's so heavy I'm convinced someone's hidden a dumbbell underneath all this foliage.

'*He's* not looking half-bad these days,' whispers Grace as we get to the back of the room.

I hate to admit it, but she's right.

Chapter 48

Apparently, nobody has informed the photographer that this is supposed to be a celebration. With sideburns like Brillo pads and a complexion so ruddy it could have been blow-torched, this guy appears to have taken charm lessons from the Gestapo.

'Right, if you'd just all move a bit closer together,' he bellows. 'Closer, *please!*'

Grabbing the arm of an elderly lady dressed in migraine-inducing cerise, he shoves her towards her neighbour. He seems completely unable to appreciate that getting this number of people into the right position isn't going to happen instantaneously.

'You bridesmaids, you need to move forward. No, not that far!' he shouts. 'Stop there. No, *not* there, backwards a bit.'

Valentina is pouting and for once I can understand why. But someone soon changes that.

'I could have sworn I saw someone like you at the last wedding I went to,' says a voice behind me which I recognise immediately as Jack's.

I hold my hand up to my mouth to try to suppress a smile.

'Bridesmaid on the left, can you put your hand down,

please,' the photographer trumpets. 'Right, let's try again, shall we?'

'If you don't behave yourself, Miss Hart, you'll be sent to the back,' the voice behind me whispers.

I try not to smirk, fearing that I will look like a professional gurner on these photos if I'm not careful.

'I can do without you trying to get me into trouble,' I lean back and murmur through my cardboard cut-out smile.

'It's hardly my fault if you can't do what you're meant to do properly,' he replies. 'I bet you were always in detention at school, weren't you?'

I'm trying to think of something witty to say in reply when the photographer instructs everyone but the bride and bridesmaids to stand down. The entire wedding party surges towards the hotel, all clearly desperate for a drink, and it becomes apparent that Georgia might have benefited from hiring some crowd control for this event.

'Looks like I'm going to have to leave you to it,' says Jack, smiling widely. 'I'll catch you later, shall I?'

Yes, please.

One of the things I am starting to learn about weddings is that the photos take such a long time that by the time they're finished, most of the guests are already pissed, and the main wedding party has all got leg cramp. Almost an hour and ten minutes after this marathon began, I'm afraid I start to get rather fed up.

'Have you seen the time?' I say to Grace, who is next to me.

'What about it?' she asks.

'It's gone five p.m. and we're all completely sober. It doesn't feel right at a wedding somehow.'

'I heard that,' says Georgia.

'Sorry,' I say, holding my hands up. 'I wasn't complaining, honest.'

Patently, I was.

'No, you're right,' she says. Then: 'Listen, Bruce,' she tells the photographer, 'from now on, let's just have natural shots, shall we? Come on, girls, where's the bar?'

She marches ahead, leaving Mr Brillo Pads hopelessly redundant, while the rest of us attempt to follow her as daintily as is practical on a beach when you're wearing two-inch heels. When we reach the terrace, I turn to Grace and take a deep breath.

'Is my mascara intact?' I ask her.

She smirks. 'Yes.'

'Hair okay?'

'Yes.'

'How about lipstick?'

'Evie,' she says, 'you look gorgeous. So gorgeous, in fact, that if you don't manage to pull Jack tonight you never bloody will.'

Chapter 49

The reception is in a huge room packed with the sort of wedding paraphernalia you wouldn't usually find outside a twenty-page *Hello!* magazine spread. There are four-foot table centrepieces made from white roses and feathers, an eight-tier cake covered in white chocolate and berries, and an enormous net above us filled with balloons.

'Aren't the feathers fun?' says my mother, approaching me with two glasses in her hand. 'I must ask Georgia where she got them from.'

'Given that your reception is being held *in a field*, Mum, I'm not sure the Full Length and Fabulous look would quite work,' I reply, taking a glass from her.

'Oh, I wasn't thinking about them for the reception,' she says. 'I thought I could get a head-dress made. You know, something a bit *Moulin Rouge*. Of course, they'd need to be in a colour to match my dress. I told you I've settled on green, didn't I?'

Whether the Isles of Scilly were ready for my mother's dress sense, I'm not entirely sure, but her unique style is unleashed on them to full effect today. She has chosen a purple poncho, a floppy sixties-style hat and a skirt so short that it should be illegal for a woman her age.

The only positive thing I could possibly say about this ensemble is that she has at least got half-decent legs. It's just a shame they're currently sporting a pair of orange paisley tights that make her look as if she is suffering from the early stages of gangrene.

'Hello,' says a voice, and I whirl around, my pulse racing. It's Jack. 'I thought you must have been swept out to sea, you were all outside with that photographer for so long.'

'Tell me about it,' I say, gazing into his eyes.

He looks back at me as if he's trying to tell me something. I just can't quite work out what.

'I'm Jack,' he says eventually, extending his hand for my mother to shake.

Oh God, *my mother*. For some reason I'd had momentary amnesia about her being present. In her mad hat. And hideous tights. And . . . *oh Mum, please behave yourself*.

'Pleased to meet you,' she says, smiling. 'I'm Sarah – Evie's mum. You're one of my daughter's ex-boyfriends, I presume?'

The woman is a liability.

'No, Mum,' I leap in. 'Jack is—'

'Oh, sorry. It's just that she seems to have amassed so many of them these days,' she adds, for good measure. 'Everywhere I go, I bump into someone she's been out with.'

'*Ha ha ha ha ha ha ha!*' I blurt out, wanting to throttle her. 'That's a good one, Mum. Anyway, er, right . . . er . . .'

I'm trying to steer the conversation around to a subject that won't let my mother embarrass me. But somehow it's very difficult to think of one.

'Well, it's great to meet you, Sarah,' says Jack. 'Although

I'd already guessed you were mother and daughter. You look very alike.'

God help me! I hope he doesn't think I've got a similar wardrobe.

'Ooh, just excuse me for a second,' says my mum. 'I'm absolutely starved.'

I'm hoping she's going to disappear to try to find something to eat, but sadly not. Instead, she almost rugby tackles a waitress passing with a tray of canapés right in front of us.

'You don't know whether any of these are organic, do you?' she asks.

The waitress, who looks like she's barely old enough to have left school, shakes her head. 'I don't. Sorry.'

'Anything with gelatine in?'

The girl shakes her head again. 'Not sure,' she says.

'Anything vegan?'

'Er, I think maybe that's a spinach one,' she says, pointing at something vaguely green perched on top of a square of puff pastry.

'And the pastry hasn't got any animal fat in?'

'I'm not really sure.'

'Mum,' I interrupt. 'Do you really have to ask all this?'

'Of course,' she says. 'And you should too, young lady, with your allergies.'

My allergies consist of one – to shellfish – and even then I haven't had a reaction to that in years.

'Now, where was I,' says my mother. 'How about the eggs – are they free-range?'

The waitress looks as though, if she's asked another question, her head might explode.

'I can go and ask Chef, if you'd like,' she offers.

My mother shrugs. 'Tell you what, I'll take my chances, shall I?' she says, and proceeds to load up a napkin with enough canapés for a small family to survive on for two days.

I try to think of something to say to Jack to distract him from this bizarre interlude, but again, I'm struggling to find anything appropriate.

'Is your bedroom nice?' I enquire, and immediately realise he might think I'm looking for an invitation to a private view.

'Not because I want to see it,' I add hastily. 'Well, I mean, I wouldn't *mind* seeing it. But, not because I want to – well, you know.' Oh God.

'Er, mine's got a veranda,' I offer. You prat, Evie. Even my mother has paused from wolfing down her canapés and is wondering what I'm going on about.

'Yes, it is,' says Jack.

'It is what?' I ask. 'I mean, what is? I mean . . . *what?*'

'Yes, my bedroom is nice,' he says calmly. 'And it's got a veranda overlooking the bay. Actually, it's spectacular. I've never been to the Scillies before and I'm starting to wonder why. It'd be nice to come back for a bit longer, some time.'

'Hmm, it is a lovely place, isn't it?' says my mum. 'And all this luxury is such a treat. I'm not used to it. My holidays are usually very different.'

Oh no. Don't mention the week clearing up pollution in Egypt. Don't mention the week clearing up pollution in Egypt. Please don't mention the week clearing up pollution in Egypt.

'I've just spent a week clearing up pollution in Egypt,' Mum announces.

'Funnily enough, a girl I work with did something similar,'

says Jack. 'She loved it. And she actually made it sound enjoyable.'

'You see?' says my mother to me. She then turns back to Jack. 'Evie thinks I'm mad.'

'I know you're mad,' I mutter.

'Well, I can see why it wouldn't be everyone's cup of tea,' says Jack. 'But I'd choose it over a week in Benidorm any day.'

'You see?' Mum repeats to me. 'That's what I think. Evie, you should listen to your friends more.'

I do not like the way this conversation is going.

'Well, yes,' I say, 'I'd choose it over a week in Benidorm too,' which isn't actually true, 'but there are lots of other places I'd rather go to instead. I'm not one of these people whose idea of foreign travel doesn't extend beyond an 18-30s brochure, as you know.'

'Well, no,' says my mum. 'Plus, you'll soon be too old anyway.'

Chapter 50

The table plan may have been hand-crafted from crystals and white gold leaf, but there is one thing I don't like about it. Jack and I are not sitting together.

Worse still, he has been put next to another bridesmaid, Georgia's Cousin Beth. Not only is she years younger than me, but with her sultry brunette looks she is effortlessly glamorous.

Still, it's not all bad. I am at least sitting next to Jim, which will give me the opportunity to find out whether he likes Charlotte's new look.

'What do you think of Charlotte's transformation?' I ask as the starter arrives.

'She looks incredible,' says Jim. 'Really different. Although I thought she looked nice before too.'

I grin.

'Every time I see you, you ask me about Charlotte,' he adds. 'Anyone would think you were trying to set us up.'

'Me?' I say. 'Nothing could have been further from my mind.'

I pause for a second while he raises a sceptical eyebrow.

'All right, if I were,' I continue, 'and I mean *if* – you could do far worse than Charlotte. She's an absolute angel.'

Jim laughs. 'Very subtle,' he says. 'But look, I know. I don't need any persuasion.'

'You don't?'

'No. I told you last time,' he says. 'I think she's lovely.'

I'm waiting for the 'but' as in, 'I think she's lovely *but* I just don't fancy her.'

'And I really like her,' he concludes.

'But?' I say.

'There's no but,' he tells me. 'I like her. Really like her. There, you happy now?'

'When you say you *like* her,' I persist, taking another mouthful of my smoked salmon and lime crème fraiche, '*really* like her, do you mean you're interested in her, you know, *romantically*?'

Even I think this sounds ridiculously twee, but I can't think of any other way of putting it.

'Yes,' he grins. 'God, what more do I have to say? Yes, I think she's lovely. Yes, I'm interested in her. Yes, I fancy her. You satisfied now?'

'You *fancy* her?' I echo, nearly leaping out of my seat. 'Really? That's fantastic! That's bloody fantastic. God, you're made for each other.'

'Hmm. I'm not so sure,' he says.

'What do you mean?'

'I mean,' he says, 'I don't think the feeling's mutual.'

I can't believe this guy.

'But it is!' I tell him. 'I promise you it is.'

'Hmm,' he says again, clearly unconvinced. 'I just never got that impression.'

177

'Oh, that's just Charlotte,' I say. 'She's hopeless. What I mean is, she can be a bit shy. You don't need me to tell you that.'

'And you think that's all it is?'

'Definitely. Leave it with me,' I say.

I can't wait to tell Charlotte the news.

Chapter 51

I don't actually need to go to the loo. But heading to the ladies after dessert at least allows me to make a long and completely unnecessary diversion past Jack's table. I straighten my dress and breathe in as I head in his direction, trying to conceal the alarming and immediate effect a large piece of cheesecake with wild berry compote has had on the shape of my stomach.

As I approach, I see Beth leaning on the table towards Jack, laughing, twirling a piece of hair round her finger and pouting so much she'd make Angelina Jolie look as if she needed lip implants. She, I notice guiltily, has declined her dessert. I attempt to breathe in even further and start to walk past, hoping Jack might catch my eye.

But he doesn't – and I bet I know why. If there were such a thing as a flirting contest, Beth would be going for a record-breaking gold medal. She's gazing into his eyes so deeply, he must have as intimate a knowledge of her corneas as an optician by now.

From the angle I'm at right now, I can't see Jack's face – despite my straining to see what his reaction is to this full-on flirtation. But from behind, I can't help thinking he doesn't look overly worried about the fact that his personal space is being invaded with all the determination of a crack military squad. I feel a stab of jealousy. And I don't like it one bit.

I force myself to snap out of it by doing a U-turn and taking another route to the loo, grabbing Charlotte on the way. It may as well not be a completely wasted journey.

'I've got something to tell you,' I say, linking her arm with mine.

'What?' she says.

'Jim fancies you.'

'So you keep saying,' she says, rolling her eyes.

'No, but this time I'm not speculating about it,' I tell her enthusiastically. 'He actually said it.'

'Oh,' she says.

It's not exactly the reaction I'd hoped for. I can only think that she doesn't believe me.

'Charlotte, honestly, I'm not making this up, or embellishing it, or anything. He *said he fancied you*,' I say. 'As clear as a bell.'

'Okay,' she says, deadpan.

'Well, aren't you happy?' I ask, incredulous. 'I thought you liked him.'

'I do like him, *as a friend*,' she tells me.

I think about this for a second.

'You're not telling me that you actually don't fancy him? As in, you *really* don't fancy him?' I ask, scarcely believing this is a plausible explanation.

'Really,' she says. 'I am saying exactly that.'

I frown. 'But he really, really fancies you, Charlotte, and he's absolutely gorgeous.'

'Well, I'm sorry, Evie, but the feeling isn't mutual,' she

says, starting to get uncharacteristically exasperated. 'I don't know what else to say about it.'

I'm struggling to know how to react to this.

'Well, I'm not going to flog a dead horse, Charlotte, but I have to say I'm surprised,' I tell her. 'He's good-looking, he's intelligent, he's really nice, and now he's admitted publicly that he fancies you. Christ, what more do you want?'

'You wouldn't understand,' she sighs. Then off she goes into a cubicle, with a piece of loo roll stuck to her heel. Before I've even had a chance to defend myself.

I decide I may as well use the loo after all, and go into the cubicle next to her. Just as I am about to come out, I recognise a voice coming from outside. It's Beth, talking to her fellow sickeningly slim and gorgeous bridesmaid, Gina.

'He's actually given you his phone number?' Gina is asking.

I take my hand off the lock and decide I'd quite like to overhear this conversation.

'I've got it right here,' says Beth, giggling. 'Hasn't he got lovely writing? Who am I kidding, hasn't he got lovely everything?'

Gina laughs now.

I put the lid down on the loo seat and sit on it to contemplate the situation. Why do I have a horrible feeling I know who they're talking about?

'So when are you going to phone him?' asks Gina.

'Depends,' replies Beth, 'on whether or not I manage to shag him tonight!'

They both collapse into giggles and, for some reason, I start to feel a bit queasy. That extra dollop of wild-berry compote was definitely a mistake. I'm dying to stay and listen in

181

on more of this but am concerned that if I don't come out soon, someone will think I've collapsed in here and try to break the door down. I turn the lock and walk over to the sink.

Charlotte, it appears, has already gone.

'Hi!' I say brightly to Gina and Beth.

'Hi!' they reply in unison.

'You two enjoying yourselves?' I ask cheerily.

'*She* certainly is,' says Gina, nodding over to Beth, and they both start laughing.

'Oh?' I say, a picture of innocence. 'Why?'

'Oh, nothing,' says Beth. 'I just hit the jackpot on the seating plan, that's all. Actually, the guy I'm next to, Jack – I think he said he knows you, Evie. Vaguely, anyway.'

'Yeah, he does,' I reply, throwing my towel into the bin. 'He does know me. Vaguely.'

Chapter 52

I'm discussing who won the sweepstake on the length of the speeches with a group of Georgia's friends when I feel a tap on my shoulder.

'Long time no see,' says Seb, with a wide smile.

'Bloody hell, how are you?' I ask, kissing him on the cheek.

'Brilliant, actually,' he says. 'And you?'

'Yeah, great. How's work?'

Seb studied physics at university and then took the traditional career route for a science graduate – by getting a job in a building society. It's not my idea of fun, but then I write stories about talented farm animals for a living. Plus, if all you were interested in was money, then you really couldn't knock Seb's career choice. The last time I saw him, he'd risen through the ranks so rapidly, he gave the impression that he commanded the sort of salary a journalist like me could only hope to achieve by the time I reach, oooh, 112.

'Work's really good,' he says. 'And your job?'

'Er, not bad,' I say, really not wanting to get onto the subject of Simon today. 'Are you still living in Woolton?'

'No, I moved last year,' he says. 'I wanted somewhere a bit bigger so I could fit my pool table in.'

I shake my head in amusement. 'Your girlfriend must be very understanding, letting you fill the house with boys' toys,' I say.

'Er, yeah. Well, the pool table arrived after she left,' he says, looking into my eyes. 'We split up last year.'

'Oh,' I say. 'Sorry.'

'No, it's fine,' he shrugs. 'It just wasn't working out so we agreed to go our separate ways. It was all amicable.'

'Good,' I say, nodding.

'It was a nice meal, wasn't it?' he asks.

'Fabulous,' I say, although as I say it, I realise the funny feeling I had earlier when I was in the loo is getting worse. I definitely don't feel 100 per cent at the moment. I can't put my finger on why, but I'm certainly not firing on all cylinders.

'Well, I must say you're looking fantastic,' I go on, determined not to show that anything's wrong. Besides, this isn't just polite conversation. I mean it. The years since university have been kind to Seb. His once baby-faced features are now more angular and grown-up, and his previously pale complexion now has a light and very becoming tan.

We spend a good twenty minutes reminiscing and catching up – in equal measures – and discover that lots of things have changed. But lots haven't either.

'I've got to admit,' he says finally, 'I was dying to speak to you today.'

'Were you?' I ask. 'Why?'

'I dunno,' he says. 'When I saw you walking down that

aisle before, well, you looked incredible. Beautiful. And it made me think.'

'About what?' I say.

'About why I ever let you go.'

Chapter 53

I decide to go for a walk to see if it makes me feel any less queasy.

But after twenty minutes of trying to stop my hair from being messed up in the wind, all the while listening to the wedding party becoming increasingly lively, I realise it hasn't worked. As I head back into the reception, I run into my mother.

'Hi, Mum,' I say.

'Argghhh!' she exclaims.

'What's the matter?' Surely my hair doesn't look that bad!

'Evie, have you been eating shellfish?' she asks, her expression full of concern.

I frown. 'I don't think so, although . . .'

Now I think about it, I did eat a couple of canapés earlier with some unspecified gunk on top of them. My eyes widen as I look at the expression on my mother's face – and I don't like what I see. I bring my hands up to touch my face, where I find all the proof I need. Apparently, I *have* been eating shellfish. And, for the first time in at least two years, it's brought me out in a reaction. Which is just about all I need on a day like today.

'Those bastard canapés,' I say. 'I didn't even want the damn things. I only ate them for something to do while I was stuck talking to Georgia's Aunt Vera.'

'Look. Don't panic,' says my mum, deciding, rather irritatingly, that she's going to be the calm and rational one. 'Let's go and splash some water on your face. It might take the swelling down. Come on, I'll smuggle you in.'

My mum and I creep through the double doors, attempting, like two very poor amateur cat burglars, to cross the room without being noticed.

I have my hand across my face as if feigning a headache, and Mum is walking three inches in front of me – the idea being that nobody will be able to see past her to get a glimpse of what I look like. Which would be fine, except for the fact that she keeps tripping me up and I've just nearly ended up face down in a nest of meringues.

When we get into the ladies, I take a deep breath and look in the mirror.

'Argghhh!' I say.

'Oh, come on, it's not that bad,' says my mother.

'May I remind you that that was exactly what you said earlier,' I grumble. 'And it's not even your face we're talking about.'

I won't go so far as to say I look like the Elephant Man, but with my swollen eyes and blotchy cheeks, I suspect he would win a beauty contest over me at this moment in time. Suddenly, the door swings open, and Grace walks in.

'*Oh my God . . .*' she says, her expression that of someone looking at a car crash.

'Just don't scream, please,' I say. 'I can't take much more of it.'

'What happened to you?' she asks. 'You look like you've been beaten up.'

'Well, thank you,' I say. 'I really needed someone to make me feel better. I've had an allergic reaction to some shellfish.'

'I thought you hadn't had one of those in years,' she says.

'I haven't,' I say. 'But that's probably because I haven't eaten shellfish in years.'

'So why did you today?' she asks.

'I didn't realise— Oh look, it doesn't matter,' I say. 'The fact is, I look like I've just stuck my head in a beehive. What the hell am I going to do?'

My mother sighs. 'There's not an awful lot you can do, except wait for it to go down,' she says practically. 'And look on the bright side.'

'Which is?' I ask.

'There are tribes in Papua New Guinea who find that sort of thing very attractive,' she informs me. 'They go out of their way to get that kind of effect on their faces.'

Thanks, Mum. Thanks a lot.

Chapter 54

In the absence of a paper bag to go over my head, Grace and I find the quietest, darkest corner in the room.

'That girl makes Valentina look like an amateur,' Grace tells me, looking over at Beth.

Despite the fact that she had the pleasure of his company for almost two and a half hours during dinner, Beth seems to have now attached herself to Jack like a leech, albeit a very good-looking one.

'Why don't you go over and break them up?' says Grace.

'What? Are you insane?' I ask her.

'I thought you fancied him,' she says.

'Yes, and it's going to do wonders for my chances when he sees me looking like the Phantom of the Opera.'

She takes a sip of her drink and studies my face again.

'It's going down already, you know,' she says. 'How long did you say it usually takes?'

'A couple of hours. I just wish it would hurry up and go dark.'

Grace takes another sip of her drink and looks into the distance.

'Are you all right?' I ask. I can't put my finger on it, but Grace doesn't seem herself today.

'Yeah, yeah,' she says. 'I'm just a bit tired, that's all. Scarlett has decided it's a good idea to start waking up for a play at two o'clock every morning, and it's all just catching up with me.'

'What, and you're not in the mood for a sing song at that time of night?' I ask.

'Funnily enough, no.'

Valentina suddenly appears at our table. 'Still puffed up, then?' she asks me.

I frown. 'Why don't you just say, "still ugly"?' I ask.

'I didn't want to hurt your feelings,' she shrugs. 'But: "still ugly"?'

I tell myself to just ignore her.

'How many people are there at this wedding?' she continues.

'Just over two hundred,' I reply.

'Unbelievable,' she says, shaking her head. 'You'd expect at least a smattering of suitable single men among that number.'

'There are loads of single men here,' says Grace.

'I said *suitable* single men,' she corrects Grace. 'There's a big difference.'

'By which you presumably mean someone with the looks of Orlando Bloom and the bank account of Donald Trump,' I offer.

Valentina tuts.

'I don't know why everyone thinks I'm so shallow,' she says. 'But yes, that sort of thing would be a start.'

'Isn't Seb single?' asks Grace.

'Er, yes, but he's just told me he's having a break from dating,' I say hastily. 'He's just broken up with someone recently and wants some time by himself.'

'That's what they all say,' says Valentina. 'I haven't met a man yet who couldn't be persuaded. Who is this Seb anyway?'

'That guy I used to go out with at college,' I tell her. 'You know, the one who studied physics.'

She pulls a face. If there's one thing certain to put her off a bloke, it's the idea that I've been there before. Hang on a minute. Why am I trying to put her off him? What does it matter to me if Valentina seduces Seb?

Oh Evie, get a grip.

Chapter 55

'You are sure everything's all right, aren't you?' I ask, as Grace and I are alone again later.

She sighs. 'Weddings just make you think about your own relationship, that's all,' she says. 'When we'd been to them previously, I would stand there, watching someone else walk past, and try to analyse whether we'd ever do it ourselves. Now that we actually have done it, I've spent the whole of today trying to analyse our marriage.'

'And?' I prompt her. 'Your marriage is okay, isn't it?'

'Oh, everything's fine, really,' she says. 'Patrick's just in a funny mood lately.'

'How so?' I ask.

She frowns. 'It's nothing in particular,' she says, 'but let me give you an example. This weekend is the first time we've had away together since the honeymoon. So, this morning, we've checked into a gorgeous room with a fabulous view and, I suppose I just expected us to . . . I don't know, slot into our usual roles.'

'What are they then?' I ask, hoping she isn't referring to anything involving nurses and doctors.

'Well, ordinarily,' she continues, 'I would be sensible and

start to hang up my clothes and then maybe say I was taking a shower to freshen up. At that point, Patrick would throw the bags down, grab my bum, say bollocks to the shower and . . . well, you can guess the rest.'

'So what happened today?' I ask.

'I'd completely unpacked and was halfway through shampooing my hair when he came into the bathroom to announce that he was going out and would only be five minutes. So, you know, I said: "Where are you going?"'

'What did he say?' I ask.

'He said he was going for a walk because he had a headache,' she tells me.

'What's wrong with that?'

'Well, for a start, isn't that supposed to be the woman's line?'

'Don't be so sexist,' I tell her. 'Look, this sounds like nothing, Grace, it really does.'

'Maybe,' she says glumly. 'But, you know his walk?'

'Yes?'

'It lasted for two hours.'

Our conversation is interrupted by the sound of someone at the microphone and, when we look up, we see that it's Georgia. She's clearly emboldened by drink, although not as inebriated as I'd expected, given that the champagne today has practically been served via intravenous drip.

'I know lots of brides are doing speeches these days, but I actually hadn't intended to say anything,' she says, slurring slightly.

'I mean, you lot have already had to listen to Pete, and my dad and our best man Phil, and I'm sure between them, that was quite enough. But then, as the day wore on, I started to think: Why let everybody off the hook that easily? Besides, anyone who knows Pete and I will know that I never like him to get the last word.'

There is a ripple of laughter.

'People used to say to me, "You'll know when you meet the love of your life",' she continues. '"You'll *just know*". Well, I was sceptical, I have to say. But I've known Pete for over a year now, and during that time, I've discovered a hell of a lot about him. I've discovered that he's generous, he's loving, he tells a good joke, he's clever, he's crap at remembering dates (so I'm not holding my breath for a first anniversary present) . . . and I know he loves me, even on the days when I'm not very loveable.'

One or two spontaneous 'aahs' come from the direction of Georgia's aunts, followed by another ripple of laughter.

'But it's not just that,' she goes on. 'The reason I did this bloody incredible thing today – and got married – is that I discovered that all those people were right. I *just knew*. If I was going to spend the rest of my life with one man, then I *just knew* it would have to be Pete.'

She turns to look at her new husband, who is at the very front of the crowd and grinning from ear to ear.

'I love you, sweetheart,' she says quickly.

He steps up to hug her and she throws her arms around his neck, still gripping the microphone.

'I love you too, you soppy bugger,' he whispers.

Grace and I look at each other and smile. Pete is clearly oblivious to the fact that the microphone is two inches from his mouth, broadcasting to the entire room what he believes are entirely private sentiments.

'And can I tell you something?' he breathes, while two hundred guests wait to hear what he's going to say next. 'Your tits look great in that dress.'

Chapter 56

This really is no good. Here I am in a place so romantic they could bottle it and sell it as a Viagra substitute.

Yet, I'm sat here talking to my mother's boyfriend like the girl without a date on prom night. In fact, I could only dream about a date on prom night, looking like this. The swelling may have gone down ever so slightly, but the blotchiness certainly hasn't. And my desperate attempts to cover it up with Valentina's face powder has just left me with the sort of pallor that would frighten small children.

'Is it just your face that's the matter, Evie?' offers Bob.

'Sorry, Bob,' I say, turning back to him and being momentarily cheered by the sight of his green bow tie and stripy boating jacket. 'It's not just that, no.'

'More boyfriend trouble?' he asks. After six years with my mother, he's more than familiar with my romantic history.

'Yeah,' I say. 'But not really . . . the usual kind.'

'Oh?'

'It's complicated this time.'

He nods and goes back to his tomato juice.

I frown. 'You're supposed to say, "Try me", or something

now, Bob,' I tell him. 'You know, persuade me to confide in you. To get it off my chest.'

'Oh,' he says, twiddling his beard nervously. 'Oh, well, obviously I'm all ears.'

'Okay,' I say, taking a deep breath. 'Well, I really fancy this guy who's here today. That is, I didn't at first because he was going out with Valentina. But then they split up and I realised I did.'

'Oh good,' says Bob.

'Except now someone else seems to have got their claws into him.'

'Oh dear,' says Bob.

'No – wait, that's not all,' I say. 'Now one of my ex-boyfriends is here and says – and I quote – that he wonders how he ever let me go. He's *really* nice.'

'Oh well,' says Bob immediately. 'Go out with him then.'

'I hadn't finished,' I tell Bob. 'I was about to say that he's really nice but I suspect in my heart of hearts he's not the one for me.'

'Oh,' says Bob.

'And that the other one is.'

'Ah,' says Bob.

I look over to the dance floor, where Beth is currently teaching Jack how to tango. She couldn't be attracting more attention if she cartwheeled across the dance floor wearing nothing but a pair of Mickey Mouse knickers.

'I see,' says Bob, and it's perfectly obvious that he doesn't. Bob's good on vegan cooking and the works of Jean Paul Sartre, but I doubt he'd ever give Jerry Springer a run for his money.

'This one you don't think is the one for you,' he says. 'What's wrong with him?'

197

'I can't remember exactly,' I say. 'It's ages since I dumped him.'

Bob looks pensive.

'It's not just a question of what's wrong with him though,' I continue. 'I guess the real point is that when I look at Jack my heart does somersaults. When I look at Seb, well . . .'

'Barely a flutter?' he says.

I smile. 'And yet he's lovely and good-looking, and he's got a good job and, he doesn't appear to have any terrible anti-social habits or anything like that. And he obviously still likes me. And I like him enough to not want him to be seduced by Valentina.'

'Hmm,' says Bob, nodding.

'So what do you think I should do?' I ask.

Bob has the look of an eight-year-old who's just been asked to explain the principles of metaphysics.

'Well,' he says, thinking carefully, 'have you asked your mother?'

I laugh and put my hand on his.

'Don't worry, Bob,' I sigh. 'By the way, I've got to know where you bought that jacket.'

'Oh, do you like it?' he asks. 'I thought it was quite dapper too.'

I can suddenly sense someone walking towards us from across the other side of the room, and when I look up, I realise to my horror that it's Jack.

'Oh my God,' I say, leaping up and grabbing my bag.

'What's the matter?' asks Bob. 'You look as if you've seen a ghost. I mean, you look *even more* as if you've seen a ghost.'

I frantically touch my eyes and can feel that they're still

puffed up – enough at least for me not to want Jack to see me this way. My eyes dart around the room. I'm desperate to find an escape route. I've got to get out of here.

Fast.

Chapter 57

I scramble past a group of tables and chairs, trying to get to the door as fast as I can. But everywhere I turn, someone blocks my path – and every one of them looks at me as if I've landed the star part in a remake of *Night of the Living Dead*. I start pushing guests out of my way like skittles, knowing that it's the height of rudeness, but thinking that I'm going to have to be excused on this occasion.

Breathless, I finally get outside into the fresh air, where the sun is setting and the Atlantic waves are crashing onto the shoreline. Flinging off my Jimmy Choos, and carrying one in each hand, I start sprinting towards a handy rock. It seems like the most fitting place for me to be at this moment in time: my own rock to crawl under.

I turn back to see if anyone is behind me and to my relief I've managed to lose Jack. I sigh and sit on the other side of the rock, looking out to sea, and suddenly feel more relaxed than I have all day. It's great, sitting here with nothing more than the waves and a couple of cormorants to keep me company.

Suddenly, I see something in the water and can tell immediately that it is bigger than a fish. I study the spot where I saw it . . . and it happens again. I cast my mind back to the guide book and realise that it must be a seal. Sure enough, a little head pops up out of the water and turns straight to me. I smile.

'What are you looking at?' I say to him. 'Do I look so bad that I'm now getting dirty looks from you too?'

'Evie,' a voice says. 'Is that you?'

I frown at the seal again for a second, momentarily wondering what on earth is going on. Then I hear footsteps at my side.

Jack's found me!

I immediately put my head in my hands.

'Don't look at me!' I squeal, realising that this tactic will probably have the direct opposite effect of the one I actually want.

'I just came to see how your allergic reaction was,' he says. 'Your mum told me what happened.'

'Oh God, thanks, Mother,' I say, my head still buried beneath my hands.

Jack sits down next to me. 'Are you going to stay like that all night, with your hands over your face?' he asks.

I lift my head up, my hands still firmly in place. 'Probably,' I mumble.

He bursts out laughing. 'Well, okay, fine,' he chuckles. 'But you must think I'm terribly shallow.'

'How do you mean?' I ask.

'Well, you obviously think I won't want to sit here and have a conversation with someone, just because they've got a few . . . spots.'

'They're not spots, actually,' I say. 'They're blotches.'

'Only blotches?' he says. 'That's nothing.'

201

'Look,' I say, my hands still over my face, 'I appreciate the sentiment, but it'd make my life much easier if you just went back to the party and practised your *Come Dancing* routine again.'

'Oh, you're kidding, aren't you?' he says. 'I can't stand all that stuff. Now, come on, Evie, be sensible. Let me see you.'

I think about this for a second. Or probably more like a minute. Against all my better judgement, I slowly peel my hands away . . . and look into his eyes.

'*Oh – my – God!*' he shrieks.

'Argghhh!' I say, and put my hands back again.

'I'm joking!' he says. 'Evie, really, I'm joking.'

He puts his hand on my arm, sending a small shockwave through my veins. Then, he slowly pulls my hands away.

'Honestly, that was a joke. I'm sorry,' he says. 'I'm really sorry. Look, Evie, I don't think it looks anywhere near as bad as you think it does.'

I grimace.

'I know you're only being polite', I say, 'but thank you anyway.'

Jack picks up a piece of rock and starts to play with it as we both look out to sea.

'I think your mum's great, by the way,' he says.

I look at him, surprised.

'Do you?' I ask. 'I mean, *I* think she's great too, but most other people would run a mile just at the sight of those tights.'

He smiles.

'Has she invited you to her wedding yet?' I ask.

'She has,' he replies. 'Do I assume from the question that it might not be the most exclusive ticket in town?'

'You could say that,' I tell him. 'I ought to warn you as well that it won't be anything like as civilised as all this. I hope you like nettle wine, put it that way.'

'It'll be worth it just for that,' he jokes. 'And you're a bridesmaid again, are you?'

'Yep, for the third time this year. I'm a serial bridesmaid.'

He laughs and looks over to me.

'Anyway,' he says, 'I'm glad to have escaped for a bit.'

'Me too,' I say. 'Although I'd assumed you were taken for the night.'

'You mean with Beth?' he asks.

'Hmm,' I say, nodding.

'No,' he says. 'She's very sweet and everything but, no, I certainly wasn't taken for the night. Not with Beth.'

Chapter 58

This should be the best news I've heard all night, but something is still bothering me. Why, exactly – if he *wasn't* taken with Beth – has he given her his phone number? I bite my lip and think about this, pretending to look for something in my bag. Should I bring it up? Just get it out on the table and clear the whole matter up at the start?

No. *No way.* I mean, what has it got to do with me? Precisely nothing, that's what. Then again, when has that ever stopped me? I'm just considering whether a way exists for me to mention this without looking like a grade A bunny boiler, when suddenly, something takes my mind off the whole issue.

His hand brushes against mine.

I can't decide at first whether it was just an accident. But then he does it again. This time, his fingers clasp around mine decisively, sending a bolt of electricity though my body. I turn and look at him, our fingers intertwined in each other's, his hand squeezing mine.

'If it's not too personal a question,' he says, looking into my eyes, 'are you seeing anyone?'

I know I should be pouting and looking seductive here,

but sadly, the only thing I can manage is uncontrollable grinning.

'It's not too personal a question,' I reply. 'And no, I'm not.'

Now he smiles.

'Are you?' I ask.

'No,' he says, shaking his head. 'As you know, I went on a couple of dates with Valentina but that's it since, well, since my girlfriend and I broke up.'

'Oh,' I say, half-wishing that hadn't come up.

There's a short pause while I think about what to say.

'Was it, you know, amicable?' I ask, more out of politeness than actually wanting this line of conversation to develop.

'Hmm. I suppose so,' he says. 'But I don't think that ever makes splitting up less of an ordeal when you've been together for a long time. We'd been an item for over three years.'

'You were in love with her?' I ask.

He thinks for a second.

'I thought I was,' he says. 'Although when I look back now, things weren't working out for a long time before we split up.'

'You don't think there's a chance you'll get back together again, then?' I ask.

'No, definitely not,' he says. 'It's taken me a long time to come to this conclusion, but I know now that we were right to go our separate ways.'

He pauses for a second. 'That hasn't stopped me making a promise to myself though.'

'Oh?'

'Well,' he says, 'there is no way I'm going to let it happen again.'

205

'Which bit?' I ask tentatively.

'The being dumped by someone I really care about bit,' he says.

I suddenly feel a little uncomfortable.

'Do you think that's stupid?' he asks, obviously sensing it.

'No – God, no,' I tell him. 'It's awful when that sort of thing happens – being dumped and everything.'

He smiles. 'You sound as if you speak from experience,' he says.

Christ, do I? How did that happen?

It strikes me suddenly that I've got two choices here. One, I can come clean. I can tell Jack that, in fact, I am the most desperately dysfunctional person he is ever likely to meet when it comes to relationships. Never been in love. Never been out with someone for more than three months. Never come close to having had my heart broken.

Or I could fudge it.

Option two seems far more attractive.

'Well, yes,' I say. 'I mean, I have as much experience as the next person.'

'Go on, tell me about it,' he says.

Oh shit. Can't we talk about something less complicated, like the Arab-Israeli conflict, for example?

'Oh, no really, I don't want to bore you with it,' I say, shaking my head as if the whole thing is all too painful for me to discuss. He raises an eyebrow and I start to think that if I don't say something soon, he'll smell a rat, and a rather big one at that.

'*Okay*,' I say. 'Well, I had this boyfriend.'

'Name?' he asks.

I scan our immediate surroundings for inspiration.

'Jimmy,' I say, hoping any knowledge he may have of the fashion industry doesn't extend to identifying the names of shoe designers.

'And how long were you together?' he asks.

'Oooh, a while,' I say. 'Yep, a good while.'

'What, two years, three?'

'Yep,' I say.

'Which one?' he asks.

'Hmm?'

'Two years or three?'

'Oh, two,' I say. 'And a half.'

He waits for me to elaborate. I pretend not to notice.

'So what happened?' he asks, eventually.

'Well, as I say, we'd been together two and a half years and, out of the blue one day, he split up with me.'

'Right,' he says.

I am painfully aware that the complete lack of detail in this story means it couldn't be more suspicious if it involved Colonel Mustard, a dining room and a bloodstained candlestick. I desperately need to fill in some gaps.

'Basically,' I say in a rush, 'he asked me to go for a walk with him in Sefton Park. Well, we walked and walked until we got to the bandstand and then he turned to me and said, "Evie, I've got something to tell you".'

More detail, Evie, more detail. I take a deep breath.

'I didn't know what he was going to say,' I continue. 'He might have been about to propose, for all I knew.'

Steady on, Evie.

'God,' Jack says.

'Hmm,' I add, and am appalled to realise I have developed a sorrowful Princess Di-style expression.

'So he held my hand,' I continue, 'and said, "Evie, I don't want to be with you any more". And you know, I would have cried but the place was swarming with teenagers on skateboards.'

Dear God, what am I saying?

Jack squeezes my hand as if to say I don't need to go on if I don't want to, and I am torn between disgust at myself and feeling touched by his kindness. Either way, my heartbeat is going into overdrive.

Thankfully, Jack is suddenly distracted by something, and I take the opportunity to breathe deeply and try to force myself to relax.

'Oh, look over there!' he says, pointing into the sea.

I scan the water and wonder what I'm looking for.

'I can't see anything,' I say.

'It's a seal!' he exclaims.

I'm about to tell him I saw one earlier, but decide against it, given that he seems to be huddling up to me to point it out. I search the water but can't actually see a seal this time. Admittedly, this is probably because I am struggling to concentrate on anything other than the curve of his forearm around my waist.

'I still can't see it,' I say rather breathlessly. 'You've obviously got better eyesight than me.'

I suddenly become aware that he is looking at me and I turn to look at him too. Our faces are no more than six inches away from each other. Then he smiles.

'What?' I ask, wondering whether I've still got some blotches or some wildberry compote stuck in my teeth.

'Nothing,' he says softly.

My heart is beating like crazy now. He's going to kiss me – I know it. I have never been more sure of anything in my life. My eyes close as he pulls me towards him, the heat from his body searing into mine. Even before we have touched, I can already sense the softness of those lips. I can almost taste his mouth, feel the wetness of his tongue . . . I'm so turned on by anticipation as our lips are about to meet that I almost feel faint.

'Eviiieee!!'

Oh God.

'Eviiee! Is that you over there?'

If I didn't know better, I'd think it was the Hound of the Baskervilles.

'Evie, we need you!'

I could happily kill Valentina sometimes.

Chapter 59

Life is supposed to be all about learning lessons, and I have learned a significant one today. Never again will I agree to carry the key card of a friend who is having her period and therefore likely to want to get into her room at any given moment for a greater choice of sanitary products than those on offer in the ladies' loo.

The friend I refer to is actually Charlotte – Valentina had simply been deputised into the search-party. Charlotte had been unable to fit said card into her own bag because, despite being exceptionally pretty, sparkly and well-matched to her dress, it was also so small it wouldn't accommodate anything other than a sample lipstick from the Clinique counter and two Kirby grips. Which, I did point out, kind of negates the object of a bag, for me.

Poor Charlottte was apologetic almost to the point of self-flagellation when she found out where I'd been for the last half-hour. Which makes me feel slightly better, but not much. Because, between Georgia's dad stopping for a chat with me, and my mum waylaying Jack for a discussion about Amnesty International's membership fees, I somehow managed to lose him again.

Which is bloody careless, I know.

'You don't get away that easily,' says a voice behind me, prompting a small somersault in my stomach.

I spin around eagerly, but realise it's only Seb.

'Pull up a chair,' I say, trying for the sake of common decency not to look as disappointed as I feel. 'Have you enjoyed the party?'

'It's been spectacular,' he says.

'Not missing your pool table?' I enquire.

'Oh, I can manage without that for a night,' he says. 'Anyway, listen. Your office isn't far from where I work. We should really hook up some time for a drink after hours. Or lunch maybe.'

I hesitate.

'Come on,' he says. 'I've never known a journalist to turn down the offer of a free lunch yet.'

'Oh, you're paying, are you?' I ask.

'Of course.'

I smile. I don't want a romance with Seb again – I'm pretty sure of that much – but being friends with one of my ex-boyfriends might be just the sort of novelty I could do with at the moment.

'Sure,' I say. 'We'll definitely do that.'

As I take a sip of my drink I spot Charlotte sitting by herself at the side of the dance floor.

'Would you excuse me a minute, Seb?' I ask. 'I just need to catch up with someone.'

'I Just Can't Get You Out of My Head' is playing and Valentina is, predictably, in the centre of the dance floor, jerking backwards and forwards in as close an approximation of Kylie's video routine as someone who is five foot nine can manage.

'Valentina appears to be having some sort of convulsions,' I say to Charlotte as I sit down next to her. 'Do you think we ought to find a paramedic or just shoot her now to put her out of her misery?'

Charlotte giggles.

'You don't feel like dancing then?' I ask.

She shakes her head and smiles. 'Even if I lost ten stones I don't think you'd ever get me dancing like that,' she says.

'I should hope not,' I say. 'There wouldn't be room for two people doing those moves. You'd end up taking somebody's eye out.'

'I just mean I wouldn't have the confidence of some people,' she says, looking now at my mum and Bob, both flailing their arms about like a pair of manic Morris dancers.

'You've got everything to be confident about now,' I say. 'You look amazing. You've lost so much weight already.'

'I've got a long way to go before I'm a Gold Member at WeightWatchers,' she sighs.

'But you'll do it, won't ask?' I say. 'You'll more than do it, I'm sure.'

She nods decisively. 'Oh, I'll do it all right,' she says, grinning. 'I've not given up my smoothies and replaced them with this blinking Diet Coke for nothing.'

Suddenly, Valentina bounds over looking like a member of Legs and Co, and dramatically plonks herself down next to us.

'Okay, I give up,' she says. 'If there is a single goddamn eligible man here, I'll be goddamn damned if I can find him.'

'Would you like a drink?' asks Charlotte.

'No,' she says. 'I'm taking it easy after Grace's wedding. Strictly between the three of us, I didn't feel so good the next day, although that was probably more down to the beef, which I bet wasn't organic. And I'd had a mouthful of Frisée with my starter which wouldn't have done my enzymes any good. I've told you I've got a lettuce intolerance, haven't I?'

Charlotte nods, then says, 'Well, it's certainly not like *you* to struggle on the man-front, that's for sure.'

Valentina pulls a face. 'You're not suggesting I'm easy, are you?' she asks.

'No – God, no!' says Charlotte quickly. 'All I mean, is that you usually have them swarming around you.'

This is apparently the right thing to say.

'I know,' replies Valentina, smiling. 'Although, can I let you both into a secret?'

'Go on,' I say. It goes without saying that Charlotte would never betray her confidence.

Valentina beams. 'I'm getting married,' she tells us.

Chapter 60

I would try not to look surprised, but it is difficult when you've just nearly choked on your ice cube in shock.

'Did I hear you right?' I ask Valentina. 'You're getting *married*?'

'Don't look so surprised, Evie,' she says. 'There simply comes a time in a girl's life when being a bridesmaid isn't enough. And I'm *there*.'

'Well, bloody hell, Valentina, that's wonderful,' I say.

'It is,' adds Charlotte, leaning over to give her a congratulatory kiss on the cheek. 'It really is wonderful. But who are you getting married to? And when is the big day?'

'Well,' she says, 'it'll definitely be before the end of next year, although I'm a bit short on some of the detail at this point. It's early days in the planning process really.'

'Okay, but like Charlotte says – who to?' I ask.

'That's the detail I'm short on,' she says.

Charlotte and I both frown.

'So you haven't *actually* found anyone yet?' asks Charlotte.

'Well, no, I haven't, but I'm not overly concerned about that part,' says Valentina. 'I mean, how hard can getting married be? Fat, ugly women everywhere seem to be at it these days. I just can't believe that with a little application it should be anything other than a breeze for me.'

'You're the first person I've met who manages to make getting married sound like taking a maths exam,' I say.

'Besides,' she continues, ignoring me, 'self-confidence is everything. That, and setting yourself clear targets. I'm a firm believer that once you decide you want something, you should go out and get it. That's all I'm doing. You should take a leaf out of my book, Charlotte.'

'Charlotte,' I say, 'please don't. For all our sakes, please don't.'

Suddenly, Valentina gasps.

'What now?' I ask.

'Him over there,' she says, pointing to the table next to the door. 'Wasn't he Grace and Patrick's best man?'

Edmund, who was indeed Grace and Patrick's best man, catches us looking over and waves at me. I wave back, conscious that Valentina's man-radar is going into overdrive.

'Yes,' I reply, with a sinking feeling.

'I *knew* it,' she says, grinning and opening up her handbag.

I flash a look at Charlotte and she knows exactly what I'm thinking. Edmund may be softly spoken, unassuming and nothing more than a solid average in the looks department. But, as someone who is also due to inherit half of Cheshire, he couldn't be more sought-after if he held the secret to eternal life. Now that I think about it, I am amazed it's taken Valentina this long to spot him.

'Do you know, I've just realised – he was looking at my legs when I did the reading,' she tells Charlotte. 'And that can only mean one thing.'

'You had a ladder in your tights?' I ask.

'*No*,' says Valentina, flashing me a look. 'It *means* he's a man with taste. Now, what else do you know about him?'

Charlotte and I don't reply.

'Well, come on,' she says. 'Spit it out. *Charlotte?*'

'He's a doctor – a surgeon,' Charlotte blusters, buckling under the pressure.

'Really?' purrs Valentina. 'That's *such* a coincidence.'

'Why?' I ask.

'I thought about going into the medical profession at one point,' she says, 'but then I realised how much of it involved wiping octogenarians' bottoms. Anything else? Come on now, Charlotte.'

'Well,' says our friend reluctantly, 'I think his father is some sort of . . . *lord*.'

'What?!' says Valentina, breathless. 'And nobody told me? Nobody *ever* tells me *anything*.'

Her hand is now in her bag, rooting around it frantically and producing such a large and random collection of belongings that its previous owner could have been Mary Poppins.

First is the hand cream, then the eye cream, face cream, spot cream and nail cream. Then comes the make-up, which emerges in the sort of quantities that a contestant in the Glamorous Tranny contest might consider a bit OTT. She opens her mirror and quickly touches up her face, giving poor Charlotte's cheekbones a prod with her blusher brush, and commenting on how much better her appearance would be if she bothered to accentuate them more.

'Right,' she says, pushing the clasp on her bag tightly shut and winking at the two of us. 'I'll see you later. Or hopefully not!'

Chapter 61

Here's what I don't get. Charlotte was determined that she *didn't* fancy Jim.

Yet at the moment, she's at the bar, sipping her seventeenth Diet Coke of the day, and chatting away to him as if he's the last man on the planet.

Valentina, meanwhile, has spent the last hour trying to convince Edmund that she's a country girl at heart – having spent one weekend in the Lake District as a Girl Guide in 1987 – and asking him to give his medical opinion of her hamstring injury. Which obviously involves her lifting her skirt up so she can put his hand on her backside.

Still, part of me admires her. Because here I am, with Jack again, and apparently totally incapable of engineering a situation where he might even think about kissing me.

'Have the bride and groom left?' he asks.

'I think so,' I say. 'Ages ago.'

'Oh,' he says.

'It's been a long day,' I sigh.

'Yeah,' he agrees. 'It has. A very long day.'

Quite frankly, I'm starting to get a little concerned. I think the moment has gone. Which is bad news for any number of reasons – not least because my blotches have near enough disappeared and if I don't look worthy of a snog now, I never will.

The final bars of Jack Johnson are played out and it can only mean one thing. It's the end of the night. Most of the guests have already left. There's a small but hardcore group settling down in the lobby for what they clearly hope will be a marathon drinking session.

But there is no doubt that the event is on its last legs and, although the staff are still smiling, they also look weary enough for it to be clear that they can't wait for us all to bugger off and let them get to bed.

'Looks like we're about to be evicted,' says Jack.

'I guess so,' I reply. I may be smiling, but I'm feeling a bit anxious. Our almost-kiss on the beach wasn't our only chance, was it?

'Well, I don't suppose the crime rate is very high around here, but can I walk you back to your room?' he asks.

'That'd be great,' I say. 'You never know, I might risk getting mugged by a passing seal.'

As we head out of the main section of the hotel and along one of the moonlit paths, the night is filled with a bizarre combination of sounds: waves against the rocks and revellers in varying states of inebriation staggering to bed.

'It's been lovely seeing you again today,' he says.

I can't help noticing that he hasn't tried to hold my hand again, like he did earlier. I move closer to him so he can if he wants to. But he doesn't.

'Yeah,' I say. 'You too.'

I briefly consider being bold enough to hold *his* hand, but surprise myself by deciding against it. I'm obviously not as liberated as I like to think. Mum would be appalled. It is a frustratingly short distance between the main hotel and my suite, and when we reach the door, Jack turns towards me.

'Good night then,' he says softly.

'Good night to you too.' *To you too?* What, have I turned into Bruce Forsyth now?

'See you in the morning,' he adds.

'Yep,' I say. 'See you.'

It suddenly becomes painfully clear that he is about to leave without kissing me. I root around in my bag for my key card and when I produce it, unkissed, I have never felt such a sense of utter disappointment. It must show on my face.

'What's up?' he says.

'Oh, nothing,' I reply, looking away and now just feeling embarrassed.

But he puts his hand on my chin and turns me back to him. Then he moves his hand to the nape of my neck, where his fingers caress my hairline; our eyes are locked, and my breathing is quickening even more.

He pulls me towards him, and as I close my eyes, our lips meet. His mouth is full and soft, and I discover that his taste is even more luscious than I could possibly have imagined. Our tongues slowly begin to explore each other's mouths. But soon the initial gentleness is replaced by something else, a hunger that's as clear in him as it is in me. Our kissing becomes more passionate, and as he pulls me in tighter, his body presses against mine.

With his hand firmly against the small of my back, he moves his mouth to the side of my neck, and the sensation of his lips against my skin sends shockwaves through my body.

Breathless, tingling, I look up into the star-filled night. This may just be the sexiest kiss of my entire life.

Chapter 62

I wake up with a smile on my face. I'm not quite sure why at first, but I just know that yesterday was a good day, that today is going to be a good day, and as for tomorrow – well, I'm feeling pretty damn optimistic about that too.

Rolling onto my back, I pull the sheet up to my chest the way Joan Collins used to in *Dynasty*. As I open my eyes, the blinds are all shut but I can already see the sun streaming through and casting patterns on the walls. I close my eyes again and picture Jack's face, which I've seen up close now. I've seen the pores of his skin, the flecks on those brown eyes, and the tiny scar next to his cheekbone.

I start to picture him undressing me. Taking off my clothes, one by one. Then kissing my neck, my breasts, my belly, my thighs.

None of that happened last night, I hasten to add. Instead, I'm here, alone. And I would like to say I feel quite angelic about that, except 'angelic' is the least appropriate description of how I feel when it comes to Jack.

Suddenly, I realise that the phone is ringing. It can't be so late that they want me out of the room, can it? I scrabble around on my bedside table, and after managing to knock everything off, including a previously untouched glass of water and the Gideon Bible I decided to read last night after I couldn't find my paperback, I finally locate the alarm clock and peer at its display.

9.30 a.m. I distinctly remember reading that check-out was at 11 a.m.

I pull a pillow over my head, but the ringing rattles through my ears like a freight train and I finally resign myself to answering the phone.

'Hhhr?' I say, clearing my throat. 'Sorry, hello?'

'Evie, it's Mum.'

'Oh, hi,' I say, realising that my voice sounds as if I've spent the entire night gargling with white spirit.

'Ooh,' she says. 'Are you hungover?'

'No, I'm not,' I say, and am almost telling the truth. Okay, so my mouth feels a bit like a bear's armpit, but it's nothing I can't handle.

'I just wondered whether you were coming on the walk this morning?'

'Yes,' I say, remembering that Jack and I had agreed last night that we'd join everyone else after breakfast for the walk Georgia has organised around the island.

'Well, we're all waiting for you,' she says.

'What?' I sit bolt upright. 'I thought we weren't going until ten-thirty?'

'That's the time it is now,' she says.

I suddenly remember that I'd attempted to set the alarm last night, but had given up on it and told myself I'd be sure to wake up in time anyway. My technical skills are never at their best in the early hours of the morning and I'd obviously managed to alter the time on it too.

'Don't worry about breakfast,' she continues. 'I put together a little doggy bag from the buffet, so you can have some of that. I've got twelve hard-boiled eggs in my rucksack here.'

Putting the phone down, I leap out of bed with the speed of a Grand National winner before running into the bathroom to splash my face with some water, scrape off the last crusty bits of mascara from last night and brush my teeth so vigorously, you'd think I was scrubbing a doorstep.

By the time I'm dressed and out of the door – in less than three minutes – I do wonder whether I should have taken more care over my appearance. Problem is, there's nothing I can do about it now.

When I arrive at the main terrace, which was where we'd arranged to rendezvous, everyone has gone. Everyone, that is, apart from Jack and Edmund, who are chatting and drinking coffee. Jack looks over in my direction and my stomach does that strange lurching thing it's been doing constantly for the last twenty-four hours.

'Fresh as a daisy, are we?' he asks, grinning.

'I'm raring to go, I promise you!' I say. 'I just had a little bit of alarm-clock trouble. Hi, Edmund. How are you this morning?'

'Marvellous,' he replies, and I can't help wondering whether some of his enthusiasm is connected to the way in which Valentina was becoming acquainted with his upper thigh last night.

'So, are we all ready to go?' I ask.

'Just waiting for Valentina,' says Jack.

'Well, good morning everyone!'

We all turn around.

Valentina is striding along in a pair of pink and white high-heeled mules, a Juicy T-shirt, and a pair of hot pants straight out of *The Dukes of Hazzard*. She is also fully made-up and looks like she's spent two hours tonging her hair.

'You're not coming for a walk like that, are you?' I ask.

She frowns. 'Why not?'

'Because you'll break your neck in those shoes, for a start.'

'Thank you, *Mum*,' she tells me. 'If you must know, I have a change of shoes in my backpack if it becomes necessary.'

In case I wondered for even a millisecond that she might have brought something practical, she turns around to display a bubblegum-coloured rucksack with the words *J'adore Dior* emblazoned across it.

'I take it you haven't got a camping stove in that,' I say.

'I have everything I could possibly require on an exhilarating morning walk,' she replies.

I look her in the eyes.

'You mean your make-up bag, don't you?'

She purses her lips and doesn't answer.

Chapter 63

Serious walkers are always looking for their next challenge. They start with the gentle slopes of the South Downs, then go for the trickier crags of Snowdon in North Wales. For the ambitious, it's then onto the Alps and, you never know, eventually they might end up taking on Everest.

But I'm discovering today they they need not bother with any of this.

Instead, there is an item at any outdoor enthusiast's disposal which could turn a very average, unchallenging walk into a positively perilous adventure. Something which could make tackling an otherwise simple piece of terrain a seemingly impossible, nay insurmountable, challenge.

What am I going on about? Valentina's bloody shoes, are what.

I can imagine no footwear less suited to a walk around the rocky shoreline of the island than her three-inch strappy mules. It has now taken us forty-five minutes to cover the sort of distance the average toddler could do in five. This is partly because every time Valentina gets one of her heels stuck between a crag, she makes the sort of squealing noise Penelope Pitstop might emit while having her legs waxed.

Then, she falls dramatically to the ground like a nineteenth-century maiden as Edmund rushes to her rescue.

I'm about to suggest to Jack that we leave Valentina and Edmund behind so we can actually make some progress, when suddenly, she steps in before me.

'Evieee! Jaaack!' she shouts from behind us. 'We can step up a pace now, if you like. I've decided a change of footwear probably *was* in order, after all.'

Valentina now has her Nikes on and is jogging along the shoreline with a *Baywatch*-esque pout. I can't help smirking as she and Edmund overtake us. Valentina couldn't be looking more smug at the moment if Jude Law were waiting at home for her with a winning lottery ticket between his teeth.

By the time we finally catch up with the others, they are all on the beach having a rest. My mum and Bob are both sitting with their legs crossed as he shells eggs into a blue bandana and she offers round her flask of dandelion-leaf tea, apparently surprised that there have so far been no takers.

Grace and Patrick are next to them and I'm relieved to see that Grace's beauty routine this morning appears to have been about as cursory as mine was. Charlotte and Jim are also here and, again, are looking very comfortable indeed in each other's company.

Georgia and Pete are holding hands and looking thoroughly loved-up, and as we arrive, the topic of conversation is whether she is going to take his surname or not.

'The thing is, when you've got a maiden name like Pickle, the opportunity to have another surname doesn't seem like such a dilemma,' Georgia is telling us. 'I thought about it for all of three seconds.'

'Yes,' says my mum, 'but as a principle, there are lots of

good reasons for women *not* to take their husband's name – not least because of what it meant historically. It's a hangover from the days when a husband was considered to own his wife.'

'I bet life was simpler then,' says Pete, before Georgia clouts him over the head with her rucksack.

'But isn't it just much more romantic?' whispers Valentina, flashing a smile at Edmund.

Bob joins in now.

'Oh, but Valentina, there's nothing romantic about servitude,' he says softly, although as he sits in his crocheted tank top with bits of boiled egg stuck in his beard, I can't help thinking that the prospect of him ever reducing my mother to servitude seems pretty remote.

'Given that women are well and truly emancipated these days, surely it doesn't hold those negative connotations any more?' says Patrick. 'That's what I tried to tell my missus, anyway.'

All of a sudden, Charlotte pipes up.

'If I ever got married, I *would* take my husband's name,' she says. 'I don't know about historical connotations or anything else, but I do know that if you really love someone, well . . . why wouldn't you?'

Grace, Valentina and I all look slightly taken aback. Because for those of us who know Charlotte, this has got to count as something of a seminal moment. Charlotte has always hated talking in big groups, and by big, I mean anything more than two people. And yet here she is, actually contributing to a debate. Okay, it may have only been one statement, but this is so far removed from what we're used to, it feels like she's one step away from being a panellist on *Question Time*.

'Well, I admit it,' says Grace, holding her hands up. 'I'm with the keeping your own surname camp. It's taken a lot of blood and sweat to build up my name professionally – so why would I want to throw that away now?'

'Hmm,' says Patrick under his breath. 'And that's so much more important than being married.'

Grace looks as shocked at this statement as the rest of us who caught it. But the ensuing silence is broken as Jim stands up and brushes down his combat pants.

'Well, everyone,' he says, 'shall we head back? I'm aware we've all got a flight to catch pretty soon.'

He offers Charlotte a hand, while everyone else starts gathering up their belongings, and we're soon heading back towards the hotel.

I don't know whether it's on purpose or not, but Jack and I somehow drop back from the group and are soon out of earshot of the others.

'I'd love to get together some time,' he says. 'You know, just you and me – no wedding or anything.'

'What, you mean you might actually be interested in me when I'm not in a bridesmaid dress? And here's me thinking you were a satin fetishist.'

He laughs.

'I'd love to get together too,' I add.

He smiles. 'Great. Good. Well, we'll swap numbers and go out some time.'

'That'd be nice,' I say. 'Some time.'

'Good,' he says. 'You free tomorrow?'

Chapter 64

Our speedboat cuts through the waves and leaves a soft spray on our faces. From Valentina's yelping, however, you'd think she was in a canoe during a gale force nine storm. Suddenly the boat bounces off a wave, and we are all thrown upwards slightly.

'Oh!' cries Valentina, and somehow dramatically lands in Edmund's arms, despite the fact that everyone else has been flung in the opposite direction.

I can't help feeling disappointed when the boat arrives at St Mary's harbour. It's not just because the time to leave this gorgeous place is almost upon us, but Jack and I are catching different flights. And it's time to say goodbye. Okay, he's going to phone me later to arrange to get together tomorrow, but leaving these islands somehow feels like the end of a holiday romance – admittedly without the tan or huge bar bill – and I just hope things will feel the same back home.

'I'm just going to nip into the shop and buy a paper before I go,' I tell Jack and he waits outside.

The queue at the counter is annoyingly long, not helped by the fact that some poor teenage oaf at the front is attempting to buy some condoms.

'Just the plain ones, is it?' asks the shopkeeper, who must be in his seventies and is wearing a T-shirt commemorating Status Quo's 1996 UK tour.

'Hmm, yeah,' says his poor customer, looking at his shoes.

'I think them ribbed ones are on special offer. They're two for one,' the man says.

'Er, okay, whatever,' says the lad, fiddling with his key chain.

'We've also just got some of these new flavoured ones in, if they take your fancy. Melon,' he reads, shaking his head. 'The things they come up with these days.'

The teenager is now the colour of a very ripe cranberry. 'The others'll do,' he says, clearly desperate for this torture to end.

'Quite right, lad,' the man agrees. 'There's sixteen johnnies in there between the two packets – and if that's not a couple of quid well spent, I don't know what is.'

At last, the queue moves forward, but as the shopkeeper launches into his views about whether a Cornish pasty really is a Cornish pasty if it's made of puff pastry rather than short-crust, I look out of the window and do a double-take. Jack has now been joined by Beth – and she's wearing a pair of denim hot pants smaller than the average bikini bottoms on a Rio beach.

He says something that makes her laugh, which she does with a flirtatious flick of her long dark hair. She leans forward and puts her hand on his arm, as they both continue laughing. She then twists her waist to remove a piece of paper from the back pocket of her shorts and appears to be consulting him about it. I may be wrong but I'm sure it's the same piece of paper that had his phone number on it yesterday.

I am rooted to the spot, wondering what the hell to do. But with the queue almost grinding to a halt, I decide there's only one thing for it. I abandon my paper and make my way outside, trying to look as casual as possible. The thing is, there's no way I'm going to say anything, but I still want to get over there to see what this conversation is all about. More importantly, I want to see what sort of guy Jack really is.

But when I'm still a few feet away, my mum grabs me by the arm.

'Evie,' she says. 'Come on, we've got to get going or we'll miss our flight.'

I look over to Jack and Beth.

'So it's okay if I phone you next week?' she asks him, flashing a set of teeth so white she's like a walking Colgate advert.

'Er, sure,' says Jack, who has spotted me looking at them.

As Beth walks away, I can't help noticing that half of the people in the harbour have their eyes glued to her perfect backside, most of which is peeking out of the bottom of her shorts. I walk over to Jack and pick up my suitcase.

'I've had a lovely time,' he says.

'Er, well – good,' I say, not sure how to handle this.

'Is something the matter?' he asks.

Yes.

'No.'

'Well, you still on for doing something tomorrow?' he asks.

Maybe there's been some misunderstanding with Beth. Maybe I didn't hear it right. Maybe I should give him the benefit of the doubt. Maybe I'm a complete bloody idiot. Maybe not.

Oh God.

'Sure,' I say. 'Give me a ring later, by all means.'

Suitably nonchalant, but not closing any doors completely. It's the only way to play it. He leans over to kiss me and I find myself turning my head slightly so his kiss lands on my cheek.

'See you,' he says.

'Bye,' I reply. And I walk away in the full knowledge that, sadly, there isn't a single soul looking at my arse.

Chapter 65

'Well, what do you think? Am I being taken for a ride or what?' I say, taking a gulp of water and putting the bottle on the ground next to me.

'I don't know, do I?' says Grace.

We are sitting outside on the grass waiting for our plane to arrive.

St Mary's hasn't so much got an airport as a field with a terminal the size of a doctor's waiting room. The others – those who are due to catch the first flight with us – are inside drinking tea and eating scones and clotted cream. For some reason, I've lost my appetite.

'Well, you're not being much help, I must say,' I tell Grace.

'Look,' she says, 'you were the one who was there. Did he *act* like he was two-timing you?'

I think for a second. 'No. No, he didn't,' I say firmly.

'Well then,' she says, by way of a conclusion.

'At least, he didn't until I saw him telling another woman to phone him. Oh God!'

'Look,' she says again, 'just wait until he rings you later today – that's what he said, didn't he? Then, when you go out with him, if you still feel the need, just ask him straight.'

'You don't think I haven't got any right to ask him about this sort of thing?' I ask. 'It's not like he's my boyfriend. We just, you know, kissed.'

She shrugs.

'If he's worth his salt he won't mind you asking,' she says. 'As long as you ask in the right way. You know, like you're not really bothered but just . . . interested.'

I nod. 'Gotcha. Have you ever thought of becoming an agony aunt?'

Chapter 66

My flat, Sunday, 8 April

I wonder if there is something wrong with my phone?

When Jack said he would call me, I just assumed it would be earlier than this. It's now 9.30 p.m. and no matter how hard I try to convince myself to be relaxed about things, I currently couldn't feel less relaxed if I were about to take part in a *Mastermind* final.

I switch on the TV and catch the tail end of a piece about some Brits being taken hostage somewhere in the third world – a story that will undoubtedly dominate the papers tomorrow. I decide to put *How Clean Is Your House?* on again. It's been playing back to back all evening on some cable channel as I've nearly worn a hole in my laminate flooring from pacing up and down.

I pick up my mobile and scroll down to his name on the phone book. Maybe I should phone him.

Or maybe not. No.

Or maybe yes.

No. Definitely not. Far too *Fatal Attraction.*

I put the phone down and decide I need to do something

to occupy myself. I settle on cleaning out my food cupboard, which bears an alarming resemblance to that of a family of fifteen from Hackney who have just been told by presenters Kim and Aggie that they have an estimated 42 billion dust-mites living in their carpet.

My flat isn't particularly messy or dirty, it's just averagely disorganised. And while I'm happy to hoover and dust once in a while, I have to admit that until today, the food cup-board hasn't really been on my radar.

I pull out a previously unopened bottle from under the sink, calling itself a 'power spray', which I can't help think-ing sounds like something you'd find at a nuclear processing plant and not just something designed to remove old bits of tomato sauce from the hob.

When I open the cupboard door, I am confronted by an array of foodstuffs that ought to have been condemned a long time ago. A packet of Bird's custard powder that has split in the middle. White wine vinegar that is now less white than urine-coloured. Loose Earl Grey tea which has never been opened and that I could only possibly have acquired by mistake instead of bags.

This is the cupboard that time forgot. No wonder Jack doesn't want to phone me. Who'd want to go out with some-one who has such a sluttish attitude to household cleanliness? Depressed by this thought, I go to have another look at my mobile again, just in case it accidentally went into silent mode without me knowing. Sadly, my phone screen refuses to humour me. I go to the contacts book, scroll down to Grace's mobile and press *call*.

'What's up?' she asks, when she answers.

'Can you do me a favour?'

'Of course. What is it?'

'Can you just phone my mobile?'

'Why?' she asks.

'Er, because I've lost it and think it might be under a cushion or something.'

'But you're phoning me from it now,' she says. 'Your number's just come up.'

'Ah,' I say, realising I've been well and truly rumbled. 'Look, Jack's still not phoned, and I want to dismiss even the tiniest possibility that there's something wrong with my phone before I go away and slit my wrists.'

'Don't be so dramatic,' she says. 'I'll do it now. And calm down, for God's sake.'

I put the phone down and wait. And wait. And I keep waiting until at least a minute goes by. This is starting to look promising. I look at my clock and decide I will time it. If three minutes pass without Grace phoning, there really must be something wrong with my phone.

They feel like a long three minutes but, sure enough, the clock ticks by and eventually they pass. I feel ridiculously jubilant. There *is* something wrong with my phone, after all! Which means Jack hasn't gone off me. In fact, he probably still likes me very much indeed. My mind starts spinning with the thought of him frantically trying to get hold of me to tell me he's booked a table at a romantic restaurant or that he's cooking a candlelit dinner round at his place. Who am I kidding? I'd be happy if he were planning a date at a sewage works.

Oh joy! Oh Jack! You still like me. You still want to go out with me. You still want to walk along beaches with me and hold my hand. You still want to let me look into those deep brown eyes. You still . . .

237

The phone rings. I look at the display to see that Grace's number has come up and I answer it.

'Shit,' I say despondently.

'Charming,' she replies.

'Sorry.'

'No, sorry it took me a while to phone back. I was busy having a domestic.'

'Is that husband of yours playing up?' I ask.

'Don't get me started,' she says.

'Is everything all right?' I am thinking back to Patrick's barbed comments in the Scillies when he accused Grace of caring about work more than her marriage.

'Hmm, listen, I've got to run, Evie,' she says. 'And don't worry about Jack. He'll phone.'

Chapter 67

My flat, Monday, 9 April, 6.30 p.m.

He hasn't phoned.

It's now 6.30 p.m. on the day we were supposed to be going out together, and as far as I can tell, I have two choices. I can sit here moping all evening about the destitute life of spinsterhood I have in front of me. Or I can phone Jack and risk looking like the sort of woman who likes making bunny stew in her spare time.

Not very appealing either way.

It has taken me nearly twenty-four hours of contemplation, but I decide, finally, to go for the second choice. It's a risky strategy but at least I'll know where I stand.

I go to the contacts book on my phone, scroll down to his name and quickly press Call before I get the chance to whip myself up into a nervous frenzy.

But the phone doesn't even ring; it just goes straight to his messages, indicating he's either on the phone to someone else (probably someone significantly thinner, bigger-breasted and more attractive than me), or he's switched off (probably because he's with someone significantly thinner, bigger-breasted and more attractive than me).

'Hi, *you've reached Jack's mobile . . .*'

Oh God, do I leave a message?

'*. . . but I'm not available at the moment.*'

Yes, I'll leave one.

'*Just leave a message after the tone . . .*'

No, I won't.

'*. . . and I'll get back to you as soon as I can.*'

Oh bugger.

'Er, hi Jack, it's Evie,' I splutter. 'Just thought I'd give you a ring because, well, you know – to see how you are. And because we were supposed to go out, if you remember. And, well, I didn't hear from you. I don't want you to think I'm a stalker or anything – that wasn't why I phoned. Er, so why *did* I phone? Well, just to say that if you don't want to go out with me, then that's just fine. But if you do, then that'd be great – even better, in fact. And in that case, well – here I am! But, well, clearly you don't, otherwise you would have phoned. So, I'll go now.'

I go to put the phone down, but hesitate.

'Whatever happens,' I add, 'I had a nice time this weekend. Just thought I should say. Bye.'

I put the phone down.

I've been stood up. I don't believe it.

That's it for me and Jack, then. Over before it even began.

But what I don't understand is that he seemed so keen.

Until you saw him flirting with another woman, Evie.

But all the signs seemed to point to him really liking me.

Apart from him giving his phone number to someone else.

But didn't he kiss me and tell me we'd get together today?

Yes, but how many other women has he done that with?

I'm simply going to have to pull myself together. This is not worth wasting another thought over. I'm just going to forget it right now. Not mention it to anyone, not allow myself to even think about it.

There, I feel better already.

Chapter 68

My flat, Monday, 9 April, 7.30 p.m.

I feel terrible.

Chapter 69

I can't believe I even considered phoning my mother to confide in her about this.

But after almost twenty-four hours of thinking about nothing else, I've just got to get a few things off my chest. Problem is, Grace has a deadline and, according to Patrick, she has told him not to call her to the phone unless it's God on the line to say He's decided to make her a millionaire.

Charlotte, meanwhile, appears to have been at the gym all night, Georgia has very inconsiderately buggered off on her honeymoon, and as for Valentina . . . well, not even if I plummeted to the depths of despair would I consider confiding in her about something like this.

'I really got the impression that he liked me,' I tell my mum, aware that I'm whining a bit, but deciding that listening to this sort of thing is all part of a mother's job description.

'There is always the possibility that something's come up,' she says.

'He still could have phoned, couldn't he?'

'Well, maybe he's been in an accident,' she says cheerfully. 'You never know what sort of state he could be in. It does happen.'

'So, let me get this straight,' I say. 'You're trying to make me feel better about him not going on a date with me by telling me he might be injured or dead.'

'Oh, okay,' she says. 'I'm not much good at this, Evie. You've never asked me about these sorts of things before.'

I sigh. That's because it's never really happened before.

The only positive thing I can possibly say about the fact that it is now late on Monday and Jack still hasn't phoned, is that my taps are now gleaming. I've spent four hours scrubbing limescale off them with a bit of old potato and some washing-up liquid, and to Kim and Aggie's credit, they really have come up a treat.

I'm starting to worry for my mental health though.

Chapter 70

My flat, Tuesday, 10 April

I really can't leave another message on his answer machine. I'm just going to have to forget him. I mean, what's the big deal? It was only a kiss. And he's only a man. So what if he's got gorgeous eyes and a body to die for and is generally lovely in every way? I wish I'd slept with him now.

Argghhh! No, I don't.

Oh, for God's sake.

Chapter 71

My flat, Wednesday, 11 April

Wednesday and still no call. What I can't understand is why Jack would have bothered saying he'd phone me, and then not do so. I mean, why didn't he just not say anything?

Valentina's wisdom on this issue isn't exactly what I want to hear.

'Some men just seem to think it's impolite not to say they'll call after they've snogged you,' she shrugs. 'They just say it to fill a gap in conversation when they've got no intention of actually going through with it. Not that I've ever experienced anything like this personally, of course.'

Chapter 72

Café Tabac, Bold Street, Liverpool, Wednesday, 11 April

I am getting over my failed romance by plunging myself into my career.

What's more, I have realised that there is only one way I'm going to get a front-page splash – and that's by going out and getting it myself. Because it is now perfectly clear that Simon is about as likely to feed me a decent story as he is to offer me a pedicure.

So, in between knocking out nibs about the quarter-finals of an OAP crown green bowling competition and the fact that the gas supply in Skelmersdale is going to be switched off for an hour on Friday, I have been doing something else. Phoning my contacts.

Okay, so not all of them have been fruitful. No, that's an understatement. The only thing which has even approximated a story was a tip about some theft allegations at the distribution depot of a toilet roll firm – which turned out to be completely and utterly false.

But, now, as I sit in my favourite Liverpool café, opposite Detective Inspector Gregg 'Benno' Benson, things are looking up.

'I've got a belter for you,' he tells me confidently, polishing off one of the three muffins I've just bought for him.

'*Really?*' I am trying to retain an air of professionalism – rather than just looking so pathetically grateful that I'm on the verge of offering to have his babies.

'Yep,' he says, reaching for muffin number two.

I haven't exactly specialised in crime reporting, but I've met enough police officers since I started this job to know that Benno is not what you'd call typical of the breed. He scoffs at the graduate trainee schemes that send recruits on media training, would never dream of dealing with the Press Office and, despite a continual stream of internal memos instructing officers to the contrary, prefers to deal with journalists directly. At least, he prefers to deal with journalists he likes and trusts. What put me in that category, I'm not entirely sure, but he claims I'm the only journalist to have *ever* spelled his name correctly in print (Gregg with two gs, not one) and that might have something to do with it.

Anyway, the story he's got goes like this: Pete Gibson, the Liverpool-born pop star with a squeaky-clean image and a string of Top Ten hits under his belt, has been arrested and bailed on suspicion of supplying cocaine.

Not just that, but he was caught at it during a drug-fuelled orgy involving several other celebrities – models and footballers. A *belter* it undoubtedly is. However, there is a problem.

'You can't run the story yet,' says Benno.

'What?' My eyes widen as I can feel the first decent story I've had a sniff of, slipping out of my hands. 'That's like Father Christmas telling someone they can't open their presents until Easter. What's the problem?'

'The problem is,' he says, 'that we suspect Gibson isn't the only one up to no good.'

'I don't follow you,' I say.

Benno has reason to believe that Gibson has been attempting to bribe a police officer to 'lose' some of the evidence that will be used against him in court. If that is the case – and he succeeds – then there is a seriously dodgy copper to deal with too.

'So why can't you just arrest them both?' I ask.

'Because,' he says, licking some icing sugar off his fingers, 'we've got no hard evidence – yet.'

'And?'

'Well,' he says, 'we need to catch them at it. So, we're following Gibson. That guy can't have a crap without us knowing about it. So if he turns up at our man's door with a brown envelope in his back pocket, we'll be in there faster than Lance Armstrong – on a motorbike.'

'So how long will that take?' I frown.

He smiles. 'I promise you, Evie, you will be the first to know about it.'

I have a terrible feeling this just isn't going to happen. There's no way this story is going to stay out of the nationals.

'Definitely?' I whimper.

'You can come and take a picture of him being brought in, if you like,' he says.

My eyes widen again.

'Benno,' I say, 'if this story comes off, you will be – without question – my absolute favourite journalistic contact. Ever.'

'Good,' he says. 'You can go and get another couple of them buns in then.'

Chapter 73

I head back into the newsroom with the same spring in my step as the reporters who exposed Watergate must have had.

'Evie,' Simon says, chucking a press release onto my keyboard, 'we need some grouting for page thirty-nine. Bash out a bit of that, will you?'

I pick up the press release and look at the headline: *Blood donor sessions – time change*.

As I dejectedly start to type out a piece about how the planned blood donation sessions at Childwall Library will now take place at twelve noon, and not 12.30 p.m. as initially advertised, I look up and notice the buzz around me. There is clearly a big story breaking.

'What is the splash?' I ask Jules, next to me.

He nods over to BBC News 24 on one of the television screens. It's the story about the hostage crisis that has been on every news bulletin and in every paper for the last couple of days.

'A load of hostages have just been released in Sudan,' he says. 'More importantly, we've just found out that one of them is from our patch. Graham's doing it.'

I look over at Graham, frantically typing out some copy

with his phone perched next to his ear, and feel a stab of jealousy. Graham has been here a year longer than me, but the stories we're assigned differ so monumentally in quality, it could be twenty years. I look up at the big screen in the newsroom to see what the BBC have got to say about it.

'One British hostage, who was released this morning, is forty-two-year-old Janet Harper, an aid worker from Lancashire,' says the correspondent. 'Her release marks the end of a terrifying ordeal which began three days ago when she was seized outside a camp in Darfur by a gang of militia men.'

It's a big story, that's for sure.

The correspondent continues: 'I have with me Jack Williamson, who runs Future for Africa, the British-based charity Miss Harper was working for when she was seized.'

As the camera pans out, my jaw almost hits the floor.

It's Jack. My Jack. Jack – who I have been cursing for standing me up. Jack – who, it would appear, has a pretty bloody good excuse for standing me up.

'Mr Williamson, have you been in contact with Janet Harper since she was released?' asks the BBC correspondent.

Jack is unshaven and looks tired, but he's still got the sort of looks that would make a nun reconsider her career choices.

'I have,' he says. 'I spoke to her about an hour ago.'

'And can you confirm what sort of condition she is in?' asks the correspondent.

'She's physically unhurt, but obviously very shocked,' Jack tells him. 'She's receiving treatment in hospital at the moment and is doing very well under the circumstances.'

'There has been some criticism of your organisation for

not pulling their aid workers out of this area earlier, in the light of the unrest,' says the correspondent.

'Yes, I'm aware of that,' says Jack. 'We were monitoring the situation carefully back home and, to be honest, we were getting increasingly concerned about it. I spoke to Janet's project director two days before she was kidnapped, and we agreed that if the situation deteriorated any further, we would pull out of there. Clearly, events overtook that. And I'm just desperately sorry we misjudged the situation.'

As the piece comes to a conclusion, I rush over to the newsdesk.

'Simon,' I say breathlessly, 'put me on this story. You've *got* to put me on this story.'

Chapter 74

Simon looks at me as if he's just realised that an irritating bout of piles he thought he'd got rid of has come back.

'In most newsrooms it's traditional for the reporters to do what the News Editor tells them,' he says curtly. 'Unless, of course, you've finished that press release already.'

'No,' I say. 'No, I haven't. But I know that guy on the telly!'

'Who?' he says. 'Michael Buerk?'

I decide not to tell him that this particular BBC Africa correspondent is about twenty years younger than Michael Buerk and happens to be Asian.

'No,' I say. 'The other one – Jack Williamson – the boss of the aid agency the hostage works for.'

'So what?' Simon shrugs. 'Who's interested in him? It's the woman we want.'

'But—' I begin.

'Look,' he continues, 'unless you're telling me you can get an interview with the woman's family and the first pictures of her in time for the second edition, then please, just don't bother.'

We both know he's asking the impossible.

'Right,' I say. 'I'll do my best.'

He raises an eyebrow and looks down my top.

'Good,' he says. 'Otherwise I've got another story here that's right up your street. It's about a missing parrot.'

My first port of call is the obvious one: Jack's mobile. I'm not expecting much, given that every time I've tried him previously it's gone straight onto Messages – and now I know that he's in the middle of the desert, it's clear why. I think he's found the last place in the world where there isn't a mobile-phone mast in sight.

'Hi Jack,' I say, when I get his message service. 'I've known blokes to go to some lengths to avoid going on a date with me, but this is ridiculous.

'Er, seriously,' I continue lamely, like I've just told a joke no one laughed at, 'I've just seen you on TV and well, believe it or not, I'm covering this story for the *Echo* and I wondered if you'd be prepared to give me a ring about it. I'll understand if you don't want to – you're probably being bombarded with press enquiries at the moment. But if you were able to, I'd be really grateful.'

I'm about to say goodbye, but something makes me hesitate.

'Just one more thing,' I say, and wonder how I can best put this. 'I'm sure you're more than capable of handling yourself but, well . . . I just hope you're okay out there. Do me a favour and take care of yourself, won't you? Bye.'

I put the phone down and don't stop to think before I pick it up again.

'Who are you trying now?' asks Graham, sitting opposite me.

'Future for Africa's head office,' I say.

'Don't bother,' he replies. 'I've already done it. They're being completely unhelpful.'

I decide to give it a go anyway. Surely when I tell them I know Jack, it'll open some doors. When I get through to Future for Africa's offices, a woman with a youngish-sounding voice answers.

'Hi,' I say. 'I'm phoning from the *Daily Echo* and was just wondering who was handling your press enquiries over the Janet Harper kidnapping?'

'What is it you want to know?' she asks.

'Well,' I begin, 'given that Janet is originally from our patch, I was wondering if her family would be prepared to give us an interview.'

'Right,' says the voice at the other end. 'I'll have to pass it onto our Press Officer – I'm just taking messages. What was your name again?'

'Evie Hart,' I say. 'I'm from the *Daily Echo*.'

'Okay,' she says. 'Got it. I'll pass the message on.'

There is something about the tone in her voice that makes me think I'd have more success if I directed my press enquiries to Lassie.

'Hang on,' I say, ever hopeful. 'There's something else.'

'Yeah?' she says.

'I'm a friend of Jack Williamson, your Chief Executive,' I tell her.

There's a short silence.

'And?' says the woman at the other end of the phone.

'Er, right,' I say. 'Well, if he phones in, will you tell him I'd love to speak to him. My name is Evie Hart.'

'Yeah,' she says. 'You said.'

Chapter 75

Graham has already contacted the Foreign Office, the UN, the British Embassy and a handful of other aid agencies working in Darfur to try for new leads.

But he's facing the problem all journalists have to contend with these days: all anyone is giving us is a succession of uniformly bland press statements which manage to ramble on for 400 words and say precisely nothing. More importantly, there still isn't a sniff of a picture of Janet Harper.

'We need to get back to basics,' Graham decides.

'How do you mean?' I ask.

He picks up a phone book and throws it at me, coming alarmingly close to knocking me out.

'Oops, sorry,' he says. 'Now, come on, let's split the Harpers between us and phone them all.'

'But there are loads of them,' I object.

'I know,' he replies. 'We'd better get cracking.'

Just as I'm about to phone the first one, a new Foreign Office press release comes through and as I scan it, something immediately jumps out at me.

'Hang on, Graham,' I say. 'This may not have to be as laborious as we thought. Are there any Harpers in that phone book from Ormskirk? That's where the FO are now saying she's from.'

'Brilliant,' he says. 'Er, let's see . . . two of them. Let's give them a go.'

Excitedly, I phone the first number, while Graham takes the second. But after two minutes of it ringing out, I realise I'm not going to be in luck.

'No answer,' I tell him.

'Me neither,' he says. 'There's only one thing for it. We need to get out there.'

At the first address, the door is answered by an old lady with the most rampant facial hair I've seen outside Knowsley Safari Park.

'What do you want?' she shrieks, peering around the door.

'Sorry to bother you, but we're from the *Daily Echo*,' I tell her. 'We're looking for the family of Janet Harper. She lives in Africa now but was born in Ormskirk. I don't suppose you're any relation, are you?'

'What?' she shouts again, holding a hand up to her ear.

'*I said*, we're looking for Janet Harper,' I say, significantly louder. 'Do you know her?'

'I can't hear you,' she bawls. 'You're not from that Church of the Latterday Saints, are you? If you are, you can bugger off. I gave up on God when Robert Redford got married.'

'No,' I say, 'we're not,' and she appears to be able to lipread that much.

'Well, if you're conmen, I'm warning you – don't even try it. I can do self-defence. I'll have my fingers in your eye-sockets before you get a chance to scream for help.'

Suddenly something dawns on me.

'Is your hearing aid on?' I ask, pointing at my ear.

'What?' she hollers.

'YOUR HEARING AID?' I holler back.

A look of comprehension washes over her face, and she reaches behind her ear to fiddle with something.

'IS THAT ANY BETTER?' roars Graham, making me jump.

The old lady winces. 'There's no need to shout, for goodness' sake. What is it you want?'

'We're looking for Janet Harper,' I say. 'She lives in Africa.'

She shakes her head. 'My niece Janice lives in Aberdeen. Is she any good?'

Chapter 76

As we arrive at the next address, it is clear that this is the hot favourite. Because, sadly, we are not the first here – far from it, in fact. There are four journalists outside already and it's almost certain there will be more on the way.

'Any luck?' I ask Andrew Bright from the *Daily Mail*.

'Nah,' he says. 'Nobody's in there, but our news desk has told me to wait until they return.'

Which is, I fear, exactly what we'll be doing.

Twenty minutes later, I look at my watch and know that Graham's earlier version of the splash will have made it onto the front page of the *Echo*, with a few late lines added in by the news desk, but not a single exclusive revelation, and certainly not a picture or interview with the family.

I've missed the second edition, along with my (admittedly impossible) deadline. I know now that my only option is to get something mind-blowingly brilliant for tomorrow. Although, judging by the conversations outside the Harper family home, that's looking as unlikely for me as it is for everyone else.

Suddenly, my phone rings, and I'm on full alert. This could be Jack.

'Evie Hart,' I say, and am taken aback by the distinct ring of hopefulness-cum-desperation in my voice.

'Evie. You still outside that Harper house?'

Great. It's not the new love of my life, it's my least favourite News Editor.

'Yes,' I say. 'Although I was planning on leaving Graham here to head back to hit the phones again. No point in two of us being here.'

'You said it,' Simon says. 'Get your arse back here. You've wasted an entire bloody morning.'

I'm sitting in a taxi on my way back to the office when my phone rings again. I'm coming as fast as I can, but Simon obviously doesn't realise that the firm that runs our company taxi account isn't exactly famed for its sense of urgency.

'I'm on my way,' I say, as soon as I pick up the phone.

But there's no reply and the line goes dead. That man really is charm personified. We're still in month one of our professional relationship and already he's putting the phone down on me. When it rings again, I decide that maybe I should be more polite if we're ever going to start getting on with each other.

'Hi,' I say, but know I'd probably sound more pleased to be speaking to the clap doctor.

'Evie, is that you?'

I almost jump out of my seat.

'Jack! Bloody hell! Are you all right?'

'I'm fine,' he says, 'but this line is terrible and I've got to be quick. Listen, I'm so sorry about the weekend.'

'Don't worry,' I say. 'I can hardly be annoyed at someone who's jetted across the world to rescue hostages.'

'I'm not sure I was that heroic,' he says. 'Look – I'm due

back the day after tomorrow. I'll phone you then, if that's okay. And in the meantime, I really am sorry. If there's anything I can do to make it up to you, let me know.'

'Now you mention it,' I say, 'there is something you could do for me.'

Chapter 77

The minute the *Daily Echo* hits the streets at 11 a.m. next day – and my story takes its place as the lead item on our website – every national newspaper in the country seems to be on the phone seeking a copy of the picture of Janet Harper. The chat with the family is also widely sought after, but it's my interview with Janet herself – conducted on Jack's mobile from her hospital bed – which has got everyone the most excited.

Everyone, that is, apart from Simon, who couldn't have been more begrudging in his praise if somebody had been holding a gun to his head. Not that that matters. The Editor himself sent one of his famed 'hero-gram' emails around the newsroom, telling everyone how great they'd done on that day's paper. And he singled *me* out in it. *Particular thanks go to Evie Hart* it said, *who has proved in spectacular style just what hard work, determination and brilliant contacts can do. Well done, Evie.*

Janet was lovely when I spoke to her, and has agreed to do a follow-up interview with me when she returns home in a couple of weeks.

She was also full of praise for Jack.

'There is no way the Foreign Office would have jumped into gear that fast if Jack hadn't been on their back from the word go,' she said. 'He really is wonderful.'

Chapter 78

Alma de Cuba, Liverpool city centre

Seeing Jack prompts the most unusual physical reactions in me. I'm talking the sort of symptoms for which other people might seek a doctor's appointment: churning stomach, racing pulse, raised temperature, that sort of thing. I could, in fact, quite feasibly be diagnosed with the early stages of malaria.

I'm pretty certain I haven't got malaria, though. I'm pretty certain that what I've got is . . . well, I'm trying not to get ahead of myself. But as I sit opposite Jack, in one of Liverpool city centre's trendiest bars on an unusually balmy April evening, it's difficult.

His skin is a shade darker after Sudan and his hair has been cut into a style which, on anyone else, would look boyish. But boyish is still the last word you'd use about Jack. He might be a sensitive soul who reads excessively and helps people in poor countries, but to look at he's 100 per cent alpha male – and has the biceps to prove it.

'So, I helped then?' he asks.

'Very much so,' I say. 'I suspect if you hadn't spoken to

Janet Harper for me I might have been begging for a trainee-ship to serve burgers somewhere by now.'

He smirks.

'I'm exaggerating about that, by the way,' I add. 'I owe you one, but I'm not going to be forever indebted to you, so don't get any ideas.'

'That's a shame,' he says. 'I'd have enjoyed thinking of ways for you to repay me.'

It's a week later than originally planned, but Jack and I have finally managed to get together and now I'm sitting opposite him, I have all the composure of a giggly schoolgirl on a date with Justin Timberlake.

The reason, I suspect, is that there are no speeches to interrupt us now. No wedding cake to be cut. No bridesmaids looking for spare tampons. This is just Jack and me.

'Do you want another drink?' he asks.

'Please,' I say, draining my glass.

He picks up the cocktail menu. 'Well, you can have a Singapore Sling, Mai Thai, Sea Breeze, Cosmopolitan, Daiquiri, Cuba Libre, Long Island Ice Tea, Klondike Cooler or indeed, any exotic combination of fruit and alcohol you want.'

'I'll have a beer,' I say.

He goes to order, but then hesitates. 'You don't fancy going somewhere a bit less . . . fancy?' he asks.

As we walk out into the street, where throngs of people are making their way from bar to bar, Jack takes my hand and I huddle up to him as if to keep warm – despite the fact that I'm actually perfectly cosy already.

In recent years, the city centre has been overtaken by lots of hip bars featuring painfully fashionable clientele and not a packet of pork scratchings in sight. Tonight we're in the mood for something different, something simpler, and as we reach a familiar door I know exactly what it is.

'The Jacaranda!' I exclaim, pulling Jack towards the bar. 'I haven't been here for years.'

'Me neither,' he smiles. 'And for good reason.'

'You mean you're not a fan of the open mike?' I ask.

'You wouldn't get me up there for a night with Elle Macpherson.'

I frown.

'Okay, a week,' he says.

As we enter the bar, we are struck by a combination of heat, noise and a heady perfume of booze and sweat. This is a bar where people know how to enjoy themselves. It isn't a bar for posing, or picking up, but it is a bar where you can drink old-fashioned booze (the kind in a pint glass) and, if the mood takes you, do the thing this place is best known for: sing.

Tonight at the Jacaranda is open mike night, which basically means karaoke with taste, in theory at least. This isn't 'Like a Virgin' territory, this is for serious musicians or those who fancy themselves as such.

As for why I like it so much, well, I have a confession to make. I used to come here to sing too. In those days, when I was at university, I fancied myself as a musician too, although I was never really a serious one. I always knew my days as the lead singer of Bubblegum Vamp (a name which I despised for the entire two and a half years of our existence) would eventually peter out when I got a proper job.

Anyway, these days, the only exercise my vocal cords get is singing in the shower and occasionally in the car, although I do less of that since I noticed the looks I attracted from other drivers. Grace saw me at some traffic lights belting out

'Suspicious Minds' once and told me afterwards that I looked as if I was having a fit.

'This brings back memories,' I say, as we dive towards two stools at the bar when a couple stand up to leave.

'You're not a singer, are you?' Jack asks.

'Don't sound so surprised,' I say. 'As a matter of fact, I used to be in a band. A long time ago, admittedly. Nirvana were in the charts at the time. God, I feel old.'

'So, are you having a go tonight?' he enquires, clearly with some degree of amusement.

'No *way*,' I shake my head vigorously. 'It's been forever since I sang in public.'

'Well, then,' he says, 'I'd say it's about time you gave it a go again.'

'I don't think so.'

'Oh, go on.'

'Believe me,' I reply. 'I'd only embarrass you.'

'You won't embarrass me,' he says. 'If you're crap I'll just pretend I don't know you.'

Chapter 79

Oh God. What am I doing?

I've sung in front of all sorts of audiences: parents and teachers at school, students at university, and many a time in front of the crowd in this place too. But after an hour of Jack attempting to persuade me to do this – and eventually succeeding – I suddenly feel desperately nervous.

My palms are unpleasantly clammy, my stomach feels very like it does after a dodgy curry and, now I'm up here, all I can think about is what on earth possessed me to agree to this. Okay, the glass of wine and two bottles of beer probably had something to do with it.

At least the band are pretty good, so much so that I'm amazed they agreed to get up here with me. I only knew the bass guitar vaguely back in my Bubblegum Vamp days after I went out with one of his friends (for four days – a particularly low point in my commitment problem).

As the opening bars begin, I realise immediately that the song I've chosen is all wrong. I saw Ruby Turner sing 'Nobody But You' live on Jools Holland's show years ago and fell in love with it immediately. But I should have remembered one of the fundamental principles of singing in public: no one should attempt to emulate Ruby Turner unless they're Ruby Turner.

A spotlight suddenly shines in my eyes and I wonder if everyone in the audience is aware, as I am, of the bead of sweat moving slowly down my forehead.

Too late to worry about it now. I take a deep breath, and the second I start singing those beautiful words, my anxiety disappears. Because, unbelievably, I actually sound half-decent.

'*No-one ever gave me anything . . .*' I lament.

I glance up and realise that people are looking up at me – and in such a way that they appear to want to listen too. I close my eyes and imagine myself singing in the bathroom, with no inhibitions, no audience, only a crackly radio and a load of empty conditioner bottles to keep me company.

It may be misguided, but I suddenly have complete and utter confidence that I sound good. No, forget good, I sound bloody *great*!

'*No one ever held my hand . . .*' I croon.

I look over at the bass player and he nods his approval. I am still nervous, but I feel on top of the world.

'*Nobody. Nobody but you.*'

My eyes fix on Jack as I sing to him with all my heart and soul. But as I'm about to start on the second verse, someone else catches my eye. Someone at the front. Someone waving.

Oh my God.

Oh fucking hell.

It can't be.

It bloody can.

It's Gareth.

Uh-oh. That last line was wonky as hell.

'*Every time that I felt lost . . .*'

Oh shit, shit, shit. Even wonkier.

I'm trying desperately to concentrate, but I can't keep my attention on anything other than Gareth, whose smiling expression suddenly bears a distinct resemblance to Jack Nicholson's in the final scenes of *The Shining*.

I'm trying my very best to sound soft and husky, but now I just sound like I've got a cold. And as people start to turn away, I look over once again to the bass player for some moral support. This time, he avoids making eye-contact, obviously wishing that he was with someone with more vocal ability. Like the Cheeky Girls, for example.

Gareth is now right at the front of the crowd and is the only person in the room swaying in time to the music, his eyes glued on me. I glance anxiously at Jack, on the far side of the room. When he sees me, he smiles encouragingly. For some reason it brings to mind the expression of my Sunday School teacher after I broke wind conspicuously in the middle of a nativity play when I was six. Even at that age, I was painfully aware that the Virgin Mary was simply not supposed to fart – at least not publicly – and no matter how sympathetic my teacher looked, my humiliation wasn't going to just go away.

As the song reaches a crescendo, I close my eyes, desperate to block out any sight of Gareth and determined that, as I reach the final, most difficult line, I'm going to give it everything I've got.

'*No . . . body . . . but . . . YOUUUUU!*'

I gave it all I've got all right.

Shame I sounded like a chicken being slaughtered.

Chapter 80

My hands shaking, I put the mike back into its stand and make my way down the steps of the stage. The applause consists solely of an embarrassed smattering – with the exception of Gareth, who is cheering me on at the front as if he's just seen Shania Twain on the final date of a world arena tour.

As I reach the bottom step, my head is swirling with all manner of thoughts: how I'm going to get past Gareth, how I'm going to get Jack out of here, and not least how I'm going to live down a performance that, a couple of centuries ago, would have been a hanging offence.

With all these matters spinning around my mind, I seem to be incapable of taking on another one: the small matter of placing one foot firmly on the ground in front of the other. Instead of gliding off the bottom step and into the arms of my adoring date, as I'd hoped when I first got up to sing, I make the sort of manoeuvre that you might expect from a knock-kneed ostrich after an alcopop overdose.

Gareth dives out of the way as my legs twist around each other and the ground hurtles towards me – until I am face down on the floor with two prawn cocktail crisps and a Budweiser bottle top stuck to my cheek.

'Evie, are you all right?!' shouts Gareth dramatically as he helps me up.

'Fine,' I tell him, brushing myself down. Nothing is broken – except my pride – although as Jack is getting the next round of drinks in at the bar, at least he didn't appear to see my fall.

'You were amazing,' Gareth breathes.

'No, I wasn't,' I say, thinking I'd have preferred him to have tried to break my fall instead of trying to flatter me now.

'Evie, you *were*,' he insists, and I notice that the rash he had last time I saw him has spread faster than a fire in an oil refinery.

'Your voice is a real classic,' he goes on. 'Very Geri Halliwell.'

'Oh, er, well, thanks,' I say. 'Anyway, I must run.'

'I've been meaning to give you a ring,' he continues.

'Right,' I say. 'Why's that?'

'Because I've been thinking a lot . . . *about us.*'

Oh God.

'Gareth, you were thinking a lot – *about us* – the last time I saw you,' I say. 'All this thinking will make your nose bleed if you're not careful.'

'Well, anyway,' he says, ignoring this, 'I know we talked about this commitment problem you have . . .'

Not any more I don't.

'And how I feel I can help you get over it . . .'

No, thanks.

'And, well, I know what you said last time . . .'

I couldn't have been clearer, as I remember.

'But the upshot is . . .'

'Yes, Gareth?' I ask politely, trying not to reveal that I'm starting to find this as irritating as chronic athlete's foot.

'Evie,' he says generously, 'I'm willing to give you a second chance.'

Chapter 81

There is a slight pause as I try to work out whether I have heard Gareth correctly.

'You're *what?*' I ask finally.

'I said I'm willing to give you a second chance,' he repeats, looking immensely pleased with himself. 'I've come to the conclusion that nobody is perfect and that your emotional detachment from just about anything or anyone is something we can work through *as a couple.*'

I don't know whether to lose my temper with him or run for my life. Aware that Jack is on the other side of the room, however, I do neither, and keep my voice on a level as I say, 'Gareth, we no longer *are* a couple.'

He pulls a face. 'Evie, I *know* that. And there's no need to speak to me like I'm some sort of psycho, either. I'm not. I'm just a normal guy who likes you and wants to make a go of it with you.'

'I know you're not a psycho,' I say, although now he mentions it, Norman Bates does seem like a more attractive proposition at the moment.

'Gareth, look,' I continue, aware that I've got to get back to Jack. 'I know it may look like I keep trying to avoid you, but I'm truly not. I just really have got to go.'

He lets out a long sigh.

'I tell you what,' I add, thinking of the only thing that might appease him, 'I'll give you a ring next week and we can talk about it then, okay?'

'I'd like that, Evie,' he says, nodding.

'I'll see you then,' I say, about to finally make my exit.

He grabs me by the arm. 'Before you go,' he says, 'I want you to have something.'

'What?' My mind flashes back to the last parcel he decided to give me in public.

'Don't look so suspicious,' he chides me. 'Just take it, please. As a present. From me.'

He hands me a little box wrapped up in silver paper and a shocking pink ribbon. I start shaking my head. I have no idea what this is, but accepting any gifts from Gareth at the moment feels dodgier than a cupboard full of porn in a Church of England vicar's garage.

'I can't accept this,' I say, and I have never meant anything more in my life.

'You can, Evie. *Please*,' he says. 'It's the earrings you wanted. You saw them when we were out together once and I remember you saying how much you liked them. I was going to buy them for you for Grace's wedding, but then you dumped me.'

I feel a stab of guilt.

'Gareth, that really is lovely of you,' I say, 'but I mean it, I just don't think it's . . . appropriate.'

'You can be so cold,' he says, narrowing his eyes.

For someone supposedly in love with me, Gareth is very good at his put-downs.

'Look, I'm sorry, but I don't want this.' Feeling terrible, I hand the box back.

But he doesn't take it from me; he just turns around and starts walking away.

'Sorry, Evie,' he says, with an expression about as genuine as a runner-up at the Oscars. 'I've really, really got to go now.'

And before I know it, he's gone. Buggered off before I get a chance to say or do anything.

Cheeky sod. That's *my* trick.

Chapter 82

'Are you sure everything's okay?' asks Jack as we jump into the back of a taxi.

'Fine. Honestly, I think I've just had a bit too much,' I say, crossing my eyes to emphasize how drunk I am and immediately realising how completely and utterly unsexy I must look.

'Lightweight,' he grins. 'Well, I thought you were incredibly brave anyway, getting up to sing like that.'

'Yeah,' I say. 'You'd have to be either brave or stupid to get up and give a performance like that.'

'Seriously,' he goes on. 'I mean, there is no way in a million years you'd ever get me up to do it.'

'Really?'

'Really. People think it's a tom cat fighting when I sing. I've never even done karaoke. In fact, I mime the hymns at weddings.'

'Ah, well, I wouldn't know that, would I?' I say. 'I'm always at the front with a bouquet in my hand. Anyway, you should try it one day – you might enjoy it.'

'Evie, I may like you enough to be persuaded to do a lot of things by you, but you will *never, ever* get me to sing in public.'

'What a spoilsport,' I sigh. 'And after I've just been through all that.'

His hand suddenly finds mine and he looks into my eyes as he slowly pulls me closer towards him. His face is an inch away from mine and I can feel his soft breath on my skin. Our lips meet, and as we begin to kiss in the darkness of the taxi, it almost takes my breath away.

Grace once told me that she and Patrick almost had sex in the back of a taxi. What constitutes 'almost', I'm not exactly sure, but I bet it's not something they get up to very often these days. The thought has popped into my head because our kissing, somewhere along the way, becomes rather more passionate than might be considered fitting under these circumstances.

Our bodies are pressing against each other's, and the fact that this is going on as quietly as possible so as not to attract the attention of the driver is only serving to make my pulse beat even faster.

Jack's hand is on my leg, and as he moves it slowly upwards, my skirt begins to gather on my thigh. I can tell from the way his kissing has slowed down that he is trying to work out whether I'm happy about it or not. So I kiss him in a way that leaves him in no doubt.

'Is it quicker going around the park?' the driver shouts into the back, and Jack and I jump apart.

'Er, yeah, that's probably the best way,' says Jack. We look at each other and smile conspiratorially.

The taxi trundles along for a couple of seconds, before Jack moves towards me again so I can just see his features lit up by the orange flicker of streetlights. His lips brush against my ear and send a shiver of electricity through me.

'Only someone I had in the back last week wanted me to go down the Dock Road,' says the taxi driver, and we jump apart again, stifling giggles.

'I think you're definitely right on that one,' says Jack.

'Well, that's what I thought,' says the driver. 'I get all sorts in the back of here, you wouldn't believe it.'

He proceeds to tell us a story about a woman whose King Charles spaniel went into labour in the back of his cab while he was trying to struggle through a mile and a half of roadworks on Smithdown Road. Jack leans over again, but not to kiss me this time. Holding my hand, he puts his mouth next to my ear.

'You haven't got away that easily,' he whispers.

I turn and kiss him briefly on the lips.

'Good,' I whisper back.

Chapter 83

Green's Gym, Liverpool, 13 May

'Hey, Charlotte!' someone shouts as we're heading into the gym.

Charlotte and I turn around and one of the instructors is jogging towards us, clutching a pile of leaflets. He's one of those annoyingly athletic people who never seem to just walk, but instead move from place to place with a permanent Anneka Rice-style skip.

'Oh, hello, Shaun,' says Charlotte brightly.

Six months ago, the idea of Charlotte being on first-name terms with a gym instructor would have been unthinkable. Now they're all practically her best friends.

'I tried to catch up with you yesterday but couldn't find you,' he says. 'You're not slipping, are you?'

'I just had a dental appointment, that's all,' she explains. 'I've been every day this week, apart from yesterday.'

'Don't worry, I was only kidding – I've seen how often you're here,' he replies. 'And it's obviously working. You look brilliant – a walking advert for this place. Anyway, the reason I was looking for you was that I'm organizing a charity challenge for next year. I'm trying to get a group of people together to do a bike ride across the Atlas Mountains.'

Charlotte is completely taken aback, but he misinterprets her look.

'No, I didn't know where they were either,' he says. 'Morocco, apparently. Anyway, the point is, it'll be great fun and we can raise money for charity. Have a think about it, won't you?'

'Er, okay,' she says. 'I will.'

As Shaun and his impossibly toned legs skip off again into the men's changing room, I turn to Charlotte.

'Do I not exist or something?' I say. 'Don't *I* look capable of cycling in the Atlas Mountains?'

She shrugs apologetically. 'I think it might just be the regulars they're asking to join them,' she says.

'Hmm. I suppose I haven't been for a while, have I?'

She smiles. 'I think that's what happens when you find someone you want to spend every minute of the day with,' she says.

'Is it that obvious?' I feel a flash of blissful Jack-induced happiness, combined with a very definite undercurrent of guilt. I know I've been neglecting Charlotte. And Grace, for that matter. Valentina I haven't seen for ages – although she does have her own blossoming romance (for that read 'shag-athon') with Edmund Barnett.

'So, Charlotte,' I say. 'Bike riding across the Atlas Mountains. Are you going to do it?'

'Do you know,' she says, 'I just might. It can't be any harder than shifting all this weight.'

'And, God, you're doing that all right,' I say.

In the ladies' changing rooms just how much Charlotte is

doing that becomes immediately apparent. As she gets undressed, this time, she no longer hides behind her big family-sized beach towels. She happily walks around in her underwear, which is now lacy and fashionable. In fact, it couldn't look less like the granny pants she used to wear – pants I dare say she'd have burned by now except for the fire hazard all that polyester must represent.

It's not just her underwear though. Charlotte now owns an item of clothing she has coveted for her entire life in the same way that other people covet Gucci jeans. A trouser suit from Next.

Okay, so it's not exactly what *Vogue* is tipping as the fashion item of the season. But it represents something crucially important for Charlotte. Because, for the first time ever, she doesn't have to go into one of those specialist outlets with euphemistic titles like *Ladywear Plus* or *Big and Beautiful*. She can just stroll down the high street, walk into any bog-standard store, and buy a suit – in a size 14. And a comfortable size 14 too.

'How much did you lose this week?' I ask.

'Another five pounds,' she says, glowing. 'Everyone warned me that the weight loss would start slowing down soon, but that just hasn't happened. It seems to be falling off now.'

It's funny, but knowing that she's another five pounds lighter makes Charlotte run faster on the treadmill. She presses the buttons until she gets to 9km an hour and is striding away on it, unafraid any more that the people behind are getting an eyeful of her backside.

As I look up into the mirror in front of me, a familiar face walks through the door and I turn to Charlotte in amazement.

'Is that Jim who's just come in?' I whisper.

She nods. 'He joined shortly after Georgia's wedding,' she says. 'I recommended the place to him. He doesn't come as often as I do though.'

'No one does,' I point out.

'Hello, you two,' says Jim, approaching us. 'How are you, Evie?'

'Brilliant,' I say, still taken aback to see him. 'You?'

'Yeah, great,' he says. 'I'm starting to think you live here, Charlotte. You seem to be on that treadmill every time I walk through the door.'

She presses a couple of buttons on the machine and slows it down to a gentle walk.

'I promise you I do go home at night,' she says, breathless. 'Although they have to throw me out sometimes.'

'Well, you put me to shame, you really do,' he says. 'I tell myself every Sunday night I'll come here a minimum of three times in the following week, but I've not hit that target once yet. I enjoy the pub after work too much.'

Charlotte giggles and it suddenly strikes me that she hasn't blushed at all since this conversation began. Okay, so she's flushed from her run anyway so you probably wouldn't be able to tell, but still . . .

'Speaking of the pub,' says Jim, 'I don't suppose . . . well, I don't suppose I could tempt you to come with me one night, could I?'

She hesitates.

'Oh, it doesn't have to be the pub, it could be anywhere you like,' he says. 'The pictures, a restaurant – whatever you want, really.'

'Yes,' she says. 'That would definitely be nice.'

'Great.' He looks pleased.

I knew it. I bloody knew it. I was right all along. Charlotte and Jim, together at last. I feel like bursting with pride.

'Only, I'm really busy over the next couple of weeks,' continues Charlotte, as my smile suddenly dissolves. 'What with the wedding and everything – there's only three or four weeks to go until that. And I've got a lot on at work. But some time we'll do it, yes. Definitely, some time.'

Jim smiles softly but he obviously knows what she's trying to say.

'I'm not trying to give you the brush-off,' she adds.

But that's exactly what she's trying to do. And all three of us know it.

Chapter 84

Jack's apartment, Friday, 18 May

A funny thing happened last night. Jack and I have been going out together an average of about five times a week since Georgia's wedding and, while the general state of euphoria I'm in at the moment is in many ways priceless, it is not having a positive effect on my bank balance.

'Let's just stay in then,' Jack said. 'We can get a DVD out and cuddle up on the sofa. If you're okay with that.'

'Fantastic,' I said. And, bizarrely, I meant it.

Before now, it was exactly this sort of thing which counted as one of my 'triggers': those little things which might seem perfectly innocuous to a bystander but were enough to make me start plotting my bid for freedom with all the determination of an Alcatraz prisoner.

I had loads of these triggers. From the sight of someone's socks in my washing basket to the suggestion of dinner with the parents, anything that could reasonably be deemed 'coupley' was enough to make me run for the hills. But apparently, as of last night, staying in to watch a DVD is a prospect I consider to be more exciting than a movie première with Brad Pitt on my arm.

Even more weirdly, it actually lived up to expectations. I loved eating the dinner Jack had cooked for me, I loved watching the crap film we'd rented, and I loved cuddling up on the sofa. No, I *really* loved cuddling up on the sofa.

There was, in fact, only one downer on the whole evening – something I can't quite get out of my mind, even now. Jack went to the bathroom and while he was out of the room, his mobile started ringing. I was about to answer it for him, when I saw the name flashing up on the screen. *Beth*. My eyes widened in shock as I sat there, letting it ring, wondering what the hell to do. It rang off as he was walking back into the room.

'Er, you just m-missed a call,' I told him, stuttering.

'Right,' he said, looking at the phone's screen. 'Thanks.'

I scrutinized his expression, but he wasn't giving anything away.

'Aren't you going to phone them back?' I asked as casually as possible.

'They'll leave a message if it's important,' he shrugged, equally casually.

I was about to ask if it was anyone I knew – just to test whether he would try to pretend it was someone else – when I stopped myself. There could be a perfectly innocent explanation. In fact, I was sure there would be. So I couldn't just go launching into a full-scale interrogation. Relationships are about trust, or so every magazine I've ever read in every hairdressers I've ever been to has told me. So I need to trust him. Definitely.

But what if he's a complete and utter two-timing cad? And I'm falling for him? Oh God. Oh bugger. Argghhh!

In the event, I kept my mouth shut and didn't ask any

more questions. Partly to avoid Jack thinking I'm a jealous control freak who doesn't want him even speaking to other women. But also because I didn't want to know the answers.

Tonight, I ring the doorbell to Jack's flat at seven having shaved my legs again (they haven't been this smooth for such a sustained period since I was three months old) and put on just enough make-up to cover any blemishes but not so much that I look over the top for an evening in front of the telly.

He answers the door wearing jeans and a T-shirt which shows off the definition in his arms to such an off-putting degree I know immediately I won't be able to concentrate on anything else tonight.

'Come in,' he says, taking off my coat as I am enveloped in a fantastic aroma, which for once isn't coming from him.

'You do like Thai food, don't you?' he says as we go through to the kitchen so he can stir his sauce.

'Love it,' I say.

Then somehow, and I honestly don't know how, something happens which brings our conversation to an immediate end. It might be the spices invading our senses or, more probably, the simple fact that this has been building up for weeks. Whatever it is, within seconds of my arrival Jack and I are in each other's arms, kissing – no, not kissing, *devouring* – each other.

With our mouths exploring each other's and his body pressing hard against mine, we stumble across the room until we find ourselves next to the breakfast bar. Jack lifts me up onto a stool, kissing every inch of my collarbone as I wrap my legs around his waist. Something takes over me as I grab his T-shirt and, determinedly, lift it over his head to expose the smooth, toned muscles of his torso.

Item by item, we undress each other until we are both almost naked, Jack is inside me and we are swept away in a bliss I can confidently say I have simply never experienced before.

The Thai red curry frantically boils over and the rice turns into mush. Dinner is certain to be inedible.

But, quite frankly, neither of us care.

Chapter 85

My flat, Monday, 21 May

We didn't move from Jack's flat for two full days. Honestly, I was waiting for the Missing Persons Bureau to turn up after an intensive forty-eight-hour search, only to find us lazing about in bed having survived on nothing but toast, black coffee and a healthy helping of lust.

Tonight, I've been on a late shift at work and so we've agreed we won't see each other until tomorrow. Apart from anything else, there is a big part of me that thinks I really ought to spend a night by myself just to prove I can do it without pining for him.

At least, that was the theory. It's now almost 10 p.m. and as I open the door to my flat and flop in front of the television, the news is on and I wonder if he's watching it too. I immediately shake the thought out of my head. I am getting concerned that I'm becoming a bit pathetic now.

Tonight, when I was covering a story about a protest by fox-hunters, it made me wonder where Jack stood on animal rights. When I went to the ladies and looked in the mirror, it made me think about him kissing my forehead last night. I even found myself doodling his name on my shorthand pad when I was meant to be taking down some quotes from a local councillor. The last time I did that with a boy's name, Duran Duran were in the charts. In short, I've been thinking about Jack Williamson more or less constantly.

But it's not all been good. Because at the back of my mind I still can't shake the nagging feeling I have about that phone call from Beth. Should I challenge him about it? Or would that make him run a mile? I'm thinking about this very issue – again – when my mobile rings.

'Just thought I'd phone to see how your evening was,' says Jack.

Despite what was going through my mind a second ago, the sound of his voice makes me smile. In fact, it makes me smile so widely, I know I couldn't look more uncool if I was wearing Clark Kent's glasses.

'Oh, fabulous,' I tell him. 'I had a succession of nutters on the phone. One wanted me to do a story about him being ripped off by a guy who'd sold him some dodgy cannabis.'

Jack laughs. 'What did you tell him?'

'I advised him to contact Trading Standards,' I say. 'What about your night?'

'Nothing like as exciting,' he says. 'I was torn between catching up with a load of work, fixing the skirting board in the living room and watching repeats of M.A.S.H. on satellite.'

'It'd have been Hot Lips Houlihan all the way for me,' I say.

'Yeah, well, she pretty much won the day,' he agrees. 'But I have to say, I had a much better night last night.'

I smile again, this time from ear to ear.

'Me too,' I purr. 'In fact, if you don't think it's too forward, I'd like to do it again some time.'

'I *do* think it's forward,' he tells me, 'and I'm very glad you'd like to do it again some time, because as far as I'm concerned, you can do so as often as you want.'

'Ah, but will I get breakfast in bed every time?' I say.

'Is that all you want me for?' he asks, sounding hurt.

'Hmm, that and your body,' I tell him.

By the time the conversation ends an hour and a half later and I'm climbing into bed, I have to force myself to think about some of the other things I'm meant to be thinking about at the moment. Benno, aka my pal DI Gregg Benson, and his story about Pete Gibson's goings-on (which I'm still plugging away at), Polly's fifth birthday next week, my mother's wedding . . . Oh God, yes – my mother's wedding!

Only three weeks to go, and while she's sorted out a woman to dye her headdress and someone to apply her henna tattoos, there are still other matters she's 'working on'.

Like invitations. And transport. And music.

Why do I think I'd be better relying on a three-year-old to organize this wedding?

Chapter 86

My mum's house, Scarisbrick, Lancashire, Friday, 8 June

I answer the door to Valentina, who is grinning madly and carrying a suitcase so big that if it had wheels you'd call it a caravan.

'Are you embarking on a round-the-world trip or something?' I ask, grabbing the handle of her case to help her hoist it up the stairs.

'If you're referring to my case,' she says, 'I promise you Harvey Nicks have some far less modest ones.'

'You don't have to justify yourself to me,' I tell her.

'I'm aware of that,' she says, uncharacteristically chirpily, 'but just for the record, I have got both myself and Charlotte to attend to today, which means I had to bring double the amount of cosmetics. We have completely different skin tones.'

I study her expression for a second.

'Is everything all right?' I ask. I've never seen Valentina smiling quite so broadly before, largely because she's worried about triggering the onset of premature wrinkles.

'Oh yes,' she replies mysteriously. 'Oh yes indeed.'

We finally get up to my mother's bedroom which, with its riot of batiks and ethnic throws, looks like a cross between a charity shop and an opium den. The overall feel of the place is shabby chic without the chic. And with six people crammed into it, it's also already starting to feel a little bit claustrophobic.

'Valentina! Lovely to see you!' says my mum, kissing her on the cheek.

Mum has spent all morning in her dressing-gown, with her red hair pinned up in tight kiss curls, which I strongly suspect are going to make her look like a Muppet when they come out.

'Thank you, Sarah,' beams Valentina. 'And how are you today? Nervous?'

'Oh no,' says Mum. 'I don't tend to get nervous. I've done too much yoga over the years – I think nervousness is beyond me.'

'All that dope you smoked in the seventies probably helped too,' I put in.

The doorbell rings again and Valentina jauntily offers to go and get it, although she's probably glad to get away from all the joss sticks, which must be clashing dreadfully with her DKNY Be Delicious perfume.

It's Charlotte, Grace and Gloria Flowerdew, my mum's friend and another of her many bridesmaids, wearing her trademark dungarees. What with my two younger cousins, Deborah and Jasmine, as well as Denise – who works on reception at the place where my mum teaches yoga – the number of people in the room is now starting to give it the air of a third-world bazaar.

'Right, Charlotte,' says Valentina, guiding her over to the edge of the bed. 'How shall we do your make-up today?'

'Oh, er, I don't mind,' says Charlotte. 'You always do it nicely. Just do what you think.'

'Right,' says Valentina, looking for some reason as if this wasn't the response she was expecting.

'What do you think, Grace?' she adds, tilting Charlotte's chin upwards. 'I reckon some soft apricot swept across her eyelids would really bring out her colouring, don't you?'

Grace, who is rummaging around in her handbag, looks up momentarily.

'Definitely,' she says, before going back to trying to locate her mobile.

Having grinned more than the average Cheshire cat since she got here, Valentina, for some reason, is starting to look unhappy. This time, she turns to me as I'm putting my own make-up on in the mirror.

'Evie,' she says, 'those colours you're using might be nice for Charlotte too. What do you think?'

Then she does the weirdest thing. She places both hands on my shoulders and leans down to look at me in the mirror as she's talking. It's the sort of chummy physical contact you might expect between two pals in their third year at Mallory Towers. From Valentina it's as suspicious as a brown parcel making a ticking noise.

'I'm sure you're a far better judge of these sorts of things,' I tell her.

She pulls away and crosses her arms, now looking really annoyed.

'What's the matter?' I ask. 'There is something the matter, isn't there?'

'Well, now you mention it, yes,' she says.

'Well, come on then, spit it out.'

'*This!*' she squeals, thrusting her left hand in front of my face, as the room falls silent.

On the third finger along she is wearing a diamond ring. No, not just any old diamond ring.

This diamond ring is so big you could use it as a paper-weight.

Chapter 87

'Bloody hell!' comes a cry from the other side of the room.

It's Denise, and she is rushing towards us. Grabbing Valentina's hand, she examines the ring while Valentina at last looks mildly satisfied.

'I was going to get one of those!' exclaims Denise in the sort of tones that make Coleen McLoughlin sound as if she's had a lifetime of elocution lessons.

Valentina's face drops. 'I don't think you were,' she says snootily, turning her nose up.

'I *was*,' insists Denise.

'No,' insists Valentina back, snatching her hand away. 'No, you weren't.'

'Honestly,' continues Denise innocently, 'it's *Diamontique*, isn't it? They had them on that shopping channel last week. They are *gorgeous*. You lucky thing.'

Valentina looks as if she's going to faint.

'Would you like to sit down?' asks Charlotte diplomatically.

Our friend dramatically perches herself on the edge of my mother's bed, the back of her hand on her brow.

'This is *not*, I repeat, *not Diamon*-whatever,' she says firmly.

'*Diamontique*,' corrects Denise, clearly oblivious to the distress she's managing to elicit.

'This,' stresses Valentina, 'is a genuine five-carat diamond, perfectly cut and one of a kind. Master craftsmen have toiled away for months to create the most beautiful, the most unique and the most perfect engagement ring anyone could ever hope to find. *And more importantly, it cost a bloody arm and a leg!*'

Poor Denise is finally silenced.

'You're *engaged*?' asks Grace, incredulous.

'Is that so hard to believe?' Valentina sounds slightly hysterical now.

'Yes – I mean *no*,' Grace flusters. 'What I mean is, you've only known Edmund for a matter of weeks, haven't you? Isn't it a little soon?'

'We're *in love*,' growls Valentina.

Charlotte leans down to give her a hug.

'Well, I'm delighted for you,' she says simply. 'You deserve it, Valentina.'

This, for some reason, seems to snap everyone into action and they all start fussing and congratulating her. When it dies and people begin to concentrate on their curlers and mascara again, I go over to Valentina.

'Well done,' I say. 'It's fantastic news, brilliant. So when did he ask you to marry him?'

'Oh, yesterday,' she says. 'It was *very* romantic.'

'Did he get down on one knee?'

'Between you and me, not exactly,' she whispers. 'We were in the middle of a particularly athletic technique I'd read about in *Cosmopolitan* at the time. But then I can't complain. I was only expecting a multiple orgasm from it and ended up with a fiancé. What more could a girl ask for, from a quiet night in?"

Chapter 88

I think the others first started to wonder about the nature of this wedding when my mother announced that we were all to just bring our own bridesmaid dresses. There were no fittings, no months of wading through bridal magazines, nothing more in fact than a simple instruction: wear purple – if you like.

I warned Mum at first that there were so many of us, we were in danger of looking like a walking bunch of grapes. But it's only now we're all here that I realize just how many shades of purple actually exist. In fact, we are a veritable rainbow of colours, ranging from Avon Lady pink to the sort of maroon you'd find on the upholstery of a 1982 Cortina.

Still, some of us don't look half-bad.

There was something about Jack being here today as my official steady boyfriend that prompted me to make what Valentina referred to in amazement as 'an effort'. I'm talking manicure, hair done by a half-decent stylist and a dress that has sent my overdraft into freefall.

Charlotte, meanwhile, is also a revelation in the dress – *the size 12 dress* – I helped pick out with her. Grace looks nice, if slightly dishevelled because she was in such a rush this morning. Although she's not pleased that Valentina has spent all morning offering her Eye Rescue Treatment.

Valentina is sporting her usual look – footballer's wife meets high-class call girl – and is already dazzling everyone in sight with the blingiest ring outside a P Diddy video.

That said, given this event involves my mum's friends too, I can't say with any conviction that the standard of dress here today is averagely high. From Gloria with her 1970s maternity smock to Penelope with her culottes, if the fashion police turned up today, some of this lot wouldn't just be convicted, they'd end up on Death Row.

Still, nobody will be surprised about this when they see what the bride herself is wearing. As we reach the front of the register office, I sit down with the other bridesmaids and the guests have the opportunity to see Mum's wedding dress in all its glory.

Bob turns towards her and smiles as if she is the most beautiful person in the world. I've always known he was slightly mad and this has just confirmed it. Because everybody else just gasps.

The most striking element of the bride's dress is that it is green and when I say green, I mean she could start traffic with it. As for the design, the bottom half is fine – full-length, swirly – but the top has a peculiar neckline that involves both a halter neck – an alarmingly low-cut halter neck – *and* collars. It is the sort of thing Margot Ledbetter of *The Good Life* would have worn to a swingers' party. The look is embellished further by a headdress made from a single enormous peacock feather which could have been raided from a Museum of Native American culture.

The registrar, an aged gentleman who, judging by his

tweed jacket, clearly isn't a fan of experimental fashion himself, looks almost shell-shocked by the vision before him and has to compose himself before beginning.

'Good morning, ladies and gentlemen,' he says meekly. 'May I start by welcoming you here on this very special day. Today, Sarah and Bob are here to offer each other the security that comes from legally binding vows, sincerely made and faithfully kept. You are here to witness this occasion and to share the joy which is theirs.

'But before we begin the main part of the ceremony, there will be a short reading by, er, Ms Gloria Flowerdew.'

Gloria nearly knocks everyone out with the overpowering pong of patchouli oil as she walks past.

'Er, hi, everyone,' she says, holding up her fingers to make the peace sign, and begins to recite the words to some poem.

It all sounds strangely familiar, but I can't quite put my finger on where I've heard it before. It's only when she reaches the main body of the text that I actually realize what she's reading.

'Thank you, Gloria,' says the registrar, at the end. 'That reading was an extract from, ah, "Baby Light My Fire" by The Door Knobs.'

There is a smattering of giggles.

'The Doors,' I whisper to him. 'Just The Doors.'

'Oh, ah, right – just The Doors,' he corrects himself, embarrassed.

The poor guy looks as if he's spent a lifetime marrying people. But I'll guarantee he's never encountered anything like this before.

Chapter 89

Outside the register office, the sun is shining and the mood is one of general elation.

'You look really happy,' I tell my mum affectionately.

'I *am* really happy,' she says, looking surprised as I lean over and kiss her on the cheek.

'What was that for?' she asks.

I shrug. 'I'm just really happy for you too.'

God, I've turned soppy lately. Even though my mother looks as if she's been playing with the contents of a dressing-up box, when she and Bob were saying their vows earlier, I actually had a tear in my eye. What that's all about, I don't know. Well, maybe I do.

As the guests start pouring out of the register office, we find ourselves in a blizzard of confetti which is, my mum spends a long time reassuring everyone, 100 per cent biodegradable.

'They're a lovely couple,' says Charlotte, appearing at my side.

'They are,' I agree. 'But speaking of lovely, you'll be getting a lot of compliments today. You look amazing.'

'Thanks, Evie,' she says, grinning. 'I never knew I could look like this, I really didn't.'

'Well, you deserve it, Charlotte,' I tell her. 'You must have done more sit-ups than Private Benjamin.'

Not only does Charlotte now spend more time at the gym than at home, but in the space of a few months she's also learned all those things that in most cases it takes a lifetime for women to accumulate: how to wax legs without the need for an epidural, how to apply lip-liner without looking like Boy George, how to paint the nails on your right hand without covering your whole arm in polish. Today is the culmination of all this. She looks slim, beautiful and – most amazingly of all – confident.

There are throngs of people on the tiny driveway and it's clear that it would be best for everyone concerned not to hang about here too long.

'Mum,' I say, grabbing her arm, 'you need to throw your bouquet before we go.'

'Ooh, right you are,' she says.

It's funny how women seem to have an instinct for these things. Within seconds of Mum getting into position to throw the flowers, a group of female guests start gathering with the sort of expressions you'd see on a pack of Cocker Spaniels at the mention of some doggie chocolate drops.

To my surprise, someone is missing. Valentina is still talking to Edmund and Jack on the other side of the drive and hasn't even noticed what's going on.

'Valentina!' shouts Grace. 'You'll miss this if you're not careful!'

As the bouquet flies through the air, narrowly avoiding an entanglement in my mother's headdress, there is a surge forwards. Some good-humoured but determined nudging begins. But nobody here has the athleticism – or determination – of Valentina.

Having heard Grace shout, she has hitched up her skirt and is sprinting towards us, elbowing guests out of the way. Grace's mum's powder-blue hat is knocked off, Cousin Denise's bouquet flies out of her hands, Gloria's kaftan ends up over her head. And, finally, looking very like an Olympic volleyball player, Valentina dives for the bouquet. Somehow, miraculously, everyone manages to get out of her way at this crucial point. Well, everyone but one person. Me.

With Valentina flying through the air, it is almost in slow motion that I can see her engagement ring getting closer, like a small comet heading straight for a crash landing . . . on my face. As it makes contact with an excruciating thump, squarely in the socket of my eye, it takes my breath away. Sharp and searing, the only thought that is going through my head as I am flung to the ground is that I have never felt anything like it in my life.

Sitting on the ground, it takes me a second to work out what has happened. Slowly, I become aware of the blood dripping down my nose, and the deep throbbing in my eye-socket.

Just as I'm wondering whether I have cartoon-character stars whirling around my head, something else strikes me. Nobody has even noticed what has happened to me. They are all too busy looking at the flowers. Watching, dazed and confused from my vantage point on the car park floor, I can just about see through the crowds.

Patrick is there – dressed far more casually today than he was at his own wedding to Grace – and is grinning at Charlotte.

'You must be next down the aisle, sweetheart,' he teases

gently, as he puts an arm around her shoulder. He points at the flowers her hands are gripped around, having beaten Valentina to them seconds earlier.

'Have you been keeping someone secret from us?' he says, laughing softly.

Charlotte looks up at him, blushing so much that her cheeks look like they've hit 200 degrees Fahrenheit. Her delight at catching the flowers couldn't be more obvious, because I don't think I've ever seen her smiling more widely in all the years I've known her. I decide to try to stand up to go and congratulate her.

But it's at this point that I pass out.

Chapter 90

'You really ought to go and see a doctor, you know,' says Jack, dabbing a piece of damp cotton wool on my eye.

'I don't need a doctor,' I say miserably. 'I need a paper bag to put over my head.'

He stifles a smile.

'It'll be fine in no time,' he says. 'Honestly, I know the swelling's bad now but these things tend to go down really quickly. It'll surprise you.'

I've had rather enough of surprises. Like the one I saw when I looked in the mirror just now. Having spent the entire morning tarting myself up for Jack's benefit, my face – courtesy of Valentina's crystal ball of a ring – now looks as if I've just done ten rounds with Mike Tyson.

Okay, so she has apologized. In fact, she was so shocked by what she'd done, she did look genuinely sorry – for at least a second. But that doesn't change the fact that my eye is so black and swollen I can barely see out of it, and I have now had the indignity of my boyfriend insisting on wiping the crusty blood away from my nose.

'You still look lovely,' he says, and as he kisses me on the lips I feel like crying. And it's not just because my head, even after enough painkillers to anaesthetize a shire horse, feels as if someone is jumping up and down on it.

Jack and I have now been together for exactly eight weeks. Under other circumstances I might have considered this an achievement, which it undoubtedly is, given my past history. But I'm just not thinking about it in those terms. Hitting the eight-week mark has happened so effortlessly that I can't imagine not hitting the ten-week mark, twenty-week mark, or any other mark after it.

It's not just that I'm not sick of him. It's that my heart leaps when I see the soap bag he now keeps in my bathroom. It's that when we wake up on a Sunday morning and he suggests we spend the day together – *again* – I can barely contain myself. It's that when he phones me at work and mentions that he can't wait to see me that night, it's the highlight of my day.

In short, I am cured. My relationship issues are a thing of the past. The only down side is that it's taken me until today to realize just how much I've abandoned other people in my life. Outside work, the only person I've spent much time with lately has been my mum, and this was largely out of necessity, given how haphazard her wedding planning has been.

Still, with the exception of her daughter looking like she's been brawling in the street, things haven't worked out too badly. The reception is being held in a field near her house, which sounds horrendous but actually isn't that bad in practice. Okay, so the marquee doesn't have organza curtains and chandeliers – because it's a former cider tent from the Reading Festival. And okay, so there's not much in the buffet if you have a particularly strong liking for red meat – but if you like mung beans and dried papaya, you'll be in heaven.

No, it's not really my mum I'm concerned about. It's Grace. She's been my best friend for as long as I can remember, and she doesn't need to spell it out for me to know something's going on between her and Patrick. When I say 'something', that is about as specific and scientific as I can get at the moment, because she's not given a great deal away aside from the odd moan.

If there's one thing I am determined to do today, it is to broach this subject. And, as difficult as it is to tear myself away from Jack, that's exactly what I'm going to do. Right now.

Chapter 91

I suppose it had to happen. I knew it had to happen. I'd just pushed it to the back of my mind to try to pretend it wouldn't. But Gareth is the sort of person who just can't help himself. Much as I bloody well wish he would.

'Evie!' he shouts, as I'm heading towards Grace on the other side of the marquee.

My heart sinks as if it's attached to a boulder.

'I was trying to catch your eye during the ceremony,' he tells me, 'but . . . God, what's happened to you?'

'Oh, nothing,' I say, touching my eye, but I feel like asking the same question of him. Gareth's skin is now so bad it looks like he's been exfoliating with a cheese-grater.

'Are you . . . all right?' I ask.

'Of course I'm all right,' he replies, picking at one of the drier bits on his chin and flicking the resulting debris to the ground. 'Why wouldn't I be?'

'I don't know, you just don't look terribly well, that's all,' I dare to say.

'I'm fine,' he says. 'On top of the world. Anyway, how are you? You never did phone me like you said you would, did you? Still, I won't hold it against you. Have you been wearing those earrings?'

The earrings he gave me in the Jacaranda are currently burning a hole in the bottom of my chest of drawers as if they're made of Kryptonite. I don't want them there, I just don't know what to do with them. I'm certainly not wearing them, but throwing them away seems a bit callous.

And, despite the fact that bumping into Gareth again is about as pleasant as a session of electric shock therapy, a part of me can't help feeling bad about the effect me dumping him has clearly had.

'You shouldn't have bought me the earrings, Gareth,' I say, trying my best to sound firm and kind, as opposed to bossy and slightly irritated. 'I know you meant well but you shouldn't anyway.'

'But you wanted them, didn't you?'

'That's not the point,' I say.

'What *is* the point then?' he asks, scratching the left side of his chin so hard it looks like it's about to draw blood.

'The point is, we're no longer together,' I tell him gently. 'And we're not going to get back together either.'

'Not *yet*,' he reminds me.

Before I get the chance to disabuse him of this fantasy, Bob appears. It was Bob who first introduced me to Gareth and I can't help but feel immensely relieved that someone else is now here to share the burden of his presence.

'Bob, congratulations!' says Gareth, patting him on the back with such force he nearly knocks him over. 'How are you keeping?'

'Er, fine, yes,' coughs Bob. 'How are you? Have you found a new job yet?'

I frown. I had no idea Gareth wasn't still working with Bob at the university.

'Oh, I've got lots of irons in the fire, put it that way, Bob,' he replies, glancing at me nervously.

'When did you leave?' I ask.

'Oh, a few weeks ago,' he says. 'I, er, decided it was no longer for me.'

Now Bob is frowning.

'Anyway,' continues Gareth, 'I'm going to go and tuck into some of that lovely food. Catch you later, Evie, Bob.'

As he heads off towards the marquee, I turn to my step-father.

'What was all that about?' I ask.

'Hmm, funny business really,' Bob says. 'He wasn't exactly sacked, but the rumour is that the Vice Chancellor and he came to a mutual agreement that he would leave and never darken their door again.'

'Why?' I ask. Gareth may be as much fun to be around as a plague of dust mites at the moment, but I never had him down as the type to be sacked.

'It's not exactly clear,' says Bob. 'All I know is that they've been trying to get rid of him for ages. He's a very difficult person to work with, by all accounts. A bit . . . well, sneaky, they tell me. But what the exact circumstances of him going were, I'm not exactly sure, except that he had a huge row with one of our media professors – a nice lady called Deirdre Bennett. Big bottom and terrible teeth, but nice. Anyway, he just seemed to go after that. No one misses him much, I must say.'

'Oh well, remind me never to rely on you to introduce me to eligible men in future,' I say.

He looks over at Jack, who's talking to my mum inside the marquee, and nods.

'It doesn't look much like you'll need it in future, does it?'

Chapter 92

By the look on Grace's mum's face, she's either got chronic wind or she's not impressed with the buffet.

'It's an *unusual* spread, Evie,' she says euphemistically. 'Not many vol au vents.'

'They've got some nice salads,' Grace offers, although Scarlett, who is in a pushchair next to us, doesn't exactly look convinced either.

'Yes . . .' replies Mrs Edwards, taking a hesitant bite out of a chick-pea patty. 'Although some of it reminds me of that stuff you put in the bottom of Polly's rabbit hutch.'

Suddenly, my own mum appears, straightening her peacock feather as she approaches.

'Is everyone enjoying themselves?' she asks.

'Absolutely,' says Grace. 'I thought your service was lovely. Have you met my mother?'

Grace's mum smiles and brushes down her dress, which looks as if it's come straight out of the late Queen Mother's wardrobe.

'Del-aighted to meet you,' she says in her best telephone voice. 'And many congratulations.'

'Oh, thank you,' says my mum, grabbing her hand and shaking it vigorously. 'I'm so happy you could come today.'

'Oh well,' says Mrs Edwards, continuing with the odd inflection in her voice, 'Ay'm here to look after the little ones, that's all. Ay'll be taking them home soon to let my Grace have some time to herself. She doesn't have a lot of time, normally, what with her high-powered job.'

'Er, yes – thanks, Mum,' interrupts Grace, before Mrs Edwards starts regaling us with how 'advanced' she was as a child.

'How's the buffet?' asks my mum. 'Ooh, you've obviously enjoyed it, Mrs Edwards.'

'Er, yes, very nice,' says Grace's mother. 'I'm more of a Marks and Spencer fan myself though, to be honest. You know – mini-quiches, sausages on sticks, that kind of thing. But er, yes, this is very nice. For a change.'

'Oh well, Bob and I don't buy any of our food from the conglomerates,' Mum says.

'From the what, dear?' asks Mrs Edwards.

'You know, supermarkets . . . chains,' Mum explains. 'We try to buy direct from the grower. It's much tastier and ultimately more economical too.'

Mrs Edwards gamely tries to hide her concern for my mother's welfare and possibly her sanity too.

'Hmm,' she says. 'I don't think that'd be practical in our case. I wouldn't know where else to get a Battenburg from, for a start.'

'Anyway, I do hope you'll excuse me so I can do a bit more mingling,' says Mum. 'Ooh, but before I go, you don't happen to have a lighter, do you?'

'Not me,' I say.

'Sorry, Sarah,' says Grace. 'I don't smoke.'

'Oh, don't worry,' says Mum. 'It's not for me, it's for Bob's

friend Gerry. And, between you and me, I think he only
wants it for his bong.'

Mrs Edwards turns to us after she's gone.

'What's a bong?' she asks.

Grace gulps.

'A type of barbecue,' I say. 'They're about to do some corn
on the cob.'

Chapter 93

Patrick is trying to give Scarlett and Polly a kiss goodbye before Mrs Edwards takes them home. Trouble is, he's clearly seeing four of them.

'Wheresh my besht girlsh?' he says, stumbling, before scooping both of them up.

'Are you drunk, Daddy?' asks Polly.

'Don't be shilly,' he says, trying to pat her on the head but missing.

'I'm not sure you fooled her,' Grace tells him after they've gone, but he ignores her and takes another liberal gulp of his beer.

As dusk starts to descend, the lights in the marquee are turned on and the four of us – Grace and Patrick, me and Jack – watch as the band prepare for their big performance. They are friends of Bob's and I can only describe them, from the one time I've seen them before, like a souped-up version of Simon and Garfunkel.

'Hey everyone,' says the lead singer, a middle-aged man in a Hawaiian shirt and hair like a mad scientist. 'Before we start, can I just say congratulations to Bob and Sarah. I can't think of a . . . cooler . . . couple.'

Everyone cheers as the band launch into the song the bride and groom have chosen for their first dance – 'Let's Spend The Night Together' by the Rolling Stones.

Bob grabs Mum's hand and leads her onto the dance floor in a half-skip as their heads bob up and down manically in time to the music. He swings her around in wild abandonment and, with both of their arms flailing like they're performing a rain dance, they set the dance floor alight in their own unique way.

'Other people choose James Blunt for their first song,' I say, shaking my head.

'Well, they're entertaining if nothing else,' says Grace, laughing. 'You've got to admit that.'

'Yep, they are,' I agree. 'Listen, I was thinking. We four should get together soon, you know.'

'What, you mean a double date?' says Grace. 'I've not been on one of those since I was about eighteen.'

'I wasn't going to suggest we go ten-pin bowling,' I say. 'I haven't got the co-ordination for a start. I thought a bit of dinner might be nice though. Jack's a great cook.'

'Tsk, Jack,' says Patrick, as he starts to sway backwards and forwards. 'It starts off being invited out and ends up with you doing the bloody cooking. I wouldn't stand for it, mate.'

Patrick is clearly trying to jest, but there is something about how pissed he is that gives him the air of an *EastEnders* hard man – and seeing that he's a corporate lawyer, it really doesn't suit him. Fortunately, Jack is polite enough to pretend he hasn't noticed.

'You're right,' he says. 'Maybe we should get the girls to do the cooking instead. The only trouble with that is that I've tasted Evie's Pasta Putanesca and I'm a bit worried I might not survive the experience twice.'

I hit him playfully on the arm and he responds by pulling me towards him and gently kissing the top of my head. As we move away from each other, I turn to look at Grace and Patrick and am a bit shocked by what I see. They are standing apart from each other and look so uncomfortable with our display of affection, neither of them appears to know where to put their eyes. Then, something strange happens. Patrick drains his glass, turns on his heel and walks away. Just like that.

'Are you going to the bar?' Grace shouts after him, clearly trying to pretend she's not as taken aback by this as we all are.

But he ignores her and continues with his swaying march away from us.

'I hope you weren't expecting to get lucky tonight,' I say. 'I haven't seen Patrick this pissed since your wedding night.'

'Hmm,' she says, forcing a smile.

'Grace, are you sure everything's all right?' I ask, but the second I say it I know now's not the time. She'd never spill the beans in front of Jack.

'Oh fine,' she answers. 'Anyway, I'm starting to think if I can't beat him I may join him. Can I get either of you a drink?'

We both shake our heads. As she walks away in Patrick's direction, I grab her by the arm, out of earshot of Jack.

'Grace, really,' I say. 'Do you want to talk?'

'No, honestly,' she says. 'It's no big deal.'

But it is starting to seem like a big deal to me. It's starting to seem like a very big deal.

Chapter 94

If I thought Patrick was acting strangely, that is nothing compared with Charlotte.

This is the first time she's drunk anything other than saccharine-packed fizzy drinks since the start of her *WeightWatchers* regime, and it has had an immediate effect. When I shared a Portaloo with her earlier she was swaying so much trying to hover that she nearly toppled the thing over mid-flow.

'Oooh,' she says, throwing her head back wildly. 'The first proper drink I've had in ages and it's made me go really squiffy.'

She's not the only one. Thanks to my black eye and painkillers I couldn't feel wobblier if I'd spent the entire afternoon on a playground roundabout.

'Still, it's not unpleasant,' she giggles. 'In fact, it's quite nice.'

I wish I could say the same thing.

As Charlotte and I head back into the marquee, the band are in full swing – and so is Valentina. Apparently not put off by the fact that they're playing a Van Morrison track, she has dusted off her old Spice Girls routine and is giving it its first outing since 1999. Edmund couldn't look more proud.

'You know,' says Charlotte, out of nowhere, 'people look at you differently when you're thin.'

'*I* don't,' I say determinedly. 'I mean, you look great and everything, but you're still the same old Charlotte to me. I've always thought you were lovely and I always will do.'

'Yes, but not everyone's like you Evie,' she says. 'Take my mother . . .'

She swallows a large gulp of her wine.

'Do you know what she said on Sunday? "*There's barely a pick on you,*" was what she'd said. I'd gone round for lunch and passed on the Yorkshire pudding and gravy—'

'What, and she nearly fainted?' I joke.

Charlotte giggles.

'But it's not just my mother,' she continues, running her hands contentedly over her new bias-cut dress. 'It's . . .'

'Who?' I ask.

She looks up at me and smiles conspiratorially.

'Men,' she whispers, giggling like a naughty schoolgirl.

'Men?' I echo, grinning. 'Go on, who've you been flirting with?'

'Ah,' she says, taking another liberal mouthful of wine. 'That would be telling.'

'Charlotte,' I say, slightly amazed, 'stop teasing. Come on, tell me.'

She shakes her head.

'Not yet,' she says.

'Charlotte!' I squeal. 'Who are you talking about? Tell me this bloody instant!'

She giggles again.

'I can't.'

'Okay, okay.' I am desperate to know, but don't want to

make her clam up completely. 'But has anything . . . happened?'

She looks into her wine glass and smiles again.

'Oh yes,' she says dreamily.

My eyes widen.

'What?' I ask.

She shakes her head again, apparently enjoying teasing me with this story as much as the story itself.

'So, have you kissed?' I ask.

'Oh yes,' she says again.

'Look here, you,' I say, exasperated, 'I am a journalist and I will get this out of you sooner or later – I promise. So, look, are you seeing him again?'

Charlotte's smile suddenly disappears and she looks very serious, and very drunk.

'I hope so,' she says. 'I really do hope so. But, I'll be honest with you, I'm not so sure.'

Chapter 95

Patrick has always been what you'd call a happy drunk. A harmless drunk. The sort of person who, after a few jars on a Friday night, does silly things with his boxer shorts and gives sloppy kisses to his male friends. Not the sort of drunk who's obnoxious. Although on the evidence of his behaviour earlier, something's clearly changed on that score.

It is because of this that I've left Jack chatting to my mum about mudslides in Guatemala and the food crisis in Malawi (glad to see they've kept the agenda upbeat to befit the happy occasion) and go off in search of Grace, who I find talking to Jim near the bar.

'Hi, you two,' I say brightly, not wanting to arouse any suspicion that I've come in search of a deep and meaningful conversation. 'What do you think of the band?'

'Brilliant,' says Jim. 'Although I think Valentina threw them earlier by asking if they knew any Christina Aguilera numbers.'

'Listen, Jim,' I say, 'I hope you don't think I'm being rude, but I wonder if I could borrow Grace for a few minutes?'

'Sure,' he says. 'I was going to try and persuade Charlotte to come and dance with me anyway.'

Grace and I go in search of a quiet table in the corner away from the dance floor. I can't help noticing as we pass that Valentina's dancing, which always involves a fair amount of arm movement anyway, tonight involves so much conspicuous waving of the hand with her ring on it that she could be directing traffic.

'What's up?' says Grace as we sit down in a suitable spot.

'I was about to ask you the same thing,' I say.

But before she gets the chance to answer, my handbag starts ringing and I realise it's Jack's mobile which, since he abandoned his jacket earlier, I've been looking after. Normally, I'd take it straight to him, but now is really not a good time so I just dig it out and press the silence button.

'What do you mean?' she asks.

'Look,' I say, 'I don't want to pry or anything, but I've noticed that you and Patrick both seem a bit . . . I don't know . . . not really yourselves.'

She bites her lip and considers this for a second.

'You've noticed then,' she says.

'Is something the matter?' I ask.

'Yes. Yes, I think there is,' she sighs. 'But, well, it's hard to put my finger on really.'

Suddenly, the phone goes off again. I dig it out of my bag, and press silence again, before nodding at her to go on.

'It's hard to put my finger on because it's no one big thing,' she continues. 'We've not had a huge row over money, or the kids or, well, anything. But we are at each other's throats a lot. Everything I say seems to offend Patrick at the moment. And he just *never* seems happy.'

'Do you have any idea what's caused it?' I ask.

'You mean do I think he's having an affair?' she says, her eyes welling up.

'No!' I say hastily. 'I don't think that for a second.'

'Don't you?' she says. 'I'm not so sure. I'm really not so sure.'

Some people, when they cry, look like they do in the movies, with a single tear cascading poetically down porcelain skin. Grace, like me, isn't one of them.

Her cheeks now resemble corned beef, her eyes are almost as puffy as my own and her nose has acquired that special beetrooty tinge that comes from excessive blowing on a six-ply napkin.

'Patrick loves you, I know it,' I say. 'God, you only had to see the way he looked at you at your wedding. Things can't have just gone from that to what you're talking about overnight.'

'You wouldn't have thought so,' she says, sniffing into her napkin again. 'But that's what it feels like.'

'I take it you've tried talking to him about it?'

'Hmm, yes. I mean, sort of.'

I frown. 'That means no.'

'I suppose I haven't wanted to confront him,' she admits.

'Well, you should,' I say firmly. 'Confront him, talk to him, tell him you love him.'

I see the hint of a smile.

'For someone who has never had a long-term relationship, you're very good at giving advice on them.'

I put my arm around her. '*Had* is the operative word,' I say. 'Commitment is my new middle name. Jack and I are so loved-up we make Romeo and Juliet look emotionally stunted.'

'Well, I'm glad,' she says. 'I really am.'

Suddenly, Jack's phone rings again. This time, for the sake of shutting the damn thing up, I decide to answer it.

'Hello, Jack's phone,' I say.

'Er, oh, hi,' says the voice of a young-sounding woman on the other end. 'Is Jack there, please?'

'Not at the moment,' I say. 'I mean, he's around but I'm not sure where he is right now. Can I take a message?'

'Yeah,' says the woman. 'Can you tell him Beth rang. Just let him know he's still got my T-shirt. I forgot to take it with me when I left this morning and I wanted to know whether I could come over and get it tomorrow.'

I freeze.

'Er, can I take a number?' I ask.

'Oh, he's got it,' she replies.

I am suddenly unable to think about what to say or do.

'Hello?' she says.

'Er, yes, no problem,' I say, and end the call.

'What's up?' asks Grace, leaning over. 'Evie, you're as white as a sheet. Whatever's the matter?'

Chapter 96

Evie, you're an idiot. No, worse than that. You're a gullible idiot.

I'd known the second I saw Jack talking to Beth on that jetty in the Scillies that something was going on. There was more chemistry between the two of them than you'd find on top of the average Bunsen burner. Then there was the phone call to his mobile the other week. And now this. So how could I have been so stupid?

I know exactly how. I've been swept off my feet to such an extent that every ounce of commonsense appears to have been swept away at the same time, and I managed to convince myself I hadn't even noticed anything was going on.

Which is absolutely ridiculous because it couldn't have been clearer if someone had put a sign up. I *knew* this was happening and just chose to ignore it!

'I just can't believe it,' I tell Grace as I storm across the floor of the marquee. 'I really can't.'

'Are you sure there couldn't be an explanation?' she says, trying to keep up with me.

'Tell me,' I say, spinning around and making my head feel as if someone is clog dancing on it in the process. 'What explanation could there possibly be? I saw it coming at Georgia's wedding. He gave her his phone number. I saw them flirting. Then, I saw her name come up on his mobile a couple of weeks ago. Now Beth has apparently left an item of clothing at his flat when she left there . . . this morning!'

Grace is obviously trying to think of something to say but is just opening and closing her mouth like a frustrated goldfish instead.

'So you weren't with him last night, then?' she asks finally, clutching at straws.

'I was busy helping my mum get ready for the wedding,' I continue, ranting so much now that I sound like Gordon Ramsay with PMT. 'Which was obviously the perfect opportunity. I just don't see what possible explanation there is apart from Beth having stayed over for a mad, passionate all-night sex session.'

'Okay, so she may have stayed over. But it might have all been innocent,' says Grace. But I can see from her face that even she can't imagine how.

'If it was that innocent, why wouldn't he have mentioned it?' I ask sadly.

'I just don't want you to do anything you'll regret, Evie,' she says, grabbing my arm. 'I know how much you like him.'

'That was before I knew – knew for certain – that he was two-timing me,' I say.

Leaving Grace next to the entrance of the marquee, I continue to look for Jack. But my mother gets to me first, calling my name out as she skips towards me, her peacock feather now bent over in a perfect right angle.

'I've hardly seen you all night,' she beams. 'Are you enjoying yourself?'

327

'Er, yes,' I say, forcing a smile. I couldn't be more transparent if I was made of Perspex.

'What's the matter?' she asks.

'Oh nothing,' I tell her. 'Have you seen Jack anywhere?'

'Oh, I meant to say, earlier: he *is* lovely, you know,' she enthuses. 'I mean, if I'd tried to speak to some of your other boyfriends about the humanitarian crisis in the Republic of the Congo they'd think I was speaking another language.'

'Hmm,' I say. 'Have you seen him?'

'And he seems very fond of you,' she continues.

I'm starting to think *I'm* talking another language.

'Yes,' I say patiently. 'But have you seen him?'

'Yes,' she says. 'I left him talking to that chap you know.'

'Which chap?' Honestly, Mum!

'You know,' she says, 'the one with the unfortunate complexion. I told him he ought to get that seen to. I met someone with a rash like that when I lived in India and he fell into a coma a week later.'

'You don't mean Gareth, do you?' I say.

'That's the one,' she says brightly.

Chapter 97

I feel an instinctive stab of horror at the fact that I've failed to keep Jack and Gareth apart. But I remind myself that this is now utterly irrelevant under the circumstances.

When I see the two of them together, the first thing I notice is their expressions. Gareth is smiling one of his increasingly creepy smiles that have started reminding me of the Child Catcher in *Chitty Chitty Bang Bang*.

Jack, on the other hand, isn't smiling at all.

'Can I speak to you a minute, please?' I say to him.

'What?' he says, frowning. 'Yeah, sure.'

'Having a nice evening, Evie?' Gareth enquires as we walk away, but I can't bring myself to do anything other than ignore him.

When we are a safe distance away, I turn to Jack and produce his phone.

'There,' I say pointedly. 'There's your mobile. Beth phoned. She left a message asking you to phone back.'

'Right,' he says, taking the phone from me without showing even a flicker of embarrassment.

'That's right,' I add for good measure. '*Beth*.'

'I heard you,' he says, and I've seen brick walls acknowledging more remorse.

'Oh, *did* you?' I am aware that my voice is starting to sound slightly wobbly in an I'm-actually-hysterical-but-I'll-be-buggered-if-I'm-going-to-show-it kind of way. 'Oh, you heard me, did you? Right. Right then. O-*kay*.'

He just ignores me, which I can't help thinking is unbelievable. Positively shameless, in fact.

'I need to ask you about something, Evie,' he says instead.

'Oh?' I cross my arms huffily. 'What?'

'About something that—' But he stops midway through his sentence. 'Why are you doing that?'

'What?'

'Pulling that funny face?' he says.

Now I really am annoyed.

'Because I'm upset,' I say, trying to control my voice as I realize I'm sounding more and more like Miss Piggy throwing a tantrum.

'In fact, I'm *bloody* upset, you deceiving . . .' I want to say *bastard*, but am concerned that might be a little too Vicky Pollard '. . . you deceiving . . . *so and so*.'

But even I think that sounds ludicrous.

'What are you talking about?' Jack looks mystified.

'I'm talking about the *thing* you're having with Beth,' I grind out.

He furrows his brow.

'Don't look like that,' I say, my head banging again. 'I know you gave her your number in the Scillies. I know she's been phoning you because I saw her name come up on your mobile. And now she's just phoned to say she left her top at your place this morning. You must think I've got the intelligence of an amoeba.'

'Evie,' he says calmly. 'You don't know what you're saying.'

330

'Oh, you're denying it then?' At this very moment I could be a Crown Court prosecutor.

'Yes,' he says. 'I am denying it. But while we're on the subject of deceptive *so and sos*, I wonder if you could clear something up for me?'

'Fire away,' I tell him, crossing my arms so tightly now my wrist has gone dead.

'You know how you told me that heartrending story on the beach in the Scillies about how you'd just been dumped? Who was it, by Jimmy, who you'd been seeing for two and half years?'

I can feel the heat rising to my neck now.

'That was a load of bollocks, wasn't it?' he says.

I'm trying to think of a suitable response but nothing is springing to mind.

'And, tell me something else,' he goes on sternly. 'Is it true that you've never, not once, been out with anyone for longer than a few weeks because you've split up with them all before then?'

Again, words are somehow failing me. Which is not something I'm used to, I'll admit.

'I take it from your silence that it is. Why did you lie to me, Evie?'

I consider this carefully and try to remember again why I did.

'It wasn't exactly a lie,' I try.

'Wasn't it?' he asks.

'Okay, well, so it was. I had my reasons,' I say. 'But let's not change the subject. I want to know how long this thing between you and Beth has been going on.'

He shakes his head. 'There *is* no thing between me and Beth.'

'I don't believe you,' I say.

He doesn't say anything, just looks at me, his eyes blazing.

'Are these ridiculous accusations your way of splitting up with me?' he asks. 'Because we've been together for as long as eight weeks now? I presume from what I've heard that that must be what this is all about.'

'Oh, they're ridiculous, are they?' I say, refusing to get drawn into anything other than the most important matter here.

'Yes,' he says, 'they are. But let me save you a job, Evie. You don't have to split up with me. I'm happy to go quietly.'

And then he turns around and starts walking away.

'So you expect me to believe that you and Beth aren't an item, but you won't even explain why she left her clothes at your flat?' I shout after him.

'I've got nothing to explain to you because I haven't done anything wrong!' he shouts back. 'Oh, and by the way, don't expect me to shower you with jewellery like Gareth did now we've split up.'

Chapter 98

In a strange way, I feel like I did on the day I lost my virginity. I remember the sensation distinctly as I walked through town, idly looking in shop windows. I felt as if a fundamental part of me had changed for ever. And I couldn't help getting an eerie, if illogical feeling that people could tell. From the shopkeeper who asked me if I had change of a twenty-pound note to the woman sitting next to me on the train reading an article about HRT, I felt as if they knew that something earth-shattering had just happened to me, that it must be written all over my face.

As I jump into the back of a taxi, I wonder whether the driver can tell that I've just been dumped by someone – someone I actually care about – for the first time in my life. I wonder if he realizes how this occurrence, so completely alien to me until now, has changed everything.

'Have you been in a fight?' he asks, studying my black eye in his mirror.

'Yes,' I say. 'I mean no . . . no, my eye was just an accident.' I stare out of the window, really not wanting to talk.

'Have you come from that wedding down the road?' he asks.

'Yes,' I mutter.

'You're the third one I've picked up from there,' he says, and only then do I realize just how late it is. 'Christ, I've seen some sights. The last one was wearing a poncho. Looked like she'd just stepped out of a Spaghetti Western.'

Okay, so maybe he doesn't know.

My head spins as I lean back on the seat and block out the sound of his voice. Just take me home, I think. Just leave me alone.

My daze is suddenly broken as the taxi beeps and swerves around something, or somebody. As I look out of the window, I realize we've just narrowly missed Grace and Patrick as they walk down the middle of the road.

'Can you stop a minute, please?' I say to the driver, and as he pulls in I push the window down.

'Do you want a lift?' I ask.

They're holding hands, but Patrick won't look at me.

'No, no,' says Grace. 'Honestly, we're going in a completely different direction. We'll flag our own one down. Is everything okay, Evie?'

I hesitate.

'I'll speak to you tomorrow, okay?' My voice is wobbling.

'Sure,' she says.

She huddles up to Patrick, but I can tell from his face that something still isn't right. I don't know what. And at this moment in time I don't really care. Somehow I can't bring myself to even think about Grace and Patrick's problems any more.

As the journey continues, it strikes me how quickly my rage, the rage that was so forceful such a short time ago, turns into something else: a dull, rising ache which already feels far more potent, and far more painful, than plain old anger. Or the lingering effects of Valentina's left hook, for that matter.

Tonight marks the end of something which, just four hours ago, I thought was the best thing that ever happened to me. It's the end that I, foolishly, never thought would come. The end of me and Jack. Jack and me. My one and only steady relationship. Almost.

The enormity of what has happened suddenly hits me and tears prick into my eyes. I try to swallow but a hard, bitter lump in my throat stops me from doing so. Instead, tears spill down my cheeks, cascading in a stream of misery.

I think of Jack tenderly kissing my swollen face earlier and telling me I was still the most beautiful woman he'd ever known. I think about how safe it made me feel. How special. How loved.

My face is soaking with tears but still they keep coming. I sit, crying, in a way I've never cried before. My chest gets tighter and tighter and it begins to feel as if someone has ripped out my heart and is wringing it, wringing it remorselessly, to squeeze out every tear.

I look out of the window but can't focus on anything except an image of Jack's face, that lovely face with its warm eyes and oh so soft mouth. It strikes me that I may never see that face again.

I put my head in my hands and, despite my attempts to hide the fact that I'm crying, a sob escapes from my lips.

'You're not going to be sick back there are you?' says the driver, looking in his mirror. ''Cos it's an extra twenty-five quid if you are.'

Chapter 99

My flat, Saturday, 9 June

I wake up with a hangover mouth, a throbbing eye and a very odd feeling about the night before. 'Odd' as in I know immediately that something is wrong, but it takes a half a second before I recall exactly what it is. When I do, my stomach lurches so hard it feels like I've been kicked by the hind legs of a donkey with a serious mood-swing problem.

I take a deep breath. In some ways, it's no surprise I feel like this, given the amount of coffee I drank when I got back last night. On top of the alcohol I'd been drinking all day. On top of the painkillers I'd taken in the afternoon. On top of the smack in the head by Valentina's sparkler.

And yet, I know that what I'm feeling isn't just caused by that lot. Because nothing is making me feel more nauseous than the recollection of Jack's words.

'Evie, you don't know what you're saying. Are these accusations your way of splitting up with me? You don't have to split up with me. I'm happy to go quietly.'

Just remembering them makes my head spin almost as much as my stomach, my thoughts being thrown this way and that in a desperate attempt to make some sense of what happened. He looked so sincere. Yet how could he be, given what Beth told me? God, I want to believe him – which can only make me a bloody fool. But what if he was telling the truth? Is it too late now anyway?

I look up at the ceiling and focus on an impressive cobweb cascading between my Ikea lampshade and the top of my curtains. I close my eyes and try to think about all this rationally.

As far as I can see, there are only two possible explanations for what happened:

A. Jack *has* been lying and two-timing me with Beth as I suspected. In which case, he's been acting like a horrible, deceiving rat for months, with no regard for my feelings. And I'm an idiot.

Or

B. Jack *hasn't* been lying or two-timing me with Beth. In which case, I publicly accused him of doing just that – immediately after he discovered, not just about my past, but also that I've been telling monumental fibs about it. And I'm an idiot.

Funny, but I'm struggling to find anything positive in either scenario.

Chapter 100

My flat, Thursday, 14 June

'Jack, it's Evie. We need to talk.'

No, no, no, that's all wrong. I sound like someone from a bad daytime soap. I have now practised so many deep, meaningful and often pathetically tearful conversations with Jack – with everything from my shower head to my steering wheel – I'm starting to wonder if I need therapy.

The problem is, I just don't know where to start. Because I have no idea whether or not he and Beth were getting it together, I just don't know what approach to take here. Do I confront him again? Or do I beg for forgiveness?

There has also been something else nagging at the back of my mind and it's this. It has now been five days since our fight and it's not as if he's banging down my door to try to patch things up. In fact, I haven't heard a solitary word from him. And I am now absolutely sure that he hasn't attempted to contact me as I have taken my mobile into Carphone Warehouse twice since Monday to check whether it needs servicing because it never seems to ring (or at least *he* doesn't). Apparently my Nokia is in such rude health it is currently on course to out-survive me.

It's been a weird few days. A numb, horrible, sick-to-my-stomach few days. And although I can't deny I've had a continual stream of visitors – everyone from Charlotte to Valentina has turned up laden with *Sex and the City* DVDs and Maltesers – there's something strange about the whole thing. I've never been surrounded by so many people. But I've never felt so alone.

Chapter 101

Liverpool city centre, Friday, 22 June

'Can I get you a drink?' he offers as we find a table in a quiet part of the bar.

'A glass of white wine would be great,' I say.

'Coming up,' he replies.

When he returns to the table, he's clutching an ice bucket and a bottle of champagne instead.

'What's all this about?' I ask. 'Have you won the Lottery? If you'd mentioned it earlier, I'd have agreed to go out with you ages ago.'

'I just thought we ought to be celebrating,' he says, smiling.

'Oh?' I reply. 'Celebrating what?'

'Celebrating the fact that two friends have been reunited,' he says.

'Were we friends?' I ask. 'I don't remember it like that.'

'No,' he says. 'You're right. Two *lovers* reunited.'

It's nice being out with Seb. I know I told myself I wasn't interested, but things have changed since then. And one thing's for sure, I can't spend another moment moping

340

around my flat waiting for Jack Williamson to call, even if it has been good for my standards of household cleanliness.

It's been almost two weeks now. Two weeks of moping, crying, hating myself, hating *How Clean Is Your House*. But enough's enough now. He hasn't phoned, he's not interested and there's only one thing for it. I've got to pick myself up and start again.

'So, I know you work for a building society,' I say, 'but tell me again what your job involves exactly?'

'Well,' says Seb, and starts to tell me again.

I'm aware I already asked him about this at Georgia's wedding. But when you're in a profession like mine, where you've got something visible to show for your efforts at the end of the day – even if it is sometimes only three nibs about library opening hours – trying to get your head around a job which involves 'determining regional strategy' and 'finding synergies to improve overall efficiency' is a bit weird.

'. . . so you see,' he concludes, 'it's all quite straightforward really.'

I get a flashback of Jack telling me about his job when we first met, but push the thought out of my mind immediately. So what the hell if Jack helps impoverished families in famine-hit regions of Africa? Big deal. Determining regional strategy and finding synergies to improve . . . whatever it is Seb improves, is probably just as interesting – only in a different way.

'You know,' he says, 'I was really gutted when you dumped me at uni.'

'*Sorry*,' I say jokingly. 'I was an idiot.'

'Nah,' he says, 'I'm sure I deserved it. You were probably too good for me anyway.'

I don't let on how much it means to me, but it is genuinely nice to hear Seb saying this sort of thing. My self-esteem has never felt as battered and bruised as it has recently, and Seb being so lovely tonight has gone a long way to cheering me up.

'Anyway, I won't hold it against you,' he continues, with a teasing wink. 'We've all grown up since then, haven't we? Things change.'

He's damn right about that one. A few months ago, the closest I'd ever got to commitment was deciding on a new colour for my living-room walls and sticking to it.

Darren Day's romantic history looked modest compared with mine. But – and I say this in all seriousness – things are different now. I have come to the realization that the only way I'm ever going to end up in a serious relationship is by trying harder, criticizing less and being much more tolerant. Not that I need to be particularly tolerant when it comes to Seb, of course.

Chapter 102

We end up in a club of Seb's choosing, a city centre haven of the beautiful, the evenly tanned and the expensively dressed. Okay, so some of the fashion ensembles in here are not always what you'd describe as *understated* style, but they definitely cost a packet. In fact, I suspect my mortgage wouldn't cover the price of the average pair of shoes here.

As we pass the doormen, Seb nods in acknowledgment and I immediately get a sense of how Charlotte must have felt six months ago. Everyone in here seems to be so skinny I strongly suspect there are hundreds of regurgitated dinners swilling about somewhere in the lavatory system of this place.

'I must remember to book in for some liposuction before my next visit,' I mutter.

'You're gorgeous as it is, sweetheart,' says Seb, putting a reassuring arm around me.

As we walk past the dance floor and Seb heads for the bar, I spot someone who, despite the regulation hot pants and strappy heels, makes me do a double-take.

'Beth,' I say, feeling very wobbly all of a sudden. 'Er, hi.'

I might have known this would be the sort of place she'd come. Although she immediately looks as awkward to see me as I am to see her.

'Hi, Evie,' she says, flicking back her long dark hair.

I smile as naturally as possible, which I think in practice is about as convincing as someone on a particularly poor chewing-gum advert.

'Sorry to hear about you and Jack,' she says.

'Right, yes,' I say casually. 'Georgia told you about it, did she?'

'No, actually, it was J—' she says, then immediately looks like she regrets it. 'I mean, yeah. Yeah, Georgia told me about it.'

I narrow my eyes, my mind racing as I scrutinize her expression. You don't have to be Sherlock Holmes to work out that Georgia didn't tell her at all. Which only leaves one other person. Jack. I feel a stab in my chest. So I was right all along.

'Right – well, nice seeing you,' I say, forcing myself to smile again, which is difficult now I know that they were – *are* – definitely seeing each other.

'Yeah, you too,' she says. And away we both go to separate ends of the dance floor.

As Seb and I start dancing, I give it my best but it's hard to get in the mood under the circumstances. Besides that, dancing here just doesn't feel as much fun as it used to, camping it up to 'Native New Yorker'. Or even singing Ruby Turner as appallingly as I managed to. I push the thought out of my head and tell myself that now, more than ever, I've got to forget about Jack.

After a while, Seb somehow gets us into the VIP room and we sit in a booth and each order a cocktail from the waiter.

'I'll need something to wash this little beauty down with,' he says, taking something out of his jacket pocket and putting it onto the table.

I watch in silent astonishment as he proceeds to chop and line up a pile of white powder with the side of his credit card and roll up a new £20 note. He then snorts it up in a movement accompanied by the sort of sound effects you'd expect from a warthog with a congestion problem.

Seb leans back with an unnerving smile on his face and powder stuck on the end of his nose as if he's dipped it in a sugar bowl.

'Er, you've missed a bit,' I whisper.

He brushes it off his nose with a finger and snorts that up too.

'Here, let me set a line up for you,' he says casually.

'Oh, no,' I say hastily. 'Honestly, I'll stick with my cocktail. Besides, aren't you worried someone will see?'

'You're joking, aren't you?' he scoffs. 'This is the VIP room. Everyone's at it in here. Come on, I don't want to party by myself.'

'Really, I'd prefer not to,' I say.

He looks at me as if he's suddenly got Miss Jean Brodie sitting opposite him.

'Come on, Evie,' he says. 'It's just a bit of fun. It'll help you loosen up.'

'No. Honestly, Seb, I'm loose enough – really,' I say, although I suddenly feel distinctly un-loose.

Mercifully, the waiter comes over to give us our cocktails and, despite his bravado, Seb puts his paraphernalia away. But over the next couple of hours, he proceeds to take his little packet of magic dust from his inside pocket to perform the same ritual three separate times.

'Did you enjoy Georgia's wedding?' I ask, trying to ignore what he's doing.

'Yeah,' he says. 'Yeah, I did. It was good to see some of the old gang again. You in particular.'

I smile.

'There were some pissed people on that dance floor by the end of the night though, weren't there?' he adds.

'Aren't there always at weddings?' I say.

'Yeah, but did you see that guy in the stripy jacket with his missus?' he adds, shaking his head and smirking. 'Those two looked like they needed locking up.'

I feel a surge of heat rising to my cheeks as I realize that the couple he's referring to are Bob and my mother.

'You're talking about Bob,' I say. 'Bob and, er . . .'

'Oh, do you know them?' he says, before I get a chance to finish. 'I hope I haven't offended anyone.'

'Er, well – no, you haven't offended anyone,' I say, shifting in my seat. 'But it was my mum and her husband you were talking about.'

'Shit!' he says, laughing. 'Christ, talk about the wrong way to impress your date!'

I laugh too. Seb wasn't to know who he was referring to. And, let's face it, it's nothing I haven't said about my mum myself.

'I have to say though,' he continues, 'I've never seen a pair of tights quite like the ones she was wearing.'

'No, you're right,' I say, chuckling. 'She's got unusual dress sense, that's for sure.'

'And that hat. *Jesus*,' he adds, rolling his eyes.

'Er, yes,' I say, starting to feel a bit uncomfortable.

'Listen, I'm just glad you haven't inherited your mother's sense of taste – or lack of,' he adds. 'You look amazing tonight.'

The compliment somehow doesn't have the same effect as his earlier ones did.

'Yeah, okay, Seb,' I find myself saying with an agitated tone. 'So my mum looks a bit unconventional. But that's the way I like her.'

'Whoa,' he says, holding his hands up. 'Just having a little joke. Sorry. I didn't mean to offend you.'

He looks like he means it. I untense my shoulders and suddenly feel a bit silly.

'No, I'm sorry,' I say. 'I didn't mean to snap.'

'That's okay.' He winks at me. 'I'll forgive you.'

I shift uneasily, but remind myself how much I've enjoyed being out with Seb tonight.

I'm just thinking about this when he leans over and, taking me by surprise, kisses me on the lips. I say he kisses me, but I can't help thinking Seb's manoeuvre reminds me of a giant octopus pouncing on its prey. He goes from nought to sixty in seconds, with full-on tongue and not a great deal of opportunity for the small matter of breathing.

I pull away, gasping for breath, and lean back on my seat. I know it's only because of the way I've felt since Jack and I split up that's making me react like this. But I still can't help it.

'What's up?' he says.

'Oh, nothing.' Then I look up and spot Beth on the other side of the room.

'I mean, I don't know,' I add.

But as Beth looks away, I realize I do know. Of course I know.

Chapter 103

My flat, Thursday, 28 June, 5.15 p.m.

I've got to admit, I'd almost given up on Benno's story about Pete Gibson, the angelic pop star with a secret penchant for cocaine and orgies.

After phoning Benno three times a week for the last two months to see whether the business with the dodgy copper has been sorted out, so I could go ahead and write my story, I started to fear that the whole thing was going to come to nothing.

Not least because I couldn't believe the nationals hadn't picked up on it yet. If I'm entirely honest, despite how desperate I have been for this story, I've also had other things on my mind more recently.

However, this evening, I get back from work after an early shift, slump in front of the television with a bowl of reconstituted noodles which look barely fit for human consumption, and the phone rings.

I recognize the voice as Benno's immediately.

'What are you up to?' he asks.

'Eating rubbish and watching *Richard and Judy*,' I say.

'Well, you need to tear yourself away from both and get

yourself down here with a snapper,' he announces. 'You're about to get your story.'

'What? Really?' In my excitement, I throw my bowl down on the couch next to me.

'But before that I want a favour,' he adds.

My heart sinks. 'You know we don't have much of a budget,' I say.

'Tsk, I know *that*, love,' he replies. 'I've seen the car you drive. No, you know my daughter?'

'Yes,' I say. 'How is Torremolinos?'

Benno and his wife had a ten-year head start on David and Victoria Beckham by naming their child after the place in which she was conceived.

'She's great,' he says. 'Now look – she wants to be a journalist. So I was just wondering if you'd be able to sort her out with some work experience or something.'

On these occasions I'm supposed to say that there's a long waiting list and she'll have to write to the Managing Editor. But this story is just too good and, even with the threat of a bollocking from Simon, I take an executive decision.

'Benno,' I tell him, 'I'll get her some work experience all right. In fact, I won't rest until she's editing the *Sunday Times*.'

Chapter 104

Green's Gym, Liverpool, Thursday, 28 June, 8.20 p.m.

We're printing the story about Pete Gibson in tomorrow's paper. In the event, the constable he was attempting to bribe was having none of it and turned out to be one of the good guys, after all. Which is fine by me, because, by itself, the fact that one of the saintliest pop stars in the UK is actually a cocaine dealer who regularly organizes celebrity orgies has got to constitute one of the scoops of the year.

The only thing is, I'm so nervous about it all, I'm now experiencing the sort of nausea I once had on a nine-hour ferry crossing in high winds. At work, they call it *the fear*, that horrible feeling journalists have just before a really big story breaks. It's a peculiar mixture of blood-pumping adrenaline because you know something amazing is about to be printed, and total knicker-wetting terror in case you've written something that will land the Editor in court. Which is never very good for your career prospects.

I've covered all bases on this three times over – as have the paper's lawyers – but at the end of the day, these are serious allegations and there is no doubt that a large helping of the brown stuff is going to hit the fan tomorrow.

So, here I am at the gym with Charlotte, trying to take my mind off things. Only it's the first time I've done any exercise in weeks and I'm starting to wish I'd brought a note from my mum to let me sit it out.

We start on the treadmills and I optimistically, and very foolishly, plump for a setting called 'World Endurance'. I plan to start off slowly, but somewhere along the way, manage to find myself in the middle of a K2 climb, along with the sort of gradient that shouldn't be attempted without crampons.

I frantically stride upwards in a movement reminiscent of Basil Fawlty's impression of the Germans and, with a mixture of panic and near-exhaustion, begin hitting the buttons like a hyperactive seven-year-old let loose on a fruit machine.

'Bloody hell!' I squeal, before slamming my hand against the emergency Stop button. The machine grinds to a halt and I lean over to rest on the side of the treadmill, feeling like my lungs are about to explode.

Charlotte giggles and when I get my breath back, I giggle too. We're both laughing now in a weird, hysterical kind of way. People are starting to look at us like we've been taking hallucinogenic drugs.

'How are you feeling these days, Evie?' she asks, when I finally manage to find a more sedate setting.

'Apart from nearly killing myself on a treadmill, you mean?' I grin.

'You know what I mean.'

'Oh, fine,' I say. 'Absolutely fine. Bit nervous about my story, but fine really.'

I know full well she's not talking about the story. And if

the truth be told, my jitters over that – even when they're making my stomach churn like the inside of a washing machine – still aren't a patch on the feelings about Jack.

But her question takes me a bit by surprise because people have stopped asking me about Jack recently. I guess three weeks after we split, it's becoming old news. Plus, it's not like I've ever given anyone much of an insight. I've only ever said the same thing as I say to Charlotte now. I'm fine. Couldn't be finer. I'm as fine as fine can be. Really, I'm very, very fine indeed.

'Well, if that's true then I'm glad to hear it,' says Charlotte, but she looks unconvinced.

'Why do you look like you don't believe me?' I ask.

She slows her treadmill down.

'We all just knew how much you liked him, I suppose,' she tells me.

'You mean you think I'm a sad act.'

'Course not,' she says. 'People just don't know what it's like to be in love with someone when it's not reciprocated.'

'God,' I say, panting. 'An outbreak of long words. What's all that about?'

'Well, they don't, Evie,' she repeats, and I suddenly realize that she looks really unhappy.

'What's up with you?' I want to know. 'I thought I had the monopoly in personal misery these days.'

'Oh nothing,' she says, shaking her head. 'I'm just premenstrual, that's all. I get upset at the slightest thing these days.'

'God, it must be bad if that includes me,' I say. 'Come on, shall we go for a drink?'

'I'll never say no to a Diet Coke,' she says.

I forget sometimes just how amazing Charlotte's transformation has been. But when she puts on a touch of make-up and pulls on a pair of jeans – which are now Skinny Fit as opposed to just Don't Fit – it strikes me how far she's come.

At the pub, we order two drinks and talk for the rest of the night, predominantly about my story. It feels good to get some of my nervous tension off my chest. Then, when last orders have been called, Charlotte brings up the thing I've been avoiding.

'Were you in love with Jack?' she asks, out of nowhere.

I take a deep breath.

'If I admitted that to myself, I really would be a dead loss, wouldn't I?'

'What do you mean?'

'I mean,' I say, 'that if the only man I had ever fallen in love with turned out to be someone who didn't want me . . . well, that'd be bloody tragic.'

'Hmm,' she says.

'Besides, I'm having a nice time with Seb,' I say.

'*Nice?*' she echoes, and I realize I sound about as convincing as Jack the Ripper's defence lawyer.

'I guess I've discovered one thing,' I say, 'that sometimes, no matter how much you want someone, no matter how much you love them, no matter how desperate you are for them . . . sometimes you just can't have them. It hurts like hell. But sometimes you just can't have them.'

I look up at Charlotte and she's wiping her eye. Then I remember something – what she said at my mum's wedding, about having kissed someone. I still haven't got to the bottom of that.

I'm just about to bring this up when the landlord comes over.

'Haven't you two got homes to go to?' he grumbles.

With the exception of a German Shepherd polishing off a packet of cheese and onion crisps at the other end of the bar, I look round and see that we're the last ones in the whole pub.

Chapter 105

Daily Echo *newsroom, Friday, 29 June*

The Editor's PA asks me to go and see him just after the first edition of the paper has come up from the press hall at 11 a.m. the next day. When I knock on the door, Frank is on the phone, but beckons me in.

'I don't give a toss about how much work your fella's done for charity, Diamond,' he bellows. 'He should have thought of that before he let his crotch do his thinking for him.'

The Diamond he's talking to is Dale Diamond, celebrity agent and staunch advocate of the What They Don't Know Won't Hurt Them school of public relations. By the sound of the protestations I can hear coming from the telephone receiver, Mr Diamond doesn't appear to be very happy with today's splash.

'You'll go to the Press Complaints Commission?' booms Frank again. 'Ha! On what grounds exactly? Causing undue distress to a dirty old drug dealer? Don't make me laugh. Anyway, I've had enough of this conversation, Diamond. I'll speak to you when you've managed to grow a brain. Goodbye.'

He slams the phone down and stands up to walk over to

his conference table, where today's paper – printed only a few minutes ago – is sitting.

'Evie,' he says, jabbing the main picture of Pete Gibson being arrested outside his multi-million pound mansion, 'this is fucking brilliant. Absolutely fucking brilliant.'

Frank Carlisle has many fine qualities as an Editor, but being able to get through a sentence without using at least one expletive is not one of them.

'Thanks, Boss,' I say, wondering if I should remain standing here like a schoolgirl in the Headmaster's office, or just sit down.

'Take a seat,' he says, as if reading my mind, and I pull out a chair from around his huge conference table.

'I've been impressed with your stuff lately, Evie,' he tells me. 'Bloody impressed, actually. You've got balls, and I like a reporter with balls.'

'Er, that's nice of you to say, Boss,' I say.

'Now, the thing is,' he goes on, 'you know we're about to lose Sam to one of the nationals?'

'Yes, of course.' Sam Webb, the crime reporter, has landed a job working for *The Times* and is due to leave in less than two weeks.

'Well, that leaves a gap,' Frank continues.

'Right,' I say.

'I only want someone in an "acting" capacity, of course,' he warns me. 'But we can review that in a couple of months' time.'

'I see,' I say.

'So, I've got two questions for you,' he goes on.

'Okay,' I say.

'Do you want the job?' he says. 'Or do you want the job?'

Chapter 106

St Nicholas's Church, Friday, 13 July

Valentina said that only a small core of the main protagonists would be here for her wedding rehearsal, which by my count today means about sixty of us. As well as seven bridesmaids, there is an entire army of people fussing over the music, the flowers, the choreography, the reading and just about anything and everything, in fact, to ensure that the Big Day tomorrow is stage-managed to perfection.

'Did you hear how one of Valentina's stylists took the Vicar to one side to request that he does his hair differently tomorrow?' whispers Grace.

I shake my head in disbelief.

'So now even the seventy-year-old curate has got to look like he's just stepped out of *Vogue*?' I say.

'Don't feel too sorry for him,' chuckles Grace, digging me in the ribs. 'He apparently asked them if they could put in some highlights for him.'

I laugh, but the truth is, neither I nor Grace – nor, for that matter, Charlotte – are in the mood for this today. Grace is putting a brave face on things, but she's undoubtedly still having trouble at home and Charlotte, well, Charlotte is just acting very strangely.

As for me, I'm trying not to mope these days, I really am. And in many ways I've got absolutely no reason to do so. Work is going brilliantly. I've landed a good job – no, a *great* job – which, as far as my career is concerned, means the world is my oyster. But there's something about being here today, when I'd originally imagined I'd be here with Jack, that is preventing me from really getting into the swing of things. Thankfully, however, the bride-to-be is getting into the swing of things enough for everyone.

'Now,' says Valentina, who has somewhere along the way acquired a clipboard, 'I'd like to practise the entrance again. I'm a bit concerned about the posture of some of the bridesmaids, *naming no names . . .*' she says, looking at me.

'Subtle as ever, isn't she?' I mutter to Grace.

'Come on, girls, off we go to the back again,' orders Valentina, and she'd almost make a convincing Headmistress, if she wasn't wearing her *Von Dutch* baseball cap and a pair of four-inch mules.

'Do try not to slouch, Evie,' she says briskly. 'I know you don't exactly have a natural sense of grace, but if you *could* just make an effort, please?'

The church is a surprisingly modest one. I suspect Valentina would have preferred Westminster Cathedral, but apparently this is where generations of the Barnetts have married, and it was Edmund's one and only request.

He got St Nicholas's Church, she got four wedding co-ordinators, a contract with *High Life!* magazine and a dress costing more than the GDP of some small states. I think, on balance, she did quite well out of the deal.

When we're at the back of the church, Valentina links arms with Federico, a former male stripper turned model and her mother's thirty-one-year-old boyfriend. He's the one who will be giving her away tomorrow.

Valentina has only met him once before and didn't particularly like him then, but given the Barnetts' fondness for tradition, she felt strongly that she needed someone – anyone, in fact – to walk her down the aisle. Well, anyone she'd never slept with, which obviously narrowed it down. A tiny bit. So Federico it was.

'Can you take over here, Jasmine,' Valentina says, foisting her clipboard on one of her planners. 'I'm needed for the important bit.'

Jasmine gives a nod to the organist and the church is filled with the opening bars of Mendelssohn's 'Wedding March'. Valentina flicks back her hair, grabs Federico by the arm and begins her walk down the aisle with a smile that says she couldn't be more pleased with herself if she'd made it to a Wimbledon final.

'Remember, not too fast,' warns Jasmine, but Valentina has no intention of speeding this up.

Even with the pews only half-full with wedding organizers, she is obviously enjoying herself too much to do anything other than a slow, dramatic walk that allows everyone the opportunity to look at her for as long as they might wish.

Valentina's mother, Mrs Allegra D'Souza, is in one of the adjacent pews and as they walk past, she lifts a glamorous hand and blows Federico a kiss through the most startlingly white set of dental veneers I've seen in my life. Federico winks back, prompting Valentina to tut and tug at his arm like a disobedient puppy.

It takes a good few minutes to get to the altar, before Valentina turns around and supervises her bridesmaids, shuffling into place at the front one by one.

'Very good, Georgia, and you too, Grace,' she says. 'Evie, *really*, if you could just take a leaf out of Grace's book, you'd be fine.'

I bite my lip and glance sympathetically over to Edmund as he stands at the front with Patrick – his best man – next to him.

We go through the vows four more times until, finally, Valentina is happy with everything.

'Now everyone,' she concludes, 'I'll see you all tomorrow, and don't be late. That includes you, pumpkin,' she adds, flashing a smile at Edmund. He leans over and kisses her on the nose, looking utterly besotted.

As people start to head for home, Valentina makes a beeline for Grace, Charlotte and me.

'Can I just say that I don't know what the matter is,' she snaps, 'but all three of you look like you're rehearsing for a funeral, not a wedding. And, yes, that includes you, Charlotte.'

'I'm just a bit tired,' she says. 'I've had a busy week at work.'

'If you say so,' Valentina replies huffily. 'Although I hadn't thought working at the Inland Thingumijig was particularly pressurized.'

Charlotte simply shrugs.

'And, Evie,' Valentina goes on, '*buck up*, will you? You've just been promoted, for goodness' sake! I mean, correct me if I'm wrong, but doesn't that mean that it might not be long before you can go and work for a proper newspaper?'

I am considering whether or not to dignify this with an answer when Valentina turns to Grace.

'Now, Grace,' says Valentina, 'what on earth have you got to be down in the dumps about? You managed to bag a lovely husband before any of the rest of us.'

'I'm all right, Valentina,' says Grace. 'Honestly. I'm just tired, like Charlotte. I'll be fine tomorrow. We all will be.'

Valentina frowns. 'Well, I do hope so,' she says, turning on her heels. 'Because God knows what the *High Life!* team will think otherwise.'

Chapter 107

'Does anybody want a lift?' asks Grace when we get outside the church.

'I've got my car with me,' I tell her.

'No, it's okay,' says Charlotte.

'Come on, Charlotte,' Grace urges. 'We go right past your flat. How are you going to get home otherwise?'

'Oh, I feel like the walk,' says Charlotte. 'Honestly.'

'Don't be daft, it's starting to rain. Tell her, Patrick, it's no trouble.'

Patrick is standing at the driver's door of his Audi, ready to go.

'Actually, I could do with getting straight back, Grace,' he says.

'What are you on about?' says Grace. 'It's on the way.'

'Really,' Charlotte interrupts. 'I'm fine.'

'See? She's fine,' says Patrick. 'Now, come on.' He gets into the car and slams the door.

'Well, if you're sure,' says Grace, looking bemused. 'I'll see you tomorrow then. Bye, Evie.'

When Grace is in the car, it reverses and speeds out of the church grounds like something being driven by Michael Schumacher.

'Christ, he's in a hurry,' I say. 'Why didn't you want to go with them?'

Charlotte shrugs. 'I really could do with the walk,' she says.

'In this rain?' I query. 'All that diet food must have got to your brain.'

She smiles.

'You're welcome to come with me, if you want,' I offer.

'Well, if you don't mind,' she says, slightly to my surprise.

'You'll just have to move a few McDonald's cartons first,' I tell her. 'And don't let my mother know you've seen them, she'd disown me.'

As I reverse out of the car park and head in the direction of Charlotte's flat with her in the passenger seat, I turn the radio on low enough for us to be able to talk over it.

'So what do you reckon?' I say. 'Are you and I always going to be the bridesmaids and never the brides?'

I'm trying to be jolly but there's something about the way it comes out that makes me sound like I want to slit my wrists.

'It's looking increasingly like it,' she says, trying to smile.

'But, hey, single isn't that bad, is it?' I say with the forced enthusiasm of a primary school PE teacher. 'In fact, it's quite fun, I think. I *enjoy* being able to go out when I like and with whom I like, whenever I like, and not have to justify myself to anyone else, thank you very much.'

'Hmm,' she says.

'I mean, who wants to get married anyway?' I continue. 'All you're doing is condemning yourself to a lifetime of conversation with the same person. How dull must that be?'

'You're probably right,' says Charlotte reluctantly. 'Being single isn't that bad.'

'And all this wedding malarkey,' I rant. 'I mean, at the end of the day, it's just a bloody big expensive party, isn't it? All that money, thrown away on one party! Think of all the other things you could buy.'

There's a silence.

'Like what?' says Charlotte finally.

'Well,' I say, determined to prove my point, 'you could go on holiday. A *brilliant* holiday. God, you could go anywhere – and fly first-class too. You could sit at the front sipping champagne and getting your bunions massaged, while the oiks in Economy battle with the lids of their in-flight meals and get snotty remarks from the flight attendants. Fantastic.'

She nods. Then says: 'By yourself though.'

I frown. 'I thought we were agreed there was nothing wrong with *by yourself*,' I say.

'Hmm.'

'Okay, let me think of a better example . . .' I pause for a few seconds to make sure it's a good one.

'Okay – just think of all the shoes you could buy,' I say.

'You sound like Valentina,' Charlotte giggles.

I groan. 'Fine,' I say. 'Then you could give the money to help starving children in Africa.'

I'd meant it to be flippant, but the second I say it, we both know I couldn't have picked a worse example to illustrate the point than something my ex-boyfriend does every day. As I continue driving silently, I look over at Charlotte, who is staring straight ahead with a very peculiar look on her face.

'Is everything all right?' I ask.

It takes her a moment before she says anything.

'Can I tell you something, Evie?' she asks.

'Of course,' I say immediately. 'Go on.'

'I'm in love,' she says.

She couldn't sound more matter-of-fact if she'd just told me she was off to the shops to buy some turnips. My mouth drops open in complete and utter amazement.

'Hey, that's fantastic!' I exclaim. 'Who with?'

She hesitates then takes a deep breath, before turning to look straight at me.

'With Patrick,' she says. 'I'm in love with Patrick.'

Chapter 108

It's done entirely subconsciously, but Starsky and Hutch have got nothing on the way I swerve my VW Golf to the side of the road, throwing Charlotte against the passenger door with the sheer force of the manoeuvre. When I'm confident I haven't accidentally run someone over, I pull the handbrake on and turn to her, barely able to believe what I've just heard.

'Patrick who?' I ask, in the vain hope there there has been a terrible mix-up and she's actually referring to some bloke who works in her local chip shop – and not our best friend's husband.

'*Patrick* Patrick,' she says.

'*Patrick* Patrick who?'

'Patrick *Cunningham*.'

I shake my head, unable to compute this piece of information.

'Let me get this straight,' I say, frowning. 'You're telling me that you are in love *with Patrick?* With *our* Patrick? With *Grace's* Patrick?'

'I know it sounds hard to believe.'

'Hard to believe? Charlotte, he's married to our best friend.'

367

'*Your* best friend, Evie,' she mutters.

My eyes widen. 'So not only are you in love with her husband but she's now no longer your friend?' I ask, incredulous.

'I didn't *say* that,' she replies.

I stare straight ahead, gripping the steering wheel.

'Well . . . how long have you felt like this?' I ask, trying to stay calm.

'From the moment I met him,' she tells me. 'Seven years, to be exact. I've felt like this ever since I first set eyes on him. I've never stopped loving him.'

The last sentence makes my blood run cold. How could I have not seen this? How could any of us have not seen this? My mind is a whirl of thoughts, not least how matter-of-fact Charlotte appears to be about the situation.

'But Charlotte,' I say, my voice torn between sympathy and exasperation, 'Patrick loves Grace. And Grace loves Patrick. They have a *family*. Whatever your feelings for him, you need to put a stop to them now. For your own sake. Because, Grace and Patrick – they're solid as a rock.'

She gives a snort of derision.

'What was that for?' I ask, shocked.

'You don't know the half of it, Evie.'

'What on earth do you mean?'

'Well, I'm just saying,' she continues. 'You speak as if the very idea of me and Patrick being together is ridiculous.'

'It *is* ridiculous,' I tell her, my voice rising uncontrollably.

Now Charlotte looks really annoyed.

'It might have been six months ago, Evie,' she says. 'But I'm as thin and . . . and fashionable . . . and attractive as anyone now.'

'What the hell has that got to do with anything?' I say.

She frowns. 'I'm just saying, the idea is *not* so ridiculous any more,' she says, her fury palpable.

I can't believe what I'm hearing. I think about Grace and the kids. I think about how distraught she's been about Patrick. I think about the fact that they've only been married a couple of months. For the first time ever, my feelings towards Charlotte are not entirely positive ones.

'Charlotte,' I say, 'you losing a load of weight has got nothing to do with this. The idea is a ridiculous one – not because you're not pretty enough for him – but because you're talking about our friend and her husband. About Grace and Patrick. Where's your loyalty?'

She gives another snort. And there's something about it which really sends me over the edge.

'Listen,' I say, turning to her, 'you need to forget this whole thing, Charlotte. Because you are *never* going to get together with Patrick, do you hear me? *Never.*'

The blood is rising to Charlotte's cheeks now.

'That, Evie,' she says quietly, 'is where you're wrong.'

'What?'

'I said, that's where you're wrong,' she continues, her face flaming. 'Patrick and I very much would get together. In fact, Patrick and I already have.'

Chapter 109

'What are you talking about?' I ask, dreading the answer.

'At your mum's wedding,' says Charlotte. 'You know I told you I'd kissed someone? Well, it was Patrick.'

I don't say anything.

'In fact,' she continues, 'we didn't just kiss.'

'What do you mean?'

Charlotte is clearly wondering whether or not she should go on. But there's no going back now – and she knows it.

'I'd . . . I'd gone for a walk to clear my head,' she says, her voice wobbling. 'I was feeling a bit drunk and – well, I found him doing the same thing. Just sitting – clearing his head. And so we started to talk. We talked and talked. And he told me things that you haven't got a clue about, Evie. That *Grace* hasn't even got a clue about.'

'And?'

'Then . . . well . . . it just happened. We started kissing.'

She pauses, unsure whether to say any more.

'And?'

She sighs. 'One thing led to another, as they say. And . . . we . . . we . . .'

'You what?'

'We had sex,' she says defiantly. 'There – you happy now? Patrick and I . . . *we had sex*.'

My eyes nearly pop out of my head.

'In the field?' I say, appalled. 'In the field when my mum's wedding reception was happening next door?'

Charlotte's lip is still wobbling, but she's not backing down.

'Yes, in the field,' she says, determined to hold her head high. 'Yes.'

'I don't believe you,' I say. But, actually, I do.

'It's true,' she replies. 'Ask him yourself if you like. But it's absolutely true.'

I am supposed to be employed as a wordsmith, but somehow words are failing me. I find myself just sitting, muttering under my breath, like a character from *One Flew Over the Cuckoo's Nest*.

'How could you?' I finally say. 'How could you do this to Grace?'

'I couldn't help it,' she whimpers, less defiant now. 'I mean it, Evie, I really couldn't help it.'

'Of *course* you could help it!' I cry.

'Let me put it this way,' she continues. 'What you're feeling about Jack at the moment: the heartbreak, the intensity, the pain – well, you've felt like that for a few weeks now. I've felt like that for seven years. *Seven long years*. You just couldn't begin to imagine what it's been like.'

I close my eyes. 'I don't think I know you very well any more, Charlotte,' I whisper. It's all I can think of.

She grabs my hand.

'Don't say that, Evie,' she pleads. 'You're my best friend. Please try to understand.'

'Do you even recognize what you've done is wrong?' I ask.

Charlotte sighs. 'I know what I've done isn't right,' she says, 'given that they're married. Of course. But I also know that doing the right thing has got me nowhere. Absolutely nowhere.'

I look into her eyes. 'Charlotte,' I say, 'you are one of my oldest friends. You know that I would do anything for you. But if you're responsible for breaking up that marriage, I don't know how I'll ever forgive you. I really don't.'

She puts her head in her hands and sobs silently. She sobs and she sobs, for I don't know how long. Finally, she lifts her head up.

'I won't break up their marriage,' she says.

'How are you so sure?'

She sniffs. 'Believe me, I'm sure,' she says, taking another pause for breath. 'He . . . he . . . made us stop almost immediately.'

'Go on.'

She shakes her head.

'That's how quickly he regretted it. God Almighty. I've been trying to kid myself into thinking it might have been the start of something. But I managed to make someone regret sleeping with me before it was even over.'

'So what happened?' I ask reluctantly, not particularly wanting the gory details but knowing I've got to hear them.

'He was so drunk,' she confesses. 'Not just drunk, actually, he could barely stand up. I can still picture him now, fumbling to zip his trousers up and virtually running away from me. And now, well, he's not even spoken to me since it happened. He *hates* me.'

Charlotte is sobbing hysterically, but I can barely bring myself to look at her. Then something else strikes me.

372

'I've got to tell Grace, you know,' I say.

She turns to me with panic in her eyes.

'Don't do that,' she says. 'Please don't do that.'

'She's my best friend,' I say. 'I've got to tell her.'

Charlotte starts shaking her head.

'No. No, you can't,' she gabbles. 'She's got two children. A family. You telling her is only going to be the fastest way to destroy that.'

I hesitate, biting one of my nails.

'But how *could* I keep this a secret from her?' I ask.

'All you would be doing is unburdening yourself,' she says. 'Tell her, and she and Patrick won't last the year.'

'How did you become so concerned for her and Patrick all of a sudden?' It comes out before I can stop myself.

'Hate me as much as you want, Evie,' she says dully. 'But what I'm saying is the truth.'

We sit in silence again.

'I don't hate you, Charlotte,' I tell her. 'I just can't believe this is happening. And I just can't see how I can keep this from Grace. I'd feel like a bloody accomplice.'

'Listen,' she says, 'don't say anything tomorrow at the very least. Not on Valentina's wedding day. It'd ruin everything. Just sit on it for a few days, then you'll realize what I'm saying is right.'

I don't know what the hell to do. Going along with Charlotte now is not something I feel particularly inclined to do. But she's undoubtedly right about Valentina's wedding day being the wrong time and place.

'A few days, then,' I decide. 'I'll think about it for a few days – that's all I'm promising.'

'Okay,' she says. 'Good.' She wipes her eyes.

'There's one thing I don't get though,' I say, partly wondering why I'm even telling her this. 'Patrick's been acting strangely since well before my mum's wedding. He's been . . . odd . . . for months now.'

Charlotte bites her lip.

'I think I might be able to shed some light on that,' she mumbles.

'Oh?'

'This is what our talk was about. Our long talk, before . . .'

'Well, what?' I say. 'Come on, spit it out.'

'Okay, okay,' says Charlotte, taking another deep breath. 'Patrick has lost his job.'

Chapter 110

Grace and Patrick's house, Saturday, 21 July

'I want to wear my bra,' whines Polly.

'You can't, I've told you,' says Grace, grabbing some baby food out of the microwave with one hand and brushing her hair with the other. 'Five-year-olds do not wear bras.'

'I bet Evie will be wearing a bra,' Polly replies. 'Won't you, Evie?'

'Well, yes,' I tell her. 'But I'm a 34B – and you're not.'

Polly pouts.

As usual, Grace's kitchen is so chaotic, it's starting to look less like the hub of a domestic household and more like the set of *It's A Knockout*. The theme to *Bob the Builder* has been blaring out for the last half-hour while Grace has galloped around ironing Polly's outfits, locating bottles of Calpol and entering into intense telephone negotiations with her mother about whether or not Scarlett should be eating with a knife and fork yet.

Grace plonks Scarlett in her high chair and starts shovelling a spoon into her mouth with a concoction on it she insists is lentil bake – but actually looks more like something you'd find splattered on the floor outside a nightclub at 2 a.m.

As Patrick wanders in, looking for something to polish his shoes with, I find myself studying his face in the light of Charlotte's revelations yesterday. He looks about as happy as you'd expect for someone who's secretly unemployed and has recently had a drunken shag with one of his wife's oldest friends.

'Well, I have to say I never thought Valentina and Edmund would end up together, did you?' Grace asks, looking at Patrick hopefully to see if he might answer her.

'Hmm,' he shrugs, pulling a duster out of the cupboard under the sink.

As best man, Patrick is due to meet the groom at his house in about twenty minutes. It won't be a minute too soon, as far as I'm concerned: just being in the same room as him and Grace, with the knowledge that I have but she doesn't, is making me feel distinctly twitchy.

'God knows what sort of marriage they'll have,' Grace ploughs on. 'I can't help thinking she'll walk all over him.'

'Maybe,' he says.

Grace flashes me an almost apologetic look as if to say: This is how stimulating our conversation gets these days. I look away immediately and start studying the nutritional information panel on the back of a packet of Cheerios.

'How does she get on with his parents?' she asks.

'Fine, I think,' Patrick grunts. 'Don't know, really.'

'Bernard probably loves her,' she continues, 'but Jacqueline . . . I don't know, I suspect she'd have preferred it if Edmund had brought someone a bit less exuberant home.'

'Hmm,' I say. 'Like Madonna.'

Patrick puts his duster back into the cupboard under the sink and walks towards the hallway, saying nothing. I hear the door to the loo shut just as Polly arrives wearing her lovely pale pink dress, through which her 'bra' – which is actually the top half of a bikini – is perfectly visible. She looks like a strange hybrid of Shirley Temple and a Kings Cross hooker.

'*Polly*,' says Grace wearily as Scarlett starts hurling her plastic bricks across the kitchen. 'What did I tell you?'

'I can't remember,' she says.

'I told you you couldn't wear that thing, didn't I?' says Grace.

'But—' she interrupts.

'No buts,' Grace says sternly.

'Yeah,' I add, starting to tickle her. 'Or we'll call Supernanny.'

Polly collapses into reluctant giggles, forcing their way through despite her being absolutely determined that she's going to sulk.

'I'd better get going,' says Patrick, appearing again.

'Daddy,' says Polly, 'can I wear my bra for the wedding? It's not a real bra, it's only a pretend one. And Grandma bought it for me because she thought it was nice and knew that it was only for me to play with really. So can I, Dad?'

Grace and I listen to all this almost speechless. If Polly is like this at five, what on earth will she be like when she's fifteen? Machiavelli?

'If Grandma bought it for you, then I don't see why not,' says Patrick, grabbing his car keys.

'Patrick!' protests Grace. 'No, she can't wear it! I could have throttled my mother when she bought her that.'

'But Daddy said I could,' says Polly, pulling a face so distraught you'd think she'd just been told she had to spend the rest of her life in a workhouse with a diet consisting of nothing but gruel and dried peas.

'Daddy didn't mean it,' says Grace. 'Did you, Daddy?'

Patrick flashes her a look.

'I *thought*,' he says indignantly, 'that Mummy and Daddy weren't supposed to contradict each other in front of the children.'

'You're right,' says Grace, with equal indignation, 'they're not. But Daddy obviously doesn't realize that *he's* just done exactly that.'

'Right,' he says, his tone getting firmer, 'but Mummy must surely accept that Daddy isn't psychic and therefore could not have been aware of whatever it was exactly that she'd said earlier.'

'Mummy *does*,' says Grace, 'but given Daddy now knows what Mummy's views were, she would be very grateful if he would back her up on this.'

He looks on the verge of throwing another comment so acidic it could melt the furniture, when suddenly his phone rings. He pauses to answer it.

'So,' says Polly, 'now that Mummy and Daddy have had a chat about it, I'm okay to wear my bra, aren't I?'

'No!' shouts Grace.

She and Polly continue their battle, as Bob the Builder chirps on and Scarlett whines for her next spoonful while banging plastic bricks on the table of her high chair. But, although so much is going on in this place you barely know where to look, I can't help focusing on one person. Patrick. Patrick is the only one who is silent, and as he listens to whoever is on the other end of the phone, he remains so, his face growing so white he soon starts to look like Christopher Lee.

Eventually, he puts the phone down.

'Who was that?' asks Grace.

'Evie,' he says, 'I think you'd better leave. I need to speak to Grace about something. I need to speak to her alone.'

Chapter 111

Knowsley Hall, Saturday, 21 July

Valentina is dressed from head to toe in the most expensive bridal couture money can buy, and she is wearing a tiara that would out-dazzle a Buckingham Palace chandelier. But something is not quite right: the bride isn't smiling.

'I don't know what I expected from the *High Life!* magazine team,' she pouts, as we pose for the first photographs of the day, 'but it wasn't one decrepit old slime ball taking the photos and a seventeen-year-old work experience girl doing the interviews.'

We're in the sweeping grounds of Knowsley Hall, one of the most impressive ancestral piles in the North of England and where – except for the church service – most of the action is taking place today.

'She is eighteen, apparently,' I tell her.

'Who?' asks Valentina.

'The interviewer. We were chatting earlier. She's called Drusilla – Drusilla von Something. Her dad's a Count somewhere in Europe who knows the magazine's owner.'

But Valentina isn't interested in Drusilla von Something's dad.

'Now listen,' she is saying to the photographer, 'how about one of me getting into the carriage with my bridesmaids close by?'

'Dear,' he snarls, 'you concentrate on looking pretty and I'll look after the pictures. Then we'll both get on just fine. Now, I think one of the bride and her father before they leave for the church would be nice. Where is your father exactly?'

'I am 'ere,' says Federico, sidling up to Valentina and putting his hand around her waist.

'You are *not* my father,' she tells him. 'He is *not* my father,' she tells everyone else.

'I know I am not *usually*,' says Federico, 'but I thought just for today, just for ze 'ere and now, zat's what I am to be.'

'You're giving me away, that's all,' she hisses. 'That doesn't alter the biological fact that you and I have nothing whatsoever to do with each other. You are here to decorate my arm, okay?'

'Okay, okay,' he says, holding his hands up. 'I get ze idea. You are so 'arsh sometimes, Valentina. But I like zat in a woman.'

Insistent that *High Life!* magazine has sent him with a list of instructions – including returning with a picture of the bride and her father – the photographer forces a reluctant Valentina to pose for a photo with Federico. The latter slings his arm low around her waist again in a pose that somehow doesn't look very paternal, given the proximity of his palm to the top of her buttock.

There is no doubt about it, Valentina has put some truly spectacular finishing touches to this wedding. The cake has been handcrafted in white Belgian chocolate and, at over five foot, it makes Michael Douglas and Catherine Zeta Jones's effort look like something from Marks & Spencer.

The dress cost so much there are semi-detached houses in parts of the country you could buy for less. And the look, according to Valentina, is elegant, but also sexy enough to ensure Edmund's pulse is just the right side of coronary failure the moment he sees her.

Of all the finishing touches though, none is more jaw-dropping than the one we're standing in front of now: her Cinderella carriage. Embedded with crystals and with four white horses at the front, I'm afraid Valentina's sense of taste has in this particular case been railroaded by her equally well-developed sense of exhibitionism. The idea was that it would befit a proper society wedding. In fact, it looks like the sort of thing Elton John might run around in, if he lived in Disneyland.

'It's quite a carriage,' says the photographer, and for a split second Valentina almost looks like she might change her view of him. 'I did Jordan and Peter's wedding and they had one just like it.'

'*Idiot*,' she huffs.

As the bridesmaids – with the exception of Grace – wait in the background, I take Charlotte to one side at the first opportunity I get.

'Was that you who phoned Patrick earlier?' I demand.

Her face flushes, but she looks defiant.

'Yes,' she says, gripping her bouquet.

'What did you say?' I ask.

'I told him that you knew,' she says. 'I told him that I'd told you everything.'

I frown.

'I had to,' she says. 'I couldn't risk you telling Grace first.'

'I told you I wouldn't, didn't I?' I whisper. 'At least not until after the wedding.'

She sniffs and shrugs.

'Whatever happens now happens,' she says, 'he knows how I feel. The ball is in his court.'

I shake my head, unable to even contemplate what could be happening at Grace's house at this moment in time.

'Ah, excuse me, ah,' says Drusilla, the *High Life!* journalist, stepping forward.

'Ah, do you think I could do my, ah, interview, yet?' she says.

'Absolutely,' says Valentina briskly. 'Fire away.'

'Ah, yah, well, okay,' she says. 'So, did you and Mr Barnett meet at a party?'

'He was best man at another wedding, actually,' Valentina tells her. 'That of two of my dearest friends, Grace and Patrick. That might be too much detail, but you don't have to mention them by name if you don't want. However, it might be nice if you did mention that I have many friends. Many dear, dear friends.'

'Ah, yah, okay,' says Drusilla, taking down shorthand notes at a rate of about six words per minute. 'And, ah, now, ah . . . do you like parties?'

'Well, yes,' says Valentina. 'Of course I do – who doesn't?'

'Right,' says the girl. 'And what kind of parties do you go to?'

'Well, all sorts of parties,' Valentina continues. 'But what have they got to do with my wedding?'

'Oh, ah, well, I'm not sure really,' says Drusilla. 'But my Editor said I should always ask about parties. She said if I make sure I ask about parties I won't go wrong.'

'You're not aiming for a Pulitzer Prize with this article then,' says Valentina.

Chapter 112

Georgia is starting to look a bit concerned. But not, I suspect, as concerned as I am.

'When do we need to head off to the church?' she asks.

'Not for another hour,' I say. 'Has Grace turned up yet?'

'Erm . . .' Georgia glances up to see whether Valentina is listening.

'You mean *no*, don't you?' Valentina shrieks. 'You'd think on today of all days she might have made the effort to turn up on time.'

'I'm sure she won't be long,' says Georgia. 'You know what she's like. She's always late – but she always makes it in the end.'

'That may be,' says Valentina. 'But there's *no way* Andrew Herbert is going to be able to do her hair in this amount of time. The man may be a genius with colour, but time travel is not one of his skills, as far as I'm aware.'

'Look,' says Georgia, 'why don't you come inside and have a glass of champers with the rest of us?'

'Fine,' says Valentina, marching off towards the main house. 'I'd had enough of David Bailey and his intrepid reporter anyway.'

When we reach the drawing room, we each take a glass of champagne and it's not long before everyone starts to relax. Even Valentina. And even me. And soon, the place takes on the hint of merry excitement that every wedding should have. As I sip my champagne and look across at Valentina, glowing with happiness and about to commit herself to one man for the rest of her life, I feel compelled to say something.

'Right,' I find myself announcing. 'I'd like to propose a little toast.'

Everyone stops what they're doing and looks over at me.

'Well, Valentina,' I say, 'we've all known you for over six years now and, like any friendships, there have been ups and downs. But there's little doubt that you are one in a million. And luckily, you've found a man who's one in a million too. Someone who absolutely adores you and someone who's determined to never let you go. And that is one of the most . . . well, it's one of the most amazing things in the world.'

My throat goes dry and I suddenly feel ridiculously emotional, with thoughts of Grace and Patrick and Charlotte, but above all Jack, whirling through my head.

I look upwards and pretend to check my mascara as tears well up in my eyes. A vivid image of Jack's wide, generous smile flashes into my head and I'm furious with myself for feeling so weepy.

'Are you all right, Evie?' asks Georgia, but as she puts her hand on my arm, it just seems to make the tears welling in my eyes even more determined to make their break for freedom.

'Yes, yes,' I say, pulling myself together. 'Now raise your glass, everyone. *To Valentina!*'

'*To Valentina!*' everyone shouts, clapping as she laps up the limelight.

'Oh look,' says Georgia, glancing out of the window. 'Here's Grace now.'

'Well, thank God for that,' says Valentina. 'Although I hope she knows she can't leave her car there in the middle of the driveway. I don't want an Audi on the wedding photos. Especially not one that's three years old.'

But as Grace's footsteps approach the room less than a minute later and the door bursts open, it's quite obvious for all to see that the wedding photos are the last thing she's interested in right now.

Chapter 113

Grace looks about as ready to be a bridesmaid as someone who has just mucked out a farmyard. But it's not just the jeans, lack of make-up and general state of dishevelment that is the most striking thing about her. It's the look on her face. As if she's about to explode.

'You,' she says, pointing at Charlotte. 'You and I have got some talking to do.'

'Grace!' shrieks Valentina. 'There's no time for talking – we need to get your hair in curlers!'

'I'm sorry, Valentina,' says Grace, 'but I've got something more important to do at the moment than get my hair done.'

'What could *possibly* be more important than getting your hair done?' asks the bride-to-be. 'The service is happening in less than forty minutes.'

Grace turns back to Charlotte.

'Do you want to do this here, or outside?' she demands.

Valentina looks horrified.

'Listen, Grace,' she says, 'I know how difficult Evie can be sometimes, but really, can't you just put your differences aside for the moment? At least until the *High Life!* team has gone home.'

Poor Valentina obviously thinks it's me Grace has fallen out with.

'Well, Charlotte, what's it to be?' asks Grace.

Charlotte's entire face and chest have turned so red it looks like she needs extinguishing.

'Grace,' she says, her mouth quivering as if she's about to say something. But nothing comes out.

'Right,' says Valentina, taking charge. 'Enough's enough. What's going on?'

Grace's face crumples.

'How could you, Charlotte?' she says. 'How could you do it after being my friend for so many years? After seeing my children growing up? After being my bridesmaid?'

Now Charlotte looks at the floor silently, her lip still quivering.

'You've acted like Miss Sweetness and Light for as long as I've known you, Charlotte. But tell everyone what you've done. Go on.'

Charlotte doesn't move and still doesn't say anything.

'No? Well, let me tell everyone instead,' Grace says. 'Charlotte has been trying to steal my husband from me.'

'What?' says Valentina. 'Grace, have you been drinking?'

'Just ask her,' Grace says. 'Ask her about attempting to seduce Patrick – at your mum's wedding, Evie.'

I bite my lip and look at the floor, suddenly aware that Patrick hasn't told her that I know. I have about 0.2 seconds to feel relieved, when Grace does a double-take.

'You knew!' she yells at me.

'The thing is, Grace . . .' I begin to protest.

'You bloody knew!' she continues. 'Jesus, I don't believe this.'

'*I* didn't,' stresses Valentina. 'Why am I always the last to know these things?'

Charlotte, shaking and red, suddenly looks defiant.

'Okay, Grace,' she says. 'How could I? Well, I'll tell you how.'

The whole room is suddenly very, very quiet.

'Because I love him,' she says. Valentina looks like she's going to pass out.

'I love him more than I suspect you've ever loved him,' continues Charlotte. 'I'd do anything for him. I'd die for him. Can you honestly say that?'

Grace doesn't answer.

'No,' says Charlotte. 'I didn't think so.'

Grace slumps onto a chair, suddenly looking very weary.

'If it means anything,' Charlotte adds solemnly, 'I did feel guilty – about you and the kids. It wasn't as if I didn't think about you and them at all.'

Grace, her face filled with emotion, stands up again and walks towards Charlotte. For a second, it looks like she's about to hug her. But when she gets within a foot of Charlotte, she punches her square in the face.

Chapter 114

'I 'ad no idea English weddings were zis exciting,' says Federico as we trundle along in the Cinderella carriage.

'Oh shut up,' says Valentina, as Georgia puts a supportive hand on hers.

The carriage has the sort of suspension you'd expect from the back end of a tractor, and whoever hired the horses at the front of the carriage just may have found the four most flatulent beasts in Britain. On the plus side, however, Valentina is somehow slightly calmer now, even though we're downwind of the most horrendous whiff outside the elephant enclosure of Chester Zoo.

She's even managed to stop hyperventilating about the fact that she's now one bridesmaid down, having had to dispatch Charlotte to Accident and Emergency. And the fact that three of her other bridesmaids now have the slight but unmistakable splatter of blood and snot – the resulting debris from Grace's punch – across their dresses.

Mine is the worst, with a big gory blob right on the front of my skirt that was only made worse by a frantic amount of scrubbing. But if I position my bouquet in a certain way I can almost cover it, and Drusilla from *High Life!* has assured

Valentina that they'll be able to airbrush any excess off before they go to print.

'Grace,' I say, as we bump up and down, negotiating a section of road with more pot-holes than a third-world dirt track, 'can we talk about this?'

'Yes, please do,' insists Valentina. 'Make friends, for God's sake. Or at least start smiling like you're all meant to.'

'I'm too angry and upset to talk about it,' says Grace, a fraction away from tears. 'Now isn't the time.'

'No,' says Valentina. 'No, you're probably right. No more drama today, thank you. But *do* smile, won't you? *Please.*'

We slow down at a set of traffic-lights, but before we get a chance to stop, the carriage starts to make a strange sound. A very strange sound indeed. A cracking sound.

Valentina's eyes widen and we all look at each other in alarm. Then, all of a sudden, the cracking sound gets louder and one corner of the carriage plummets to the ground, catapulting bridesmaids and posies and satin shoes and veils and tiaras into all directions.

'What the fuck—' cries Valentina as she bangs her head on the windowframe, completely forgetting her role as the demure bride.

'What ze 'ell is going on?' shouts Federico.

We climb out of the carriage and the sight before us doesn't look promising at all.

'The goddamn bloody goddamn wheel has broken,' screams Valentina, apparently directing this tirade at the driver.

He scratches his head and looks exceptionally calm about the whole thing, which is completely inappropriate in the circumstances.

'Oh dear,' he says.

'Well, what are you going to do about it?' she asks hysterically.

He shrugs. 'Not sure really,' he says. 'You can't just call the AA with one o' these.'

Valentina fans her forehead.

'So how do you propose I get to the church?' she growls.

He shrugs again. 'You could always hitch-hike, love.'

Chapter 115

We'd thought at first he was joking. But with everyone we know already in church with their mobile phones switched off and not a taxi in sight, hitch-hiking suddenly became the only option.

So we split ourselves into two parties, and my group piles into the rear of a van belonging to a fish merchant just on his way back from the wholesalers. Having left the house smelling of Vera Wang, we arrive at the church smelling of *eau de haddock*.

But for the other group – the bride and her 'father' – we reserve a vehicle we all agreed would *almost* pass for a wedding car – if the *High Life!* photographer and the video man catch her at the right angle, that is.

'You might need to do a bit of editing of this,' I tell the video man as we wait outside the church for them to arrive.

'Why?' he says. 'What is it she's coming in exactly?'

'Er, you'll see,' I say. 'Just do your best, will you?'

As Valentina and Federico's vehicle comes into the driveway head on, nothing at all looks amiss from a distance. It's only when it has to make a right turn to park that all becomes clear. The video man and the *High Life!* photographer gasp so dramatically, you'd think they'd both just received a sharp kick in the groin.

'Tell me she's not in a hearse,' breathes the *High Life!* photographer. 'She *can't* be in a bloody hearse, surely?'

'Like I said,' I tell him, trying to retain a sense of calm, 'if you photograph her getting out from the front, it could easily look like a wedding car.'

'But what about the flowers in the window?' he asks. 'They're arranged to spell out RIP BILLY.'

'I know, I know,' I say, realizing we must be presenting one of the biggest challenges to his professional career to date. 'But they've said we can shove those in the back with the coffin for a couple of shots. Come on, we'll have to be quick.'

As Valentina emerges from her hearse, beaming from ear to ear and apparently unfazed by the fact that she's just shared her journey with a corpse *and* Federico, I start to see her in a whole new light.

'I'm bloody impressed,' I say to her as we stand at the back of the church, ready to go in. 'You're taking all this incredibly well.'

She smiles.

'Well,' she says. 'It suddenly struck me on the way here: I'm about to get married. Why would I let anything else bother me?'

Chapter 116

I strongly suspect that I'll never be able to go to a wedding again without thinking about Jack.

It's not just the fact that our brief but oh so sweet courtship both started and finished at occasions just like these. It's also that everything weddings are meant to represent – love, commitment, happiness – are things I now honestly believe I'm never going to find with anyone else.

I know that sounds about as positive as the average suicide note, but I'm just being realistic. I mean, why would I find love with anyone else when I hadn't even come close beforehand? I had my chance and I blew it. Simple as that.

'What's up with you?' Seb asks when we get to the reception. 'You looked as miserable as sin throughout that whole service.'

'Nothing,' I say. 'I'm fine. Absolutely fine.'

'Well, I wish you'd cheer up. You're putting *me* in a bad mood,' he says.

'Sorry,' I mutter.

'Don't worry,' he says, leaning over and whirling his tongue around my ear with all the subtlety of a St Bernard devouring a lamb chop. 'You can make it up to me later.'

He puts his hand on my backside and squeezes it as if he's trying to determine the ripeness of a Gala melon.

'Don't, Seb,' I grimace. 'Not at a wedding.'

In fact, not wanting to be groped is something I can only partly put down to the occasion. It's also because, despite trying very hard to make this work, I can now barely look at Seb without wishing he was somewhere else. Like Outer Mongolia.

As the guests start to pour into the main dining room of Knowsley Hall, it quickly becomes evident that the bride's and groom's camps aren't mixing. I'm not sure why it happens exactly and I'm sure they're not doing it intentionally. It's just that those in the groom's party seem to feel a little ill-at-ease speaking to anyone who isn't wearing a twinset and pearls; ditto the bride's party and anyone without a facelift.

I haven't eaten anything all day, but as I turn down a smoked salmon canapé for the fourth time, I realise I couldn't feel less like eating if I'd just had three super-sized McDonald's.

'I'm just going to the gents for a bit of a pick-me-up,' whispers Seb, winking. 'To get me through the speeches.'

I'm sipping my champagne when I feel a tap on my shoulder.

'Whatever happened to Charlotte?' asks my mum.

Today's outfit consists of a purple velvet culotte suit and matching Robin Hood hat, the feather of which made several guests sneeze throughout the entire ceremony.

'It's a long story,' I say.

'Well, as long as she's okay,' Mum says.

'She will be,' I reply, not entirely confidently.

When Seb returns, he looks slightly taken aback to come face to face with my mum. Sarah often has this effect on people, but they don't usually greet her with quite the same look of distaste.

'Hello,' she says brightly. 'I don't think we've met. I'm Sarah, Evie's mum.'

'Hi,' he says dismissively, and grabs the last glass of champagne for himself from a passing tray.

'I think you were at Georgia's wedding, weren't you?' Mum continues, smiling. 'You might not remember me, but I was there too.'

'I remember you all right,' he sniggers, and turns away.

At first, Mum looks a little thrown by his comment. And I'm so startled that, for once, I can't think of anything to say.

'Well,' she says, forcing a smile, 'I'm sure I'll see you later. Enjoy the rest of the day.'

When she's out of earshot I turn to Seb.

'Don't take the piss out of my mum,' I say, in a tone that makes it clear he's unlikely to get his tongue anywhere near my ear canal again.

'Oh, come on – all I said was I remembered her,' he says carelessly.

'You said: *I remember you all right*,' I tell him.

'Well, Christ, how could I not have, the way she looked?'

'Why are you so obsessed with the way people look?' I ask. 'My mum is a wonderful person – and if you'd bothered to speak to her, then I'm sure you'd have discovered that.'

'What-*ever*,' he says, sounding like a stroppy teenager. 'Christ, when did you become such a bloody drag? Anyway, it was just a joke.'

He takes another swig from his glass, apparently finding

the whole thing more entertaining than a trip to the seaside.

'I know,' I say matter-of-factly. 'But the thing is, Seb, I just don't get your jokes.'

The smile is wiped off his face in a second.

'I suppose,' I continue, 'I don't want to see you any more. I'm sorry.'

'You're dumping me at a wedding?' he asks, incredulous. 'I haven't even had my dinner yet.'

'I'm sorry, Seb,' I say. 'But I'm in love with someone else.'

'You?' he sneers. 'In love? Ha – don't make me laugh.'

'It's true,' I say forlornly.

'Evie, it'll last five minutes, just like they all do,' he says, turning dramatically on his heel.

I watch as Seb storms across the room and heads for the door, before I sense someone next to me and turn to look. The video man is happily filming away as if he's gathering footage for a David Attenborough programme.

'Do you *mind*?' I snap. 'Can't a girl expect a little privacy when she's dumping someone these days?'

'Oh, sorry,' he tells me. 'I was just told to film as many guests as I could.'

Chapter 117

I'm starting to think I'm more likely to bump into the Yeti than Grace during this wedding.

I've spent the last half-hour searching for her, desperate to talk things through, and all without success. Then, just when I'm starting to think she might have left, I spot her across the other side of the room, talking to Bob. I immediately make a beeline for them but am stopped in my tracks by a familiar voice – a voice that is about as pleasing to the ear as the sound of chalk scraping across a blackboard.

'Evie! Looking amazing, as ever.'

I turn around and see Gareth outside on the balcony, pulling on a Marlboro with the sort of suction you'd expect from a top-of-the-range vacuum cleaner.

'I don't want to talk to you, Gareth,' I say.

This is the first time I've seen him since he decided he was going to tell Jack all about me, my past and those bloody earrings.

'Oh, why not?' he says. 'Not over that business with the earrings? And your, well, your *commitment problem*. I hope I didn't put my foot in it.'

'You told Jack about that deliberately, didn't you?'

Gareth shrugs, trying to look cool, but the vigour with which he's scratching his face again suggests he's feeling anything but.

'I just didn't think he was right for you, that's all,' he mumbles.

'Oh, and why not? Because I liked him more than you?'

'You don't suit being angry, Evie,' he says, wagging his finger at me.

'Gareth,' I begin, deciding maybe I do want to talk to him after all, 'can I speak to you bluntly?'

'Of course,' he says.

'I've tried to be nice to you,' I tell him. 'I tried to let you down gently. I tried not to have to tell you that if you were the last animal, mineral or vegetable left on the planet I'd still rather spend a night indoors watching *Countdown* by myself. I've said I'm sorry for dumping you countless times and, quite frankly, I'm not going to say it again. Because now I'm not sorry. Now I'm *glad* I dumped you. I just wish I'd realized earlier what a sneaky little toad you were.'

'So, let me get this straight,' he states, frowning. 'You're saying you really, really won't agree to go out with me again? Like, really?'

I snatch the cigarette from his hand and slowly stub it out on his pink polyester tie. His eyes widen in disbelief.

'Gareth,' I tell him, 'I think we're finally starting to understand each other.'

Chapter 118

As I approach Grace and Bob, she straightens her back and I realize my presence is about as welcome as an outbreak of avian flu at Flamingo World.

'Evie!' says Bob when he spots me. 'Grace and I were just comparing honeymoons. Our three weeks in Colombia sounds rather different from the Maldives. We loved it, of course. But I have to say I'm secretly rather jealous of their flushing toilet.'

'I bet,' I nod.

'By the way,' he adds, 'I saw you talking to Gareth there. I finally found out why he left work in such strange circumstances.'

'Oh, why?' I ask.

'You know I told you there was something funny going on between him and Deirdre Bennett, my colleague? Well, it turned out they'd had a very brief fling.'

'Wasn't this the lady with the big bottom and terrible teeth?' I ask.

'That's the one,' says Bob. 'Not that that put Gareth off! By the time he left, he was virtually stalking her. Even bought her some strange rubber underwear from one of those

401

funny shops – you know the ones I mean. That was when the Vice Chancellor stepped in to tell him to either put a stop to it or leave. Fortunately, he decided on the latter and Deirdre hasn't heard anything from him since, ooh, about when you started dating him actually. I think you'd do well to steer clear of him, personally.'

'I think you're right, Bob. But listen,' I continue, 'is there any chance I could speak to Grace for a second? By ourselves, I mean.'

'Of course,' says Bob. 'I was about to go and find your mother anyway. I'd left her telling one of Edmund's aunts all about the wormery she's installing. I'm not sure it was quite Lady Barnett's thing.'

As soon as Bob is out of earshot, I get straight to the point.

'I'm sorry for not telling you, Grace,' I say. 'I really am. But I only found out last night and, well, I just wanted to get the wedding over so that it didn't ruin things.'

She sighs. 'It's a bit late for that now.'

'I know,' I say.

'So you *were* going to tell me?' she asks.

'Well, yes, I think so,' I say, realizing immediately that I could have made life easier by just saying yes.

'What do you mean *you think so?*' she says. 'You're supposed to be my best friend. Best friends can't keep secrets like that from each other.'

'I know, I know,' I say. 'I'm sure I would have told you. But it wasn't as simple as that. I was worried about what it would do to you and Patrick. I mean, I knew things had been . . . tricky . . . recently and I was scared that just coming out and telling you might have – well, made things even trickier.'

402

'Don't worry about it,' she says, sniffing. 'You're not the only one who finds it difficult to tell me what's going on.'

I hesitate. 'You're talking about Patrick losing his job, aren't you?'

'Oh,' she says despondently. 'You knew about that too.'

'Sorry,' I say, lowering my head. 'That's all I know though. I don't know why or what it's all about or anything.'

'He confessed everything earlier,' she says. 'He lost his job months ago, just after our wedding. That's what's been wrong with him.'

'But why?' I ask.

'They made him redundant,' she sighs. 'I know – unbelievable, isn't it? I'd always thought of redundancy as something that happened to, I don't know, miners and car workers and . . . well, not lawyers. Not Patrick. But he was just called in one day, told there had been a downturn in business and the firm needed to do some cost-cutting. Then he was out on his ear. Just like that.'

'God,' I say lamely. 'No wonder he's been in a bad mood.'

'He's been going out doing the odd bit of freelance stuff,' continues Grace, 'but nowhere near enough to pay the bills in the long term. What I can't believe though, is that he couldn't even bring himself to tell me. What sort of wife must I be?'

'Don't be ridiculous,' I say. 'You're a brilliant wife and Patrick loves you. You do know that, don't you?'

She sniffs again and doesn't answer.

'You know exactly what happened between him and Charlotte, don't you?' she asks.

I nod. 'Yes. She told me. She also told me it was over in seconds and he couldn't get away from her fast enough.'

403

Grace's lip starts trembling.

'Still doesn't change the fact that he had sex with one of my friends.'

I put my arm around her.

'I know, sweetheart, I know,' I say. 'But don't let this destroy your marriage, Grace. Please don't. For your own sake and for the kids.'

As I say it I don't completely know whether what I'm telling her is good advice or not. I mean, she's right. Her husband had sex with her friend. How could anyone forgive that? And yet, something deep down tells me that, ultimately, that's got to be the right thing to do.

'I guess I've got a lot of thinking to do,' she says. 'It's still so raw. I need to have a long think about what I'm going to do.'

'Well, for God's sake blow your nose first,' I say, and lean over to hug her.

She wraps her arms so tightly around me, I'm struggling to breathe.

'Thanks, Evie,' she says. 'I love you.'

'I love you too, Grace,' I say.

Suddenly, Patrick is by our side. He looks terrified – of Grace and of me.

'Do you mind if I borrow my wife, Evie?' he says. 'I've got some serious making up to do.'

Grace looks up at him.

'I'm not taking anything for granted, Grace,' he says, 'but I will do anything – *anything* – for you to stay with me. For you to forgive me. I know I don't deserve you, but I'm nothing without you, Grace. I mean that.'

Chapter 119

'Well, it's a hell of a wedding, anyway,' says Georgia, as we share her make-up bag in the ladies. Her cosmetic collection is a combination of £3.99 Rimmel lipsticks and face powders that probably cost more than gold dust.

'Makes yours look distinctly tame, doesn't it?' I say, sweeping a blusher brush across my cheeks in an attempt to revive some colour in them. 'No physical fights, no coffins, no marital bust-ups. It was all a bit boring, really.'

'Thank God,' she laughs. 'Although, give Valentina some credit. She's really taken it all on the chin. Speaking of which, how are you feeling these days, Evie?'

'How do you mean?' I ask.

'Well, I heard you were still a bit upset over Jack,' she says. 'And we've not really had a chance to talk about it, have we? I haven't even seen you since your mum's wedding.'

'I'm fine,' I say. 'Honestly, Georgia. These things happen.'

'Well, if it means anything,' she continues, 'Beth said he's been moping around work ever since it happened.'

I pause.

'Beth?' I repeat.

'Yes, Beth. You know – my cousin,' she says.

Jane Costello

'Yes,' I say. 'I know your Cousin Beth. I just thought you said "he'd been moping *around work*".'

'I did,' says Georgia. 'They work together.'

'Really?' I am slightly confused. 'God, I had no idea. I mean, I'd worked out they were seeing each other, but—'

'Seeing each other?' echoes Georgia. 'Evie, they're not seeing each other.'

I frown.

'They *work* together,' she explains. 'Only since very recently, mind you. Beth's always wanted to work in the voluntary sector and she got chatting to Jack about the charity he works for at our wedding. He told her there was some administrative position coming up, so she phoned him on the Monday and started work there about a week later.'

'So, she's still working for them now?' I ask.

'Yes,' says Georgia, 'but there's nothing going on between the two of them, I promise you. I know that for certain because Beth has fancied him from day one but he's refused to even acknowledge it. He clearly just isn't interested in her. And she does nothing but complain about it.'

I shake my head.

'But why wouldn't he have told me she was working with him?' I ask.

'Probably because he's a man,' Georgia says dismissively. 'Pete's had deaths, pregnancies and a sex change among his colleagues without bothering to tell me about any of them.'

That might explain the phone number exchanges. And the missed calls on the mobile.

'But that doesn't explain something else,' I tell Georgia, as she zips up her make-up bag. I tell her about the call from Beth that I picked up during my mum's wedding. About how

406

she'd left her top at his flat that morning. How could she explain *that*?

'I really don't know,' she says, looking puzzled. Then: 'Hang on, this was the night of your mum's wedding, wasn't it?'

'Yes.'

'Well, she couldn't have been with him the night before, because we were all at my Uncle Tom's fiftieth birthday party. I was with her all night. In fact, we stayed at the hotel.'

My heart sinks. I don't know what the explanation is for what she said on the phone. But I do now know that I publicly accused Jack of two-timing me when he was completely innocent; did so when he'd just discovered I'd lied to him about my past, and then failed to even pick up the phone afterwards to say sorry.

I have never had such an overwhelming urge to burst into tears.

'Hey, love,' says Georgia. 'Don't get upset.'

'Sorry,' I gulp. 'But, oh God, Georgia. This is a disaster.'

Chapter 120

Edmund has given Valentina the biggest and best wedding money can buy, but he's saved the thing that will probably mean most to her for last. He's been taking ballroom dancing lessons. It means that Valentina gets to perform possibly the most professional, the most impressive and certainly the most downright flashy first dance in history.

Naturally, she's chosen the tango. And as the dance ends to rapturous applause, with her and Edmund nose to nose, she pulls a rose from between her teeth and kisses him like a comic-book heroine who has just been rescued from a gang of marauding ne'er-do-wells.

The guests now start to pour onto the dance floor, including Bob and my mother, whose particular brand of dancing immediately terrifies some of the elderly and infirm in the party.

I pick up my bag and decide to go outside for a walk in the grounds. The breeze is soft and warm and when I find a decent log, I plonk myself down on it and look into the sky, feeling utterly distraught. Tears prick into my eyes again as I think about what Georgia told me earlier.

'You lot have got it easy,' I say, between sniffs, to a couple of sheep munching away at some grass in front of me. 'You don't have to deal with having your bum groped in front of other wedding guests and being stalked by psychotic ex-boyfriends. And certainly, you don't have to deal with screwing things up with the one man who ever meant anything to you. At least, I don't think you do.'

I really have lost it now. I'm sitting here, blubbing my eyes out and talking to a group of farm animals about my emotional difficulties. The fact that they appear to be pretty attentive listeners really isn't the point.

I don't know how long I sit here for. Certainly it's a good while – it honestly could be hours – and somewhere along the way the two existing sheep are joined by another handful.

I am just starting to feel like Little Bo Peep when suddenly I hear voices behind me. When I turn around, Valentina, Grace and Georgia are marching towards me.

'I hope there aren't any cow pats around here,' says Valentina, holding her hem up in disgust. 'These shoes are Christian Louboutin.'

'Valentina,' I say, 'aren't you meant to be mingling or something?'

'Yes, Evie,' she says, 'I am. But we're here because we're worried about you.'

'Me?' I repeat, waving them away. 'Surely I'm the least of everyone's worries today. Really, I'm fine.'

'Well, we don't think you are,' says Georgia. 'In fact, we think you're less than fine.'

'We think you're pining,' says Valentina. 'For Jack.'

'You make me sound like a Labrador,' I say. 'Anyway, whether I'm pining or not, there's nothing you can do about it. I've buggered it all up – big time.'

The three of them exchange glances and couldn't look more conspiratorial if they were all called Guy Fawkes.

'Maybe, maybe not,' says Georgia.

I raise an eyebrow.

'I've just been in touch with Beth,' she tells me. 'The top she was referring to when she spoke to you on the phone was actually a T-shirt. A charity T-shirt that she needed for a fun run she was taking part in the following day. That T-shirt *hadn't* been left at Jack's flat. It had been left in Jack's office.'

I groan. 'Do you have to even tell me this?' I ask. 'I mean, I feel like enough of an idiot anyway without having all the horrifying details rubbed in.'

'I just thought you'd like to know,' says Georgia. 'That, and something else.'

'Oh God,' I say.

'According to Beth,' continues Georgia, 'for two weeks after your row, Jack spent the whole time pacing up and down the office, agitated, and clearly torn up.'

'So why didn't he phone?' I whine.

'One might say that should have been up to you,' points out Grace. 'The misunderstanding was all yours – not his, Evie.'

'Fair point.' I slump back onto my log.

'The thing is, he might have,' Georgia persists, 'but something put a stop to that once and for all.'

'What?' I ask.

'My little minx of a cousin told him about you and Seb. About her seeing you in that club.'

I cast my mind back to the club and Beth witnessing Seb's big sloppy kiss. It sends a shiver down my spine just thinking she might have relayed that back to Jack.

'Oh God,' I say. 'Do you really have to go on with this torture? Really, do you have to?'

'Well, we have got something *good* to tell you too,' Grace pipes up.

'Please do,' I say.

'Jack loves you!' she announces

'Oh, I wanted to say that bit,' whines Valentina.

I scrunch up my nose.

'What?' I say. 'How can he love me? And how the hell could you know?'

They all look at each other again, each one grinning from ear to ear.

'The thing is,' says Georgia, 'once I'd spoken to Beth, we weren't going to leave it there, were we? I mean, what sort of friends would we be to just not do anything?'

My eyes widen. 'So what did you do?' I ask, slightly hysterically.

'We phoned someone,' says Valentina, clapping her hands like a three-year-old. 'In fact, we phoned—'

'You might want to come with us,' interrupts Grace, grabbing me by the hand.

Chapter 121

The first thing I notice when I walk into the ballroom is that the music has stopped; virtually the only thing I can hear is my own heartbeat, which is now hammering away as if I'd just run up five flights of stairs.

The next thing I notice is Jack. Standing there, on the other side of the room, and the only person in the place wearing jeans, a T-shirt and, most bewilderingly, holding a microphone. I can see some guests out of the corner of my eye exchanging baffled looks and I glance at them for a second as if to say: 'I haven't got a bloody clue what's going on either.'

'What . . . what's happening?' I splutter.

'You'll see,' says Grace, smirking.

Then the music starts, the unmistakable opening bars of a song I recognize instantly. Jack lifts up the microphone and feedback screeches through the sound system, prompting a sharp collective intake of breath from everyone in the room.

'Sorry,' he says, and I suddenly realize that he looks terribly nervous. 'Although you might think that sounds good compared with what you're about to hear.'

Georgia giggles.

'Evie,' says Jack, 'we haven't spoken for a while now. That was partly due to pride on my part – and I'm guessing it was the same for you too.'

He's right across on the other side of the room, but our eyes are locked as if we're inches apart.

'I also thought . . . well, I thought you'd found someone else,' he says. 'Now I know – thanks to your friends – that's not the case. And that *you* know I was completely faithful.'

I try to swallow. I can't. I'm frozen to the spot, simultaneously terrified, confused and exhilarated, and desperately trying to keep this tearing emotion inside me in check.

'But the thing is,' Jack continues, 'given that I didn't phone you, I guess I need to do something to prove just how much I feel about you. And – although it's a shame that the only thing I could think of makes me look a complete and utter prat – there really is only one way to do it.'

There isn't a person in the room who isn't nudging, whispering and speculating about what he's saying. I flash a look at Grace and she grins. Jack starts slowly walking towards me and, with lightning running through my veins, I hear Ruby Turner's backing singers launching into song.

Then, to my complete amazement, so does Jack.

Jack Williamson, a man who has *never* sung in public – a man who *swore* he never would – is singing. He's singing to *me*.

His voice is deep and ever so slightly off-key, but I don't think I'd care right now if he sounded like a castrated seagull.

As Jack sings, the guests who were initially wondering what the hell was going on, now start to get into the swing of things – and one or two even stand up and begin swaying, as if they're at a Queen concert. Someone actually holds their lighter up.

By the time Jack has walked all the way over to me, I am totally unable to determine whether I should laugh, cry or just pass out with the sheer insanity of it all. Either way, when I touch my cheeks, I find they are soaked with tears.

Jack looks into my eyes to sing the final line and we're so close now I can see the contours of his face in the sort of detail that I never thought I'd see again. It takes my breath away.

'Nobody . . . but . . . you.'

He puts the microphone down on the table next to me and pulls me towards him as I wipe away my tears. With applause echoing all around us, Jack leans forward and our lips meet.

It is the sweetest, deepest, happiest moment in my twenty-seven years on this earth. And right now, right at this moment, I know I'm going to say something I thought I'd never say to anyone. Ever.

I pull back and I look at Jack, my Jack, my shaking hands clutching his, while I search for my voice.

I find it. And I whisper to him.

'Jack. I love you.'

Epilogue

Three years later

'You know,' says Valentina, admiring her profile in the mirror, 'I had my doubts about wearing a bridesmaid dress at eight months' pregnant, but I should have known, if anyone could carry it off – I could.'

I can't help smiling to myself. Valentina may have been married for three years and be about to bear her first child for Edmund, but some things never change. So are you a little bit surprised? That they're still together, I mean? Well, don't worry – I suspect a few others are too.

Let's face it, when they first met, it didn't take a cynic to recognize that Valentina appeared to be as romantically attached to Edmund's Gold Card as she was to Edmund himself. But, somewhere along the way, a funny thing happened: she fell in love with him. Whether it was when she witnessed him saving a man's life on their honeymoon, or when they found out baby Paris (Orlando if it's a boy) was on the way, I'm not entirely sure. But it happened all right – and the Barnetts couldn't be happier. Which from Valentina's point of view is fantastic, because divorce is *so* last year.

The door to our hotel suite opens and Polly walks in.

'Where's your mum?' I ask, slightly nervously. I may have been fully expecting Grace to be late, but it doesn't make me feel any less jumpy about it.

'Just coming,' says Polly, who at eight is so grown up now. 'You didn't really expect us to be on time, did you?'

'Soooo sorry!' says Grace, bursting through the door and ushering Scarlett in with one hand and her bags in with another. 'I've been trying to get out of the house for an hour but my mother phoned to ask if I wanted anything from Debenhams while she was in there. Then she phoned to ask if I wanted anything from M&S. Then John Lewis. Then she phoned back to ask was I absolutely sure I didn't want anything because M&S had some lovely paté in – she knew it was lovely because Maureen Thomas from church had some the last time she was round there and it had real Cointreau in and . . . Oh look, the upshot is: *sorry*. Now, where do I get changed?'

Okay, so they got off to a shaky start, but Grace and Patrick haven't looked back since the early events of their marriage. It took a while for Patrick to win Grace's trust back, but once he'd got a new job and she moved to a new law firm (with a new female boss who couldn't be less like her old one), things just started slotting back into place – and a good place at that.

'Right,' says my mum, straightening her turban – which along with the three-quarter pants she's wearing makes her look like she's just appeared out of a magic lamp. 'I can't be hanging round here all day. I've got guests to greet. See? See how responsible I can be?'

I go over and kiss her.

'You're right,' I say fondly. 'At least about you needing to get going. The responsible bit I'll reserve judgement on.

And make sure Bob gets here on time, will you?'

Georgia brings the champagne over to top me up again.

'Bloody hell, not too much!' I say. 'Or I'll be doing the splits on the dance floor later – and I'm leaving that to Valentina.'

'You don't think the fact that she's eight months' pregnant might stop her this time?' asks Georgia.

'Oh, it'll just make it all the more impressive.'

Georgia laughs – and I realize it's a while since I heard her do that.

She and Pete separated last month, an event which would make any future bride, even one with an unshakeable belief that they're doing the right thing, think twice. Neither have been bitter, or acrimonious, or anything other than completely sensible about it. But that doesn't mean it hasn't hit both of them hard. Which just goes to show that two good people don't always make for a good marriage.

With twenty minutes to go, I head into the bathroom to touch up my lipstick and Valentina follows me with her own extensive cosmetics collection.

'One of the hotel staff just passed this in for you,' she says, handing me an envelope.

I put down my lip brush and open it, while Valentina starts tonging her hair for the fifth time today.

'God,' I say, reading it.

'What is it?' she asks.

She leans over to read with me.

Dear Evie

Well, it's been a long time, that's for sure. I'm sorry about that. I know you kept trying to get in touch with me after

Valentina's wedding and I'd like you to know how grateful I was about that. But I also hope you understand why I didn't return any of your calls and emails. Things were very difficult. Emotionally I was a mess – and more importantly, I began to realize that what I'd done was unforgivable. That was why I took that job in Scotland and left without saying goodbye. I just needed to put some space between me and, well, everyone really. Anyway, Valentina phoned and told me about today and I could have jumped for joy when I found out (except I'm twelve and a half stones again now so it's not so easy any more!). The point is, I was delighted – more than delighted, in fact – ecstatic. And while that doubled when I received an invitation from you, I hope you understand why I had to decline. It wouldn't have been fair on anyone – particularly Grace – for me to have come. That said, I wondered if you'd like to meet for coffee some time, just you and me? I miss you terribly and I'd love to catch up, next time I'm back in town, although I'll understand if you don't want to after all this time. My mobile number is still the same.

Anyway, nobody deserves to be happier than you, Evie. So good luck, and all my love, Charlotte.

'Oh Charlotte! Do you think I've got time to phone her now?' I ask Valentina.

'Absolutely not, there's only a few minutes left,' she says, fiddling with my hair. 'Do it later, or tomorrow. After this long, one day isn't going to make any difference.'

The bathroom door opens and Scarlett and Polly poke their heads around it.

'You two have got the prettiest dresses I've ever seen, no competition,' I tell her.

'Come on, Auntie Evie,' says Polly. 'It's time to go. Bob's here to escort you down the aisle.'

I walk out into the hotel room and look at the clock. She's right. Two minutes to go.

'You look beautiful, Evie,' says Bob, appearing at my side. 'I feel so proud.'

We link arms, and with my bridesmaids behind us, we head downstairs until we reach the door to the room where the ceremony is taking place. I can already see Jack standing at the front waiting for me, and my heart leaps.

'Well, you've proved someone wrong, anyway,' says Grace, straightening my veil.

'Oh?' I ask her.

'My mother,' she says, grinning. 'She said this morning she never thought she'd see the day when Evie Hart walked down the aisle.'

'You know, Grace,' I whisper, as the guests hush and the music starts. 'I couldn't agree with her more.'